Greed & Stuff

Also by Jay Russell

Celestial Dogs (1996)

Blood (1996)

Burning Bright (1997)

Waltzes and Whispers (1999)

Brown Harvest (FORTHCOMING)

Greed & Stuff

Jay Russell

St. Martin's Minotaur

New York

www.minotaurbooks.com

ISBN 0-312-26168-3

First Edition: February 2001

10 9 8 7 6 5 4 3 2 1

For Rosie,
who arrived early:
Hey, little baby

Acknowledgments

THANKS TO Gordon Van Gelder, who is much too nice a guy to be working in publishing. But I'm glad he does.

As ever and always, thanks, love, and everything else to Jane for putting up with it all.

One

A tasty silence took hold of the room. Marconi studied the freshly cut pack of cards like a diamond-cutter sizing-up a virgin facet; like a fastball hitter anticipating that spinning orb of horsehide; like a karate black belt preparing to become one with the sweet spot in a soon-to-be-chunks, foot-thick breeze block; like . . .

Oh hell, like a weekend poker player determined to drive his buddies to distraction.

"Spit it out, ya' bastard," Conlon demanded.

Marconi nodded, smiling his greasiest publicist's smile. I could feel my cholesterol count rise as he picked up the cards. "Okay, here it is: Movie titles are wild."

"For this I'm skipping an AA meeting?" Bill Morris said. He took a long slug from his rum and coke. He was kidding, I hope.

"What the hell is that supposed to mean, movie titles are wild?" Elliot asked. "What kind of fershlugginer game is this?"

Elliot was always using *Mad* magazine words like "fershlugginer" and "potrezebie." He thought it made him a character. His screenplays suffer from a painfully similar dearth of imagination. I saw Hall wince when he said it. When Hall opened his mouth Marconi raised an eyebrow—Luke is in awe of Hall Emerson; there has to be someone, I suppose—but Hall didn't say a word, just mashed another cheap cigar between his lips.

"How long you been saving this baby up?" I asked.

Marconi winked at me.

"So how does it work?" Elliot pleaded.

"Oh, for Christ's sake, use your brain," Conlon said. "Which movies have playing cards as part of their title?"

Elliot looked stumped. Frankly, you'd expect more from someone who got paid two million dollars for his last script. Okay, maybe not someone who got paid two million dollars by Joel Silver.

"*One-Eyed Jacks?*" Conlon prompted. Elliot still looked blank.

"Marlon Brando," I added. And no one pays me two million dollars.

"Oh, yeah," Elliot said, nodding.

"*King of Hearts,*" Marconi suggested.

"Whatever happened to Alan Bates?"

"Isn't he dead? Or is it just his career?"

"Same difference."

"*Jack of Diamonds,*" Hall muttered. "Though you'll observe the knave has two eyes."

"Boy, I don't remember that one," I admitted.

"George Hamilton. Zsa Zsa Gabor."

"Ahhh," we all said at once.

"My dad ghosted on the script. Not his proudest moment. He always claimed Zsa Zsa blew him under a commissary table while he ate a chopped liver sandwich. And that was the only payment he ever got."

"Was she any good?" I asked.

"I asked him once. All he'd say was: 'She ain't chopped liver.' "

"Any others?" Elliot asked. He still looked worried.

"*Ace in the Hole,*" Conlon suggested.

"Nope. Got to be the exact card name," Marconi said, starting the deal. "Anyway, the real title's *The Big Carnival.*"

"There must be a *Queen of Hearts,*" I said, trying to remember.

"Of course: but surely that's our Kathie Lee."

"Not anymore. Regis is better off without her."

"There was a *Thief of Hearts.*"

"That's no help."

"Definitely a *Three of Hearts,*" Conlon said, drawing a roomful of blank stares. "Billy Baldwin."

"Remind me: Is he the untalented one, or the unbelievably untalented one?"

"Daniel's the merely untalented one. Billy's the one who couldn't act dead with his head blown off, a tag tied to his toe, and Jack Kervorkian as the attending physician."

"Don't you guys ever get tired of Baldwin brother jokes?" Elliot asked.

"Not me," Conlon said.

"Me either," I agreed. "They're eternal: like mother-in-law jokes or traveling salesmen jokes."

"Or any Baldwin brother movie," Conlon added. "In the far, far future, when only giant roaches and Dick Clark are left to scamper across the radioactive remains of the Earth, there will still be Baldwin brother jokes."

Marconi and Emerson nodded. Elliot sighed.

"So about this wild card nonsense. Do projects in development count?" Morris asked. Trust an agent to suggest such a thing.

"Yeah," Marconi conceded. Then he held up a finger and flashed his oleaginous grin at Morris. "But not if they're in turnaround." Everyone knew Morris had spent six months trying to get Brad Pitt to commit to a script called *Ace of Spades*. But after *Meet Joe Black* Pitt was avoiding death movies like the plague.

"Bastard," Morris grumbled. Serves him right for having that name and working for CAA.

"I don't like this at all," Elliot said, studying his hand. "I'm much better with TV shows."

Maybe yes, maybe no, but he turned out to be the big loser. Which in our friendly little poker circle only left him a C-note down on the night. Chump change to a two-million-dollar man. Not that it stopped him from grumbling about it as he poked through his alligator skin wallet. I think Elliot Feinstein is the kind of guy who'd pay up in penny rolls if he could. I'd been down on the night, but made up for most of it with five sevens in that last hand. God bless Marlon Brando, though not for his acting. Or his kids.

"Same time next week, gents?" Conlon asked.

"Not me," Marconi said. "I got to go down to Phoenix for some sci-fi thing."

"What are you pushing?"

"I'm stuck with this Schumacher nightmare. I've got to convince two thousand fat, smelly *Star Trek* geeks that the guy who ruined Batman is now God's gift to science-fiction movies. Cyberpunk, yet. Who makes this stuff up?" He glanced accusingly at Elliot.

"How bad is it?" I asked.

"I just told you it's a Joel Schumacher film, didn't I?"

"Right. Sorry," I muttered.

"Marconi cheats anyway. Stupid wild card games. What about the rest of you?" Conlon asked.

"I'm in," Morris said. "The wife looks forward to these games more

3

than I do. If it weren't for our nanny-cam, I might suspect she's having an affair."

"Maybe she's shtupping the nanny."

"That wouldn't be so bad. I like a little girl-on-girl action."

Hall flicked his ash in an affirmative way and grunted. Elliot whined some more about losing, but said he'd be there. For all his money, I know he hasn't got many other friends. I half suspect he's the kind of guy who'd *attend* sci-fi conventions if he didn't write the damn movies.

"How 'bout you, Marty?"

I pulled on my sports coat, straightened the cuffs, neatened my collar. I ran a hand through my Rogaine-assisted hair and struck a Hollywood pose. "Do you really think that a man who stars in a network action drama—not to mention the newly anointed spokesperson for Schmears 'R U.S., the nation's fastest growing chain of bagel-and-muffin cafés—has nothing better to do with his weekends than fritter them away playing penny-ante card games with the likes of you?"

"Seven-thirty?" Conlon asked.

"Sounds good," I said, and made for the door.

"And Marty?"

I turned around.

"Only Rupert Murdoch and people who take his money think that Fox is a real network."

"Didn't you just do some doctoring for Warner? That teen horror soap thing?"

"You'll have to be more specific than that," Morris interjected. "You just described Warner's entire schedule."

Conlon turned a sophisticated shade of red that clashed with his walls.

"Pot. Kettle. African-American," I said. "Seven-thirty next week."

As I walked toward my car, I heard a low rumbling noise and glanced up at the skies. I expected to see a thunder cloud, but you could nearly see stars through the glow of a relatively thin LA haze. I could almost imagine how the place looked before Carl Laemmle stole it from the Mexicans.

"Marty," the rumbling articulated and I turned around. Hall Emerson limped up the sidewalk toward me, one massive hand raised in the air. Emerson was a huge man and he walked like John Wayne the morning after prostate surgery. Marconi once told me that Emerson suffered the injury in a motorcycle accident some years before. He often gamboled about with an elaborate walking stick—it had a silver wolf's head for a handle—though the item always struck me as more of a prop or affectation than a medical necessity. Everyone acts in LA, whether they have a SAG card or not. Indeed, the best performances in town are rarely captured by the cameras; they take place everywhere you look, an entire city as theater-in-the-round. (And yes, I realize that Shakespeare said it first. Fortunately, he's out of copyright.) Emerson didn't have the cane with him tonight, but the stub of his filthy stogie remained wedged between the fingers of his raised hand in good, Churchillian fashion. I detected the brief flash of an acknowledging smile through his salt-and-pepper beard and mustache when he saw me stop and wait for him to catch up.

Though we'd been playing cards together for a year, I couldn't say that I knew Hall Emerson all that well. I got invited into the weekly poker game by way of Jon Conlon, who I met when he came to do some repair work on my TV series, *Burning Bright*. Conlon is one of those guys who no one who's not in The Business has ever heard of, but who makes a nice chunk of living by fixing the writing that the big names can't be bothered to do right. Nice enough for a million dollar house in Hancock Park, anyway. Seven figures makes a fellow happy with his anonymity.

Hall, on the other hand, is a more familiar name, if only by association. Not so much for the dozen or so scripts he's had produced, none of which, it must be admitted, is especially memorable. Or even the multitude of TV writing he's committed. Rather, Emerson is Old Hollywood: celluloid runs in his veins. His father, Frank Emerson, was a moderately successful screenwriter in the forties and fifties. Emerson Pere, it must be admitted, was no great shakes of a scribe either, but he hung out with lots of interesting people and ended up with a bigger rep than his work alone might have accorded him. Hall inherited some of his dad's prestige, along with his big schnoz, and even enjoyed a brief period of flavor-of-the-month back in the seventies. He picked up a reputation as a bad boy at the time, though I don't know that he did anything more than get his picture taken with Dennis Hopper or have lunch with Bob Altman. I do know that he'd fallen on tough times of late. But in an age when Dennis Hopper appears in car commercials and Robert Altman directs John Grisham movies, being the fifty-year-old son of a once-famous screenwriter doesn't count for a whole lot.

And in the land of the golden la-la, fifty is at least twenty-five years too old. Especially if you're an actress or a screenwriter.

Hall was breathing hard by the time he caught up to me. But then, he's a big man—in both size and demeanor—and always seems to be breathing hard. It didn't stop him from shoving the cigar between his lips as soon as he stopped, and resting a meaty hand on my shoulder. Hall's got some of that Orson Welles presence, crossed with Hemingway looks by way of Sterling Hayden. There's clearly enough of him for two medium-sized men, and sufficient facial hair to equip an entire writing staff with fashionable Vandykes. Yet he's not exactly fat, just big. And imposing.

Casting a shadow somehow smaller than himself, Hall is Hollywood to the bone.

"I wanted to catch a private word with you," he said. He gave my neck a little squeeze with the word "you" and I heard my collarbone creak.

"Sure, Hall, what's up?"

"Got a few minutes? I know a place just around the corner. They never close."

I casually glanced at my watch: 1:30 A.M. We'd been playing poker and drinking beer since nine. I already shouldn't drive, though even at this hour it would take me half an hour to cruise back to my place in Hermosa Beach. Not to mention that I had a breakfast meeting to dot the *i*'s on the deal with the bagel-and-muffin mogul and his people in Beverly Hills in less than eight hours.

"Sure," I said.

And such is how long stories begin.

"Just around the corner" proved to be a good mile walk. I should have been LA-snooty that we didn't take a car, but the night air tasted unusually fresh, sullied only by the rancid poots from Hall's cigar. Other than a few half-hearted exchanges about the game neither of us said much as we strolled up the quiet streets. Needless to say we were the only pedestrians about, though the same would likely have

6

been as true at two in the afternoon. We agreed that Elliot was an idiot, entirely undeserving of the vast sums of money thrown at him by even dumber producers, but there was no real venom behind our bitching. Elliot did, after all, have the good grace to leave his money behind at most of the games, however gracelessly he actually lost.

"Fact that the bastard can't bluff's paid my electric bill twice already this year," Hall guffawed.

It occurred to me that someone who can't pay his utilities might be better off not playing poker, but who am I to judge? Been there, done that, postdated the bouncing check.

The place Hall led me to was one of those nondescript neighborhood bars that, on a cloudy day or a dark night, could pass for an empty storefront. No neon Bud signs or beer promotions dangling in the smoked glass windows, and only the peeling remnants of a stenciled sign above to give the place a name. Steamers or Streamers—I couldn't even tell. It had the look of a serious drinker's bar.

Hall nodded at a big bartender with a bowling ball head and Chia Pet hair. Plugs, I assumed; an aspiring actor, no doubt. Every ex-con with a twice-busted nose fancies himself Eddie Bunker these days. The guy practically smiled back at Hall, not so much out of friendliness, I think—Steamers/Streamers was the kind of place where *nobody* knows your name and you're *never* glad you came—but because even in the most unlikely of places, people always seem happy to meet Hall. As if he has some secret gland which exudes a "good to see ya" pheromone. Perhaps he should have been an actor, and not a writer. I know I could do with a little of that eau d'presence.

We ordered a couple of bourbons with Buds back. Frankly, I would have felt gauche ordering anything else in such a place, like those pathetic bastards who order veal cutlet off the tiny "American" menu in Chinese restaurants. When in Beijing and all that.

The only other patrons I could discern through the gloom were a shopworn, middle-aged couple in a booth who looked like they'd wandered in from *Days of Wine and Roses,* and a semitoothless old geezer at the far end of the bar who might have been a waxwork prop that came with the place for atmosphere. Except he moved once every minute or so to spill a little bit more amber liquid into his mouth. And shake his head from side to side regretting, it seemed, just about everything it was possible to regret. You might think a man with his own television series would feel disgusted by the sight of such a creature, but once, not that long ago, I readily envisioned myself coming to a not very different end. Who's to say I still won't? I didn't have to ask Hall how it was he knew about a bar like this, because in that same once upon a time I would have known, too. Maybe not Steamers, but another place, interchangeable in look and purpose, twelve blocks the other way. And two dozen more like it, strategically located in any part of town I might happen to be. That's simply the nature of being a sad and lonely fuck in a happy place like The City of Our Lady of the Angels.

And everywhere else, I suppose.

"Been a while?" Hall asked. Before I could question his question, he raised one bushy eyebrow (actually he only had one, straight across) and managed to take in the entire bar with a half-flick of his eye.

"Not so long," I told him. "Not long enough."

"Pretend we're slumming."

"Pretend?"

He let out a raucous belly-laugh that rolled around the room a few times before bouncing back like a boomerang. It was enough to rock Jack Lemmon and Lee Remick out of their stupor in the corner. They stumbled from the booth, arms around each other's waist, and slipped out the door. Gappy, at the end of the bar, didn't blink.

Hall drained his bourbon and called for another. I was happy to sip mine—though sipping liquor it most certainly was not—and shook the bartender off. He brought two more anyway, took the money out of the cash Hall left on the bar.

"So, what's going on Hall?"

The big man grabbed another full-to-the brim shot in his fist, raised it toward his lips, then changed his mind at the last moment. He placed it gently on the bar without spilling a drop, picked up his beer and drank that instead.

"The devil on Sunday," Hall said.

"And angels on horseback with gossamer wings."

"Huh?"

"Sorry, I thought we were free associating."

Hall drank his bourbon. Chased it with the rest of the beer.

"It's a movie. *The Devil on Sunday.*"

"Don't know it," I told him. "Should I?"

"John Dall, Ann Savage, Tom Neal. Connie Clare."

I shook my head. "Doesn't sound like a David O. Selznick production."

"Hmmmph. Hardly. Could have made it a dozen times, even in 1950, for what it cost to burn down Atlanta on the back lot. Buzz Day directed it."

"I don't recognize that name, either."

"No reason to. Billy 'Buzz' Day. What a hack. Though he started out as a Max Castle protégé."

"Really."

"My old man wrote it. *The Devil on Sunday.*"

"Ahhh," I said. As if I now knew why Hall Emerson was talking about this to me at two in the morning in a seedy bar when I had bagel-and-muffin money to make in the morning.

"The screenplay, at least. Based on a short story by a hack named Rheems. Crap, really."

"The story?"

"Bad pulp fiction. You can hear the tinkle of ankle bracelets on every musty page. Smell the shoe gum."

"Hell of a thing for a TV shamus to admit, but I don't know what shoe gum smells like. So is the movie any good?"

Hall paused, glanced at me from the corner of his eye, and signaled for more bourbon. He never took that eye off me as the bartender refilled his glass and slipped more cash out of the pile, just offered a weary half-smile.

"Not bad," he said. Then raised his glass and tossed back the shot. "The old man could do a day's work when he was so inclined, and the bottle didn't beckon, especially if it was hardboiled. 'Course, you got to get offered a day's work before you can do one."

Hall started looking toward the bartender again, but I slid my still-full shot glass in front of him, took a sip of beer for sociability's sake as he downed it.

"Things a little slow?"

"Freeze frame more like."

"What's the problem?"

"The problem," Hall said, slapping his hand down on the sticky bar, "is that I'm too fucking old for this town."

"Who isn't?"

"You're making out all right."

"You think that's anything other than dumb luck? If I hadn't stumbled into the Jack Rippen mess, managed to expose the dirty dealings at Celestial Dog, would anyone have taken a second look at me for a job? Two years ago you had to be a trivia master just to know my name. I'd still be skip-tracing and running down subpoenas but for the fickle finger of fate. Hell, I never even wanted to act again, and here I am starring in a network—sorry, *Fox*—show. You can't figure this town, Hall."

"Yeah, I know. Hell, I'm second generation: it should be genetic. But it still pisses me off."

"You doing anything at all?"

"Doctoring some syndie shit. And I'm 'collaborating' on a few projects. Know what that means?"

I shook my head.

"I do all the writing while some twenty-year-old takes the meetings, the money, and the credit."

"I sympathize, Hall, I genuinely do. But Hollywood's a bitch and that ain't never gonna change. Like you say, I can't complain at the moment, but you know what? I sent in the renewal slip on my PI license just in case. I don't mean for PR reasons, either. So who ever feels secure here?"

He harrumphed what I took to be agreement, looked again toward the bartender, but didn't order another round. Highlights of the day's baseball came up on ESPN and we watched in silence for a while. The Dodgers lost. Quelle surprise.

"I can talk to my producer," I said as the baseball was replaced by Motocross. Who watches this stuff?

"Heh?"

"About some work on *Burning Bright*. I think the scripts are pretty well set for the season, but there may be something. You know, there's always room for another story consultant."

"No thanks, Marty. Really. I didn't intend to go off on that tangent and I'm not looking to scrounge work off you. Though I do have a favor to ask."

"Shoot."

"It's *The Devil on Sunday*. They're remaking it."

"You're kidding."

"Nope. It's an indie project, but there's real money there. Believe me, I checked that out first."

"You're involved?"

"They asked. Kevin Ryan Paul's producing. You know him?"

"Vaguely. Never trust anyone with three first names. Jan Michael Vincent's owed me money for years. He always ducks when I walk into a room. Wasn't Paul the guy who produced the *Rat Patrol* movie?"

"That's him. Not big on imagination, I admit, but he gets stuff made."

"Huh," I said. Paul, to the extent I knew his work, was a shit-merchant, but then who am I to judge? One critic, after all, described *Burning Bright* as the *Cannon* of the nineties. I don't see it, but I started a diet the day I read the review.

"I've got first shot at the script. Paul's got this idea that he can play some publicity off the fact that my dad wrote the original."

"Sounds thin."

"No, Marty: Not eating sounds thin. *The Devil on Sunday* sounds like a paycheck."

"So go for it," I said.

"I am. But I've got a problem. The video version of the original is incomplete. It's on one of those dire labels and they've taken no care with the print. I have Frank's copy of the original script and it runs a good twenty minutes longer than what's on tape. I've also heard that there's at least one scene they shot that the old man didn't write. I've read descriptions of it, so I know it exists, but it's not on the video *or* in his script. I'd like to see the whole shot version if I can. And any extra footage that might exist."

"You try any of the local archives? I hear UCLA is pretty good."

"Yeah, they don't have it. I went to the AFI, too, but they're a bunch of prissy snots."

"What about Paul?"

Hall made a face. "He's not *that* interested. I think he came by the rights cheap and likes the idea of doing something dark. Apparently *dark* is the new black."

"I'm sorry, I have no idea what that means," I said.

"I don't either, but Paul says it every time we meet. Maybe I *am* too old for this business."

The bartender was making closing-up movements and a glance at my watch revealed that it was past two-thirty. I stifled a yawn, but Hall waved for one more bourbon. The bartender hesitated—he wanted us out—but it was the kind of place where he'd rather have the extra two bucks. It didn't take Hall long to drink it in any case.

"So what is it I can do for you, Hall?"

"Fox has a hell of a vault and according to *Variety*, they once distributed *Devil*. It was part of a library they bought out before Murdoch came along. I made some calls, but I can't seem to get anywhere with their archive people. And I sort of had an incident with a Fox exec a couple of years back. I think I may be persona non grata over there."

"Hmmm. Was this the famous studio chief's wife at the County Museum incident?"

"You heard about it, huh?"

"Hall. Her silicon implant ruptured. Medical students across the country read about it every day. Hell, they dramatized it on *ER*."

"They work with the same exec and she's his ex now. And it really wasn't my fault."

I laughed out loud, and even Hall had to smile. The bartender removed our glasses and whatever money was still on the bar.

"So you want me to track down a print of *The Devil on Sunday* if I can."

"Would you mind?"

A pretty small favor, really. A phone call or two at most. "Not a problem, Hall. I'll check into it on Monday."

"The thing is if you could make sure and ask if there's any footage beyond what's in the print. I'm really interested in that lost scene. They may keep stuff like that someplace separate."

"Hey," I said, standing up and straightening my jacket, "Marty Burns is on the case."

He smiled and thanked me, but he didn't exactly look reassured. They never do, even when the cameras roll. A lesser fellow might nurture self-doubt.

We walked back toward our cars in silence. There's nothing quite like LA at night: you can almost believe it's a real place. But then you look up and see the Hollywood sign on Mt. Lee. Hall and I shook hands at Conlon's and Hall thanked me again. I watched him drive off in a beat-up yellow Nissan, buzzed open the locks on my Lexus but paused to take a deep swallow of the nearly-fresh night air.

The Devil on Sunday, I thought.

And angels on horseback with gossamer wings.

Two

The Sunday meeting with Schmears 'R U.S. went swimmingly, which is to say I came away with an inked deal and a gross of mixed bagels. The only downside was that I spent the whole rest of the day with "Do You Know the Muffin Man" buzzing through my head. Oh, yeah: and the mix came with a dozen blueberry bagels. Frankly, I believe that even cinnamon raisin raises serious issues of bagel propriety, but then I've been told I'm a purist. Truth be known, I'm a bialy man at heart.

It was an off couple of weeks for shooting *Burning Bright*. In the good old days, when I was a child star on *Salt & Pepper*, the networks used to commit to as many as thirty-six episodes for a season and you pretty well spent nine months of the year filming with barely a day off to hone your addictions. Nowadays, a full season is only twenty-two weeks and the programmers are too scared for their overpaid jobs to green light more than nine episodes at a time. The show's ratings have turned a little soft lately, especially among women eighteen to thirty-four (admittedly, I've always had a problem about going soft with this group), and so it was thrice annual wait-and-see time while The Suits weighed our fate over their expensive lunches. On the other hand, we do really well with male smokers over thirty-four, and since Matt Groening already has *two* Fox shows running and can't possibly come up with another in time for the new season, I reckoned we were pretty safe. Though you never know.

Looking at the bright side, an off-week meant sleeping in until a reasonable hour on Monday morning. After two seasons of blown lines and missed marks, my producers have learned better than to schedule my scenes for too early in the day, but mercilessly, I'm still expected to be in makeup by eight. Let my people go, why don't they?

I read the *Times* and forced down a bagel or two—it was going to take some real acting to sell these sandbags—then tried calling the studio to find out if they even had a print of *The Devil on Sunday* in the library. After fifteen minutes of various voice mail menus and recorded messages, and with no trace of a human being on the horizon, I hung up and decided just to go in and talk to someone live and in person.

Pete waved me on through the studio gate and I doffed an imaginary cap to him as I drove by. I did it every day and it always evoked a laugh. Pete, I feel, needs to get out more. I decided it was going to be a good day when Calista Flockhart tried to pass me on the inside as we made for the parking lot, and I cut her off. She had to brake sharply before she plowed into the big windows at the front of the commissary. She wailed her horn at me, but screw her—it wouldn't hurt her scrawny ass any to stop in for a bite.

Our production offices were quiet, with only the secretaries around to answer the phones and work on their screenplays. With a renewal decision in the air everyone was lying low or hedging their bets by pitching projects elsewhere around town. The place had that feel of a school building during summer holidays. I just had to hope that we all got promoted to the next grade. Though I don't have an office of my own—they offered me one, but what the hell would I do there?—the executive producer does and he's never around. Of course, not being around is more or less what executive producers do. (Strictly speaking, I am one of the co-executive producers of the show: a title about as meaningful as Vice President of the United States, and conferred strictly as a bookkeeping ruse. I am not, however, *the* executive producer, the person who earns the most for doing the least. Still, where would America be if we didn't all have something to aspire toward?) I pointed at the office door and raised a quizzical eyebrow at the exec's PA, a big blonde named Jennifer who rolled her eyes in a you've-got-to-be-kidding look and waved me in. I winked at her, but she'd already turned back to her script. I know for a fact it's a musical, so her PA days are nowhere near their end.

The office had the look and smell of a suburban model home, but all in brown leather. It contained everything you could possibly want but was painstakingly designed to have no functional value (sort of like an executive producer, come to think of it). So infrequently had the office been used that my feet left impressions in the thick carpet where I walked. I'd have to remember not to murder anyone in here—though the body might turn to dust before it was ever discovered. Hmmm, an idea to mention to the story editor, though it's a bit too *Columbo*.

I don't know what I was thinking when I came in to make the call, but it obviously wasn't in tune with the condition of life in the modern world. I tried to phone the film library, but naturally I could only get into the same voice mail system as before. The fact that I was calling from a location on the lot made no difference at all. No reason that it should, I suppose. Carefully retracing my footprints in the shag, I went back to the PA's desk.

"Can I interrupt?" I asked. I wasn't fond of talking to Jennifer, because she had an unnerving way of speaking, drawing out her words like she was pulling taffy.

Jennifer held up a finger and I waited as she finished typing a brief dialogue exchange. I read the words on the screen over her shoulder. Looked like she was working on a horror musical parody. *Screamin' in the Rain.* Good luck, honey.

"How can I help?"

"What do you do when you want to talk to somebody around here? All I can get are these stupid recorded menus on the phone."

"You're not using the directory numbers, are you?" she laughed.

"Well, yeah."

She looked at me like I'd taken a dump in public. She shook her head slowly. "You'll ne-e-e-ever get through on those. That's for *them.*"

"Them?"

"Civilians," she whispered.

"So how do us veteran insiders make phone calls?"

"Uhhh," she clucked. *Mommy, how do I tie my shoe?* "Just use their ce-e-e-ell phone number and leave a message."

"I don't have a cell phone number. This isn't someone I know."

"Then E-mail," she told me.

"You're kidding."

"No one *e-e-e-e-ver* answers their voice mail, much less the phone. It's a status thing."

"Oh," I said. I must indeed have looked like a little boy lost, because she saved her work on the computer, stood up and took me by the hand.

"Now, who is it you want to talk to?"

"I'm trying to get ahold of someone over in the film library."

"The film library!" God, now I'd done it. "Wha-a-a-a-t in the world for?"

"I was sort of hoping to arrange a screening. At least, find out if they have what I want to see."

"Well, they're completely useless. I don't think they even have E-mail."

I wasn't about to admit to her that I don't either, though I must be the last one in America. For Christ's sake, I'm co-executive producer!

"So what would you suggest?"

"Salma?" she called out to another PA/would-be scenarist across the room. "Do you know the number of anyone over in the film library?"

Salma issued a theatrical shudder and shook her head. "They're creepy over there. You know they got no E-mail?"

"I *kno-o-ow*. They're *cra-a-a-azy*. How would you get in touch?"

Salma made another face.

"I mean if you *ha-a-a-ad* to," Jennifer added.

"I think you got to go over. In person like."

Jennifer raised her hands in an "I surrender" gesture and shrugged at me.

"Is this the way the whole studio runs?"

The two women nodded at me, a little sadly.

"How the hell did Murdoch ever get rich?" I wondered aloud.

"Newspapers," Jennifer told me. "They're a mu-u-u-uch better business."

Salma had to make three calls, all to cell phones, to find out exactly where the film library was, and even then the answer came via E-mail. That little "bing!" the computer makes made me wish I could get some. If I'd realized what a to-do this was going to be, I'd have just asked Pete at the gate. I mentioned this to Jennifer and she nodded enthusiastically.

"Oh, yeah," she reported, "Pete's ve-e-e-ery good about answering his E-mail."

I have a bad feeling that I'm not going to like the twenty-first century one little bit.

. . .

I was going to do the proper LA thing and drive across the lot to the library, but Ally McBeal was loitering near her car, giving me the hairy eyeball, and I didn't want to risk a game of chicken with her. I could have flagged down one of those little golf carts that race around, but I feel vaguely silly riding in them, like an old lady in an airport, so I decided to do my arteries a favor and take a stroll instead. Though the *Burning Bright* offices were in hibernation, the rest of the studio was abuzz. Made an action-adventure star wonder some about his renewal status. At one point I got stuck behind a whole line of cars and carts and teamsters with dollies, as a security guard on a motorcycle blocked traffic to allow Chris Carter's motorcade to pass. A couple of beefy grips even took off their baseball caps as a mark of respect to the Lord of the *X-Files*. It's like *Harsh Realm* never happened. Now *there's* an executive producer.

For no particular reason, I expected the film library to be in some old studio warehouse, all dusty and dark with piles of beat-up film cases scattered about. In fact, it was one of the newest buildings on the lot. The walls of the lobby were lined with glass-framed movie posters old and new. If they were originals they had to be worth a small fortune. A Perky Young Thing (male) sat at the reception desk wearing headphones and stared, as everyone in the world does these days, at a large computer monitor. I assumed at first he must be typing up dictation, but as I approached I saw he was watching an old movie on the screen. Something with Spencer Tracy that I didn't recognize. He flicked at his mouse, removed the 'phones and offered me a PYT(m) smile.

"May I help you?"

"Yeah, my name is Marty Burns and . . ."

"Oh, we all know you here, Mr. Burns. Love that *Burning Bright*."

A *very* Perky Young Thing.

"Thanks, thanks very much. From your mouth to the head of programming's ear."

"Oh, not to worry. I think they'll renew," he said. "You can win back those eighteen to thirty-fours with just a tweak or two to the format. You know, I write a little bit on the side—well really it's my *main* thing, though I *will* act. I'm just doing this job until I, you know, break through—and anyway I'd love to send you some ideas."

"Wow. Terrif. Can you leave them on my voice mail?"

His face sank like a Kevin Costner picture.

"I came by because I wanted to arrange a screening of something. An old movie."

He strove to maintain his PYT demeanor as he turned back to the computer, but I could see I'd dealt him a blow. If he wasn't so obviously a smart-ass bastard I might have felt sorry for him.

"What is it that you want to see?"

"*The Devil on Sunday*. Pretty obscure, I think. I don't even know if you'll have it."

"Buzz Day," the PYT said, even before he started to type it in. "1952."

"You've seen it?"

"It's okay. It's no *Detour,* but there are some good, kinky thrills. It's been years since I watched it."

"I never even heard of it until recently."

"There was something in the *Reporter* about a remake. You up for a part?"

"Huh? No, no. Just curious about it." I wasn't about to go explaining my life to this twerp.

"Here we go. We do have a copy in the vault, but there's no video or digital version available."

"What does that mean?"

"All the originals, the actual movies on film, are kept in a special vault off-lot. There are a few around town that do the storage for all the studios. The negatives are kept separate from that, but even the film copies are pretty delicate. We keep video copies of a lot of things on hand here and try to show those where we can. Saves on wear and tear. And we've just started a process of converting everything to digital so we can store it on computer. That way there's no physical copy at all and we can zap it anywhere in the world."

"Sounds swell."

PYT shrugged. "None of it looks as good as the original celluloid, of course, but it's a lot cheaper. They're big on that, don't you know. And projectionists are a pain in the ass to keep around."

"So how do I actually get to see *The Devil on Sunday*?"

"Normally, you need special permission to get something like that out of the vault, but I mean, for you they'll do it, of course. Thing is, I can put in the request, but Sylvie will still have to sign-off on it."

"Sylvie?"

"She's the archivist. But she's out at the moment. I can go ahead and order the copy up 'cause, like I say, for you I know there'll be no problem. But it's not here right now so I can't set you up."

"How long is this going to take?"

"Might be able to arrange it for later today. If you want to use your influence."

"Use it or lose it," I told him.

"I figured. I'll E-mail the details to you."

"I heard you don't have E-mail here."

"Hawwr. We just don't give out the address to every hairy dick." He offered a slight titter.

What a fucking world.

"How 'bout you call me when it's set up." I was about to give him my own number when I remembered he was an *idea* man. "Better yet, call and leave a message here."

I left him Jennifer's cell phone number. Not her private number, which she'd reluctantly given me, but her primary work cell phone. I had her back-up work number, too, but I hoped this would be good enough.

"Can do!" PYT chirped.

"One other thing," I said. "I'm especially interested in any additional material that may be in the library."

"How do you mean?"

"You know: outtakes, cut scenes, extra footage. Anything like that."

PYT shook his head at me, though it seemed to physically hurt him to have to do it. "I never heard of anything like that for *Devil on Sunday*. Sylvie would know for sure, but I don't think so."

"Can you make certain and check? With Sylvie or the vault or whoever might know?"

"I'll make a note," he said, and literally did so while I watched.

"Aces," I declared and gave him a big thumb's up. It was my new catch phrase, straight out of *Burning Bright*; one of the writers' big new ideas to perk up the ratings. Their first idea had been to revive "Hot enough for you?" my ancient ain't-he-a-riot line from the days of *Salt & Pepper*. I made it clear that pigs would fly and Dan Quayle become queen of England before I would allow that to happen.

"Yeah," PYT said, shaking his head. "I would definitely lose that 'aces' bit. That is far and away my first big idea."

I tucked my thumb away and took my leave.

A note on my windshield informed me in block letters: I KNOW WHERE YOU LIVE ASSHOLE. It wasn't signed, but it had to be McBeal or one of her scrawny minions. I tossed it.

I drove off-lot to a nearby Mexican joint where the cervezas are as cold as the carne asada is hot. There are no piñatas dangling from the ceiling, you can sit all day long sipping your beer and reading your newspaper, and they never, but never, play mariachi. That last is far and away the most important quality in a Mexican restaurant. After three Coronas, some deep-fried ice cream, and as much of the *LA Times* I can bear to read in a day, I checked in with Jennifer. I called her from a pay phone by the little caballeros room because I don't care what everyone else does, I'll be damned if I'm going to carry one of those mobile cancer projectors on my person. I'm just afraid that soon there'll be no more pay phones because Superman and I will be the only ones left using them. Anyway Jennifer, God bless her, answered her phone on the second ring. PYT had already gotten back to her—ah, influence and its happy, happy use—and arranged for me to see *The Devil on Sunday* at five o'clock pending my confirmation. That left me with the entire afternoon to fritter away, but then "Fritter" was my mother's maiden name. My uncle Corn had a miserable childhood.

"Tell him that's okey-doke," I said.

"He also said to tell you that, hold on a sec let me check this . . . okay: Too many earth tones. He said you'd understand. Does that make any sense?"

"Only in LA. Thanks heaps."

"No earth tones," I muttered, then nodded at a passing waiter who eyed me suspiciously. Probably figured pay phone users tip for shit. (Probably right.) But who the hell did PYT think he was fooling, trying to pass off old *Miami Vice* guidelines as a big idea? Though I did note with some concern that I was wearing brown suede shoes. ("Caramel" the salesman had told me.)

Fuck it. *Burning Bright* might not be racking up the Emmies, but at least I wasn't co-starring with Cheech Marin.

. . .

They sent me over to the main building where all the Suits hang out. I'd only been there once before, for the round of hearty handshakes which accompanies the launch of every new series, and I felt conspicuously underdressed amid all that Italian silk. I found myself looking at the various Suits' shoes and noting that not a one of them wore caramel. Or butterscotch. Or any other earth tone. Damn that PYT!

Screening rooms intimidate the hell out of me. I suppose it's because I've never had a good experience in one. Then again, I appeared in so many awful movies back in the days of my declining youth that statistically, there was little chance of my attending a truly happy screening. The worst, I think, was for *Teenius,* one of the first big film roles I landed not long after my TV career tanked. I was still young enough to play fresh-faced-and-spunky and some whiz kid at Warner cast me as the supposedly smartest teenager in the world. At the time, Warner had in mind to take on Disney for the kiddy comedy market, and grabbed up Dean Jones and Kurt Russell as the headliners. The shoot was a fiasco, though, with a director whose main interest was the admittedly mature-looking fifteen-year-old who played my puppy love interest. For reasons that now escape me, I was invited along to the initial screening for the studio head. At the end of ninety agonizing minutes, graced by not so much as a chuckle or pity titter from anyone present, the lights came up and the studio head glanced around the room, his hateful, black eyes alighting on me (Jones and Russell having long since vanished, and the director already languishing in rehab). I tried to smile at him, but the muscles in my face wouldn't obey. The big cheese didn't say a word, just stared at me. Then he reached out, closed one eye and slowly drew a circle in the air around my head with his finger. Around and around and around. Then he curled the finger in, as if he was shooting an imaginary gun.

I swear I felt the bullet pass right between my eyes.

The other thing about screening rooms is that they're always freezing cold. Summer, winter—it doesn't matter. You could have bred penguins in the room they'd sent me to view *The Devil on Sunday.* Years before, an old PR flack explained to me that the temperature control was very deliberate and ever had it been so.

"Better they should lose a toe or two to frostbite than fall asleep on a picture," he said.

Such is the wisdom of Hollywood.

There were two short aisles of very plush seats—more like United Airlines first class than any multiplex I've ever endured—and I sat down front row center. A telephone handset was cradled neatly in the armrest, but there wasn't any drink holder. Of course, the floor wasn't sticky either, so I couldn't complain. I thought maybe I needed to let the projectionist know that I was ready, but as I reached for the receiver, the lights started to dim. Just as well, because what are the odds that the projectionist answers *his* phone?

As the credits rolled and the sub-Miklós Rózsa score kicked in, I had the faint feeling that I must indeed have seen *The Devil on Sunday* before. I couldn't exactly remember it—and maybe I was just thinking of two dozen other similar films I'd no doubt watched back in the days when late-night TV was chock-full of neat old movies instead of infomercials and reruns of sitcoms starring stunted minority children—but something about the picture definitely rang a few bells. John Dall plays a petty grifter who wanders into a lonesome Texas town posing as a traveling preacher man. He meets up with Ann Savage, who's just a little *too* femme fatale for Nowheresville, Texas, and who uses her womanly wiles—in the form of some pretty daring cleavage for 1952—to enlist Dall's help in knocking off her brutish, ranch-owner husband, played by Cecil Kellaway in what amounts to a replay of his role in *The Postman Always Rings Twice*. Little does Dall know that Savage is setting him up so that she can get off with the real love of her life, one hundred percent USDA psychopath Tom Neal. *But . . .* little does *Savage* know that Neal is playing *her* for a patsy, because he's got a capital *h* hard-on for Lizabeth Scott, the local reverend's lovely, if somewhat vivacious, not-so-little girl. In the course of arranging hubby's demise, Dall encounters Scott and falls hard for her, after which the two of *them* scheme to do bad stuff to Savage. Basically, the plot is an extremely vicious circle of cross, double, triple, and quadruple-cross with the various paramours declaring that they'd take on the world for each other, while busily lusting after the next sucker in line. Predictably, it ends in a bloodbath, though I couldn't quite keep track of precisely who killed who, the twist being that only Kellaway is left alive. And there's just a hint, in the film's very peculiar final close-up of Kellaway, that he engineered the whole shebang. In any case, for its many narrative failings, at only sixty-eight minutes *The Devil on Sunday* sure as hell *moves*.

As the lights came up and I kneaded my frozen digits to restore circulation, I could see where there might be interest in remaking the film. Noir never really dies, and *The Devil on Sunday* is about as dark as it gets. The world it evokes is one lacking even the *idea* of sunlight. Amazingly, for a story set in the wide open spaces, there's barely a scene that takes place outside of dingy, little rooms. I realize this was likely a function of no budget for location shooting, but it gives *The Devil on Sunday* a disturbingly claustrophobic and sweaty feel. The quality of the acting is variable, but Neal is a very convincing psycho—a kind of Hays Code Hannibal Lecter—and Anne Savage was nothing if not well-named. Not too hard to imagine someone like Linda Fiorentino taking on the part today. The ending, with everyone shooting each other in one small room, prefigured the likes of Tarantino by decades, and the Texas setting offered that perfect Cormac McCarthy feel. I could easily imagine *The Devil on Sunday* being John Woo's favorite movie and wondered who they'd lined up to direct the remake. Whoever it was would doubtless bring the sex to the fore, but I doubted they could make a film more out and out sexy than old Buzz Day had managed. Even if Buzz wasn't exactly a master of continuity.

Actually, I started to wonder about some of the gaps in plot logic. Low-budget filler of the type *The Devil on Sunday* was cranked out to be often failed to concern itself with the finer points of narrative exactitude, but watching *Devil* I did feel like maybe something was missing. For one thing, a sprite waitress who threatens to throw a monkey wrench into everyone's little plots—played well by Connie Clare—virtually disappears from the movie just when her part starts to get really juicy. And everything that follows goes a little haywire. On the one hand it adds to the movie's generally alienated quality, but at the same time it doesn't feel right. Hall had specifically asked me to try and track down any lost footage and given the holes in the story, it wasn't hard to believe that something was missing from the print I saw. I had, however, checked my copy of Leonard Maltin before coming in and noted that sixty-eight minutes was his listed running length, too. So maybe it was just a slapdash production. I mean, if such matters don't bother the geniuses who make the hundred-million-dollar stinkers they crank out today, why should it have mattered to the one-take wonders of fifties' back lots?

"Mr. Burns?"

My reverie was interrupted by a gravelly voice from the entrance to the screening room. A small, middle-aged woman with grayish hair and glasses that dangled from a chain around her neck blinked at me.

"Hi," I said.

"I'm Sylvie Braun," she called across the room to me. "I maintain the studio archive."

"Oh, right." She continued to stare at me from the doorway. "You can come on in," I said with a smile. "I don't bite. Hard."

The woman ducked her head inside the door, as if to take a good sniff before entering, and screwed up her face. Do I offend, I wondered?

"Would you maybe be kind enough to come out here?" she asked.

What the hey, I can play cooperative. I moseyed over to the exit and followed the archivist a little way up the hall, closing the door behind me. She sat down on a plush bench in the corridor—it was more like the lobby to the screening room's theater—and patted the seat next to her.

"Sit, please. And thank you. I don't like going in there. I'm a little susceptible to colds. My mother died of pneumonia."

"Sorry," I said, a bit puzzled.

"Never mind. I just came to check that everything was okay. I'm sorry I wasn't available to speak with you earlier. Did Benton take care of you? You saw what you wanted to see?"

So the PYT's name was Benton. From the way she said it, I knew it had to be his first name. Sometimes the whole universe suddenly makes perfect sense.

"Yes, Benton was very obliging." Why mention that he pitched at me? He wasn't *that* annoying.

"Very good. I think maybe you're the first person ever to ask to see *The Devil on Sunday*. Since I've been here, anyway."

"And how long is that?"

She scowled at me, and it occurred that perhaps my question was a tad rude. Like, So just how old are you, lady? I tried to cover.

"I mean to say, how well do you know the picture?"

The scowl deepened. Now, I'd insulted her professional credentials. Still, I was a "star" so she put on a brave face.

"It's not a personal favorite, if that's what you mean. I've always found the chic for film noir a little overdetermined. I'm partial to musicals myself. Give me *The Band Wagon* or *Meet Me in St. Louis* any day. But, of course, I am familiar with the film."

"Of course. What I was wondering really is, is that the whole film? I mean is that the only version?"

She put her half-glasses on the end of her nose, looked me up and down carefully *over* them, then took the glasses off again. "Yes, Benton mentioned that you were interested in any additional footage that might exist. I did check with the vault and they have nothing beyond this print. The film, you understand, wasn't originally a Fox production, it was acquired as part of a library some years later in a corporate takeover, so original production materials likely wouldn't be amongst our collection."

"So this is it?"

Braun breathed out an indulgent sigh. "I didn't say that. I said this is all we have, which is really what you asked."

"So there *is* more?"

"Not to my knowledge, but I repeat that film noir is not my specialty, and I must admit that *The Devil on Sunday* is not a work I've studied in any depth. I did a brief reference search before coming over to see you here and I found one listing for the film at seventy-three minutes, which suggests there is, or was, some additional footage. But these sources aren't always accurate. Do you have reason to think that something is missing from what you saw today?"

"A friend who knows about it suggested to me that there may be some extra scenes. And watching the movie—I don't know, it's kind of choppy. And the story seems to go a little funny about halfway in. The waitress character . . ."

"Connie Clare. She died," Braun said.

"Well, everybody dies, don't they? Isn't that the point? I mean, other than Cecil Kellaway, who's the one actor you'd really pay to see get plugged. And people ask how *I* can have a career."

"No, I mean the actress, Connie Clare. She died during the shooting of the picture. She was murdered."

"No kidding?"

Braun looked at me as if to ask why she would kid. And in all fairness to her, she did not have the twinkly-eyed look of the practiced prankster. I feel even the most joy-buzzer phobic could take her hand without the slightest worry.

"It *is* what the film is best known for, to the extent that it's known for anything at all."

"What happened to her?"

"She was strangled. It raised a stink at the time, but of course, she made so few films that she's very little known today."

"Wow. I guess that's why the picture's so disjointed. They must have had to shoot around her for some of the stuff."

"That could be. Like I say, I don't know it well enough to offer you definitive information."

"What if I wanted to find out more? Where would I go?"

Braun looked very put-upon and sighed deeply again, as if this is what she'd been waiting for.

"I can research the film for you, of course. I have a lot on my plate at the moment, but if it's not a terrible rush . . ."

"Well, that would be very nice, but I don't mind looking into it myself. We're not shooting at the moment . . ."

"It's those eighteen to thirty-fours, isn't it?"

Christ on a crutch! "Uh-huh. So I've got some spare time and nothing special to do. If you could maybe point me in the right direction."

"There are many good libraries in town. UCLA is probably your best bet, but there's USC if you can be bothered to schlepp over there, and the Directors Guild. But really, if I wanted to know something special about a movie like this, I'd talk to Harry Blanc."

"Who's he?"

"He runs Blanc's Noir—I know, it's a terrible name—on Hollywood Boulevard. It's a collector's shop. Posters, lobby cards, stills. All that crap. He sells some dirty movies, too, if you know to ask, but only old ones. Who could get excited by such things?"

"It's a strange old world. I knew a fellow who got off on the credit sequence from *Pettitcoat Junction*." Sylvie shook her head. "You know, the bit suggesting that the girls are swimming naked in the water tank? It's . . . skip it. Does this Blanc guy, um, you know, speak English or geek?"

Braun nodded, understanding immediately. "He's a *collector*. He smells a little, but basically he's all right. He knows his stuff. If you want to wait, I'm sure I can set you up with a film professor who'll know this material, but honestly, probably not as well as Harry."

She wrote down the address for me and I thanked her. As I started to go, something occurred to me and I turned back to Braun.

"The waitress. Connie Clare. You said she was killed."

"Strangled."

"Who killed her?"

Braun put her glasses back on her nose, studied me over them, took them off again.

"You'll like Harry," was all she said.

"Martha Vickers. But with *class*."

That was Harry Blanc's assessment of Connie Clare when I saw him the next morning. I drove to Hollywood when I got up at nine, only to find that Blanc's Noir didn't open until eleven. Fortunately there's a Ship's in the neighborhood where I whiled away an hour drinking coffee and making toast. Ship's provides a toaster in every booth, so you can do it yourself, fresh. I do have a toaster at home and have been making my own toast for many years now, so it's not like it's a novelty, and I'm not sure what you pay a restaurant for if not to have them cook your food for you (I mean, how would it be if they dropped a raw chicken and some hot water on your table and told you to make your own goddamn soup?), but there's something kind of neat about eating out and making toast at the same time, so go figure. Still, it's not as good as the old automats. Am I the only one who remembers those great old Horn & Hardart baked beans? (Of course, they did bake them for you.)

After breakfast I walked up Hollywood Boulevard, an old stomping ground that I'm fortunate enough not to have to stomp on too much these days. I used to know many of the hookers here by name, though it was strictly a professional thing. That is to say *my* profession—scumbag PI—and *not* theirs. Although . . . never mind. I'm not ready for *This Is Your Life* just yet. Disney may have rebuilt the El Capitan, but unlike Times Square, they haven't managed to turn Hollywood into a theme park yet. The Boulevard remains a bastion of decay, depression, and depravity. And that's just the *d*'s. The *f*'s I don't like to consider.

You want to know the worst thing for me about walking down Hollywood Boulevard? I mean, other than having "Celluloid Heroes" resound in my head for the next three days? (Which still beats "Do You Know the Muffin Man?" by a country mile.) It's those damned stars on the sidewalk. Tourists really do come just to stare at them and take pictures—though I think even the Hollywood Chamber of Commerce would have to admit that they are a singularly unimpressive sight—but I can live with that. It's the stars themselves. Or rather, the ones that aren't there.

Like mine.

As with the Oscars, you don't earn a star so much as you buy one. Or have one bought for you by the industry machine. The sidewalk stars are dished out according to who can pay for the PR at the right time. Who's got something big to push or needs a kick in the publicity ass. That's why the stars are about as meaningful as those "ID cards" you scam as a kid to try and prove that you're old enough to buy Night Train. Everyone knows it's bullshit. That's why Ray Davies could sing in such a heartfelt way about the place.

So why the hell does it bother me so much?

I think it's because I nearly had one. A star, I mean. No kidding. Back when *Salt & Pepper* was (briefly) in the Nielsen top ten, and my catchphrase "Hot enough for you?" was sweeping the nation— okay, lightly feather-dusting—our producer, loathsome sitcom poo- bah Manny Stiles, walked into my dressing room one morning with a more-shit-eating-than-usual grin on his cratered moon of a face.

"Boychick," he said, slapping me on the butt, "we're getting you a star."

I didn't have a clue what he was talking about and was more concerned with the sweaty hand which had not left my ass, but Manny explained that he'd fixed it for me—and my catchphrase—to be immortalized forever in the concrete memorial that is Hollywood Boulevard. I was thrilled, of course, and immediately told everyone I knew about the impending honor. The fact that some bratty kid in a forgettable, flavor-of-the-month sitcom could conceivably be ac- corded such status should tell you all you need to know about the worth of those stars. I remember some skepticism at the time from my colleagues, but because Manny had previously secured a star for Kooky, the chimp who featured in *Ape Over Ewe,* most doubts were allayed.

For weeks, I pestered Manny for details of when the big day was going to be. Manny, who was not a nice man at the best of times, got more and more fed up with me, not least because *Salt & Pepper*'s ratings took a hit and kept on falling as awkward adolescence made mincemeat of my few endearing features. Being about as bright as Manny was kind, I continued to badger him even as talk of cancellation drifted down to cast level. Finally, at the end of a particularly bad day of shooting, with the network vultures all but visibly circling overhead, I threw a ten-on-the-Joan-Crawford-scale tantrum, center stage, demanding to know when I was getting my star. With everyone staring—and more than a few drooling, eyes ablaze with delight—Manny walked up to me.

"Sonny boy," he said, "when dogs shit stars, you'll have your place on Hollywood Boulevard."

I honestly don't care about such things today—I've seen and been through far too much—but I still can't look at those pathetic little stars without thinking back on what might have been and what actually was. How close I came to the stuff of dreams, and where I ultimately landed. You must know that endlessly repeated Oscar Wilde line about how we're all in the gutter, but some of us are looking at the stars. Well, the thing about Hollywood—about the Boulevard which bears its name—is that what Wilde said is still true, especially when you're too down to be able to look up.

That's the kind of stuff that descends on me when I go back to Hollywood. And as if on cue, a mangy skeleton of a mutt crossed my path like a black cat, and took a long piss on Doris Day.

Town without pity or what?

Harry Blanc recognized me before I could introduce myself. He was sitting on a stool behind the counter, talking to another customer, but he literally dropped off in midsentence to run over and greet me. He had me signing publicity stills from *Burning Bright* and, remarkably, some faded PR stuff from *Salt & Pepper* before I knew what hit me. The other customer looked me over carefully as he huffed out of the store, but there wasn't any recognition in his eyes. Fortunately, I'm used to that. Harry didn't even blink as the potential cash sale departed.

Blanc's Noir was a mess. There are a slew of "nostalgia" and collector-oriented shops in Hollywood, and they all look about the same: fifteen-watt bulbs dangling from frayed cords; piles of manila folders leaking glossy stills from floor to ceiling; and movie posters, yellow and brown and obscenely overpriced, plastered up and down the walls. Harry's shop looked as if the cops had just tossed it, and it smelled like your aunt's mildewed attic. God alone knows how the man made a living out of it—I suppose those awful prices have something to do with it.

Harry Blanc, as Sylvie Braun had warned me, was notably odorific in his own right, a less than pleasing melange of fast food, sweat, and Brut 33. He was fat, of course—the guys who run these shops always are—and a few minutes either side of fifty. His stringy hair was plastered in a particularly unsuccessful comb-over which not only failed to disguise his baldness, but also accentuated two bulbous cysts on his pate. His clothes, at least, looked clean, though where he got a *Manimal* T-shirt—in what looked to me like mint condition—only his haberdasher and Simon MacCorkindale know for sure.

It quickly became clear that while Harry Blanc might not be a babe magnet (though who can say? The world is invariably more bizarre than I ever suppose, especially on Hollywood Boulevard), he knew his movies like nobody's business. Before I could broach the subject of *The Devil on Sunday,* he grilled me about my own, less than memorable film career.

"Is Kay Lenz as nice as she looks?" he practically begged.

"I wouldn't know."

"But you worked together."

"I don't think so," I told him. Kay Lenz?

"You co-starred in *Maisy Day.* You had a love scene!"

"Oh, shit," I said. The memory hit me like a falling safe. I'd have bet a hundred bucks that my co-star had been Susan Saint James. She *was* really nice. "Those were drinking days," I explained to him.

Before he could pick the scabs off the rest of my lost years with his razor blade curiosity, I explained that the Fox archivist had sent me and why I was there. That's when he compared Connie Clare with Martha Vickers.

"Martha Vickers. Nope, can't get a picture. Help me out."

"Carmen Sternwood in *The Big Sleep.* Lauren Bacall's kid sister. The hophead in the porno sting."

"Oh, yeah," I said. "She was cute."

"Married to Mickey Rooney."

"Wasn't everyone?"

Harry liked that.

"Vickers never quite hit it, neither did Clare. Clare had big girl bubbies, though."

I'd never heard a man his age use "bubbies" to refer to a woman's breasts. Tits, hooters, headlights, gazongas, melons, all of that, sure. But bubbies? It was kind of sweet, even coming out of this smelly fat guy's mouth, and I suddenly looked at him a little differently. Though I was more convinced than ever about the babe magnet thing.

"I understand that *The Devil on Sunday* was her last film," I said.

"Had to be, didn't it? Got killed while they were making it."

"That's what Sylvie Braun told me."

Harry walked across the shop and went to one of a dozen identical looking piles of folders, and running his finger down from the top, readily found and pulled one out. It held an old through-the-Vaseline studio glossy of Connie Clare in a shimmering, semitransparent drape of a dress that proved she did, indeed, have big girl bubbies. In all honesty, it hadn't struck me so much in the course of watching the film, but then she wasn't in it all that long.

"Raped, beaten, strangled, and dumped. They found her body in a parking lot down in south central. Supposedly she had a thing for black men's why the cops never cleared the case."

"What's that got to do with anything?" Clare had kind eyes, but looked like a million other blond wannabes. Hard to find fame in those features.

"Just the times, I suppose. If you think things have really changed. You ever read any James Ellroy, Walter Mosley?"

"I've seen the movies," I explained.

"Not the same. There was a big to-do at the time. *Devil on Sunday* got some press out of the killing, but it didn't help."

"The picture wasn't a hit?"

"Might have earned its money back. Didn't do much for Buzz Day. He ended up directing puppet shows on TV. Picture had some other troubles, too."

"Such as?" I asked. I handed him back Connie Clare's photo. He delicately stashed it back in its folder.

"Supposedly, the fellow who wrote it was bearding for someone else. On the blacklist at the time. Pretty common."

"Frank Emerson was a front?" Hall's father.

"Never been clear what was going on. I've read all the books about the time, and a few names have been thrown up. Dalton Trumbo for one. Emerson always denied bearding, and no one else claimed it even after most of these things got straightened out after McCarthy and that bunch went south, but the story's out there."

"Huh." I'd have to ask Hall about this. "And do you know anything about missing footage or lost scenes from *The Devil on Sunday*?"

"You mean like a director's cut or something?" Harry laughed, spitting some as he did so. "A Buzz Day director's cut. Wouldn't that be a thing? DVD might sell two copies, counting me."

"Sylvie Braun mentioned that there's some discrepancy on the recorded running times for the movie. And someone else told me they read about some scenes which aren't on the video."

Harry scratched his comb-over, then his nose. He shook his head. "I never heard of anything like that. Could be possible there's a different cut of the thing, but I don't know where you'd ever find it. If you saw the vault copy, you saw what's there. Video company likely pulled their version off that or off an old TV copy if they was walking a thin legal line. The chances that any other copy of something like *Devil*'d be out there are pretty damn slim. One might turn up in an attic someday, but that's nothing to bank on. And like I say, I try to know about these things and I never heard of any lost scenes."

I thanked Harry for the information and signed a few more things for him before I left. As I was walking out the door he called me back into the shop, handed me an envelope. I looked inside and saw it contained the still of Connie Clare.

"Why don't you have that? Souvenir of your visit to Blanc's Noir. Look at them bubbies some more before you go to sleep."

And he winked at me. I suspect he may never have winked at anyone before. I pray he never does try it on a woman.

I unenthusiastically thanked him again and beat a hasty retreat. I might look at that glossy again—might even check out her bubbies; I admit, I'm that kind of guy—but with Harry's pathetic wink imbedded in my memory, it was the last thing I'd ever want to do before I went to sleep.

Three

I'd intended to call Hall Emerson on Tuesday morning, though I didn't have a whole lot to report. It would be fun to chat about *The Devil on Sunday* and what he thought he could do with the material—it's one of those movies that's more entertaining to talk about afterward than it is to actually watch—but it didn't look as though any of the footage he was hoping to find still existed. Harry Blanc definitely seemed to know his stuff—however sad his brand of stuffing might be—and I felt like I'd done Hall as good a turn as our limited friendship demanded in seeing the movie *and* Blanc. I waited to actually phone, because while I might not be a morning person (though on Tuesday I was up at a positively early-birdlike eight-thirty), Hall was a writer. I've known a few in my day, and not a one of them was ever any use before lunch. The reason so many writers wear beards is that they're too goddamn lazy to shave. And the ones who do always seem to miss the same spot under their chins.

So I was just hanging around, watching morning TV and debating where to go out for my lunch, when the phone rang. I let the machine screen it, heard the dulcet tones of my agent, Kendall, and picked up. Kendall is one of the few people in the world who I am always happy to talk to. I never dreamed that such a thing could be said about an agent, but then Kendall isn't your garden variety pond scum in a power suit. In fact, if I wasn't so afraid of blowing our professional relationship, I might have harbored a dirty thought or two about her and those wonderfully unfashionable little denim skirts she wears.

Not to mention how she couldn't stop laughing on the one, drunken occasion when I did make a slurred, oh-God-please-tell-me-I-didn't-do-that pass at her.

You have to be sensitive to these kinds of subtleties if you want to be a successful New Man in our complicated world.

"I didn't wake you, did I Marty?" were Kendall's first words.

I swear, we could have made beautiful music together.

"No, I'm up. I set my alarm because Sally Jessy is confronting the contradictions of late capitalism in a global information society this morning. Sarah Michelle Gellar and Ike Turner are her special guests."

"Sounds like a keeper."

"Tape's a-rolling, baby. I'll send you a dupe."

"Groovy," Kendall chirped. I *think* she was laughing with me. She's so straitlaced that sometimes even I can't always decide if she doesn't do irony at all or is living an all-encompassing, post-ironic joke at the world's—and my—expense. Whatever, she's a great agent.

"So what's happening with the show? Any word from on high?"

"Nothing yet, Marty. I've tried to get some sense of how they're thinking, but mum is very definitely the word for now."

"Is that a good sign or bad?"

"Hard to say. You know that the VP for Ongoing Series Development just got the chop?"

"Again? Which one was he?"

"She. She was always the one in the middle."

"Oh, yeah. The one without a nose." Like prancing animals on the veldt, many midlevel Suits travel in packs. It gives them the illusion of safety, but when the lions get hungry, the gazelles still get their throats torn out.

"I believe she did actually have a nose. It just wasn't very prominent."

"It was one of those little upturned, piggy things. Made me kind of sick."

"Well, don't give it another thought, because she's gone now."

"I always wondered what she did on the beach, how she could wear sunglasses? What did she perch them on?"

"You're sure right about that."

"Okay, she could wear contacts out of the sun—if she needed glasses I mean. Or get that corrective laser surgery. But in the sun? She's screwed isn't she?"

"Marty . . ."

"And how could she hope to succeed in this burg if she couldn't go wear cool-looking, designer shades? I mean, it goes it with the Suit, doesn't it? Who was gonna take her seriously?"

"She's history, Marty, so don't dwell on it. They've already replaced her, repainted her parking spot and told Pete at the gate not to let her pass. And the new guy has a honker big as a baby chick."

"Well, I suppose that's okay then. Wait, how big *is* a baby chick?"

"Big enough. The point is, the change has pushed the decision process back a few days. They've brought the new guy in to live or die on the decisions the big wheels make on this final round of options. They always cover themselves with a sacrificial lamb or two. If I was a betting woman, I'd lay"—I could hear Kendall deciding how honest to be with me in the silence; she's really a terrible liar (so how does she survive as an agent?)—"sixty-forty they pick up the last nine episodes."

Ouch. Too much honesty. "I was hoping for better," I confessed.

"You're getting killed by those damned eighteen to thirty-fours."

"There's the worst-kept secret in town."

"In any case, you know that I'll call you as soon as I have even an inkling of how it's going to go. I still have my spies, you know."

"Right. Thanks."

"I'm actually calling now about a completely different subject. Well, maybe not *completely* different."

"What's up?"

"I had a call this morning from Kevin Ryan Paul."

WHOOP-WHOOP-WHOOP! Synchronicity alert.

"Say what?" I barked, playing it Marty Burns-cool.

"Do you know him?"

"I know . . . of him. I'll explain in a minute. What did he want?"

"It would seem that he's ready for preproduction on a project called *The Devil on Sunday*. Independent money, he says, but fixed-up with New Line on the distribution end. I'd take that with a giant salt shaker, but never mind. One of the actors he had signed for a meaty, secondary role suddenly dropped out on him. He'd like to meet with you to discuss the part."

"Oh, man," I said.

"What is it, Marty?"

I explained to Kendall about Hall Emerson's request, and the fact that I'd screened the original just the day before.

"Hmmm. Tiny little world isn't it. Maybe Emerson mentioned your name to Paul," Kendall suggested. "He said this literally just came up. And you know how these things work."

"Could be," I said, though I couldn't see Hall talking me up. "Did he mention what the part is?"

"Only in general terms. He's messengering a script over to me later. He said it was very dark."

"It's the new black, you know."

"No, it's not. Latino is the new black. I think we may even be getting very close to white as the next new black. Maybe, *maybe,* dark was last year's black. But Paul doesn't have to know that for his money to be green. And green is always black."

"Did he talk numbers?"

"Not to so many decimal places. But he certainly sounded interested."

"You think I should meet him."

Another silence, in which I could hear Kendall tapping her fingernails on the arm of her chair. Last time I was in her office I noticed that the wood is scarred with little, half-moon indentations. I'd always assumed it was the office cat.

"Paul is talking about shooting during what would be your normal hiatus. You know that there's nothing else lined up right now. Let's assume the best, that Fox picks *Burning Bright* up for the final nine. What happens after that if the demos don't improve? If we're sweating a midseason pick-up . . ."

"Which we are," I muttered.

"Which we are," Kendall agreed, "then the honest truth is we're gonna shvitz us an ocean come the end of the run."

Shvitz? Maybe my sweet, goyish, Midwestern Kendall had gone LA after all.

"You don't exactly fill a man with confidence."

"Well, sometimes that's my job, but sometimes I'm here to tell you what's what. It's not fun, you know."

"I can imagine. So what you're saying is that it couldn't hurt to cover my ass if there's no fourth season."

"No pain at all. If you don't like it, you don't do it. Simple enough?"

I sighed. "Nothing ever turns out that simply, Kendall."

"I know. But why not meet Paul?"

"Do you know him?"

"We've schmoozed. He'd like to be a big player, but I don't think he's got the chutzpah." Definitely a trip home to Kansas for Kendall this Christmas. "He's not more than a . . . five on the lizard meter."

"Five?"

"Six."

"Six?"

"Maybe six and a half."

"Kendall . . ."

"I don't think he makes seven. Most days. I hear he's good to his mother."

"Did *he* tell you that?"

"Who remembers sources? So tell me what you're thinking."

I was thinking that something smelled funny about the timing of all this. I was also thinking that I'd grown accustomed to a certain comfort in my lifestyle and wouldn't want to go back to lunch debates where the point-counterpoint was baloney versus tuna.

And if only because of Hall Emerson, I was more than usually curious about the remake of *The Devil on Sunday*.

"Go ahead and set up a meeting," I told her.

"Great!"

"We'll see," I said.

"Oh, Marty, don't be such a Gloomy Gus all the time."

"I'll try, Kendall. But I'm Popeye, you know? I yam what I yam."

"What you are is a pain in the tuchis," she declared, and said goodbye. But Kendall pronounced it "took-us" so she wasn't ready for her bat mitzvah just yet.

And old Gloomy Gus is nobody's fool.

I rang Hall just after noon, but there was no answer. Not even a machine. Good on him, I say.

Lunch turned out to be a sandwich at a seaside café in Hermosa. I can walk out my door, up the beach, and enjoy an avocado club and fries in full view of the roaring ocean and the smell of semitreated waste which floats down from the leaking pipes of the big plant at El Segundo. Beats baloney any day, though I am still partial to a nice tuna melt.

While I was sitting there, enjoying a postprandial Sierra Nevada Pale Ale and watching the dirty terns scavenge what edible bits they could from the dusting of Styrofoam and aluminum that litters the beach edge, a fan approached me. At least, I always assume they're fans until they speak. You never know. Unless you're really famous— and a show on Fox don't cut it—you don't actually get approached that much in LA, except maybe by tourists. The celebs who want to be seen, and complain about their lack of privacy afterward, know where in town to go to get it. Like junkies who know their street corners. The rest of us manage just fine.

This guy was short and fiftyish with glasses, silver-flecked hair and two little girls in tow. He was wearing shorts and a sporty polo shirt that screamed "California!" but he had the whitest, worm-belly legs imaginable. Hairy, too. He cocked his head like a jackdaw and squinted at me from a distance of a couple of yards, while the girls played ring-around-the-rosey about him.

"Aren't you Marty Burns?" he asked.

"I am," I cooed, eyelashes aflutter. I like to play it humble.

"I like *Burning Bright,*" he said, clearly a little nervous.

"Would you be willing to be cloned?"

He laughed. God bless him, the perfect audience. (Naturally: he was well past thirty-four; probably a smoker.)

"Ann and Kate here are as close as I come," he said, indicating the two girls. They paused briefly in their game to glance up at me, but were singularly unimpressed because they went right back to ringing rosey again.

"I like how the show reminds me of the TV I enjoyed years ago," the guy went on, suddenly emboldened. "It has an interesting retro quality, but without all the knowingness that goes with most retro stuff. Do you know what I mean?"

What he meant was: We recycle old scripts from *Hawaii Five-O.* What I said was: "Thanks, thanks very much. I appreciate that."

We nodded at each other for a little while, both smiling nervous half-smiles. His girls were clearly getting impatient and he was about to go when a tanned, blond, college-age kid who'd been listening from a nearby table stood up and came over.

"So you're that Burns dude?" he said. *"Burning Trite."*

Uh-oh, I thought.

"Bright. Burning Bright," I said. I went for levity: "And yea, I am he."

"Your show really sucks turds," the kid smirked. And walked away.

I was really going to have to start taking these demographic issues more seriously.

Using all my actorly skills to sustain my grin I looked up at my remaining fan. He looked ashen, as if it was his fault that the other jerk had insulted me. I shrugged at him, trying to broaden the grin into a legitimate smile. Like Slappy White trying to play Othello, it was a bad idea, and the man slumped away, though his daughters remained happy as clams in clean, cold water.

And there you have fame in a nutshell: One minute they're buttering you up like a Thanksgiving turkey, the next they're greasing your rear to fuck you up the ass.

I quite literally spent the rest of the day puttering around the house. I putter extremely well—I've had offers to turn pro. Twice more I tried to call Hall Emerson, with no answer either time. I read for a while, watched some old sitcoms on TV (mercifully, *Salt & Pepper* is out of the syndication loop at the moment), sat on my genuine red-wood deck and stared at the sea. I still don't know what's so fascinating about it, but like most people I can spend hours looking at the water. Along with the moratorium on baloney, the best thing about recovering my acting career and the very nice money that comes with it, was being able to afford a house on the beach. I'm not one for lying out on the sand or actually frolicking in the surf, but give me an ocean view at twilight with Tom Waits playing in the background and a frosty brew or two in the foreground and I'm as happy as Robert Downey Jr. in Peru. You almost—*almost*—don't need cable when you've got the sea.

Kendall rang just as it was getting on time to think about dinner. Pizza? Chinese? The world is my take-out oyster.

"What's your schedule look like for tomorrow?" she asked.

"Breakfast at Tiffany's, dinner with Andre . . . you know, the usual."

"Marty, do you do anything at all with your time?"

"My entire life is mental preparation for those demanding moments when the cameras roll. I live only for experiences to draw upon for my art."

"That's a no, then."

"I don't have anything to do, Kendall. What's going on?"

"I've spoken with Kevin Ryan Paul again. By the way, I lied earlier. He's a definite seven-plus."

"How's that?"

"On the lizard scale. Sorry."

"It's okay, I assumed. He's a producer, isn't he?"

"He'd like to do lunch tomorrow. I have to confirm with his PA if it's a go."

"Man, that's quick."

"Mmmm. He seemed very anxious. Insists he needs to nail down the cast to please the money men."

"I don't know if I like the sound of that."

"Me, either. But let's see what he has to say. Are you still game?"

"Let me just check my book. Um . . . oh, I don't know, Kendall: There's a really good *Dick Van Dyke Show* on tomorrow at noon. The walnut episode."

"You know, Marty, when you say you're going to check your book, it's *not* meant to be *TV Guide*."

"I'm hopeless, Kendall. But you know that."

"Yes, I do. Shall I confirm?"

"Yeah, go for it."

"Marty," she said. And paused.

"What?"

"If you don't like this guy, if you don't get a good hit off him, then just pass and don't worry about it. I'll find you something else."

"There something about this you're not telling me, Kendall?"

"No. Just remember what I said."

Kendall gave me the details and said goodbye. I was a bit disconcerted by her final comments, but some nice moo shoo chicken and barbecue pork fried rice took care of that. I called Hall one more time, but still got no reply. The rest of the evening was spent watching Dodgers baseball (though now that they are, like me, owned by Mr. Murdoch, I don't enjoy it as much), drinking Anchor Steam and munching on blue corn chips and guacamole.

I tell you, this fast-lane Hollywood lifestyle is going to be the death of me.

Kendall arranged for me to meet with Paul at Blönde, the trendoid restaurant du jour on Montana in Santa Monica. And, no, I don't know why those two little dots hover over the "o" either. Me, I would have stuck an accent over the "e" and gone with a Dagmar theme, especially those humungo sandwiches. Perhaps Blönde is the owner's name or his girlfriend's hair color or he's a big Debbie Harry fan. What do I know from catering?

I'd not been to the restaurant before, and though I didn't make the top ten of celebs and movers/shakers dining on an average Wednesday afternoon, I can't say I liked the look of the joint. The walls were covered with oddly cut shards of light brown—hell, maybe *they* were blond—wooden panels. The jagged edges and sharp spikes of the paneling were echoed in all of the decor. The tables, too, were peculiar shapes: irregular polygons of different types, but each featuring a spiky wooden claw jutting out from one or more edges, like the spiny back of a triceratops. It was okay if there were only two or three diners, but any more than that and you had to beware of impalement. The waiters (and I didn't spot a single waitress) also wore dusky, brown vests with little velvet spikes jutting up over their shoulders. They were all blonds, with gelled, spiky hair—what the hell was the deal here?—and wore identical, granny glasses, each with different colored lenses. There was something disquietingly Norse about it all, though I took some comfort from the sight of the very un-blond, sans-spiky, Mexican busboys. Some facts of life in Southern California are immutable.

I thought I'd arrived on-the-dot, fashionably business lunch late at twenty-three minutes past the appointed hour, but Paul wasn't there yet. So I'd already been back-footed. To play it right, I should have then gone to wait in the bar and let Paul sit down first, but a) I hate those stupid power games; and b) I was scared I'd end up on the pointy side of the table (I bruise easily). So I let the maître d' lead me to my seat. He presented a drinks list of cocktails with silly and/or cute names that seemed more appropriate to a college bar—Heat Ray? Swamp Monster?—but I waved it off and ordered an Anchor Steam. To fit in, I should have passed the time fiddling with a pocket organizer or talking into a cell phone, but since I don't own either, I settled for my usual course of self-amusement: I carefully stripped and peeled the label off my bottle of beer. Cheap Date Burns, they call me.

When Paul walked in at thirty-seven minutes past the hour—I'd have to note that time for future etiquette—not only did *he* have a cell phone no bigger than a playing card plastered to his cheek, but a small entourage followed in his wake. He must have been a regular or the maître d' was very smooth, because Paul didn't even break stride as he came in. Walking backward all the while, the maître d' neatly stepped in front of Paul, and matching the producer's pace, led him up the aisle to our table, smiling all the way. The guy had the chair opposite mine out and ready for ass without Paul even having to pause. If Synchronized Sitting ever makes it as an Olympic event, these boys are odds-on for a medal.

Paul didn't make eye contact with me as he sat down, so absorbed was he in his perhaps legitimate phone call. "No way, baby," he said three times and winked at me as I looked him up and down. Paul was a squat bulldog of a man, thick around the neck and wrists (not too thick to prevent a Rolex from dangling), but well-built rather than doughy. His short, black hair was gelled enough for him to get a waiter's job, though mercifully spike-free. Natty, yet casual, his gray linen suit and open-necked pink silk shirt caused me to rethink my resistance to PYT Benton's earlier, earth tones advice: Come home Don Johnson, even Cheech is forgiven. Paul wore little Dutch boy clogs on his bare feet. I don't feel that men should wear clogs (I don't know *how* women wear them; what keeps them on?), but then I think nice shoes are one of the other worthwhile perks of earning big money.

"Pay or play, sweetmeat, that's the name of the tune. Same as it ever was," Paul spat into his phone, then in a single, undoubtedly much-practiced motion, flicked it off and tossed it into the air, where it was caught by one of his still-standing sidekicks. Ricky Jay couldn't have done it neater. I was still marveling, thinking about applause, when he stuck a big hand out and offered me a wide-as-Celine-Dion's-ass smile.

"Hello, Marty. It's a genuine pleasure to meet you."

"Kevin." I nodded back at him. His hand was ever so slightly sweaty, mine was dry as a bone. Hmmm.

"I can't tell you how happy, really happy, I am that you agreed to come." He turned to the big dude—bodyguard? chauffer? personal trainer?—who'd caught the phone. "Am I happy?" he asked him.

"I can't remember the last time you were this happy," the guy admitted.

"See?" he said to me. As if Phone Dude's testimony had been Clarence Darrow's summing up in the Scopes Monkey Trial.

"Happy is as happy does," I offered, enigmatically Gump-like.

"I always say that," Paul told me sincerely, still holding onto my hand.

Phone Dude didn't sit down, merely took a few steps back from the table and leaned against the wall, hands folded over his crotch like a soccer player defending a free kick. Paul's other two companions did sit. The remaining straight edge of table was grabbed by a small man with a shaved head, all dressed in black. He was introduced to me as Kant, though I'm guessing at the spelling. He didn't say a word the entire time, so I can only assume his name wasn't "Can't" as in the contraction for not being able to speak. I think there's an agency in town that rents guys like him out by the hour. The remaining member of our little bridge party was an Irish setter redhead with truly lovely features, but so wafer-thin as to either suffer from a menu's worth of eating disorders or be a method actress up for the lead in *Schindler's List II: Life's a Gas*. She got stuck at the spiny end of the table, but was thin enough to sit between the danger points.

"I'm Sade," she said, offering up her no-need-for-X-ray-specs hand. She pronounced it to rhyme with "blade" (as in thin-as-a), informing me: "You spell it like the singer. But *I* pronounce it the way it looks."

Actually, to me it looks like the Marquis with the whips, but at least I'm sure of the spelling. And to be fair to Paul he looked a bit embarrassed by her. Why he had to bring her along at all, except in order to be *seen* with an entourage, is yet another Hollywood mystery.

The waiter brought drinks for Paul and his companions without them having to order. Kant looked particularly grateful for this. If you drank a Burnished Nail, you'd probably feel the same. I had another Anchor Steam. "Let me, before anything else, tell you how much *Burning Bright* means to me," Paul said. He sipped a glass of red wine.

"It's . . ." Paul gazed up at the ceiling, quickly looking away from the spiky mobile that dangled there, then at his companions, then impossibly earnestly at me. "It's like a visit *home,* every week, in prime time. Beautiful, man. Truly beautiful."

"That's . . . very kind," I managed.

"And frankly, you're perfect in it. Ten out of ten. Eleven even."

"Ten out of eleven?"

"*Kidder.* Eleven out of ten."

"You're far too kind." Had this guy never seen *Spinal Tap*? Or had he not realized it wasn't a real documentary?

"Huh? Huh?" he said, nodding. His laserlike gaze briefly slipped as he shot Sade a look. I think maybe she'd blown a cue.

"Yeah," she suddenly spurted. She again took my hand in her rat-wing claw. "Can I tell you something?"

"There is no voice I would rather listen to at this moment."

Paul smiled. Lord have mercy, I think he believed me.

"Sometimes I play with myself when I watch," she whispered.

Thank God I hadn't just taken a drink or I'd have done a spit take for sure.

"Pardon?" I managed.

"Burning Bright." She fluttered her eyelids at me. With her big head and emaciated body, the action nearly sent her tumbling over. "It makes me . . . come."

"Oh," I said. "My."

"Huh? Huh?" Paul repeated.

I extricated my hand and looked around for the March Hare or the Mad Hatter or the Queen of Hearts. But all I could see was the Walrus and the Carpenter at a corner table along with their lawyers and an executive vice-president from Paramount, so I waved to our waiter.

"Menus? Now? *Please?*"

I did what I do in every restaurant, no matter how swanky or greasy, which is glance around at the other tables and see what the food looks like before ordering. It was only then that I realized that virtually no one in the place was eating. There were plenty of glasses, sure, and phones and laptops and scripts piled high. But barely a plate of food to be seen.

Blönde wasn't an *eating* restaurant; it was a *Business* restaurant.

Well, fuck it, I was hungry. I might not get a part in *The Devil on Sunday,* but damn it, I was coming out of this with a full tummy.

The cuisine was SoCal Nouvelle, which means it all tastes like pesto, it's draped with unidentifiable greenery, and the portions can only be detected with an electron microscope. Paul clearly didn't expect to eat, and didn't touch his fish sliver when it came, but ordered because I did. Sade, who I wouldn't have believed had a functioning epiglottis, ordered plankton soup which the waiter balanced precariously on a table spike. Perhaps the customers didn't order for fear of tipping over their plates. Kant ate what they stuck in front of him. I don't know what it was, but I could smell the basil.

"So tell me about *The Devil on Sunday*," I prompted, tucking into my chicken-pesto-whatever. Surprisingly, it wasn't bad.

It must have been set up ahead of time, because at precisely that moment Phone Dude stepped in and handed the cell phone to Paul. "Eisner," he mouthed. I've never been much at reading lips, but if Marcel Marceau had been as crude a mime, he'd be working in the escargot factory today.

Paul hesitantly reached for the phone, then held his palm out in a "stop" gesture worthy of Diana Ross. "I'll call him back later," he said. "Marty Burns is more important."

Phone Dude nodded approvingly, then turned away and mumbled something into the tiny handset before tucking it away. If Michael Eisner was on the other end of that call, I was the Little Mermaid. Paul had even less subtlety than Blönde's decor. Producers: Can't live with them, can't plunge a fileting knife just beneath the clavicle and slowly trace a painful, deep incision to a point above the pubis and . . .

Actually, there's no good reason why you can't do that. Never mind. *"The Devil on Sunday,"* I tried again.

"What can I tell you? It is a great property. Dark with a capital 'd.' Do you know dark? Do you understand dark? 'Cause I sense that you do, Marty."

"I keep telling people it's the new black," I said.

"Unbelievable. Un-, pardon my French, *fucking* believable. I knew you were my man, Marty. I knew it." He turned to Sade, who was staring rapturously at me and nodding her head. I kept one nervous eye on where her fingers might be wandering to. "Did I say Marty Burns was the man?"

"Totally."

"You still haven't told me the man for what? My agent never got that copy of the script you were supposed to send."

"Administrative detail. We're putting the finishing touches on the latest rewrite. No point in you reading yesterday's news. She gets a new draft hot off the printer. Count on that."

Kant started to choke at that point, as if he couldn't swallow Paul's words either. We watched for a few seconds as his waxed pate went from sun-bed-tan to pass-the-defibrillator-red. I don't know the Heimlich maneuver, though I've always meant to learn, and calculated the likely success of on-the-job training. Fortunately, Phone Dude stepped up and slapped Kant across the back hard enough to knock him out of chair and under the table. Thank God he wasn't facing the spikes or it could have been bloody. When he came back up he seemed to be breathing fine, the redness fading from his dome. He waved his thanks at Phone Dude, who resumed his place against the wall. Kant offered a mildly embarrassed shrug and went back to his lunch.

No one else in the place even looked up, and Paul continued as if nothing had happened.

"I see *The Devil on Sunday* as a cross between *L.A. Confidential* and *The Usual Suspects*. Huh? Huh? Only darker."

"They have to be able to see the pictures on the screen, you know."

"Yeah, yeah. I think there's a hunger out there for this material that never goes away. It's got sex and violence, but without the bang-bang big stuff that draws bad press. It's too personal for that. No one's going to see this and start shooting up their high school. Capish?"

"It's the good kind of violence."

"Marty, I feel like we've got one mind."

Between us maybe, and hard as it was to believe, I think it all belonged to me. "Thank you, Kevin," is what I said.

"Have you, uh, ever seen the original? The Buzz Day version?"

"You know, I think I have. I used to watch a lot of late night television."

"It's nothing. Not a patch, not a piss squirt on the underpants of what I have in mind."

"That's quite an image."

"I have kind of a way with words, if you don't mind my saying so. I did write the script after all."

"*You* wrote it?"

"I had the original to work with, of course, but it was nothing. Just a pencil sketch on which to base my oil painting. A hummed ditty which I used to compose a symphony."

"Sounds pretty good."

"Marty. It's fucking fantastic. I know I can't bullshit you and I wouldn't try. You might think I'm just blowing my own horn . . ."

For some reason that brought a titter from Kant.

"Blow, Gabriel, blow," I said.

"But I know what I want for this project—I've got a vision—and I wouldn't trust anyone else to deliver it. How could they see what's in my head?"

They could hold a candle to one side and peek through the other ear . . .

"Impossible," I told him.

"Impossible. You said it."

"So no one else had a hand in the script?" Hall Emerson's face floated in my head.

"Not a soul."

"Huh," I said.

"I mean there were earlier drafts, of course. I tried farming out a few bits, looking for some punch up. You know how it goes. But really, for all intents and purposes, this script is a hundred percent me."

"And the director?"

"That's a bit of an open question right now."

"The director is an open question?"

"I planned to lens it myself . . ." Lens? Who, other than *Variety*, uses that term? "But it was taking on more than I could chew. With the writing and producing."

"Overextended."

"Precisely. There's only so much of me to go around."

"And what goes around, comes around."

That threw him, but I smiled, so he nodded agreement.

"I'm very close to inking a deal for the director, but I can't talk about it."

"I see," I said. Okay—fine by me. I didn't want anything to do with this asshole or his picture.

"Okay," Paul said, looking as if I'd just applied electrodes to his nipples. "Because we got this synchronicity thing going here—we're thinking like one person—I'll let slip to you. One word: Gamma."

"Mmmm," I said. Gamma?

"Huh? Huh?"

"I really appreciate you sharing that with me," I said. *What the hell is Gamma?* I wondered.

"Huh? Huh? Mum's the word." He turned the key on his locked lips and tossed it over his shoulder. I swear Sade was about to go looking for it under the table.

"I'm a pyramid, baby. The death chamber is sealed."

"You're terrific, you know that Marty? *Do* you know that?"

"Fortunately, I never tire of hearing it."

"I just hope we can do business. I know we can. *The Devil on Sunday* needs you. *I* need you."

I passed on dessert; frankly, I couldn't take any more artificial sweetener. Paul promised again that Kendall would have a copy of "his" script by end of business that day and I promised to give it all the consideration it was due. I got a two-handed shake from him, and as he walked away he stopped, looked at me and touched his forehead, then pointed to mine, then touched his again.

"One mind," he said, and winked at me.

"A terrible thing to waste," I said. He smiled and gave me a thumb's up. I returned the gesture and in my best Marty Burns, PI-manner gave him a hearty "Aces."

His smile collapsed in a heap at his chin. Man, I definitely had to have a word with those writers.

In the corner, the Walrus and the Carpenter toasted the completion of their deal with oysters on the half-shell.

I beat a hasty retreat.

Four

I took a walk down the Third Street Promenade after my meeting with Paul, thinking the sort-of-fresh air might clean the producer and his entourage out of my pounding head. It wasn't that long ago that the pedestrianized street was dominated by schlock variety stores selling T-shirts so thin you couldn't have bunched the cotton tight enough to make a usable Q-tip, and cheap Mexican cafés and tacky secondhand bookstores. It was nice. Now, of course, there's nothing but posh chain clothing stores with too much space between the aisles, thirty-seven branches of Starbucks, and gleaming, dueling Borders and Barnes & Noble Superstores (each with its *own* coffee bar). The street's thronged with desperate consumers, street performers—what is the deal with those guys who paint themselves white or bronze and pose as statues? *That's* entertainment?—and stallholders selling cappuccino, just in case that Borders or thirty-seventh Starbucks is too far to get to. The atmosphere sent my I've-just-spent-ninety-minutes-with-a-producer headache into overdrive, so I cut across on Arizona to walk back up Pacific and gaze upon the sea. It must have been feeding time for the bums or coffee break (maybe all those Starbucks are for them?) and I found a deserted park bench in a prime spot near the old Camera Obscura. Against my better judgment and pounding cerebellum, I played back the highlights of my lunch with Kevin.

Paul and his crew made me sick, but the truth is that he's par for the course for his species. If the cardinal virtues are your thing, you shouldn't be in the entertainment business to begin with, so I wasn't surprised or bothered by the man's latent reptilian qualities. More disturbing was that Paul had been awfully vague on any details regarding *The Devil on Sunday*. Okay, actual production was some ways off, but Paul hemmed and hawed about any specifics. And to not have a director on-line at this stage was madness. All I could figure was that Paul really did want to direct it himself, but his money men cut him off at the knees and he was scrounging for someone else. I don't know what the hell he meant with that "Gamma" crap.

More interesting, though, was his claim to having written the screenplay himself. Now, there's an old saying: Birds gotta fly, producers gotta lie. But why would Paul lie so baldly about Hall's involvement? Emerson had only brought this whole thing up to me because he was supposed to be working on the script. I suppose Paul might just have got caught up in an ego-moment and exaggerated his own wonderfulness, but it's a pretty stupid and unnecessary lie to dump on a measly character actor. And with Hall specifically in mind, I had asked Paul point blank about the matter.

Birds gotta fly . . .

An old guy whose loose skin flapped off his body like folds of soggy paper towel jogged past looking for all the world like he was about have a heart attack, followed close behind by a bronzed blond goddess so tight and buxom you could have bounced nickels off her ass and into low earth orbit. I watched, grinning like a village idiot, as she chased the old man down the path toward the pier.

I'd rather kiss Jim Carrey than admit it, but sometimes I really do love LA.

I reported in to Kendall as soon as I got back home. Nothing I say ever surprises her—she told me she once lost the strap of her best leather purse to one of those pointy Blönde tables—so I was taken aback by her little intake of breath at my mention of "Gamma."

"You're sure he said Gamma?" Kendall asked.

"He said mum's the word and that he was only telling me about it because he felt we had a special connection."

"Marty . . ."

"That it was like we had one mind."

"Marty . . ."

"I felt it, too, and it was pretty amazing. At times I thought I could really *see* inside his head. It was like a factory warehouse outlet store in there."

"Marty!"

"What?"

"Gamma. What did he say about Gamma?"

"Uh, I dunno. He just mentioned the name, like I should get down on my knees and genuflect. Or jerk off. Should I have?"

"You don't know who Gamma is?"

"Suddenly I'm turning all red here. Who's Gamma?"

"Do you watch television, Marty?"

"I watch my show sometimes, when I can stand it. I try to avoid the whore-with-a-heart-of-a-gold episodes, which makes it tough. I don't watch *60 Minutes* anymore, though I know that's bad of me. But looking at Mike Wallace makes me nauseous. Don't you think he should retire? Or be forced into euthanasia or something? Like Edward G. Robinson in *Soylent Green!*"

I could hear Kendall's exasperation building. God, I how love jagging her wires: big fish, tiny barrel.

"Have you ever seen the I-World ad?" she asked. "The one where the universe turns out to be a giant computer and the little girl turns out to be the whole universe?"

"With the flower aliens and the atom bomb ice cream sundaes?"

"That's the one."

"That's really cool."

"*That's* Gamma."

"Wow."

"He also had an exhibition at MOCA last year. The one with the lines that snaked around the block, remember?"

"I must have missed that. Is MOCA a coffee bar or the museum that's downtown?"

She ignored that. "The show was amazing. And it's only a whisper, but rumor has it that Gamma was brought in to work on the new *Star Wars* and walked out after slapping Lucas in the face over Jar-Jar Binks."

"Good for him! Who'd have guessed a comic sidekick could be *more* obnoxious than Rob Schneider?"

"So Gamma is white hot. If Paul really has a line on him, then *Devil on Sunday* is definitely fast-lane. That's if Paul wasn't blowing smoke up your ass."

"I do have a no smoking sign posted, but I recognize that it's difficult to enforce the regulations."

"Are you sure you're not interested, Marty? This project is suddenly sounding better to me."

"I don't know, Kendall. Paul scored higher on my reptile scale than he did on yours. I know I don't like him."

"This is business, not personal."

"You ever see *The Godfather,* Kendall? That can be a dangerous distinction to make. Has he sent you a script yet?"

"Nothing so far today. Should I give him a nudge?"

"No, let's see how long it takes for something to appear. I'm funny in that I have a thing about expecting people to live up to their word."

"Gee, sometimes I wonder if you're in the right business."

"Me, too. And more than sometimes. But let's just see what happens. I promise I'll look at the script when it arrives. You can try and twist my arm some more if we think there's something interesting there."

"Okay, that's fair enough."

"Kendall . . ."

"What is it, Marty?"

"This Gamma guy. Him being so hot and all and me not even knowing his name. Am I, like, terminally unhip?"

There was a pause, lengthy enough for me to re-evaluate my self-image and play a couple of slow hands of clock solitaire.

"Not *terminally,* no," she finally said.

"Okay. Thanks, Kendall."

Not terminally. Bless her little can't-lie-for-shit heart.

Worried that my finger was no longer on the vital pulse of our great popular culture, I spent the rest of the day sprawled in front of the television. I saw Gamma's I-World ad three times. It really was pretty cool.

I tried to call Hall Emerson again, but there was still nobody home.

The phone rang in the middle of the night. I was so deeply asleep and confused at being woken, that I picked it up before the machine could.

"Yum," I mumbled. I'd been dreaming about food.

"Hall Emerson. What ya doin'?"

"Uhhh"—I cleared my throat, checked the time—"doilies. Making lace doilies, Hall. In fact, the whole sewing circle's here. *Stop stealing my thread, Thelma!* What else would I be doing at three in the morning?"

"You're a pistol, Marty Burns, a regular Sig-Sauer."

"Yeah, well, I'm shooting blanks right now. What's the matter? Why are you calling?"

I heard the receiver clatter to the ground on the other end. Then I heard Hall yell at someone and a dimmer, angry voice answer back. A moment later he came back on the line.

"Fuckin' bastard! Tried to grab my drink right up off the bar. Right off it. I'm still drinking it." Then to whoever he was arguing with: "Ya bastard!"

"Hello? Hall?"

"Marty? You need to talk to me. I mean, I need to talk to you. You know. I . . . FUCKIN' BASTAAAARDS . . ."

The phone dropped again. I heard more shouting in the background, and some glass breaking.

"You gotta talk to me, Marty." Emerson was panting for breath, slurring his words rather badly. I had a picture in my head of him with blood on his face and glass in his beard.

"Hall . . . can't it wait until tomorrow? It's a little late and . . ."

"They're fuckin' me to death, man. Do you know what that's like? They got their razor dicks way up inside me, man, and they're humping away like I'm some cheap Hollywood whore. Hump. Hump. Hump. They're bleedin' me down, man. There ain't gonna be nothin' left if they don't stop."

"Hall . . ."

"Paul. He's doin' me. Doin' it *to* me. I . . . I gotta get him. I gotta get what he owes me. He's fuckin' and fuckin' and I'm dry as a bone, baby."

"Hall!"

"Whuh? Marty?"

"Where are you?"

"I don't think I can hang out here. They're not too happy with me. I busted up some shit."

"Where. Are. You?"

He gave me a proximity in Sherman Oaks. I knew a twenty-four-hour diner not far away.

"Can you get there, Hall? Will you be able to find it?"

"Yeah. Yeah, I . . . yeah."

"Give me, ah, thirty minutes or so."

"Fuckin' me, man. Hump, hump."

"Thirty goddamn minutes, Hall. I have to drive up. Not to mention *wake* up and get dressed."

I heard the phone drop and then more yelling. I hung up, threw on some dirty clothes and trudged out to the car. I wouldn't have bet money on Hall being in that diner when I arrived.

But he surprised me. Hall sat in a corner booth, back against the window, legs up along the bench, pouring something amber into his coffee from a stainless steel hip flask. His walking stick rested against the edge of the table. He was the only customer in the place and the waitress eyed him unhappily, but a big plate of uneaten food—the smoked salmon special, very generous with the Bermuda onions—suggested that she was more interested in the potential tip than in Hall's after-hours imbibing. She looked less thrilled when I sat down and ordered only a cup of joe.

"You found it okay," I said.

Hall half-shrugged, pushed the flask my way as the waitress set the coffee cup down on the table and topped off his.

"No thanks," I told him. "It's a little early for me. Or late. I'm not even awake enough to be sure."

Hall mumbled something.

"How's that?"

"I said, 'Decent of you to come.' "

I cleared my throat, then said: "You'd have done the same for me."

The way he looked at me from under his bushy eyebrow suggested that that was hardly the case. But I knew that already.

"You seem a little calmer than you sounded on the phone."

"Eye of the storm."

"Hurricane or late night drizzle?"

"Bastard bartender pissed me off. Some crap about closing time," he said with a throaty laugh.

"No service ethic in this service economy."

"Don't try to humor me, Marty."

"Okay," I said. I felt very tired. "So what do you want?"

"You're a boozer, aren't you? Or used to be."

"I've had some issues," I said. Hall practically bared his teeth at me. "Yeah, I used to drink too much. I still drink, but not nearly so much. Not in public, anyway."

"Thought so. You got the look. It gets burned-in around the eyes. You do a twelve-step?"

"Nah. I don't think I'm actually an alcoholic. Just a problem drinker. Or a drinker with a lot of problems, I don't know. I used to put it away pretty good, and I surely did drink away a few jobs, maybe even a woman or two, but I don't think I ever drank anything I couldn't afford to lose. Or wanted to keep. I tried an AA meeting once, but I didn't really need it and the coffee sucked. And a guy like me, who won't even join in for "Take Me Out to the Ball Game," I couldn't buy into the heavy duty line they sell. But like I say, I'm not much of a joiner and I probably didn't need it. I suppose the fact that I'm still here is proof."

Hall nodded. "I'm probably a drunk."

I blinked in response. Hall smiled.

"If you'd have said that was the first step to recovery, I'd have hit you. Thanks."

"I'm not much for solving other people's life problems. You're a smart guy, Hall, though sometimes you make like you're not. You know what to do if you want to. And if you don't want to, it won't make the slightest bit of difference what I say."

"Why did you drink?"

I glanced out the window. Nary a car to be seen on Ventura Boulevard. A white cat, its eyes silvery in the streetlight, stared back at me from atop an *LA Times* vending box. I considered what kind of answer could possibly address the question.

"Just the pitch," Hall prompted, "not the whole script."

That made me smile. I probably would have told him it was none of his business if he hadn't said that.

"Same reason as every other boozer I've ever met: I hated something about myself and wanted to get someplace where I didn't have to think about it, remember it. If you can't afford a Lear jet and an island, or intensive psychotherapy or a receptive blonde, a bottle will do."

"And you don't hate that thing about you anymore?"

I thought about it. Thought about the failed promise of my youth, the wasted years and empty days. I thought about the selfishness and self-pity, the sense of injury and unfairness at the world's hands which I'd cradled and nurtured like a baby for so long. Until I came to see that the world was too big and too wondrous to give a shit about me. I looked for the cat outside, but it was gone.

"I think I accept it now," I told him. "I know I don't like every-thing about myself, but I've learned not to hate it all. Or maybe I've found new things to like, I don't know. Does that sound too AA?"

Another semishrug.

"What can I tell you, Hall? I'm not so unhappy these days. It's sim-ple as that, though I bet you don't like hearing me say it. I used to hate happy people when I wasn't one. Through luck or skill or sheer bloody-mindedness, I don't know, I found a place for myself. Unhappy people need a refuge, happy people get by with other things."

"Is it 'cause you got back into the business? The series and all that?"

"No," I said. I was very certain about this. "The money and the celebrity are a delight, there's no denying that. And a pretty beach house and a nice car and cash in the bank keep a lot of midnight bogeymen at bay. Only rich people overestimate the fabulousness of money. But the truth is that's still only the symptom. The cause is elsewhere."

"That's good. That's good for you." Hall glanced at his coffee, decided to take a swig straight from his flask instead. A long swig. "I'm full of hate."

"You said someone was fucking you over."

"They're all fucking me over. I'm the cunt of honor at a Roman orgy."

"Now you do sound like a drunk."

"Fuck you, too," Hall said, pounding a fist down on the table. He caught the edge of his spoon and we both watched it take flight and land on the floor three booths away. The waitress made a noise with her tongue and teeth, but didn't come over.

"We're not in AA, Hall. I'm not your partner or your sponsor or even your friend. We're Saturday night poker buddies and you've probably taken more pots than I have. It's the middle of the night on the wrong side of the Hills and my bed's down in Hermosa Beach. And it's a whole lot softer than this bench."

"You're saying you don't give a shit."

"I'm saying the thing I hate most about drunks is the self-pity. I know because I've still got a garden shed full of the stuff neatly packed in boxes for the rainy day that'll surely come. So I don't need any of yours, though it's generous of you to want to share."

Hall chewed on that for a little while, so I chewed on the lox. Not bad at all.

"You're okay, Marty," he finally said. He managed a weak grin.

"It's my most serious flaw. Weak jaw notwithstanding."

"Double chin, too."

"That's why I haven't touched the cream cheese."

"Kevin Ryan Paul's dicking me around."

"Do tell. And he seems such a sweetheart."

"I thought you didn't know him?"

I told him about my lunch date with the producer and his interest in me for *The Devil on Sunday*. I also told him that I'd seen the original picture and passed on what I'd learned—or failed to learn—about any missing footage.

"Aw, hell, you're more than okay. Shit, I didn't mean for you to do all that. Shit."

"When I get my teeth into something I like to chew it up. Hold-over from my days as a real PI. I may move slow and not be very bright, but I like to see things through. So you didn't tell Paul about me?"

"No offense, but the thought never crossed my mind."

"None taken. Funny him calling me like that, though. If you didn't put the idea in his head."

"Somebody must have, 'cause Paul doesn't get ideas on his own. I don't think he's even a carrier."

"He must have some cortical activity. According to Paul he wrote the script for *Devil*."

"Motherfucker!" Hall screamed, and pounded the table again. This time a water glass bounced off and smashed on the floor. The waitress scampered over, looking pissed. I peeled a ten out of my wallet and put it on top of Hall's deuce.

"Hope that covers your trouble," I said to her. She scooped the money into her apron and nodded. While Hall sat there fuming, she got a dustpan and mop and cleaned up the glass, then retreated behind the counter. I could have done with a top-off on my coffee, but I wasn't about to ask now.

"Fucker couldn't write his name in the snow if he had *two* dicks," Hall spat. He breathed hard through his open mouth, spittle-flecks speckling his gray beard. "Bastard couldn't dot an *i* with a howitzer."

"Is it your script, Hall?"

"Of course it's my fuckin' script, not that he's paid me for it. All he's got is a draft—he had to see it right away, he said. Should have known I couldn't trust him. Should have learned by now."

"What do you mean?"

"I worked with the motherfucker before. Three-quarters of *Rat Patrol* is mine. I don't know who did the rest, but it wasn't Paul."

"You didn't get a credit for that?"

"Course not. Paul took it, he always does."

"Did you go to the Writers' Guild?"

Hall laughed an unpleasant gurgle. "What Guild? We didn't even have a contract, no paperwork at all. Paul paid me cash."

"Christ," I muttered.

"Five G's. You know what he sold that baby for? Two-fifty. And he took the same again when film rolled."

"Why? Why would you let him get away with that? Why in the world would you work with him again? Jesus, Hall, you're a professional."

"I need the fuckin' money, what do you think? I'm fifty-three years old and I look sixty. I'm not the new black and I never will be again. Paul's not the only one I do this shit for. You think those baby faced motherfuckers can really write the shit they say they do? No way. There's lots of bastards like me sitting in the dark in back rooms cranking it out for 'em. It's a sweatshop operation, like the sneaker companies. 'Cept you don't got to go to Vietnam or Indonesia to find the workers. They're right here in studio apartments in Palms and leaky-roofed shacks in the Hills."

Hall finished off whatever was in his flask. He turned it upside down and pounded the lip against his palm, then licked the drops off his hand.

"Classy, Hall."

"Fuck 'em all but six," he said.

"Why don't you just go public? A story like this—producer steals poor writer's work—will play big in this town. Hell, you could get a book deal out of it. Cover of *Vanity Fair*. It'd pay way more than the short money you're taking from Paul and his ilk. Use your head, man."

"And then what'd I do? Think I'd ever land another gig if I turn on a guy like Paul? At least now I get the odd real job. A rewrite here, a syndie episode there. I narc out Paul, and all the others like him—and you know that deep down they're *all* of them like him—they wouldn't spit on me if my heart was on fire."

"Is what you got that much better?"

Even beneath his bushy facial hair, I could discern the Elvis-like upturn of Hall's upper lip. "Easy for a man with a beach house to say."

I threw up my hands and slumped back in the booth. "I don't know what you want from me then."

"What I want," Hall said, pointing his finger at me, "is another drink. I know another place nearby, what do you say?"

Without waiting for an answer, he got up and headed for the door. He called out a hearty " 'Night, darlin' " to the waitress, who shook her head at his back.

Hall stumbled as he walked down the two steps to the street, caught himself just before falling over. He staggered as he walked one way up Ventura, changed his mind and reversed course.

I had no reason in the world to go after him. Hall Emerson was a sputtering bomb on a downward trajectory, heading for a messy ground zero. No reason to go after him and get cut to ribbons by the shrapnel.

I threw another five on the table as I got up to catch him before he disappeared into the night.

"I'm sorry," I said to the waitress, as I went past.

"That man needs help," she told me.

"Who doesn't?" I asked.

Cast your bread upon the waters, as the saying goes, and a giant mutant duck will eat it and then shit on your head.

The after-hours joint that Hall led us to wasn't elegant enough to qualify as a dive; it was more like a belly flop. I had no choice but to order a real drink, which I didn't want and barely sipped. I didn't cotton to the idea of touching my lips to the patently dirty glass, and was terrified at the prospect of having to use the toilet.

Hall had put down two bourbons and was chasing them with a flat, brown liquid that purported to be Pabst Blue Ribbon but smelled like yesterday's collected backwash. Hmmm, maybe it *was* Pabst Blue Ribbon.

"You thinking about taking the part?" Hall asked me.

"In *Devil*? Not really. I mean, I'm supposed to be getting a copy of the . . . your script. But Paul didn't do much for me, even before you told me about him. My agent's kind of keen though, 'cause Paul mentioned this Gamma character . . ."

"Gamma!"

"You know him? Her? It?"

"Him. Yeah, he and Paul whore together some. Most of the time, he don't live on this planet."

"Whatever. I said I wouldn't say no until I saw the script. But I mean, no way I'm going to touch it now. If he's screwing you over what do I need with him?"

An odd look came across Hall's face. If he hadn't been so drunk, the raw calculation of it might not have been so readily apparent.

"Don't turn the gig down for me," he said.

"It wouldn't be for you."

" 'Cause maybe you string Paul along, you could actually do me some good." Hall looked up at me tentatively. "If you were so disposed, that is."

"I don't know, Hall, what are you suggesting?"

"You could maybe let him know that you know that I wrote the thing. Or had a hand in it or something. Maybe that could squeeze some money out of him."

"I don't see it. Paul seems pretty keen on me for the part—the part I still haven't seen . . ."

"Gotta be Wilkins, the hubby. Cecil Kellaway in the original."

"I think that's what he said."

"I don't see you for the psycho. And I know you're not the lead."

"The words they'll put on my headstone."

"It's a nice role. Small but showy. I done good with it."

"Fine, but the point is Paul can get anyone to play it. My name on the credits doesn't put ass in seats. I try to lean on Paul, especially for something as nasty as ripping you off, and he'll go find another boy for the part. He sure as hell won't 'fess up."

"Maybe. But why'd he come to you in the first place?"

"That I don't know. I'd like to think it's talent and charisma, but I stopped believing in Santa Claus when I saw Ma and the Easter Bunny do it doggy-style one Christmas Eve."

We sat in silence for a while. Hall signaled for another bourbon, I smiled at the bartender to indicate I was okay. He didn't smile back. I think maybe he'd lost the instructions.

"There's something else," Hall said after a while. "About *The Devil on Sunday*."

I waited for Hall to continue. He took his time, but I had no place to go. The night was past shot to hell at that point.

"You saw the original?"

"I did."

"What'd you think?"

"It's not bad. You can see that it was shot for thirty-nine cents, but it holds up pretty well. Definitely has an edge to it. Old Frank Emerson could write a line or two of dialogue."

"No," Hall said, staring me square in the eye. It was the most sober he'd looked all night. "No, he didn't."

"Sorry?"

"He didn't write a word of it. *The Devil on Sunday*."

"So who did?"

Hall went back to studying his glass. He finished what was inside and called for another. It came—and went—just as fast.

"You ever see any of Frank's pictures?"

"Not that I could name. I mean, I probably have, but I don't know offhand."

"They're almost all shit. One or two touch the mediocre, but it's a stretch. Except for *Devil on Sunday*."

"Which he didn't write." I remembered Harry Blanc's rumor that Frank Emerson had been fronting for a blacklisted writer.

Hall nodded. "Mac Stans is the real writer."

"MacArthur Stans?"

"Yup. He was a red and on the blacklist at the time. Writers on the outs used other writers to cover for 'em. Gave up the credit, but split the money down the middle. Was a way to keep eating, keep working."

"And not a bad deal for Frank Emerson," I noted. "Self-respect notwithstanding."

"Not bad at all. Hand a typed script in to the producer and pocket a check. And self-respect, too. He was made to feel a hero for playing the front. A brave man. It was a risk, after all, in that climate. In those weird times."

"The nostalgia guy I talked to told me he'd heard stories that your dad was a beard or a front or whatever. But no one had ever taken credit for the script. Why wouldn't they have set the record straight after all those years?"

"I don't know for sure. It was something between Stans and Frank. Some agreement. I never got to ask him about it before he died. I figured if they were happy with it, it wasn't for me to mess with. And hell, Paul only came to me 'cause he thinks Frank wrote the original. So why fuck with a cherry ain't been popped?"

"I suppose," I said. But it still seemed queer.

"But that's still not all of it."

"Christ, Hall, I hate soap operas. Especially in prime time. Just tell me what you mean to tell me."

Yet another bourbon. I was given a fresh drink regardless of my feelings on the subject.

"What'd you think of Connie Clare?" Hall asked. A peculiar look came over him, though the previous hint of sobriety had evaporated faster than the bourbon in his glass.

"Hard to say," I replied. "Her part was so small. I liked her looks. Very nice . . . bubbies." I chuckled to myself at using Harry Blanc's phrase.

"She was my mother," Hall said.

My chuckle turned on me like a cornered animal. I poured the drink down my gullet, dirty glass and all.

"Oh," I said. "Sorry. Jeez."

Hall's hands were trembling. He tried to steady them by clutching the edge of the filthy bar.

"She died . . . was killed during the making of the picture. She was murdered."

"Yeah, I know. I'm sorry, Hall. About her having nice . . . I'm really sorry."

He shook his head. "I can barely remember her. I was so little when she got killed. When they were making *Devil on Sunday*. After . . . Frank didn't like to talk about her. He didn't even keep pictures of her around the house. He just made like she . . . never was."

"Must have been rough for you."

"It was gonna be a big part for her, a big break. She'd only done a couple of walk-ons before that. A flash of her in *Kiss of Death*. A line in *Slightly French*. I think . . . Frank fronted for Stans to help her get the role. He got drunk one night and admitted something like that."

"Her scene in *Devil* is a good one," I said.

"But there was more! That's what's in the original script that I have, the scene I've read about. They shot it before she was killed. That's what I wanted you to find, the missing footage."

Hall was sniffling now, and wiped at his eyes. I didn't much care to see this.

"I'm sorry, Hall, but there's nothing there. I did try."

"It's all there is of her," he bellowed. "I got nothing else, nothing. One flash, one line, one scene. There's more. There's got to be something more, and I want it!"

"I'm sorry," I whispered. As if it was my fault.

Hall was crying now and it had sobered him up just enough to be embarrassed.

"Christ in hell, look at me," he bawled. "A blubbering old drunk. A piece of shit, crying like a baby, drunk."

As if shot through with electricity, he bolted out of his chair and ran for the door. I started after him, but felt something hard and cold clamp around my arm: the bartender.

"You still owe for the last round," he said, his fingers merging with my own flesh. I dug into my pocket, found only a twenty and tossed it on the bar. He let me go to snatch it up.

I ran out after Hall, grabbing up the fancy walking stick he'd left behind, but saw nothing and no one on the quiet, early morning street. I heard brakes squeal in the distance, but couldn't even be sure from which direction the sound had come. I jogged to one corner, then back to the other. No sign at all of Hall Emerson.

I looked up and saw a giant duck waddling away, its bowels emptied, a happy quack on its smirking beak.

Five

I didn't get up until well after noon the next day. I'd had bad
dreams in the night, though I couldn't remember anything more
about them than that they featured Hall Emerson. I planned to call
him later in the day, to satisfy myself that he was all right, but I'd
also decided that I'd had enough of him. I felt bad for the guy,
sure; tough enough growing up in Hollywood and in The Business—
I know how that goes all too well—and being the son of a murdered mom couldn't have been an easy ride. At the same time, I
suspected that Hall was one frighteningly short step away from the
alcohol abyss. I liked playing poker with him well enough, but what
I'd said to him was the honest truth: We weren't best friends and I
was not willing to take on the mantle of his guardian angel. For
him to have been burned once by Paul and gone back for more
sounded to me like a man cruising for a bruising. Though I didn't
say it to Hall, some people drink not only to escape things but
to punish themselves as well. I didn't care to delve deep enough to
learn what Hall's motivation was or why. I'm not sure Hall did,
either.

I luxuriated in a lengthy shower, followed by a healthy repast of
Cap'n Crunch and skim milk, Pop Tarts, and coffee. Breakfast is,
after all, the most important meal of the day, even if you eat it as late
lunch. I checked the answering machine and found a message from
Kendall. She reported, with mock shock, that there was still no script
from Paul, but that she'd been asking around and there seemed to be
something to the producer's claim that Gamma was interested in directing *The Devil on Sunday,* so she hoped I'd keep an open mind.
Frankly, after last night's episode with Hall and what he had to say
about slimy Mr. Paul, not to mention our lunch at Blönde, my mind
was pretty well shut. But I'd wait to spring that on Kendall. Especially
as she hinted, in that obscure and delicate way that agents have, that

there might be bad news coming about *Burning Bright.*

"Don't panic," she said, "but don't buy anything expensive."

Swell.

Having conducted business for the day, I retreated to the chaise lounge on my sundeck for a much deserved nap. I briefly considered the idea of a beer for companionship, but the rancid smell of the dive in Sherman Oaks lingered in the back of my nose so I settled for a frosty root beer instead. In any case, I dozed off having drunk no more than a sip. By the time I woke up again, the day wasn't just shot, it was riddled with bullets and left in the gutter as an example to others. I had that dopey, underwater feeling you get when you've slept too long, and even a quicker, colder, second shower didn't clear the cobwebs. Deciding it might be nice to get out of the house for a while, I grabbed my car keys. As I was heading out the door, I remembered that I had really ought to give Hall a shout, but I couldn't bring myself to make the call. Between the lazy fogginess that filled my head and the emotional lethargy induced by the thought of talking to him again, I copped out. I'd call him *after* dinner, I figured, when he'd more likely be in anyway.

In truth, I didn't call him when I got back, either—I had a good excuse worked out, I just can't remember what it is now—but it wouldn't have made any difference.

Hall Emerson wouldn't be answering his phone, or anything else, ever again.

Jon Conlon called me with the news on Friday.

"Hall's dead, did you hear? Topped himself last night."

"Oh, fuck," I said. "Fuck, fuck, fuck, fuck."

"He owe you money or something?"

"Fuck," I said once more. Because it's exactly and entirely what I was thinking.

"Wow, that much?" Conlon asked.

"He didn't owe me money. Aw, Christ. What the hell happened?"

"They found him in his car is what I heard. Apparently, he locked himself in the garage, stuffed the cracks, cranked the engine, and took the gas pipe, as they used to say. That's about all I know. I got the story from Elliot. So you know the structure was clumsy, it was half-again too long, and characterization was nonexistent."

"I don't think that's even a little bit funny, Jon."

"Ah, I suppose not. Sucks doesn't it?"

"I should have called him last night," I said, as much to myself as down the phone line.

"Hall? What for? I didn't know you guys were buds."

"We aren't—weren't—exactly. He . . . oh, it's an Elliot-length story and it doesn't matter. I mean, it does. Oh, I don't know if it does or not. Ah, shit, Jon."

"Hell, Marty, I didn't think you'd take it so hard. I didn't realize you guys even spoke outside the poker games. You barely speak *during* the games."

"Yeah, I know. We just . . . we found some mutuality of interest only recently. I don't—didn't—know Hall that well. Jeez, you probably know him better than I did. How are you feeling?"

"Oh, well, I feel sad for the guy, of course. Hall could be a blast, though I was never all that sure what to make of him, you know? I never could decide if he was authentic or maybe a little too big a poser. That beard and that voice of his and that ridiculous walking stick . . ."

I glanced toward the corner of the living room, where the stick he'd left behind in the bar sat waiting to be returned. I felt something hard form in the pit of my belly.

"I'm not saying he wasn't an interesting guy," Conlon went on, "but I always thought there was something about him I didn't get. But I don't know if that . . . call it an absence, was something to do with him or with me."

"You don't think it was just the booze?"

Conlon hesitated. He breathed into the phone so hard, I had to pull the receiver away from my ear. "I know he had a problem with it, but no, I know lots of sots. Occupational hazard, don't you know. I knew Hall when he was boozing less, too, and I felt ambiguous about him even then. I'm not speaking ill of the dead, mind, we're just talking. You, me and the lamppost."

"Absolutely."

"Hall had a weird way of seeing things. I wouldn't call him an idealist or a romantic, 'cause he was too bitter at heart for that. But he expected the world to work in a certain way, and that expectation didn't correspond to the reality that people like you and me deal with. He once got fucked over on a TV project for some syndie outfit—

anybody else would have seen it coming a mile away; I bailed on the thing at first sight—so when the shit sure enough hit his dinky little fan, I asked him what the hell he had been expecting. You know what his answer was? 'One ort of decency.' And this from a guy who grew up in town!"

"Crazy," I agreed.

"I can dig that kind of mindset, you know? I respect it, and I never forgot those four words because they're, like, a damn noble philosophy of life. But I can't say that I understand it coming from someone with a life in The Business. It's like there was a fatal short in Hall's wiring, you know? He was DC in an AC world. And I'm not talking sexual preference."

"What did Elliot think about . . . what happened?"

"Oh, he trotted out the usual Elliot clichés. You know, something like what happened will probably turn up in his next script. Aw, I'm being unfair. He did say that he wasn't that surprised."

"Huh. What about you?"

"Am I surprised?" Conlon thought about it for a while. "Yeah. I know Hall was having a tough time of it financially and that his career was somewhere between dumpster and landfill, but even with the booze, I never saw him as the type to kill himself. I think . . . it doesn't fit his notion of decency or honor or whatever it was he was looking for or expecting from the world."

"It doesn't feel right to me, either," I said. "And I just saw him the other night."

"Really?"

"He was seriously upset about another deal that had gone sour, but . . . you know, I wouldn't have been half so surprised if you'd told me he was in jail for killing someone else."

"Anyone in particular?"

"I'm just expressing a   ιracter."

"You know that old li   er Hill about his movies? 'When someone puts a gun in ,   ᴧharacter is how many times you blink.' "

"Yeah? When's the last time *he* made a decent picture?"

"When's the last time Hall did?"

"Point," I said.

We hung on in silence for a while. Then Conlon said, "I guess this kills the game for tomorrow."

"I should think so, yeah."

"So it's doubly tragic."

"Jon . . ."

"I already bought the cold cuts and beer."

Conlon was laughing, but the sound was a man whistling past the graveyard. I still couldn't take it and hung up the phone.

But why, oh why, hadn't I picked it up and made that call last night?

The cops came to see me on Saturday. Or rather cop, singular.

"Detective Khan," I said upon opening the door.

"You remember me. I'm flattered."

"I wish it was something I could forget."

He nodded and mercifully said no more about it.

Carl Khan was part of LAPD's Celebrity Affairs Division. Or so he'd once told me. I learned later that he more or less *was* the Celebrity Affairs Division, and that it was something less than an official designation. Khan was a very slick, very smart detective who knew how to talk to and unruffle the feathers of the rich, famous, and rich and famous who occasionally rub up against trouble in town. I'd met him in the course of his investigation of a stalker. The psycho wasn't after me, but after "Baby" June Harvey, another ex-child star I'd briefly been involved with. It was an ugly and horrible incident culminating in two deaths to which I'd unwittingly and ashamedly contributed through my instinctive chuckleheadedness. Khan had proved surprisingly decent throughout the episode despite my own rank stupidity.

"I take it you know about Hall Emerson," he said.

"Yeah," I sighed. "Why don't you come on in?"

We retreated to the comfort of the sun deck. Khan slipped off his Armani jacket and draped it over the back of a chair, lovingly smoothing any creases.

"You want a hanger for that?" I asked. "Maybe a trouser press?"

"Wire or wood hanger?"

"What am I, Christina Crawford?"

"It's okay," he said and smiled. He nodded at the open bottle of Sierra Nevada on the table. "I'll take a beer though."

"Aren't you on duty?"

"It's only bribes I can't take on duty. Unless they're really big. Anyway, you gonna report me?"

I fetched the man his ale.

"Nice," he said, taking a healthy swig. "Though I'm normally a Coors man."

"In that jacket? I don't think so."

"Don't judge a book by its cover."

"Or a movie by its poster?"

"No, that you can judge. Especially the ones that have the little pictures of the cast running along the bottom."

"Yeah," I said, "it was always bums like O. J. whose mug was down there."

"Case closed. Or not, as the case may be."

We clinked bottles. Yet another in the seemingly endless panoply of beach volleyball tournaments was heating up on the sand a hundred yards from my property line. Khan took a healthy interest as four bronzed wonders appeared on center court. One babe popped her bikini top as she dove to the sand, revealing spheres considerably firmer and larger than the volleyball itself. And somewhat less natural, I should think. The biggest cheer of the day went up from the crowd.

"Yowza!" Khan offered. "This beats the hell out of watching golf on a weekend afternoon."

"It's a setup," I said.

"Hah?"

"The sponsors rig it. At least one girl loses her top every Saturday. It keeps people watching. See? She's got a Pepsi tattoo just above her left tit."

"I'll be damned. Ain't nothing on the up and up, is there?"

"I don't know, is there? You're the cop."

Khan tore his gaze away from the girls on the beach and studied me closely. The good humor had all drained from his face.

"Tell me about Hall Emerson," he said.

"What is it you'd like me to tell? I didn't know him all that well."

"You know that he's dead."

"Yeah. We played poker. One of the other guys we play with told me he killed himself."

"That's the working assumption."

"Do you have reason to doubt it?"

"Do you?"

"I don't know anything about it. I heard he was found in his car with the motor running. Did he leave a note?"

"No note," Khan said. "But a whole series of Post-its stuck up around his bungalow with your name written on them. Any idea why?"

"I did him a favor. Or so I thought."

"I seem to recall that you were doing Baby June a favor. Or so you thought."

Ouch.

"I'm a slow learner, Detective. And that's a pretty low blow."

"I apologize," Khan said. "When's the last time you saw Emerson?"

"Wednesday night. He called me up in the middle of the night, drunk as a skunk. He wanted to talk."

"What about?"

"Hall thought he was being messed around on a script. He said that a producer was screwing him over."

"Kevin Ryan Paul," Khan said.

"Yeah. You know about this?"

"And did you talk to Emerson? On Wednesday night?"

"Yeah, I went to see him. We ended up in an after hours toilet in Sherman Oaks. Hall . . . had a lot of issues."

"He was a drunk."

"I don't know. Pretty close to it, at best. He definitely had a drinking problem. Whether it was the cause or symptom of his other woes, I don't know well enough to say."

Khan watched a little volleyball, but I don't think he was paying any real attention. He tapped his beer bottle against the table before taking another big slug.

"You say you didn't know him well."

"We played poker on Saturday nights. For the last year or so. The game predated me."

"But he called *you* in the middle of the night, out of the blue, to sing you a tale of woe?"

I explained to Khan the details of my interactions with Hall over the past week. His request for the favor, my checking out of the original *The Devil on Sunday*, Paul's interest in me for a part in the remake, Hall's disgruntlement over Paul's treatment of him and his general bitterness toward the world. I told him that Hall wanted to find the missing footage of his murdered mother, but I didn't mention how he broke down in drunken tears. Nor did I go into the fact that Hall admitted to me that his dad had bearded the script—it somehow didn't seem pertinent. Or right. But I was as straight as I could be about everything else, including how badly I felt about not calling Hall to see if he was okay on Thursday. The day that he killed himself. I had nothing to hide from Khan, after all.

The detective turned back to the volleyball as he took in all that I had to say. He held up his empty bottle and asked: "Can I have another?"

I went inside and grabbed another beer out of the fridge. I turned around and found Khan standing on the other side of the counter separating the kitchen from the dining room. He pulled up a stool and sat down unbidden. I popped open his beer and dropped it in front of him. I didn't want another for myself.

"Damned volleyball babes are too distracting," Khan said. Then: "You met with Paul on Wednesday?"

"Yeah, we did lunch at Blönde."

"Ugh, I hate that place. I ripped a pair of trousers on one of their damned tables."

I snorted in acknowledgment.

"Did Paul mention Emerson to you?"

"Nope. And I deliberately gave him the chance. I was wondering if Hall hadn't recommended me for the part, but Paul didn't even acknowledge that Hall was involved with the project. Just the opposite if anything."

"Tell me what you think about Kevin Ryan Paul."

"On the record or off?"

Khan rocked his head back and forth, thinking about it. "On," he decided.

"He's a producer," I told him.

Khan nodded. "Okay, off the record."

"He's a producer," I told him.

That got a laugh. "You don't like him."

I let out a long breath before saying: "I try not to shit where I eat, Officer. Or if I do I try only to excrete tasteful little pellets that can pass as capers in a pinch." Another chuckle from the cop. "I'm . . . in negotiation with Paul for a part in his new picture . . ."

"*The Devil on Sunday* remake."

"Yeah. I don't know if it's going to happen or if I even want it to happen, but it would be pretty goddamn hypocritical of me to say anything too awful about the guy if I'm maybe going to bank his shekels and shake his hand."

"But . . ."

"But between you, me, and Roger Ebert, Paul's a scumbag. He strikes me as a bargain basement Don Simpson and it wouldn't surprise me one solitary bit if he ends up booked on the same kind of deep-six holiday. But you didn't hear it from me."

"You think he's got a habit?"

"No. I mean, I have no idea. All I meant was that he's the type to get caught up in the emptiest notions of Hollywood flash and glamour. My impression is that Paul's in it for the lunches and the girls—and who knows, maybe the drugs—and would be much happier if only you didn't have to turn out the occasional movie at the end to make it all work."

"So how's he different from anyone else in town?"

"Touché, mon inspector. Like I said: He's a producer."

Khan did some more thinking while he drank his beer and I stood there watching him. The phone rang and Khan raised an eyebrow, but I waved it away. The machine in the other room picked it up.

"I've already spoken with Kevin Ryan Paul," Khan told me.

"Really?"

"His name figured prominently in the materials we found in Emerson's place. So I went to see him last night."

"And what do *you* think of him?"

"He's a producer." Khan rolled his eyes and threw up his hands. I laughed. "But he had an interesting story to tell. He says that Emerson had been harassing him for weeks. He admitted that he hired Emerson to do a polish on *The Devil on Sunday* script, but that Emerson was a drunk who couldn't type two intelligent words. He said he approached Emerson because Emerson's father wrote the original movie and he thought that there might be a PR angle if the son was involved with the remake. Paul was a little shy about it, but he also thought he could get some play out of Emerson's connection with the Connie Clare murder."

"Figures," I muttered.

"It's neither here nor there, however tasteless it might be. Paul insisted that Emerson never came up with more than a few pages of work for him, that Emerson was too erratic and too caught up in the drinking to be any good."

"No, I don't believe that. Emerson had a problem for sure, but he was no twenty-four-seven drunk. And I admit I don't know, but Hall struck me as the kind of guy who could crank out pages in a drunken stupor in a pitch black room if he was on a deadline; he was one of those kind of writers. It's how he earned his bread for a lot of years."

"Well, you say yourself you didn't know him too well. It doesn't take a lot to bluff your way through a weekend poker game where everybody's drinking."

"I suppose it's possible."

"Paul says that Emerson started to threaten him. That he made drunken calls in the middle of the night—and we definitely know that he made those, don't we?—promising to rearrange Paul's face for screwing him over. Paul even reported one of the threats, though it didn't get followed up."

"He made a police report?" I asked.

"Sure enough. Efficient as LAPD always are . . ."—Khan cleared his throat—"it's not the kind of thing that goes to the top of the pile. But it is there on the record, I checked. Paul told me he probably wouldn't have pressed charges anyway because of the bad publicity, but he was nervous enough about the man to want the incident noted."

"I am surprised," I admitted.

"Are you? You said that Emerson was pretty upset when you met him the other night."

"He did say he'd caused some damage in another bar. When he called me. It's why we had to meet someplace else. And he did seem to have a short fuse."

"He also had a less than pristine past."

"How do you mean?" I asked.

"You know that Emerson had a record? Did some jail time?"

"No, I had no idea."

"If it had kicked out sooner, Paul's complaint might have got higher priority. It's only in the course of this investigation that we went ahead and checked his background. He did eight months on an assault beef in 'seventy-three. He beat up a guy in a bar."

"That's an awfully long time ago."

"I agree. But it does show history. He had a couple of minor drug

73

busts, too. Did some more time, though nothing since the seventies. There was some suggestion of, oh, unsavory associations as well."

"What does that mean? What would a savory association be in Hollywood? Even Julie Andrews has flashed her tits."

"Emerson had some drug connections with a biker crowd, though again, this goes back some years. It's all narcotics related. And I've never forgiven Julie Andrews for doing that. Though I've always hated Blake Edwards. What could she see in him?"

"You don't paint a pretty picture, Detective."

"Like you in the media, we police offer but a mirror to the society of which we are a part."

"Is that line in the new police handbook?"

"Page one, in bold. Right after 'Don't beat black suspects if there's a camera around.' "

"Can I ask you a question, Detective Khan?"

"If you can bear to gaze in the mirror of my reply."

"Why are you telling me all this?"

"Am I boring you?"

"Not at all. But is there something suspicious about Hall's death? Do you have reason to believe that he didn't kill himself?"

"I don't believe anything and I have no reasons. I'm engaged in a standard investigation following a death. That's the official answer. Unofficially, it's not a lot different. There's nothing to immediately suggest anything untoward. It sure looks like a suicide. Toxicology takes a couple of days, though, so if he was doped up and dumped in the car, we'll find out."

"And what do you think?"

"The only thing that annoys me is that the guy didn't leave a note. Lots of suicides don't, but the ones who go out like this usually do. Especially this guy being a writer and all. Wouldn't he have one last story to tell?"

"I suppose."

"Would you have characterized Emerson as suicidal?"

"I don't know. I was talking about this with my poker buddy who told me the news."

Khan took a pad out of his pocket. "Which one was this?"

"Jon Conlon." Khan made a little mark in his pad. "Neither of us thought Hall was the type to kill himself."

"Even after his behavior the other night? When you went to see him?"

"I don't know what to tell you. I'm no expert on the subject, or on human behavior in general for that matter, but Hall seemed more angry than depressed. Though it's hard to tell through all that booze. And I'm not sure what it means, anyway."

Khan nodded, tapped the edge of his notebook against the counter, finished his second beer.

"Another?" I offered.

"Nope. Two's my on-duty limit. And I still have to go talk to another one of your poker friends."

"Who?"

Khan glanced at his pad. "Elliot Feinstein."

"Have fun," I said.

"You don't like him? I thought that sci-fi thing he wrote was pretty good."

"It was *Red River* in space."

"Yeah, but the alien cattle drive was pretty cool."

"Oh, Elliot's all right. In fact, he'll love talking to you. Just watch out, because everything he does ends up in a script sooner or later. Elliot has imagination issues. He bought a Ferrari and then wrote a race car movie. He lost a bundle in Vegas and wrote a gambling script. If you're not careful, there'll be a cop like you in his next story."

"That sounds okay. I see maybe a slimmed-down Travolta playing the part. Or possibly Keitel."

"Be careful what you wish for, Detective. 'Cause more'n likely the bastards will cast some talentless hump like me."

Khan thanked me when he left, but he looked positively broken-hearted.

When I remembered to check the phone message an hour later it turned out to be none other than Kevin Ryan Paul. Even as I was bad-mouthing the guy to the cops, the producer was sweet-talking my machine about *The Devil on Sunday.*

"Great lunch, Marty, you positively knocked my socks off. Knocked 'em right off. I'm barefoot, baby, and my feets are cold. And Sade, she's practically ready to throw me over for you. You dog. Just wanted to touch base and keep those lines of communication open. Connection, baby. You and me. Huh? Huh? And don't you worry: Your agent will have the script first thing Monday morning. Take it to the bank."

The thought occurred to me then that there's something to be said for keeping your valuables under the mattress.

Six

H all Emerson's funeral took place on Tuesday at a cemetery near Tustin. I've never liked Orange County; not only because of its honestly-earned reputation for far-right politics, but because of Disneyland. Maybe it's just me—it must be, because umpteen zillion tourists can't be wrong—but the place gives me the creeps. I've always hated Disney cartoons and characters. I hate the fact that you can't swing a dead mouse in a shopping mall without hitting one of their damn stores. And as for Uncle Walt, with that pedophile mustache and his union-busting, anti-Semitic ways, well, he was as nasty a piece of work as this town ever produced and that's saying something. And while I admit to a perverse fondness for the Country Bear Jamboree, all the rest of that "imagineered" animatronic crap in the so-called Magic Kingdom leaves me cold as an Icelandic nun in a Popsicle factory.

Also, I once got sick on Mr. Toad's Wild Ride.

(It's neither here nor there, but I used to think the world could be divided into two kinds of people: those who preferred wry, cynical Loony Tunes, and those who liked happy-sappy Disney pap. My own sympathies, of course, were always with Chuck Jones and Michael Maltese and the Merrie Melodies bunch, but now that there are as many Warner Bros. stores as Disney boutiques, and Bugs and Daffy and the Tasmanian Devil stare ubiquitously back at you from watch faces and cereal boxes and Christmas cards, I am forced to concede that it's all just corporate mush, so a pox on all their houses. Thank God Tex Avery didn't live to see it.)

I drove down to the funeral with Jon, Elliot, and Marconi of the poker gang. Bill Morris didn't make the service. He had a longstanding lunch meeting with Adam Sandler, and wasn't about to cancel for any mere funeral. "Hall's gonna be dead for a while," Marconi reported him saying, "Sandler's money in the bank *now*. I'll do the respects thing later." At least he sent flowers.

Morris was clearly not alone in his sentiments, because the funeral was a poor show. Death is never a high-concept pitch in LA, and Hall was too much on the outs with the ins to merit the kind of attention that might make a celeb drive-by worth a shot at a photo in the *Times*. A rent-a-priest was there to handle banalities at the grave, but even with the four of us there were barely a dozen mourners. Three middle-aged men in black suits stood together, occasionally exchanging whispers and giggles. I recognized one of them as an old TV writer I'd known from my *Salt & Pepper* days. It occurred to me that they might be part of some poker circle from days gone by. Opposite them was another, less formal but no less precisely tailored group of bearded men in biker leathers. They were about the same age as Hall and the suited writers, and looked very uncomfortable. One of them, a gray-haired guy with a beer belly-length beard, stared solemnly at the open grave. Every so often he'd still his nervously shifting companions with a flex of his pinky.

The only female in attendance was a slight, elderly woman with a stoop and a cane. Her gray hair was pulled tightly back in a bun, though stray hairs broke free like bits of stripped wiring. She sniffled and sobbed, dabbing at her wrinkled cheeks with a fistful of tissues.

Detective Khan was there, too. Whether out of duty or responsibility (they're not the same things, at all), I didn't know, but I nodded at him when we arrived and he returned the greeting.

And to my considerable surprise, Kevin Ryan Paul was there, along with his entourage. Sade looked better in black—the long sleeves hid her emaciated arms—but Kant tried to get away with a Leonard Cohen thing that simply didn't work with his big bald head. Phone Dude was there, too, but he stayed with the car. Paul gave me a big wink and a thumb's up that defined "inappropriate." Everyone turned to sneer at me, so I glanced at Elliot with a what-the-hell's-the-matter-with-you look. Elliot whimpered and poked me in the back.

The rent-a-priest delivered his spiel like a man worried about time running out on his parking meter. He read off index cards and twice referred to Hall as Hal. The guy also had a speech defect, á la Elmer Fudd, and about halfway through the eulogy, Marconi got the giggles. I don't know if Hall was even religious—he sure didn't strike me as the type—but every time the priest implored us to "pway" for the "deawy depawted," Marconi all but fell down laughing. He tried to cover with a cough at first, but that just made things worse. As the others started to shoot ever more vicious glances our way, Conlon kicked Marconi hard in the shins. But then Conlon caught the giggles, too. One of the biker types edged over our way looking like he had a brand new tire chain he wanted to try out, but before anything too ugly could get going, everyone's attention was diverted by the arrival of a white stretch limo. A liveried driver emerged and dashed around to open the door, extending his hand to assist the passengers inside. There was a long pause while everyone, priest included, held their breath waiting to see who was going to emerge.

A dainty, black-gloved hand snaked out and placed itself in the chauffeur's. An exceptionally well-turned ankle in a stylish black shoe followed, leading a length of leg that Cyd Charisse in her prime might have envied. The leg just went on and on—I heard Elliot emit a squeak—and just when you'd have sworn it couldn't go any farther without an NC-17 rating, the hem of a black leather micro-thing (really, it's unfair to the vast majority of women's clothing to label it a skirt) arrived to save a visit from the Vice Squad. A second, equally impressive limb appeared—bilateral symmetry, nice or what?—and then the rest of the lady emerged.

The legs were no bait-and-switch deal.

If she was an actress I'd have known her. No one in Hollywood could look like that and remain a secret. She had Sigourney Weaver's stature, Jessica Lange's eyes, Michelle Pfieffer's nose, Julia Roberts's lips, and Liz Hurley's cleavage. And I bet they all gave it up to her willingly. She moved like a panther, and I don't mean Eldridge Cleaver. All around me in the cemetery flowers sighed with jealousy and shed petals in despair. I swear you could hear the sound of blood rushing into penises, and nails scraping at the lids of coffins from inside graves. If you could bottle this woman, Coca-Cola would be out of business tomorrow. Forgive the superfluity, but *wow*.

"Dear Santy," Conlon whispered, "I know what I want for Christmas, and it ain't no train set."

She had flowing, rich red hair and didn't acknowledge the fact that everyone was staring at her; didn't play any coy eye games or suppress an ain't-I-the-creamed-corn smile at the corner of her lip. She merely stood aside as the driver reached down again to help a second mourner out of the limo.

If the woman was a cat prowling around for the kill, the old man was the carcass after the panther had eaten, the vultures had picked through the leftovers, and the worms had got down to the serious business of stripping bones. He was old and looked it. Hell, old was young compared to this guy. His skin was mottled and chapped, with liver spots denser than the grain on 35mm film stock, though he tried to hide it all beneath an unconvincing Hollywood tan. He was bald as a pumpkin, but with lots more lines. And he had a kind of depression where one side of his face should have been. On him, it didn't look good.

Oh, yeah: and he was wearing a white suit.

The priest waited while the woman took the old man's withered hand and led him graveside. The man wore a Panama hat which he failed to doff as he approached the coffin. He was also big on gold jewelry: three fancy rings, a dangly wrist bracelet, and something around his scrawny neck that Mr. T must have hocked. I happened to glance at Paul, who stood there slack-jawed while Kant whispered into his ear. Sade's eyes flicked back and forth between the panther goddess and her own anorexic frame. She didn't look happy, but then if she was, she wouldn't be that thin to begin with.

The rent-a-priest, too, was rather taken by the sight of the arrivistes and only got back to his index cards when the old woman who'd been sobbing hissed at him. He fumbled through the remainder of the service and asked if anyone present wanted to say anything before the casket was lowered into the ground.

A nervous silence descended on those gathered, broken only by the old woman's sniffles. This was the saddest bit, I thought: A man's dead and no one but a stranger to speak at his funeral. I would have loved to break the silence myself, but what could I say? I hardly knew Hall. And I've always been useless without a script.

Just when it looked like the priest was going to wrap things up, the biker-type with the long beard, raised his hand.

"Yes, pwease go ahead," the priest implored.

The biker looked very nervous—though he, too, had a hard time taking his eyes off the young woman with the old man—as he stepped around to the top of the grave. He had little hands, with fat sausage fingers bearing half a dozen rings. He gently rested one hand atop Hall's coffin, caressing it at first, then tapped it gently such that his rings evoked a kind of bongo beat. He closed his eyes, raised both hands to the sides of his mouth, and after taking a gasping breath, let loose with an inchoate roar they must have heard all the way up in Tarzana. When it was over, he touched the coffin again—with real tenderness—then nodded his thanks at the priest and returned to his place beside the other men in leathers. Two of them had tears in their eyes and the third patted the bearded man on the back and nodded.

"Anyone ewse?" the priest asked, a little desperately.

There were no other takers.

After a few more index-carded words, they lowered Hall into the ground. The old woman approached the grave first, tossing a handful of dirt atop the coffin. I saw her mouth a goodbye, then she tossed a flower in and walked away. A line formed as people crossed themselves or sprinkled dirt or just said adios in their own way. It was only after I knelt down and let a handful of earth sprinkle through my fingers that I realized that the couple from the limo hadn't joined the queue. Indeed, as I looked up, the vision of splendor was already back inside the car and the driver was assisting the old thing in after her. I rejoined the poker circle and we watched the limo pull away.

"Who the hell was that?" I asked.

"Do you have to look like the old guy to have the money to get that kind of girl?" Marconi said.

"Where would you go to buy one even if you did?" Conlon added.

"Amazon dot com?" Elliot suggested.

It took a full minute before the three of us realized it was a joke. And a pretty good one at that.

I guess that's why Elliot rates the big money.

"Hey, Marty Burns," Paul called a little too loudly across the lingering mourners. I could bet that *Burning Bright* wasn't about to grab any new viewers out of this bunch. Paul left Sade and Kant behind and took me by the arm. "Got a minute?"

I told the others I'd meet them back at the car and strolled away from Hall's grave with the producer.

"I didn't realize you knew Hall Emerson," Paul said. I couldn't decide if he was being sincere.

"Only a little. Enough that I felt bad to hear . . . you know."

"Damn shame. He used to be a talent."

"I am a little surprised to see you here," I said.

"How's that?"

"I understand you and Hall had some problems. Something about . . . aggravated assault was it?"

Paul put on an expression as if I'd suggested that his mother had taken on the entire sixth fleet. He slapped a hand to his heart to cover the wound I'd inflicted.

"Someone's been telling you stories."

"A cop."

Paul shook his head fiercely. "A misunderstanding over a deal. You know how these things get exaggerated, the stories that get around."

"The *detective* told me that you filed charges against Hall."

"No, no, no. Charges? No. Not really. I asked merely that a . . . situation be noted. For the record. It was strictly for leverage. That's the way things work in this business, you know that."

"I've never had a police complaint filed against me. At least, not by anyone in The Business."

"But you're a sweetheart, Marty, everybody knows that. With a man like you, who needs leverage? But all that is water under the bridge. Hall is a terrible loss. A tragedy for everyone who knew him. So have you been thinking about *The Devil on Sunday*?"

A man with a weaker neck might have suffered whiplash.

"I'm a deep thinker, Kev," I said. He winced at the "Kev," but didn't let it faze him.

"I could tell that about you, Mar." Touché. "And I respect the hell out of it. But let me add a little something to that deep pool of your thoughts . . ."

"A little chlorine to counteract the pee?"

"Precisely. Not only are we now a cunt's hair away from signing Gamma on the dotted line, but inked, notarized, and in the safe is a commitment from Lissa Torres for a key role. The Connie Clare character from the original."

"Lissa Torres."

"Huh? Huh?" Paul nodded.

Lissa Torres is the hot young thing du jour, thanks to her role as a sexy werewolf in *Lupé Garou*, one of those godawful Warner shows of the sort that Conlon is always script-doctoring. The shtick is that she turns all furry every time she gets horny; and she gets horny at least once an episode. The eighteen to thirty-fours eat it up like Lay's potato chips. The dumbed-down bastards. You can't pass a newsstand without seeing Lissa Torres's face—and usually a good bit of the rest of her (and she has several very good bits indeed)—staring back at you from one magazine cover or the other. I hated to admit it, but it was pretty impressive if Paul had lined her up for *The Devil on Sunday.*

"That's pretty impressive," I told him.

"Huh? Huh? And of course, you'd have a love scene with her. *Nude,* of course."

I cleared my throat. "Nude?"

Paul flashed me a don't-be-an-idiot glare. "Lissa nude. Not you."

"Phew."

"Let's be realistic, after all."

"Those words are tattooed on my butt."

"So, sounding good? Do we have a killer project here, or what?"

"You know, my agent's still waiting on a copy of the script."

Paul grabbed my bicep so hard, I thought perhaps he was having a heart attack. "What? You didn't get a copy of the script?"

"Not yet."

"Unbelievable. Do I have to do everything myself? Can you get decent help in this town? Are these people gonna be the fucking death of me?"

"I don't know, Kev."

"Marty, your agent will have that script by end of business today. You can count on that. Heads are gonna roll."

"Now is this script the one that Hall wrote?"

We'd been strolling in a slow circle around the cemetery as we talked. Paul froze in his tracks.

"What do you mean?"

"Didn't Hall write a draft of the script? Isn't that what your . . . misunderstanding was all about?"

Paul thought about it for a little while, nodding to himself as he did so. The nod morphed into a rigid head shake.

"I'm not one for speaking ill of the dead, that's not the cut of my jib. And I certainly don't want to say any such thing here, on the day when the man is being lowered into the ground. But Hall did not write that script. I gave him the chance to do it, because he wasn't untalented when he was on his game and because of his connections to the original movie, but Hall couldn't and didn't deliver. Simple as that."

"How come you didn't mention any of this at lunch the other day?"

"I didn't know you knew Hall. If you'd asked me, I'd have told you the same. Listen to me, Marty: If you knew Hall, you must know that he had his troubles. I took a chance giving him a shot at *The Devil on Sunday*. I did it . . . you know what happened when they shot the original picture? The murder of Connie Clare?"

"Yeah, of course. She was Hall's mom."

"So you know it all. Good. Well, maybe you don't know that my uncle produced *The Devil on Sunday*. George Gaines. Uncle George, he personally cast Connie Clare in that part, and for the rest of his life he felt a little guilty, a little responsible for what happened to that girl. Uncle George was that kind of guy. The way I see it, Uncle George would have wanted me to give Hall a shot at the remake. If only because of his mother and what happened to her during the shoot of the original."

"George G. Gaines was your uncle?" I asked. Bloody hell! Just how incestuous is this miserable town?

"Of course. That's how I landed the rights to *Devil*."

"And you felt you owed something to Hall because of that?"

"I don't like to pray at my own shrine, but I have to tell you this, Marty: That's the kind of guy I am. Maybe it's crazy in this business, maybe it's suicide—pardon the expression and God rest his soul—but I gotta be me."

"You're something special, Kev," I said.

He kicked the dirt in an unconvincing, aw-shucks manner. If there'd been an open grave handy, I'd have whacked him in the head with a shovel and dropped him in. Though I suspect even maggots might turn their noses up at such an offering.

Paul again swore up and down that Kendall would get a copy of the script that day. I saw no more reason to believe that than anything else he'd had to say, but we parted with a smile. Paul wanted to give me a hug, but I managed to duck out of it with only a pat on the back as collateral damage.

Conlon, Marconi, and Elliot were waiting for me at the car. Everyone else had left, and the three of them had loosened their ties and their attitudes.

"What was that all about?" Jon asked me.

"I'm being wooed."

"I know Paul," Conlon said. "He's the kind who fucks without kissing."

"When they circumcised that bastard they threw the wrong bit away," Marconi added.

"Is that an anti-Semitic crack?" Elliot asked.

"Strictly anti-producer."

"Oh, that's okay then."

"I don't plan to kiss him or fuck him," I said, "and I don't want to know anything about his dick."

"Speaking of sex," Marconi said, "do you know who that noseless old bastard with the leather bombshell was?"

"Not a clue," I said.

"Mac Stans."

"*That's* MacArthur Stans? Jesus."

"Yeah, one of Hall's old writer friends told me after the service. Pretty neat, huh? I didn't even know he was still alive."

"You sure he was?" Conlon asked.

"I wish I could have shook his hand," Elliot said. "He's a truly great man."

"I don't know, who can say what might drop off if you shake him."

"Well, there was one piece he could have dropped that I'd have gladly taken with me. Damn, she had legs all the way up to her . . . I'd pay Elliot's money for a taste of what's between 'em. God, I love red hair. *Natural* red hair."

"Natural, unnatural, *super*natural. I'd do her," Marconi added.

"Hell, I'd do her with Elliot's dick," Conlon said.

"You guys," Elliot said.

Such was the level of repartee all the way back to LA.

Everybody had business to attend to in the afternoon, but we arranged to meet again that evening at Conlon's place for an informal wake. My business consisted of a check-in phone call to Kendall—still no sign of a script as of three o'clock—and a haircut at a salon in Manhattan Beach. I used to go only to places that charged less than ten bucks for a trim, but at risk of putting on airs and affectations, that just didn't feel right for someone with his own TV show. Now I don't get as good a cut, but they charge me half a C-note, give me cappuccino, and stick my glossy on the wall next to Alex Trebek. It's not a total loss, though, because there's a better than average deli in Manhattan Beach where I sat on the patio and had a nice Reuben sandwich and a Coney Island knish. People kept staring at me, which I've gotten used to again since *Burning Bright* went on the air, but it was only when I glanced at my reflection in the chrome napkin holder that I realized the attention probably had less to do with celebrity than the strip of tissue paper wedged in my collar. So there's another bonus with your fifty dollar trim.

I mused over my conversation with Kevin Ryan Paul. I certainly hadn't expected him to be at the funeral and still wasn't sure what to make of his presence there. His version of his history with Hall didn't match up with what Detective Khan told me about the situation. Okay, so given Hall's death, maybe Paul wanted to soft-pedal any disagreement he had with the writer to make himself look better. Maybe he was afraid that he would somehow look like he contributed to Hall's suicide by his treatment of the man. But why show up at the funeral? There was no one there for him to impress—hell, there was hardly anyone there at all. There was no press interest, no PR angle that I could make out. Was it possible that he honestly felt bad and simply wanted to pay his respects?

Christ, if I wasn't careful I'd start thinking he had a heart and a mother and paid his fair share of taxes.

I also wondered what Mac Stans was doing at the funeral. Hall had admitted to me that Stans was the true author of the script of the original *Devil on Sunday,* but hadn't mentioned any other connection to the old man. I suppose the fact that Frank Emerson had fronted for Stans back during the blacklist suggested a pretty close connection. Maybe Stans had known Hall when he was a little boy. Bimbo notwithstanding, the old guy didn't look too good, though; Hall must have rated pretty high in his estimation to get him out and about for the funeral. I wondered if Stans knew Kevin Ryan Paul. The two didn't talk at the funeral as far as I noticed, though Paul did look pretty stunned when the old geezer emerged from the limo. George Gaines must have known that Stans was the pen behind *The Devil on Sunday.* It only figured that Stans and Gaines were acquainted. Of course, Paul wasn't even born at the time, so there was no real reason that he and Stans should know each other. Though it was all just a little too in-the-family that Gaines was Paul's uncle. But then, the depths of Hollywood inbreeding make even Prince Charles look small-eared.

I don't know what difference any of it made anyway. I had no interest in Paul's offer for *Devil on Sunday,* even with a naked Lissa Torres on the plate. Kendall's enthusiasm was flagging with each passing day that the script failed to materialize, though she did continue to hock me about the wonders of Gamma.

And ultimately, Hall was dead. Still and forever dead. So what was there to do?

Other than go to a wake.

"Jon," Elliot slurred, already drunk, "if I go, I want *you* to throw the party for me. You put on a great funeral."

Conlon smiled. "I'd be happy to, Elliot. But when *you* kick, there's gonna be a lot of competition for biggest party."

"Aw, that's really sweet," Elliot said, and stumbled off to refill his glass.

"How 'bout you Marty? Can I cater your wake when you go?"

"I'm not going anyplace," I said.

"Oh, really? You got some inside knowledge or something?"

"As a youth, I sold my soul to Manny Stiles for sitcom stardom *and* eternal life. Of course, there was a catch."

"Pray tell."

"Manny kept the syndication rights on both counts."

"There's a lot of bastards out there," Conlon said.

We drank to that.

Conlon's girlfriend flitted around, pouring wine and bringing out fresh hors d'oeuvres from the kitchen. Elliot had brought his wife—Christ, but he'd married a shiksa; with that upturned little nose, I bet Elliot's mother sat shivah after the wedding—who perched in a corner with Bill Morris's current paramour, a wannabe Latina pop star who Morris swore was the new Jennifer Lopez. To me she looked more like the old Gloria Estefan, but I don't know from rock and roll. Morris was kibitzing with Marconi who came stag. I always half-suspected that maybe Luke swung in more than one direction, not that Jerry Seinfeld thinks there's anything wrong with that. Hell, it's probably just sound career grounding if a publicist can take like he gives.

"So how did lunch go?" Marconi asked.

"I might as well have gone to the funeral," Morris said. "Sandler didn't show."

"What happened?"

"Some bullshit about a clash in his diary. He sends his manager instead. And David Spade."

"Oh. Well, Spade's a nice guy I hear."

"Yeah, he's terrif. Very funny gentleman. But when you order lobster and they bring you fish sticks, it's kind of hard to enjoy your meal."

I hadn't realized that Conlon invited partners, not that it mattered to me. I wasn't seeing anyone at the moment, and certainly wouldn't have dragged a casual date to such an event. At first, I was annoyed, but after a little while—and with Elliot so quickly tanked—I decided that it would have been too damn depressing with just the five of us there.

Not that the evening was meant to be a rollicking good time.

The doorbell rang and Conlon opened it for a middle-aged couple. It took a moment before I recognized the man as one of the older writers who had attended the funeral. Indeed, it was the fellow who I recalled from *Salt & Pepper* days, though his name continued to elude me. Conlon, gracefully, rescued me from my potential embarrassment.

"Marty, I think you might be acquainted with Don Grady."

"Don," I said, shaking hands. "It's, uh, been a long time."

"Two lifetimes at least. This is my wife, Sarah."

I shook her hand, too, and she smiled as she took it, but studied me oddly. She was pushing sixty minimum, with more nooks and crannies in her face than an English muffin, but she had a vital, self-confident air about her. She also had a serious case of turkey neck going, but wore an open collar blouse that suggested it didn't bother her in the slightest. It also suggested just a bit more than I perhaps needed to know about her cup size.

"You seem to have landed on your feet again, Marty," Grady said. Without a great deal of warmth in his voice.

"Yeah, it's a nice change from stepping on other people's toes. You'll have to forgive my asking, 'cause as you say, more than one lifetime has passed, but are you someone whose insole I trod on way back when?"

"Maybe a kick or two in the shin," Grady said. "Nothing crippling, though."

He smiled, but I had a feeling he was being polite under the circumstances. I honest-to-God couldn't remember well enough to be sure.

"And, uh, you got anything in development at the moment?"

Grady's smile turned a little warmer. "You've become very diplomatic in your old age. What you mean is: Am I still plugging away? No, I've retired from the business. We have a little spread up toward Thousand Oaks, paid for by thirty years of sitcom writing. Sarah paints and I play computer games and surf the Net."

"Doesn't sound too bad," I said. "You don't do any writing anymore?"

"Just for myself. Short stories, the odd poem. I occasionally publish in small literary magazines, university journals. Beats the hell out of hacking out one-liners for Don Adams."

"You write for *Get Smart?*"

"No such luck. I had a hand in a few episodes of *Check It Out.*"

" 'Fraid, I don't remember that one. But I have some blank years."

"Take a number and count your blessings."

"Still, where can you go after Barbara Feldon?"

"Amen to that."

"So how well did you know Hall?"

Grady let out a big sigh. "We used to be pretty close. I met him years ago, when we were both working on projects for NBC. Those were good days, though Hall already had a big yen for the hooch. We got to be climbing buddies."

"Pardon?"

"Rock climbing. Me and Hall used to light out for Chatsworth or Joshua Tree. Nothing like a day on the rocks with your life hanging on your fingertips to get your mind off the industry bullshit."

"I'll take your word for it."

"Haven't done it for some time, of course. I've got arthritis now. Hard enough to grip a mouse much less a rock face. And Hall, well, he just sort of drifted away."

"You see him lately?"

"Funny thing is, I ran into him not more than three weeks ago. Max Roach was playing at Catalina in Hollywood. Sarah and I caught the early show, and found Hall propping up the bar. I have to say, the years and the booze hadn't been kind."

"You surprised by, you know, the suicide?"

Grady swirled his drink, watched the little waves until they subsided. "Hell, yeah," he said. "Hall was a guy who always had troubles. You know a man who drinks like that must. But he had a gusto about him, too. Used to see it out on the rocks. We'd drive out there five, six in the morning and sometimes Hall'd be hungover as could be. But he got out on that face and he was all there, pure focus. There were routes we'd try that I'd think were too much for us, that sometimes I'd want to quit halfway up. Hall would never have it. If you started a route with Hall, goddamn it you finished it. It was just the way he was. But . . ."

"Yeah?"

"People change, don't they?"

"Do they?"

Grady looked me up and down. "I think they do."

Sarah had gone to get some food, and came back just then with a heaping plate. Grady eyed it up and said: "That looks pretty good." I expected him to help himself to hers, but he just wandered off to get a plate of his own. Sarah ate happily, not offering me a bite either.

"You don't remember me, do you?" she asked, stopping to take a swig of her Diet Coke.

"Ahh, I have to admit you look vaguely familiar. But in all honesty, no, I don't remember you. Have we met?"

"You felt me up once."

I could hear the sudden scream of an incoming projectile. It sounded really big and I knew where it was about to hit.

"I beg your pardon?"

"You copped a feel."

"I copped a feel."

"Of my tit."

"Your . . ." The air raid sirens were wailing now.

"Don wrote an episode of *Salt & Pepper*. It was the one where you fooled your little buddies into doing your homework for you. And then you lost it and couldn't answer the teacher's questions because you hadn't actually done the work. Very sixties, very moral. Don could knock those out in his sleep."

"God, I was a scamp."

"Actually, you were a monster. Don and I had just got started getting serious and he brought me along to the set to show me what it was like. To impress me a little. I was good-looking at the time, with a hell of a rack. You were an obnoxious little bastard so full of yourself that your nose was running. You cornered me behind the catering table and grabbed my tit. I dumped a bowl of ambrosia salad on your head."

"And I had Manny Stiles fire Don," I said, closing my eyes, suddenly remembering. BLAAMMM! Direct hit.

"Yes you did."

"Christ," I said. I dropped my head into my hands. "I don't know what to say. I'm horribly sorry."

"Ancient history. I just thought you should know."

"I'm really sorry," I said again.

"You don't seem like such a bad fellow now," she said. "Though you're no Don Adams." She wandered off after her husband.

I stood there for a while, shaking my head. If Elliot hadn't had to push me out of the way as he ran to the bathroom to puke, I might be standing there still.

". . . so there's Hall, sprawled on the sofa, naked from the waist down. The hooker's on her knees trying to make something, *anything*, happen down below so she can get the hell out of there, while he's chopping coke on a cheese board with his Writers' Guild card. And that's when the cops bust in."

"Oh, no," Marconi groaned. The rest of us were laughing, shaking our heads.

"Right?" Conlon continued. "So Bob Mitchum's upstairs and when he hears the cops, he goes right out the window. Just jumps out. He's so messed up he doesn't even realize he's on the second floor, but the lucky bastard lands in the hedges, gets straight to his feet and takes off down the road buck naked."

"What about Hall?" I asked.

"Hall, as he himself told it, was never a lucky bastard. It was Mitchum's coke, Mitchum's hooker, and unfortunately Bob Mitchum's gun."

"You didn't mention any gun."

"Yeah, well, Hall didn't know about it, either. So, the cops bag the coke, send the hooker off—with a C-note they boost out of Hall's wallet, never mind she's already been paid—and take Hall in on drugs and firearms charges. And all the time he's screaming, 'I didn't even come, I didn't even come.' "

"So how'd it end up?" Morris asked.

"Hall did sixty days in County on a plea bargain."

"I remember that," Don Grady said. "It cost Hall a big score with Paramount."

"Unlucky," Conlon said, shaking his head.

That seemed to be our general assessment of Hall Emerson's life: unlucky. It's not the word most people might associate with a man who earned his living writing movie and TV shows, living in LA, and hobnobbing with the rich and famous. But all things considered—from his start as a murdered mother's child, to his end as a lonely, broke suicide—Hall didn't have the best run of the cards. Though if luck really is the residue of design, there's certainly an argument that Hall was the architect of his own crapped-out ruin of a life.

Elliot was sacked out in Conlon's recliner—his wife had already taken a taxi home, having left in a perhaps overly theatrical huff; I don't think I envied Elliot his home life—but the rest of us sat around, trading remembrances of Hall. Conlon had gone to the trouble of renting a few of the movies that Hall had written in his prime, and left them running on the television set in the corner with the volume turned down low. In the quiet, as we sat there musing over Hall Emerson's unlucky life, the words he'd written could be dimly heard in the background, like the ghost of a conversation on crossed phone lines. It was all that was left of him, really.

"Who was the older woman at the funeral?" I asked. "The one who was sobbing."

"Melly," Grady said. "Hall's ex-wife. Very ex."

"Melly?"

"Short for Melinda. I can't recall her last name, I know she re-married. It sent Hall on a bender about ten years ago. Melly . . . ?"

"Dougherty," Sarah Grady said.

"That's right. Melly Dougherty. Sarah always remembers these things." Grady smiled at his wife and she squeezed his hand. "She and Hall had a rocky relationship. I guess that goes without saying or she wouldn't be an ex. She was a good few years older than Hall. He always said he liked a woman with experience."

"Do you know Mac Stans?" I asked.

"Not really. I know his story, respect the hell out of his work. I didn't know he knew Hall. I don't think Hall ever mentioned him to me, or I'd remember. I was stunned when he showed up at the funeral with that woman."

I eyed Conlon, expecting a line about Stans's companion, but Jon was caught up in watching the movie on his TV. I think it was a little too late for anyone to feel an urge toward snappy patter. Marconi was about to drain his glass, then thought better of it. He got up and grabbed a bottle of wine and refilled all the glasses.

"One last drink," he announced. "To Hall. And to better luck."

"To Hall," we all toasted.

People drifted off shortly thereafter. The Gradys left first, then Bill Morris and the pop star. Marconi hung around long enough to finish whatever wine was open, then he took off, too. Conlon's partner started cleaning up the aftermath, but Jon told her to go to bed.

"I'll clear it up in the morning, Suze. Besides," he said, pointing to Elliot snoring in his chair, "the biggest mess is going to be here all night."

She said goodnight and then it was just me and Jon. And Elliot in the corner. Conlon poured us a pair of cognacs. Very nice stuff.

"Good bash?" Conlon asked me.

"Given the circumstances. I agree with Elliot: You can do his wake when the time comes."

"We could kill him now, get a head start."

"How would you do it?"

"Smother him? Say he choked on his own vomit?"

"Where's the vomit?"

"We could puke down his throat after he was dead."

I made as if to consider it, then said: "Nah. It's be a waste of good cognac."

"Another time maybe."

"Don't kill him without me," I said.

We clinked glasses.

"So how would *you* do it?" Conlon asked.

"Kill Elliot?"

"No. Yourself. Would you do it like Hall?"

I swirled my brandy, thought about it. "I don't think so."

"How then? You must have thought about it, everyone does."

"Yeah, sure. But I'm not really the suicidal type. I'd be long since dead if I was. God knows I've had motive *and* opportunity."

"I think it would have to be pills for me," Conlon said. "I don't think I could do the violent stuff. Though I thought Hall could."

"Why?"

"He was a gun guy. Had a whole collection. Liked to shoot, hunt, all that manly, Hemingway shit. I think he always wanted to be John Huston or something."

"Don Grady says they used to rock climb."

"See? I'd have figured Hall for eating a gun or crashing a car. Much more his style. Drive off a cliff, maybe. He liked those big gestures, in his scripts and his life. Sucking fumes from an LTD in a garage just ain't big. In fact, it's about as small as you can get."

"You talk to the cops?"

"A detective came by, why?"

"He ask you if you thought Hall was the suicidal type?"

"Yeah, I told him the same thing I'm telling you. A little cleaned-up maybe."

"How did he react?"

"Just nodded. He wasn't here more than ten minutes. Why?"

"Nothing," I said. But I wondered what Carl Khan might be thinking about Hall's death. Maybe I'd try to find out.

"Another drink?" Conlon offered.

"No, I should get going. It's late." But I didn't make any move. "Pills, huh?"

"What?"

"You'd do it with pills?"

"I think so. If I was going to do it."

"I suppose that would be my choice, too. I guess we don't think big."

"Maybe. But *we're* sipping brandy while Hall's lying cold in the ground. So what's big amount to?"

"I suppose."

We sat there, listening to Elliot snore. The videotape had run out and white noise static filled the screen of the TV.

"You wouldn't ever do it, would you?" I asked. "Top yourself?"

"I don't think so," Jon said. "Though I know people who have. That's probably why I wouldn't, no matter how bad it got. What's left after is awful."

I nodded.

"Besides, I've got my art to keep me sane."

"Your art, huh? What are you working on this week?"

"Episode of that *Xena* rip-off. I'm gonna steal Elliot's Amazon line."

"Here's to art, then," I said.

"And sanity."

"And Hall."

We clinked glasses.

Seven

I vaguely remember waking up sometime in the early morning hours, tasting the inside of my mouth, and going back to sleep. I feel it would have been an insult to Hall's memory to get up before noon on the day after his wake.

By the time I showered, it was one-thirty.

I called Kendall, flirting with her secretary, Taisha, until she could come on the line. Taisha and I have one of those weird relationships where we trade endless double entendres on the phone without actually having the slightest romantic or sexual interest in each other in person. It's the kind of thing that only happens in office life, and I suspect it is now seriously verboten under sexual harassment law. Fun, though. At least until she sues me.

Kendall didn't apologize for keeping me waiting. For one thing, it wasn't that long, and for another, she knows that I know she doesn't play stupid games and gets to the phone as soon as she possibly can.

"I got a package from Kevin Ryan Paul," she said.

"You're kidding. He sent the script?"

"Well, now, I didn't say that did I?"

"So he didn't send the script."

"He sent . . . something."

"What did he send you, Kendall?"

"I got a big box of chocolates." Kendall's diabetic. "And a big bunch of flowers." Allergies, too. Huh-boy. "And seventeen pages of dialogue."

"Seventeen?"

"Mmmm. Maybe it's his lucky number. I assume that they're meant to be your bits, but the pages are out of the middle of the script, so I don't know what to make of the context. Oh, and they're on fax paper, just that little bit smudged, making them not quite, but nearly impossible to actually read."

"Oh, he's a prince, that boy. I saw him again yesterday, you know."

"What? Where?"

"Hall Emerson's funeral. I'm not sure what he was doing there. If I didn't know better, I'd think he was waiting for me. He tried to talk up the picture some more."

"That sounds appropriate."

"Oh, yeah; made a big hit with the other mourners. Then again, maybe Kev's a trendsetter. You know: 'Have your people call my people. We'll do death.' "

"*Kev?*" Kendall said.

"Yeah, it really seemed to irk him. I'm going to try and remember to use it if I see him again."

"It's a wonder you never got drafted into the diplomatic corps. So what did *Kev* have to say?"

"Shmooze one-oh-one with a shmear on the side. Oh, yeah: he dangled a nude Lissa Torres at me."

"How's that?"

"Paul says Lissa Torres is signed, sealed, and delivered for *The Devil on Sunday*. He promised me a nude love scene with her, though he was careful to emphasize that the naked bits would all be hers. You think maybe I need to tone my butt?"

"With all due respect and affection, Marty, I think maybe you're beyond tone deaf. What did you tell him?"

"I didn't say anything. You know me, I'm the master of empty conversation."

"Yes, I know. This is a very interesting development, though."

"Ooh, I don't like that tone of voice. That's your gentle way of saying: The rectal exam won't hurt *that* much."

"Have you read the trades this morning?" Kendall asked.

"Not unless you're talking about the Dodgers' new pitching acquisition."

"Gamma has signed on to *The Devil on Sunday*."

"So?"

"*So,* Kevin Ryan Paul has got a hot young director, a sizzling young star—naked and well-proportioned, I might add—and a project made in hype heaven which he is practically begging you to appear in."

"I've also got a dead screenwriter friend who just might have been driven to the grave because Kevin Ryan Paul screwed him from here to Palookaville and back."

"There is that," Kendall mumbled. "You know, there was also a sidebar story about Hall Emerson in the *Reporter*."

"What? What did it say?"

"I think Paul must have planted it. It talked up Emerson's connection to the original picture—his mom and dad and all that—and had a couple of quotes from Paul about the remake."

"Pithy, no doubt."

"*Pithed* is more like it. I thought it was kind of a funny piece though."

"How so? You don't mean funny ha-ha."

"No. You know how the *Reporter* slants every story—it helps to read between the lines. But it wasn't a very flattering portrait of your friend Hall. It made him sound kind of sleazy. I thought it came a little close to speaking ill of the dead."

"Can you save it for me?"

"Will do. And let me call Paul's office again and try to get the rest of the script, if it exists. You want me to send you what I have?"

"Do I get the chocolates, too?"

"Taisha's already eaten them. You still haven't got a fax, have you?"

I rolled my eyes. "Who the hell would want to fax me?"

"I do!"

"You know I don't like stuff like that. It's too . . ."

"Convenient?" Kendall suggested. "Up-to-date? Sensible?"

"Intrusive," I said. God, I'm a miserable old fart.

"Okay, I'll have the pages messengered over right away. The article about Emerson, too."

"Isn't that expensive?" I asked. "I could come by for them."

"Martin Burns. You are the star of your own television series. You earn a great deal of money each and every week, of which I take a very happy percentage. Not to mention the fact that messenger charges are a deductible business expense. So stop thinking so darn small and quit acting like a schlemiel."

"Sorry, Kendall."

"You'll have the pages in less than two hours. Call me if you hear any more from Kevin Ryan Paul."

Suitably chastized, I exercised some of my vast wealth to order a pizza for lunch while I waited for the messenger to appear. I hate being told off by Kendall, especially when, as is usually the case, she's right. I do tend to think small-time; it's a holdover from years of living on the edge, with nothing more than a nail-studded baseball bat by the door to keep the debt-collectors away. Kendall has lectured me on numerous occasions that if I want to be a star again, I have to act like one. The public don't want their icons small and humble, but big and brash. The thing is that I lived that big, brash life my first go-round the celebrity mill and I know how addictive, and how dangerous, the lifestyle can ultimately be. I played the self-indulgent, me-me-me star in those *Salt & Pepper* days, and it created a monster who felt up any girl who tickled his fancy and had fired any decent man who got in his way. I swore back and forth and up and down and in and out (and whatever it is you do in the fourth dimension) that I wasn't going to let that happen to me again. I've been lucky enough to get a second bite of the cherry, but I'm not going to go spitting pits into people's eyes.

Still, perhaps I can safely be a little bolder in my approach to celebrity life. No reason not to enjoy the perks and advantages I'm fortunate enough to be able to claim. Surely, there's a halfway point between living like Leonardo DiCaprio and Mahatma Gandhi.

But I ain't buying no stinking fax machine.

The pizza beat Kendall's messenger to my door, but not by much. Especially given that the pizza place is five minutes away and Kendall's office is in West Hollywood. Though the pizza—even topped with spicy pepperoni and jalapeños (and extra cheese)—proved less painful to my digestion.

The pages, as Kendall said, were on the blurry side but decipherable. The dialogue, of course, didn't make the slightest bit of sense. But then that's the industry standard these days. Why talk when you can have a computer simulate an explosion? I couldn't make much of the part or the film from the snippets Paul sent, though a love scene was very explicitly described, so I assumed that the characters involved were meant to be Lissa Torres and me. The sex scene took place on the chrome counter of a closed diner, which sounded cold on my tone-deaf butt, but rife with cinematic potential (If just a tad too reminiscent of the Nicholson-Lange kitchen sex in the remake of *The Postman Always Rings Twice*). There was nothing remotely like the scene in the original *Devil on Sunday,* but the Connie Clare character *was* a waitress in a diner. Maybe, had Clare lived, such a scene was intended.

The pages didn't tell me much more about the project than I knew before. Obviously, the script was still in a rough state and Paul only sent this material along because a) he felt he had to in order to prove some legitimacy; and b) he wanted to sell me with the sex scene. The pages that were there didn't suggest any great reverence for the value of the word, but then they were too meager to provide a meaningful overview of the movie. In fact, the best thing that came out of the envelope was a York Peppermint Patty inserted by Kendall to make up for the chocolates that Taisha had gobbled.

Is she an agent or what?

The script excerpt did get me thinking about Hall again. For all of Kevin Ryan Paul's protestations about the writer's failure, I couldn't help but wonder how many of the words in front of me came out of Hall's pen. There remained an enormous discrepancy between what Hall claimed to have written and what Paul said he delivered. Having now spent a fair amount of time with the producer, I tended to believe that Hall's version was more likely to be true. I certainly would love to see a copy of whatever Hall had given to the producer. Not to mention the copy of the original script of the first *Devil on Sunday,* ostensibly by Frank Emerson but really written by blacklisted Mac Stans, that Hall told me he possessed.

And then I realized that, with a little exertion of that celebrity muscle Kendall had urged me to more vigorously exercise, I just might be able to do so.

"Mr. Burns," Detective Khan said down the phone, "what can I do for you?"

"I was just wondering if I might be able to tempt you with a couple more on-duty drinks this afternoon."

"Any reason in particular?"

"I, uh, want to talk about Hall Emerson."

"What about him?"

"I have some questions and, well"—for Christ's sake, exercise that celebrity muscle—"a favor to ask of you. But the drinks are on me."

"I see. Well, I'm actually off-duty as of . . . fifteen minutes ago. So there's no drink limit whatsoever."

"That's okay."

"But I'm really not that thirsty."

"Oh."

"Pretty hungry, though. You work up a hell of an appetite in CAD. Fame and the policing thereof is hard work."

"Tell me about it," I said. "Well then. How about I buy you dinner this evening? Drinks included."

"I should warn you, I've got expensive tastes."

"I know, I've seen your suits. I don't mind. As long as it's not Blönde."

"And I often eat three courses."

"I'll bring my credit card."

"And an aperitif."

"I thought you weren't thirsty?"

"Suddenly I feel parched."

"Where should we meet?"

"You're not a vegetarian are you?" Khan asked.

"Does the Pope eat Big Macs in the woods?"

"Great. I know just the place!"

"I sure hope you like steak," Khan said as we sat down.

The restaurant was a little joint, upstairs in a minimall in Mar Vista. The restauranteurs probably called it a Marina location, but trust me, it was Mar Vista. The waitress was one of those pert little things who bounce rather than walk and all but have "will fuck for fame" tattooed across their foreheads. I could tell that she recognized me immediately—it's a look you come to know—but to her credit she didn't presume to address me by name, nor did she mention any possible acting aspirations during the course of the meal. It might not have earned her a part, but combined with the fact that she didn't insist on telling us *her* name, it was enough to garner a good tip.

The menu was printed on a small piece of white cardboard, though given what it said I don't know why they bothered to hand them out at all. Steak was what they offered. And fries. That's it. There *was* a choice of soup or salad. And crème brûlée or peach mousse for dessert.

But it was steak and fries for the main course. Though they did ask how you wanted it cooked. Set price, of course; and pretty *well* set for a minimall in Mar Vista.

"I guess this is what eating out was like under Stalin," I said.

"Believe me, the Ruskies never had food like this."

"What if you don't want steak?"

"You go someplace the hell else."

Fair enough. Fortunately, I like a nice hunk of dead cow, and I have to admit it doesn't come much nicer than what we were served. The entrecôte was so lean, the cow must have had its own personal trainer. And so soft and tender that it must have read scores of self-help books. The meat didn't just melt in your mouth, it formed a meaningful relationship with your tongue and whispered that it loved you. If it told me the check was in the mail, I would have believed it.

"What do you think?" Khan asked, though the bastard already knew the answer.

"If a steak like this asked for my daughter's hand in marriage, I'd gratefully hand her over. Hell, I'd give her to white slavers for this bad boy."

"The chef here knows his beef. I've tried to find out where he gets it, but even with a gun to his head, he only smiles and shrugs. I'd shoot him, but I'm afraid I'd never taste its like again."

"These fries ain't bad, either."

"Pommes frites," Khan corrected.

"Doesn't that just mean fried potatoes?"

"Yeah, but they taste nicer if you say it in French."

"Pommes frites," I tried.

Damned if he wasn't right.

I'm not much of a wine guy, but Khan wanted some, and between us we polished off two bottles of merlot with the meal. We chitchatted while we ate, with Khan spinning carefully edited tales of life in CAD. I tried to cajole some names out of him to go with the exotic stories, but since I was already paying for the best steak dinner in town, what could I bargain with? Khan ordered a brandy to top things off, but I just had coffee. He looked a little disappointed in me.

"So you've greased me up pretty good here, Marty. Though none of it was on that steak. Damn, I could have another—don't worry, I won't. What's the favor you're looking for?"

"Have you come to any conclusions about Hall's death?" I asked.

Khan swirled his brandy as he thought about it. "Not officially, no. There are still some *i*'s to dot and *t*'s to cross. But off-the-record, it's a done deal."

"You're sure it's a suicide."

"I'm not sure of anything, Marty. That's the nature of the work. But I can't find any evidence to suggest that Hall Emerson didn't climb into his car and suck down carbon monoxide till he died. The toxicology report—and we are talking unofficially here, just a cop and a TV star eating some steak and drinking some wine—didn't show anything out of the ordinary. Your friend's blood alcohol was point sixteen, but that's not all that high for a serious boozer. And if anything, that kind of blood alcohol level is typical of a suicide. He might have been drunk enough that he indulged a passing, dark fancy and then couldn't change his mind about the situation when he still had a chance."

"No drugs in his system?"

"Why do you think there would be?"

"I don't know, I'm just asking."

"Traces of cannabis, but nothing unusual. No barbiturates, if that's what you're thinking."

"That is what I was thinking."

"Why do you think someone killed Emerson? That is what you're after, right?"

I let out a long breath. "I've just been talking to people—friends and colleagues and such—and not a one of them saw Hall as the suicidal type. He was in the midst of a disagreement, too, of a potentially very unpleasant variety."

"With Kevin Ryan Paul."

"I'm not pointing any fingers, but I'm concerned that something might be overlooked."

"A good cop could take that as an insult, you know."

"I didn't mean it as one."

Khan laughed. "I know. But you do realize that we look into these things very carefully. That is pretty much my job."

"I'm not casting aspersions on you, detective."

"Fair enough." Khan leaned forward and interlaced his fingers on the table. "You used to work as a licensed investigator, right?"

"Feebly."

"Well, but you did it. What kind of work you do?"

"I did . . . shit work. I did shit work."

"Subpoenas? Workers' comp?"

"Yeah. And repo. Sub-rosa on a good day."

"Okay, that's all right. You must have seen the odd complicated case along the way. Conflicting witness statements and evidence. One guy's word against the other."

"Sure."

"And how did those cases usually resolve? I bet it was with the simplest possible explanation. Parsimony is the path to follow. Occam's razor, my friend. It still provides the closest and best shave. Fuck Victor Kiam. And lacking any objective evidence to the contrary, the barber of Sepulveda says that Hall Emerson took his own life." Khan leaned back and finished his brandy.

"I suppose," I said.

"So why don't you look convinced?"

I thought about some of the other . . . *incidents* I've been involved with in my life, the incredibly weird shit I've seen. None of it was remotely simple and Occam's razor would snap like a plastic picnic knife on a diamond if you tried to use it against them.

"It's just my face," is what I said to the detective. "You're not still bothered by the lack of a note?"

"A lot of things bother me: the traffic on Lincoln Boulevard, anything having to do with the Clippers, Regis Philbin. You know, I don't think a million would be enough to make up for having to sit so close to that bastard. But I strive to be a reed in the wind."

"Pretty goddamn poetic for LAPD."

"We're a widely misunderstood breed."

"Uh, huh."

"Not every suicide leaves a note, you know."

The bouncy waitress came and refilled my coffee. Khan indicated that he'd have a cup, too. Along with another brandy.

"What becomes of Hall Emerson's effects?" I asked.

"Well, they should go to the next of kin once the investigation is completed. And it pretty well is. Trouble is, we can't find any. Emerson wasn't married, though there's a couple of exes, no kids. One of 'em was at the service. The old lady who kept bawling?"

"So I understand. Has she asked about his stuff?"

"Nope. I interviewed her the other day—Dougherty's her name

now—and I don't sense that they remained close. Though she made quite a fuss at the funeral. Still, some folks feel they have to put on a show. You should have seen my Aunt Gerty when Uncle Mel popped. Emerson's ex might get his stuff in the end if she wants it and no one else turns up. Either that or his landlord gets to keep it."

"Is there any chance that I could take a look at what's there?"

"Now why would you want to do that?"

"Curiosity. But also I want to see if any of the work Hall did for Kevin Ryan Paul is among his effects."

"What does that do for you?"

"I've been offered a part on Kevin Ryan Paul's new movie. Hall supposedly wrote an early draft and I'd like to see the pages. It's just to help me decide about the role."

"That's very interesting," Khan said.

"Is it?"

"Not your reason, which almost sounds credible, though not quite. But the fact that you asked. 'Cause you're the second person today to do so."

"What? Who else wants to look at Hall's stuff?"

"A gentleman by the name of MacArthur Stans."

"Goddamn!"

"Except his request came via his attorney."

"What did you say?"

"I said I'd take it under advisement. So advise me: Why would an old buzzard like that be interested in Hall Emerson's effects? You'd think that living blow-up doll of his would keep him more than occupied."

"I . . . don't know."

Khan smiled weakly. "You're a very bad liar, Marty. How'd you ever become an actor?"

"There are plenty who say I never did." I thought about the story Hall told me about the authorship of *The Devil on Sunday*. I didn't like to break his confidence, but then again, if he wasn't dead, I wouldn't have to. "And you're right, I do know. Or I have an idea."

I told Khan about Hall's relationship to Stans. Or rather, his father's relationship. I couldn't do more than vaguely speculate on Stans's interest in Hall's stuff, but assumed it had something to do with *The Devil on Sunday* and fears that Stans's involvement in the original might somehow come to light by way of Hall's effects.

"That's interesting," Khan said, "if unenlightening. I don't really understand why Stans has kept the secret all these years. I can see why Emerson *Père* wouldn't have wanted the world to know that he hadn't written one of his best scripts, but what was in it for Stans? Especially with *all* of the Emersons now dead."

"I don't know," I admitted. "Hall said it was something personal between the old guys, but didn't say what. I don't know that he even knew. So are you gonna let Stans see the stuff?"

"Probably. He's got some pretty high-powered lawyers who it's not worth getting into a kerfuffle with. They're the types who share a country club with the DA. But I'll only let them in after you take a look."

"Really? You sure it's okay?"

"This way you can tell me if you see anything there that I missed. And hey: Stans's lawyers didn't take me out for entrecôte."

"I haven't paid yet, you know."

"No, but you're gonna."

Truer words were never spoken.

Khan said he'd arrange for me to have a look through Hall's stuff the following afternoon, but then called me back to say that it would have to wait until Friday. When I checked in with Kendall she said that there was still no decision about *Burning Bright* from the network. Not a good sign, but also not much I could do about it other than worry. I got the feeling that Kendall was delicately preparing me for the worst, but she got all huffy when I challenged her about it. Which worried me even more.

As Khan reminded me, I did used to make my living—woeful as it was—as a private investigator. I was never very good at it, but it's the kind of business where you don't have to be good to make money. Unlike TV detectives, real ones rarely if ever use their guns, never meet beautiful damsels in distress, and encounter few mysteries that are harder to solve than the connect-the-dots puzzles on coffee shop place mats. It takes neither brains nor get-up-and-go to serve a subpoena, or sit in your car outside the house of a worker's compensation claimant waiting for him to lift up his kid or his groceries or, if you're lucky, a refrigerator, so you can videotape the slob doing things that his injury claim insists he can't. It's repulsive and depressing work, but it's not hard. The only real danger is that some janitor with an allegedly bad back will come running after you with a baseball bat if he catches you taping him waltzing with his Amana. And even the most simple-minded investigator soon learns the ins-and-outs of gathering basic information.

So dusting off and putting on my old PI hat—I mean that in a purely figurative sense—I love gray fedoras, but just try wearing one and looking inconspicuous, especially in LA (unless you're Matt Drudge)—I set off bright and early on Thursday morning. Even though Detective Khan was satisfied that Hall's death was a suicide, there were still a few outstanding questions that gnawed at me. If not necessarily about Hall's death, then about his life. I've spent most of my adult life trying to get over and past the burdens of my past, of my misguided youth. I couldn't help but wonder if those same kinds of burdens—unique, surely, to the horrible business that is show business—were what finally drove Hall to the end of his rope. It had to be more than one weaselly producer and a busted script deal that sent him over the edge.

A job for a private investigator, surely. I'd have to see if I couldn't find one someplace.

I did what I always do when I need some basic information: I went to the library.

I take it that there's lots of information available via the Internet these days and I probably should buy a computer and get on-line along with the rest of the lemmings, but frankly the idea appeals to me not at all. If I'm going to while away the hours of my life in front of a screen, it's going to be a proper television, goddamn it, turned to an honest-to-goodness network. Call me old-fashioned, but a remote control with a mute button is all the interactivity I need. I suppose that if I were still in the investigations business I wouldn't have any choice but to plug in, but I'm not so I do. And I don't.

I went to the library at UCLA. Where I found row after row of computers waiting for me to type in my questions. I think I'm a man out of time.

When I explained what I wanted to a librarian—the sign on her desk identified her as an "information retrieval facilitator"—she went right to *her* computer. After several minutes of clicking and typing and rapping her fingers against the side of the monitor while she waited for an answer, she told me that the information I wanted wasn't available on-line.

I resisted the temptation to shriek, "Ha!"

"It is now on CD-ROM," she said, "but we have it on order. I'm afraid you're stuck with looking at microfilm for the time being."

"I like microfilm," I declared with a smile. Which garnered me a very suspicious look.

The librarian—I mean the facilitator—set me up in an otherwise deserted microfilm room. The machines, with their dim screens and outstretched arms pleading to be spooled, looked like castoffs from some cheapo fifties sci-fi flick. The squeak of the microfilm as it unfurled beneath the lens sounded like a plaintive cry; a sad whale's song as if from some cast-off childhood squeeze toy that had been outgrown. The lyrics to "Puff the Magic Dragon" played on the jukebox of my mind. I wanted to pat the side of the machine and say, "There, there."

Fortunately, I came to my senses and started scanning the pages of fifty-year-old issues of the *Los Angeles Times*. The librarian had accessed a master index to provide me with a list of specific dates and page numbers.

I was looking for information about the murder of Connie Clare. Clare's death, obviously, was a key event in Hall Emerson's life, but it also figured into the eventual shaping of *The Devil on Sunday*. When I'd asked Jon Conlon what he knew about the incident, he shrugged and said that Hall had never discussed it with him. I'd mentioned it to Kendall, too, because she has a good knowledge of motive trivia, and Hollywood tragedies are sort of a hobby of hers. She knew Clare's name, but only as another of the many dud fireworks who'd failed to ignite in the firmament of filmland.

All but one of the references that the librarian found for me were on the same spool of microfilm, containing issues of the *Times* from May through July of 1950. They were in a bunch starting with June 6, 1950: the day that Clare's body was found. Her murder didn't make the front page, but it got a prominent headline—STARLET STRANGLED—on page two, along with a tacky, studio publicity shot. According to the report, Clare's semiclothed body was discovered in an unpaved parking lot behind a filling station near Vermont and Jefferson by a "colored" janitor on his way to work. The story reported that there were indications of an "assault," which I took to mean that Clare had been raped, and that no suspects had been arrested as of yet. It mentioned that Clare had bit parts in several B movies, but had recently landed a "starring role" in the George G. Gaines production of *The Devil on Sunday,* still being filmed. There was a quote from Gaines about the "tragedy" and what a terrible indictment it was of a society that had lost its morals. "Ironically," Gaines was reported saying, "it is this very societal dilemma which *The Devil on Sunday* seeks to address." There was no mention of either Frank Emerson or Hall, but considerable play given to the fact that no one could explain what Clare might have been doing in the black part of town.

A follow-up story in the next day's paper, on page five, reported that police had developed solid leads in what it called "the *darktown* slaying of actress Clare." A homicide detective was quoted saying: "We expect an arrest within a matter of hours." There was another quote from Gaines about the tragedy, and another mention of *The Devil on Sunday.* This second story did note that Clare was the mother of a two-year-old boy, and was accompanied by a small photograph of Hall as an unhappy looking toddler, perched on someone's knee, a hairy hand with a gaudy pinky ring supporting his chest. The caption read: "Baby Hall crying for murdered Mom, starlet Connie Clare." Hall was a ripe butterball with chipmunk cheeks and bald as Bruce Willis. I tried to find some nascent piece of the man I knew in the photo of the child that was, but I couldn't spot it. Maybe the tears?

The third reference to Clare, three days later, was a three paragraph entry in the paper's police diary, reporting that a suspect in the Connie Clare case had been interviewed and let go. An unnamed police source was quoted as saying that other leads were being actively pursued.

The final mention of Clare on the spool was a single paragraph note on the "Deaths" page, with the details of her memorial service. Nothing at all about the crime, Hall, or *The Devil on Sunday.*

I made copies of of the pages then rewound the microfilm, not much the wiser for what I'd read. But then, that's about status quo for the *LA Times* right on up to the present day. There were no real details about the murder and no indication of the nature or course of the police investigation. Frank Emerson's name didn't appear at all, and Hall was clearly mentioned as a hook for readers' sympathy. The paper wasn't salacious about the suggested sexual assault on Clare, but reading between the lines, there was a wink and nudge to the reader regarding the fact that the body was found in a black neighborhood. But then maybe that was just typical of the era.

I threaded the second spool onto the reader. This one dated back to 1947; the reference the librarian gave me was to December 17. I spun the reels until I found the correct issue and page number, but I couldn't find any mention of Connie Clare in the stories. I was looking at the entertainment pages, which were remarkably similar to the "Calendar" section of the modern *Times*: the same vapid puff pieces about actors and new films; same studio-sanctioned publicity snaps; same reviews and commentaries bemoaning how good things used to be and how awful they are today. When I couldn't find anything about Clare, I assumed there was an error in the index, but I scrolled back a page just out of curiosity.

And found a photograph of Connie Clare, attending a gala premiere with none other than "award-winning screenwriter" MacArthur Stans. Clare was only mentioned as Stans's companion, but the two of them were dressed to the nines, looking for all the world like the Tom Cruise and Nicole Kidman of their day.

No Frank Emerson to be seen.

I went back to the librarian and asked her to check for references to Mac Stans in the *Times*.

"MacArthur Stans? The writer?" she asked.

"Yeah."

"You're joking, right?"

"I don't think so."

"Hmmm," she emitted, shaking her head. "Look at this."

She clicked her way through a bunch of screens and then typed Stans's name into the computer. It took a minute or two, but the screen filled up with listings. The librarian raised an eyebrow at me, then went to the next page and then the next.

There must have been five hundred entries for Stans. Maybe more.

"Are you looking for something in particular?" she asked.

"I'm not sure," I said.

"What class is this for?"

"Life and Death one-oh-one," I said, and thanked her for her time. A terrible thing for a TV star to have to confront, but it looked like I just might have to read a book.

. . .

I popped into Barnes & Noble in Westwood, but couldn't find much on their film shelves that didn't pertain to either *Star Wars* or how to break into The Business. I cruised over to a local bookshop in Brentwood and had better luck, though there was still more devoted to George Lucas than is healthy. But that's true of the world at large. There were lots of screenplays and three whole shelves of books about how to write (and more importantly, *sell*) a script, but only two books about screenwriters. One of them had a section about Mac Stans, so I bought it. I also found a turgid-looking history of the blacklist era which had lots of entries on Stans in the index, and picked that up as well. The kid at the counter sort of recognized me.

"I know you," he said, giving me The Look.

"Thank you. Thank you very much."

"Chuck Norris!"

"Ah, no."

"Right, right. Oh, wow, you were on Howard Stern, weren't you?"

"Bababooie," I said.

"Cool. And you read, too."

"Howard likes to give pop quizzes."

"I heard that, man. Cool."

I was going to pay with a credit card, but I couldn't bear to have the kid see my name.

"Hey, you got a pay phone around here?" I asked. The kid looked horrified. I patted my pocket as if there was something in it other than lint and Juicy Fruit. "My battery's dead."

"Nads," the kid said. I don't know what it meant. But he offered to let me use his cell phone.

"I'm going to mention this to Howard," I told him.

"All right!"

I dialed Jennifer's cell phone number at the *Burning Bright* office, and was amazed when she answered. I'd spoken to her earlier in the day and asked her to try and track down some information for me. She'd had success and I wrote down the address she read to me on the bag containing my books. I thanked her and then thanked the kid as I handed back his phone.

"Reseda, huh?" the kid said. He read the side of my bag. "I got an aunt who lives there."

"Yeah, Howard's thinking of buying a house in the area."

"No way. Too righteous."

"Too true," I agreed.

The kid looked thrilled when I left, clutching the phone to his chest. I can't help it, I spread sunshine everywhere I go.

The sensible, not to mention polite, thing to do would have been to call first, but one lesson I did learn from my PI days is that if you give people half a chance to blow you off, they will almost always take it. Of course, you do want to know if the person you need to see is actually home, so I called Melly Dougherty's number and hung up as soon as an older-sounding woman answered. Satisfied that the trip might not be a total waste of time, I cruised up the 405 toward Reseda.

I used to dread making the drive up to the Valley through the Cahuenga pass, not so much because of the traffic, but because my old Subaru—I still keep it as a remembrance of things past—would huff and puff like a tubercular big bad wolf trying to ascend to the top. Pathetic Geos and ancient Volkswagen Bugs would merrily pass me by, and big rigs would crawl up my slow-moving ass as I pushed the pedal to the floor trying to reach forty mph in the slow lane. Of course, those days are now far behind. I barely need to tap the gas of my big, black Lexus to go flying up the freeway in the lap of leather luxury. The damned thing only gets about fifteen miles to the gallon, but such is half the pleasure of being a degenerate American on top of the world at the start of a new millennium.

At least in theory; the afternoon traffic was so bad that, with a rush of adrenaline, I managed to gun the engine to fifteen mph at one point. And even the air conditioner struggled to filter out the thick stench of midday smog. I glanced up at the sight of the Getty Center at the top of the hill, and reminded myself yet again that I should do more artsy stuff for my own good. I couldn't remember the last time I'd been to a gallery or museum.

That's a lie: I can remember but I'm ashamed to admit it. I went to the Bra Museum at Frederick's of Hollywood sometime in the mid eighties. I found it most enlightening—and very uplifting, of course— but I have a feeling that doesn't count much toward my cultural IQ.

At one point as I crawled up the hill, I came shoulder to shoulder with a fat guy in a Subaru exactly like mine. He was alone in the car, patting the steering wheel, and talking to it; offering encouragement, I surmised, though for all I know he was singing along to the soundtrack from *Flashdance*. I smiled with brotherly encouragement at him when he flicked a glance my way, but he must have thought I was being haughty because he flipped me the bird in response. I forgave him, because as one who's been there I can testify that Subaru drivers know not what they do.

With the help of my ever-trusty Thomas Guide—for my money the greatest book ever published (not counting the *Salt & Pepper* novelizations, of course)—I found my way to Melly Dougherty's address in Reseda. I don't know why people live in Reseda, but then I'm at a similar loss as regards most of the Valley. Bits of Sherman Oaks are okay, and I once spent a great night in Eagle Park with a pair of twin (but not identical, damn it) sisters, but the rest of it? Forget about it. Reseda is one of those suburban sprawl blight zones out of a Spielberg film that inevitably turns up in the news as the locale of a mass shooting in a high school or a post office. But then, I suppose that describes an alarming chunk of the country these days.

The Dougherty place was your standard-issue, suburban ranch house with a shake shingle roof that will ignite like lighter fluid come the next firestorm. The lawn was overgrown and the garden badly tended, with various bits of party detritus visible in the shrubs. A newish Chevy Blazer gleamed in the driveway, though the macadam was stained with the Rorschach patterns of ancient oil leaks. I parked right in front and saw the curtain twitch as I strolled up the path. Melly Dougherty stood waiting for me on the other side of the screen door.

"Yes?" she said.

"Mrs. Dougherty, my name is Marty Burns. I apologize for dropping in like this."

"I recognize you. I don't much like your show."

Another satisfied customer. And this from a supposedly safe demographic.

"I was hoping I could talk to you about Hall Emerson."

"You made a bit of racket at the funeral. I thought it was rude."

"I do apologize for that. It embarrassed me as much as it did you. I am sorry."

"What do you want here?"

"I wanted to ask you a few questions about Hall. I was . . . a friend of his."

"Why are you coming to me? We've been divorced near a dozen years."

"I'm sorry to bother you, but . . . well, there isn't really anyone else. I've talked to his other friends as best I could, and he doesn't seem to have any other family. There's some stuff which has been bothering me since he died and I guess you're about my last hope."

She snorted at that, though whether with derision or humor, I couldn't be sure. In any case, she opened the screen door and waved me inside.

The house matched the garden in lack of tidiness. The place wasn't filthy, but whoever did the cleaning could do with a refresher course. Hall's ex steered me toward the kitchen, then did an abrupt about-face and pushed me into the living room. But not before I noticed the bottle of Scotch that stood open on the kitchen table. She didn't stagger or slur, but the scent that wafted off Melly Dougherty suggested that the hootch wasn't being employed merely as room freshener.

"Excuse the mess," she said, offering me a seat on the couch next to a stack of newspapers. "I haven't been in a mood to clean since Hall passed."

"I understand entirely. It's a very difficult time."

Melly started to sit, then shot back up. "Can I get you something? Some coffee or a soda?"

I let out a long breath. "I've had one of those days, I tell you. Would it be presumptuous of me to ask if you have anything harder? I know it's a bit early but . . ."

"Say no more."

Melly went back to the kitchen and came back with the Scotch and two glasses. I didn't much fancy the stuff, but thought having a glass in her hand might soften the old girl up a little. She poured us each a healthy measure.

"Happier days," she said, raising her glass.

"Here, here." I swallowed a mouthful and put the glass down on the coffee table. "Phew, that's better."

"It always is."

Melly Dougherty had the look of a drinker, but not a drunk. Her long, thin face was pinched and wrinkly, her nose dotted with burst capillaries. She wore old-lady jeans—the kind with enough spare room to squeeze a bag of groceries into a back pocket—and a plain white blouse that could do with a date with a bottle of bleach. But she wasn't dirty; didn't have that committed alcoholic's glazed-over look in her eyes. Like her ex-husband, I reckoned she tiptoed down that tightrope of controlled insobriety. But then again, maybe she really was just having a bad week after Hall's death. People are funny, don't you know.

"How well you know him?" she asked.

"Hall? We used to play cards. Poker."

"He owe you money?"

"Huh? No, nothing like that."

" 'Cause if you come looking to collect, you can forget it. I've got nothing to do with Hall's debts."

"No, he didn't owe me. In fact, the cops mentioned that you were about the only person who might have a claim on Hall's estate."

She laughed. "And what estate might that be?"

"His stuff, I mean. He obviously left some things."

"I can't imagine there's anything Hall had that I would want. Sometimes I think there never was."

"How long were you married?"

"Six years. We were together almost twice that long, though."

"And you said you've been divorced for twelve years?"

"Yeah. I remarried a year after that. Bob passed year before last. Lung cancer."

"I'm sorry."

"He smoked forty a day. Stupid old man."

I took another sip of Scotch. "I understand that your divorce was, uh, not entirely amicable."

"What difference does that make?" Melly asked. She took a bigger slug of her drink.

"I don't mean to be overly personal. I was just wondering if you had much contact with Hall in recent times."

"We didn't talk for years after the divorce. You cool down, though; you get older. We still had some mutual friends and saw each other from time to time. Saw a bit more of him recently. You married?"

"Huh? No, I'm divorced, too. Couple times, actually. Long time ago, though."

"So you know how it is."

"I haven't spoken to either of them in decades. Seems to work for everyone involved."

"No kids?"

"Thankfully no," I said. Christ, who was doing the investigating here? "You?"

"Nope. Hall wouldn't consider it. And I was too old by the time I got together with Bob."

"Did Hall not like kids?"

"Nah, he was pretty good with them, really. My sister's boys loved him. But Hall wouldn't hear of it when I raised the subject of us having a family. He said he didn't understand himself well enough to be raising anybody else. But I thought he'd make a fine father."

"You think his attitude maybe had something to do with his own upbringing? What happened to his mother?"

Melly narrowed her eyes at me, and put her Scotch down.

"What do you want here?" she asked.

I leaned back on the couch, drummed my fingers on the pile of papers. "I'm not really sure, Mrs. Dougherty," I admitted. "Hall asked me to do him a favor right before he died. It had to do with his mother. He wanted me to help him find some film of her. I think he was looking for something beyond what might be on that film, but I'm not sure what he wanted. I don't know if he knew."

"Hall was always looking for something . . . other than what he had. A shrink once told him he was looking for the ma he lost as a baby."

"What did Hall think?"

"He broke the guy's nose on the spot. And then he wrote a movie about a psychiatrist who murders his patients. The shrink tried to sue the studio for a story credit."

"And what do you think?"

"I don't. I spent ten years trying to make sense of Hall. It wore me down at the end. Hall could be an exciting man. He was big and brave and bold, and he liked to live out near the edge. I used to like it, too, but I was younger then. No osteoporosis. Now, the edge is staying awake late enough to catch Jay Leno's monologue."

"I understand that Hall had some police troubles a while back."

That drew another squint. "Who's talking about that?"

"No one. I just wondered if that was part of his life on the edge."

"Just some foolishness."

I waited for something more, but there was nothing coming. I tried another subject: "Do you know Mac Stans?"

"I know who he is."

"Do you know why he was at the funeral?"

"I've never met the man."

Not exactly an answer to my question, but I let it pass. "Did Hall ever talk about Stans? Indicate that he knew him?"

"Not that I recall."

The phone rang then; Melly picked up the cordless and walked into the kitchen to have her conversation. I glanced around the living room, got up to look at the framed photos on a shelf by the window. They were shots of Melly and a bear of a man with long, gray hair seated at tables on what looked like a cruise ship. There were half a dozen of them, almost identical, except they were at slightly different tables in different years, the couple aging visibly from shot to shot.

"We liked to go on those cruise liners up to Alaska," Melly said, putting the phone back in its receptacle. "Bob had an appetite, and they serve you four meals a day. Plus snacks. And a midnight buffet."

"Sounds nice," I said. Sounded awful, actually.

"Good times. I don't go now that Bob's gone. Couldn't enjoy it."

"Did you speak with Hall recently, Mrs. Dougherty? Before his death?"

"Three, four weeks ago maybe. He'd come by sometimes, share a drink."

"Did he talk to you about his problems? About work?"

"He'd try, but I wouldn't hear it. I hate Hollywood and everything having to do with it. I don't go to the movies and I only watch TV 'cause that's the world, ain't it? That business of yours never done nothing good for us. No, Hall and me'd talk mostly about the past. Pretending times were better than they were 'cause even if they weren't they beat what we got now."

"Let me just ask you this: Do you think Hall was the type to commit suicide? Did it surprise you?"

"I don't surprise easy anymore," she told me. "And I think Hall was the type to do just about anything. Any damn thing at all."

• • •

Suitably depressed and largely unenlightened by my visit to Reseda, I hied myself back out of the Valley. A headache of the sort I hadn't felt in some time was insinuating itself in a spot at the back of my skull: it was the pain I used to get when I worked as a PI and found myself overwhelmed by the miserable problems of the people I was investigating. The headaches I get from working in The Business are more front-of-the-head oriented. They aren't any nicer, but I sure as hell haven't missed the old kind.

I attempted to assuage the pain with a thick shake. There's a fifties-style diner on Santa Monica, just off the freeway, that serves mediocre food but fabulous shakes. We're talking Britney Spears thick here. I grabbed a booth, ordered a large vanilla from Tiffany, my sassy waitress in tortoiseshell glasses, and waited for that stainless steel beaker of ice cold heaven to arrive. In the meanwhile, I thumbed through one of the books I'd bought earlier in the day.

The book about screenwriters was written by a "contributing editor" to *Entertainment Weekly,* so I was immediately dubious of what it might contain. It offered a kind of pantheon of screenwriters, broken down into headed sections of minibiographies. Mac Stans was in the *"Better Than Their Words"* section, along with Dalton Trumbo, Abraham Polonsky, Ring Lardner Jr., William Faulkner, and Raymond Chandler. I gathered that the idea was these were writers who were more interesting for themselves than the actual movies they wrote. Stans was described as one of the real heroes of the Red Scare era. He wasn't one of the so-called "Hollywood Ten," like Trumbo, but was one of the big fish ratted out in front of the House Un-American Activities Committee in 1951. Stans was called before the committee and refused to answer a single one of their questions; he wouldn't even agree to swear an honesty oath. Instead, he read a long and highly-charged statement regarding the shameful infringement of human rights that the committee hearings represented.

And most famously, he called the committee chairman, J. Parnell Thomas, "a bilious, flaccid prick."

Stans was immediately cited for contempt of Congress and spent a short time in a federal prison. He was among the most untouchable of those blacklisted when he got out, branded as Mac Stalin. He nonetheless managed to get by writing behind beards, including two Academy-nominated films. There was no mention, of course, of Frank Emerson or *The Devil on Sunday* among his credits, but looking over the work Stans did both before and after his HUAC experience, I had to agree with the book's author that his scripts have not stood the test of time. He had a propensity toward preachy, demagogic writing of a most unsubtle variety. As if Clifford Odets had scripted movies for Stanley Kramer.

Of course, the reason that Stans was and remained so highly thought of—the punchline to the Red Scare story, as it were—was that he never had any communist, or even left-wing, leanings of any sort. Stans and a HUAC stoolie had hated each other for years and though most of the figures named to HUAC did have some involvement with "red" causes, Stans was named purely out of spite. The author of the bio pointed out that most historians of the era agreed that Stans could easily have proven his All-American Boy credentials to the committee, as well as his longstanding enmity with the witness, but simply refused to do so as a matter of pure principle. He was a hero because he stood up for what he believed was right, without regard to personal cost. In an era in which big name stars and directors in much more secure positions happily narced everyone they knew, Stan's steel-like integrity was all the more remarkable.

History, of course, always makes it own judgments. Rats like Elia Kazan and Edward Dmytryk might have made better pictures, but who can look at Kazan today without smelling cheese? I remember how much I loved *On the Waterfront* until I learned what Kazan had done; now I can't bear to watch the damn picture (though I'll always be in love with Eva Marie Saint). You never know how you'll act in a situation until you encounter it, but I like to think that if similar circumstances ever arose, I'd be a Mac Stans and not a Dmytryk or a Kazan. Trouble is, I suppose everyone likes to think that.

Out of curiosity, I checked the book's index for Frank Emerson's name, but it wasn't there. Though his entry was pretty short, I noted that Hall was included.

The heading? *"Lost Boys."*

Eight

Carl Khan woke me with a call on Friday morning to say that he couldn't go to Hall's place with me, but that it was okay for me to visit on my own if I didn't mind.

"You sure that's kosher?" I asked.

"You're not planning on eating shellfish in there, are you?"

"No, I mean: Is it okay for me to just go in?"

"We've already got everything we need for the investigation, and I'm giving you my permission. Needless to say, you won't remove anything from the premises."

"No, of course not."

"Well, then, have yourself a rip-roaring good time. Though I don't think you will. You can pick up the keys from the desk sergeant here at the precinct."

Which was simple enough. Khan was based in a West LA station house which was conveniently on the way to Hall's rented bungalow. In fact, while "bungalow" has always had a modest connotation in my head, it proved a bit grandiose as a description of Hall's place. The house had four walls and a proper roof, so I don't know that "shack" is strictly appropriate, but Hall's abode had to be the kind of place etymologically vital to the coining of the phrase "shacked-up." It just looked like someplace you'd go for a quick round of illicit, sweaty, and ultimately unsatisfying rumpy-pumpy. The thing is, the house was located in an otherwise swanky canyon road on the basin side of the Hills. Just below it sat a row of big Victorian houses which must have dated from the early days of LA; a few hundred feet farther higher up and you got to those glass-and-stilt horrors which, *please* God, will be the first things to crunch when the Big One hits. But there in the middle, at the end of a twisty, upscale (and uphill) lane, on a conspicuously undeveloped plot of land, sat Hall's dump. And adjacent to it, the much nicer, better built garage where Hall must have said his short goodbye.

How utterly, revoltingly LA.

A strip of POLICE: DO NOT CROSS tape barred the door; Khan told me to tear it down, though I felt guilty doing so and looked to see if anyone was watching me. I slipped the key into the deadbolt, but found it was unlocked. LAPD on the case. I unlocked the latch and went inside.

The living room and kitchen were the mess I expected them to be, with pizza boxes and take-out bags strewn about, and the effluvia of bachelor life—and rotten food—thick in the air. The cops had probably dug through the stuff and been none too delicate in the doing. There was several months' worth of the *Times* piled precariously in one corner, and scores of magazines everywhere. Lots of film and entertainment stuff—I didn't know anyone still read *Rolling Stone*— but gun and biker magazines, too. And one square little coffee table was piled three-feet-high with gardening magazines. I glanced out the window at the overgrown lawn and rain forest-thick tangle of ugly weeds that covered the property, and scratched my head. Perhaps Hall had led some literally Edenic fantasy life. Maybe he just liked pictures of pretty flowers. Have I mentioned that people are funny? In any case, though I pawed through the various stacks of paper, I found nothing of particular interest to me. I glanced at the pile of videotapes which went two-thirds up the side of one wall just long enough to learn that Hall had an evident fondness for MGM musicals, John Ford Westerns, and anal-sex-oriented pornography.

Given the wretched condition of the building, the jungle of the garden, and the mess in the first two rooms, I thought perhaps I'd passed through a dimensional portal when I opened the door into Hall's bedroom. It was the only other room in the house and was half again as big as the living room. And it was immaculate.

A small, single bed—a daybed, really, but neatly made—stood against the wall right by the door. The rest of the walls were custom built, floor-to-ceiling bookcases, stuffed to the rafters with nary a volume out of place. A large oak desk dominated the far end of the room and behind it a beat-up leather chair. A small Apple computer sat on a return beside it, with three large file cabinets arranged behind that. The desk was as tidy as Richard Gere's hair, with not even a stray paper clip cluttering the work top. Papers were neatly stacked in file trays, and the desk blotter—I've never even owned a desk blotter—was doodle-free. The whole room looked and smelled so clean, I swear Intel could have manufactured microchips in there. However messy Hall may have been in his life, he was obviously a Felix Unger in his work habits. I wondered how he coped with the schizophrenic qualities of the different parts of his existence.

I started thumbing through the documents on his desk. For no good reason, I carefully kept them in the exact order in which I found them. There were a lot of bills, all unpaid, going back several months, along with a couple of notices from collection agencies. Hall obviously reserved his doodling for these, because several were adorned with red ink renderings of outsized male genitalia. He owed money on his car, his utilities, and all his credit cards. I picked up one of his MasterCard bills and scanned the items he'd bought, but it suddenly made me feel creepy to do so. What difference did it make how Hall spent the little money he clearly didn't have?

There were a couple of file folders on the desk marked with the names of what I took to be works-in-progress. One contained an outline for a science fiction series about a detective who solves mysteries in virtual reality; the other, titled "Light in the Darkness" held the first few pages of a film script. The setting was described as LA in 1954, and the dialogue had a hardboiled feel, but there wasn't enough of it there to make sense of what it might be about. There was nothing at all on his desk relating to *The Devil on Sunday*.

I turned to the filing cabinets, which were as neatly organized as the rest of the work space. The drawers were meticulously labeled and in strict alphabetical order. Copies of all of Hall's movie and TV scripts were there, along with the contracts and legal documents associated with each project. I went straight to *D* and found files for *Delvecchio* and *The Devlin Connection,* but not *The Devil on Sunday*. Then I noticed a drawer marked "In Development" and looked inside.

And Bingo was his name-o!

There were only four files in the drawer and three of them were single-sheet thin. The fourth, *The Devil on Sunday,* was Yellow Pages–thick. And we're talking Greater LA here. I found a sheaf of handwritten notes, but couldn't decipher more than the odd word per page of Hall's graphically challenged chicken scrawl. The bulk of the file consisted of two neatly printed copies of the script of *The*

Devil on Sunday. A quick browse through a copy suggested that the script was complete. These weren't merely odd, selected pages—which Kevin Ryan Paul indicated was all that Hall had provided him—but 135 pages of fade-in to fade-out. There was no cover sheet or title page and it suddenly occurred to me that perhaps these were copies of the Mac Stans/Frank Emerson original, so I sat down at the desk and started reading. By the end of page five, having found references to *The Simpsons* and Microsoft, I knew it wasn't.

It appeared, as Hall had complained that final drunken night, that Kevin Ryan Paul had given him a royal reaming. Whether or not Paul was using any of Hall's work remained to be seen—I still hadn't read any more of Paul's script than those few, badly faxed pages—but the evidence of my eyes said that Paul was a liar at the very least.

That is to say: a producer.

There was nothing else in the file; no contract with Paul, or letters or legal documents of any kind. No paper trail back to the producer about the script. I dug around some more among the papers on Hall's desk, but couldn't find any incriminating evidence. I glanced at the computer, and thought about turning it on, but there wasn't any point. The cyber-age has managed to pass me by. I wouldn't have a clue how to find my way around Hall's files. Indeed, though I looked at the computer back and front, I couldn't even figure out where the "on" switch was. PlayStations are as technical as I get.

I felt a little seedy doing it, but I poked around under Hall's narrow bed. God knows what I expected to find, but other than a beat-up pair of no-name sneakers, there was nothing but a copy of *Captain Corelli's Mandolin.* I could see where it wasn't the kind of thing Hall would want to be seen reading in public, but I wondered about giving it the *Hustler* treatment.

As I perused the book titles on Hall's massive shelves, another idea struck me. Hall's organizational scheme was entirely alphabetical. Fiction, nonfiction, comic books—they were all lined up in meticulous a–z order starting at the top of one corner of the room and finishing at the bottom of another. I found the *E*'s and ran my finger along the edges of the spines. I found several volumes by Ralph Waldo and *Mr. Nice Guy,* a cheesy-looking memoir by Keith, but nothing by Frank Emerson. Then it hit me.

"Duh," I said, shaking my head.

Hall was manifestly precise about these things; the anal orderliness of the room was testament to that fact. I walked across to the *S* shelf, and wedged between Eddie Stankey's autobiography and *The Hunter* by Richard Stark I found an oversized, black volume with no writing on the spine. I pulled it out and saw that it was a bound copy of the original script of *The Devil on Sunday*. Though Frank Emerson's name was on the title page, the real author, of course, was MacArthur Stans.

I did a bad thing.

I'd left the file with the copies of Hall's script out on the desk because the thought occurred to me as soon as I saw there were two: *Who'll miss one?* I walked back to the desk with the original Stans's script still in my hands, and stared down at the open file. I took out one copy and laid it atop the bound volume. I wanted to read them both, but knew I couldn't do it sitting there in the dead man's bedroom. "Needless to say, you won't remove anything," Carl Khan had said to me.

A streetwise cop like him ought to know that *everything* needs to be said.

I put the file with the remaining copy of the script back into the drawer, but as I did so I noticed the title on one of the thinner files: *Better Red Than Dead*. I pulled it out and gave it a quick glance, saw it was a proposal for a TV miniseries about the Blacklist. I got more curious. Feeling guilty but determined, I closed the file, scooped it up along with the two screenplays and tucked the bundle under my arm.

On the way out, I took a long, last look at Hall's tiny bed. I pictured the big man lying on it and knew he couldn't have done a lot of entertaining there. The bed was so small it would be tough even to amuse yourself, if you know what I mean.

"Lonely bastard," I said out loud. To myself. Or to Hall, maybe.

I closed the door quietly behind me.

I wanted to spend the afternoon reading the scripts, but the phone was ringing when I got home and the LED on the answering machine was blinking like a Tourettic hooker. Daniel E. Rostovic was on the other end. Or rather, his secretary. No one but me makes their own calls. I once asked Dan what the middle E in his name stood for. "I dunno," he said, "works for David E. Kelly, don't it?"

You'll have gathered, thus, that Dan is the producer of *Burning Bright*.

"Crisis meeting. Now!" Daniel E. screamed.

"What are you, kidding? I'm talent, what do I have to do with anything?"

"You're co-executive producer, or have you forgotten?"

"Why should I be different from everyone else?"

"We're circling the wagons. We may need signatures. Today!"

"Oh, man," I whined. Since when did wagon trains haul along notary publics? But I agreed to drive in to the office.

When even a poor, co-executive producer has to pay for his meta-phorical baguettes, you *know* there ain't no such thing as a free lunch.

The meeting dragged on until six o'clock. What it amounted to was an epic dissection of a men's room rumor that Fox had decided to close shop on *Burning Bright*. No definite word had come down, but from the Suits' urinal to God's ear, as they say where the big boys go wee-wee. I have no idea why they needed me to be there, other than to cast sullen looks my way. The actors always get blamed when the chop comes. I didn't say three words the entire afternoon, and in the end I didn't have to sign a thing. There was a lot of talk about Plan B, though it all sounded pretty desperate to me. By the time Dan called it quits for the day, I was almost as exhausted as I was bored. I felt like I *should* have felt depressed, but I imagined that would come later. Coming out of a four hour meeting with a roomful of TV execs is like surviving a 7.0 earthquake: You're too much in shock and grateful just to be alive to worry about the ruins of your life.

I gave Kendall a call but only got through to her voice mail. I left a grumpy message.

Back to the car, where I cranked the engine and the A/C and reclined the seat. My head hurt and try as I might, I couldn't get myself to concentrate on what it might mean to me to lose *Burning Bright*. I glanced over at the passenger seat, where I'd left the scripts I'd lifted from Hall's house.

Nothing there.

I sat up and turned around. There was nothing on the back seat, either. Or on the floor. My heart started to race as I felt around underneath the seats. I found three dimes and an empty can of Mountain Dew, but no screenplays.

A groany noise formed somewhere between my bowel and throat.

I got out of the car. The more I thought about it, the more certain I was that I'd left the two scripts on the passenger seat. I'd forgotten to take them into the house when I went home; remembered thinking that I *should* put them inside when I got back into the car to drive to the studio. But I'd been too lazy.

Feeling panicky, I went back into the office to check that I hadn't somehow carried them in with me. There was nothing in the conference room, though, or anyplace else I could remember being. I even checked the toilet stalls.

When I'd got into my car after the meeting, I'd turned off the alarm with my clicker. The doors had definitely been locked and the alarm chirped off at me. The windows weren't broken, and nothing else had been taken.

But the scripts were gone.

"Fuck, shit, fuck," I yelled, and pounded my fist against the roof. *Now* I felt depressed.

A fat man was sitting on my sun deck. I didn't even notice him when I first walked in; nothing was amiss in the house. It was only when I went to get a drink out of the fridge that I saw him sitting out there. He'd helped himself to several of my beers. And his associates, two large men in biker leathers, had polished off the best part of a bottle of Jack Daniels. And a whole bag of genuine Pennsylvania Dutch Bavarian pretzels I'd been saving for a special occasion. They hadn't even left crumbs in the bottom of the bag.

"Nice view," the fat guy said. He was bald on top with a long gray beard. It took a minute for me to make the connection: it was the biker dude who'd howled his eulogy at Hall's funeral. His two companions wore the uniform, but I didn't think they were the same pair who'd been with Howling Wolf at the boneyard. I could be wrong, though.

"How'd you get in?" I asked.

"We're not in. We're out."

"You're drinking my booze."

"Might have brought it with us. For a picnic. We just strolled on up from the beach. You couldn't even call it breaking and entering since we're not inside. Trespassing, maybe. Class E misdeameanor."

"Those are my pretzels."

"You got a receipt? Certificate of authenticity or something?"

One of the big guys crumpled up the bag and tossed it over the rail.

"Trespassing *and* littering. You boys do live on the edge."

The litterbug took a step toward me, but the fat guy gestured for him to keep back. The big guy made a growling noise.

"You don't need to know where we live. You don't need to know a lot of things."

"Who are you?" I asked.

"Call me Gabbo."

"That your Christian name?"

"I ain't no Christian."

"You don't look Jewish."

"That some kind of crack? You an anti-Semite?"

"Forgive me, I didn't mean to offend," I said.

" 'Cause I don't care for that kind of shit. Never again is what *my* people say."

Oh, brother: the biker from Chabad.

"Who *are* you and what the hell are you doing here?" I asked.

"Just stopped by for a little drink, a little chat. Admire your view."

"You were a friend of Hall's."

Gabbo swirled the backwash around in his bottle of Anchor Steam. Sucked it down.

"Me and Huck went back a ways."

"Huck?"

Gabbo nodded. "You don't know much about him, really, do you? Maybe that's for the best. Maybe it should stay that way."

"Listen: if you're a friend of Hall's . . ."

"No, *you* want to be listening to me, sitcom boy: Don't be asking no questions about old Huck. He's gone now and that's all there is to it, all you need to know. You ain't no one to be asking after what went down in the once upon a times. Just you stick to your little TV adventures and leave Huck's people and Huck's life alone. You understand that?"

"I think you misunderstand . . ."

"Nope," Gabbo said, "I understand everything I need to. You keep your yap shut and your honker out of Huck's business. And ours. 'Cause otherwise . . ."

Gabbo signaled to one of the big men, who scooped the bottle of Jack up off the table and hurled it at my big glass patio door. The bottle exploded when it struck, sending bits of glass flying. I ducked and covered up. Gabbo didn't even blink.

Amazingly the glass door was intact.

"Goddamn," Gabbo said. "You losing your arm, Pud."

The big guy who'd thrown the bottle looked positively abashed. He kneaded his right shoulder with his left hand. "Rotator cuff's all shot to hell," he muttered.

"Double glazing," I said, marveling at the door. "Cost a bundle."

"Money well spent," Gabbo agreed, standing up. He walked over and tapped on the glass with his knuckle. "But remember . . ."

Gabbo turned around to face me. He raised his knee up and kicked backward, driving the heel of his boot into the glass door. It smashed to bits.

"What don't get broke the first time, can easy go all to pieces later on. Know what I mean?"

"I think I can decipher your code," I said.

"Good sitcom boy."

Gabbo patted me—hard—on the cheek as he walked by and departed down the steps to the beach. His associates followed, the bottle-tosser still working on his shoulder. *"Rotator cuff,"* I heard the other scoff at him as they walked away.

I watched them walk away down the beach. I got a broom and started cleaning up the mess.

I was sitting in my living room, ignoring the Dodgers as they lost on TV, still wondering what to make of Gabbo's unpleasant visit when the doorbell chimed. Pizza delivery boys and Jehovah's Witnesses notwithstanding, I don't get a lot of visitors. But then I hadn't been expecting the biker crowd, either.

About the last thing I would have dreamed of was Lissa Torres standing on my front step. Well, I might have dreamed of it, leaving a stain on the sheets, but I didn't expect it.

"Oh," I quipped.

"*Hi*, Marty," Lissa said. She smiled and a thousand angels began to sing. "I hope you don't mind me just appearing like this, out of the blue, but I *really* wanted to see you."

It wasn't very professional, not to mention polite or cool, but I stood there and gawked at her. Lissa Torres was someone to gawk at. Not a lot over five feet tall, she personified the notion that big things come in small packages. Blonde and bronze, her features chiseled by an Italian master, her teeth white as moonlight, her body courtesy of Richard Avedon, Lissa was every dirty old (and young) man's dreams made flesh. She stood there, literally glowing in the twilight. So radiant was she, that I swear I started looking around for hidden key lights. I didn't think anyone could look that good off a soundstage.

Hubba-hubba, as they used to say. (And as I, obviously, still do.)

"Would it be okay if I came in for a little while?" she asked, crossing my threshold.

"Absolutely," I said to the evening air. I shook it off, closed the door, and followed her inside.

"This is great. I'm renting up in the Hills right now, but I'm thinking about buying a beach place. The surf is just *so* relaxing, you know? But Malibu's *such* a cliché. It's . . . oh my!" She saw the big empty space where my glass door had until so recently bravely held back the sea breeze. "What happened?"

"Um," I muttered. I wasn't about to get into it. "Flying fish?"

"What?"

"Industrial accident?"

"Industrial accident?"

"Workers revolt."

"Pardon?"

"I broke the glass," I said.

"Oh. That's a shame. Nice view, though." She stepped outside. A fresh wind blew in off the ocean, but the unsubtle scent of bourbon lingered about the deck. Lissa didn't mention it.

"Can I get you something? A drink?"

"I'm just a girl who can't say no. Whatcha got?"

"Plenty of beer. There's probably some wine around if you want, but it might not be very good. Or something softer."

"Or *harder?*" she asked. And yes, it sounded *exactly* as dirty as you imagine.

"Whatever you want."

"Got a Diet Coke?"

"Er, regular. I can't stand the taste of diet sodas. Fortunately I have a fast metabolism so it doesn't matter."

"You're lucky. I'm always watching my figure."

"Nice work if you can get it." Christ, what's the matter with me?

Lissa giggled. I got the drinks and brought them outside. Lissa sat in the same chair that Gabbo had occupied. It looked better on her.

"You must be wondering why I'm here," she said.

"Never look a gift horse in the mouth, as they say. But then you're no Mr. Ed."

"I'll take that as a compliment."

"That's how it was meant to come out. I'm hopeless without a script."

"*Tell* me about it. You wouldn't believe how often I fluff my lines."

"I think the audience might be a little more forgiving of you."

" 'Cause I'm a dumb blonde?"

"Because they're too busy drooling over how gorgeous you are."

"You're sweet," she said.

"Not that I'm complaining, but, um, what are you doing here?"

"I wanted to meet you."

"Yeah?"

"For *ages*. And when Kevin mentioned that he was after you for *The Devil on Sunday*, well, I just about died."

"God forbid I should be the cause of such a tragedy."

"I thought I could help you make up your mind. That maybe if we met and hit it off I could persuade you to come on board the picture. I could maybe, you know, talk you into it. I'm told my oral abilities are impressive."

Lissa had slipped out of her shoes and slithered down in her chair. She stretched her legs out and pointed her toes at me. The nails were painted a revolting color, but frankly she could get away with whatever she wanted. She drew her knees up and sat in a decidedly unladylike, Sharon Stone way, God bless her. I found myself at a loss for words, if not drool.

"How are your eighteen to thirty-fours?" I finally managed, clearing my throat.

She looked puzzled, glanced down at her chest—rather larger than thirty-four to this normally keen eye—as if I'd said something dirty or asked her an overly personal question. Then she wrinkled her nose in perplexity. And cuteness.

"Huh?"

"Your demographics. *Lupé Garou*. No problems with your eighteen- to thirty-four-year-olds?"

"Oh-no," she laughed. "No, our target audience is twelve to eighteen. Everything else is gravy."

"I envy you," I said. Envy, covet, lust . . . what are those other sins? Lust is the only one that mattered to me at the moment.

"I don't believe that. God, you've been a star for*ever*."

"I don't know about that."

Lissa touched laid her fingertips on my arm. "Do you know how much I loved you in *Salt & Pepper*? God, I had the biggest crush on you."

"You weren't even born when *Salt & Pepper* was on."

"I used it watch it in reruns. I grew up in Chicago and TBS used to show it at four o'clock every day. God, how I used to dream about you."

"You must have grown up pretty deprived then."

"Hardly. I'd run home from school to watch the show. I used to fantasize that I was Penny Pepper and that you were really in love with *me*. I can remember actually shivering with pleasure imagining you asking if it was, you know, *hot enough for me*."

"This must be a terrible disappointment for you."

"Not at all. You've kept your boyish good looks."

"You been to an eye doctor lately?"

"Nothing wrong with my eyes," Lissa said. "Or the rest of me, I'm told."

She got up and walked—no, the only word for it is sauntered—over to where I was sitting. She knelt down, resting her elbows on my legs. I could smell tropical fruit in her hair and Opium behind her ears. She looked up at me, wet her full red lips, blinked her big, brown, teddy bear eyes. Flutter-flutter-flutter went my heart. And one or two other organs.

She unself-consciously unfastened the buttons of her thin cotton blouse, placing my hands on the warmth of her perfect, soft breasts. Her nipples were as dark and hard as Hershey's Kisses.

"Hot enough for you?" she breathed into my mouth.

To paraphrase the unsinkable Molly Bloom: *Heck, yeah!*

. . .

I'm not a Hollywood stud or a wannabe. Unlike too many of my colleagues, I'm not in The Business primarily for the pussy. I ran that treadmill when as I was a teen star and I'm old enough now to know that there's more to life than notches on the headboard. I don't go for one-night stands or quickies in the location trailer with slavering groupies and aspiring actresses. But even so, when a walking fantasy like Lissa Torres drops her perkier-than-double-espresso tits in your hands and her pretty head in your lap, it takes more spine than I've got to say: "What kind of a boy do you think I am?"

And while I'm not the kiss-and-tell sort—a type I generally disdain—there's no honest way to summarize the events of the evening other than to observe that Lissa Torres fucked and sucked me raw.

"Jesus!" I said, having sent Elvis out of the ballpark not once, not twice, but three times. I think it'd been twenty years. "Moses, Mohammed, and Buddha, too. I'll even give it up for L. Ron Hubbard. Woo-woo-woo!"

Lissa giggled. I would have joined her, but I didn't have the energy. "I'm hungry," she said.

"Kitchen there," I said, pointing. "Can't move. Save self."

"You want anything?"

"IV saline."

"Is that in the fridge?" she asked. Ruining—and at the same time, *saving*—everything.

Ah, Hollywood. Ah, humanity.

"Just some juice, please."

"Okay." She took a playful nip at my cheek, then scooted off the bed. I couldn't have scooted with a Rolls-Royce jet engine rammed up my ass.

I lay there, looking over my bedroom as if I'd been teleported to some foreign country. Everything looked different, better, *nicer* in my postcoital haze. I felt drained, yes, but relaxed, replete . . . satiated. Damn, I felt good.

And then my brain switched back on. The bastard.

It started when I caught sight of a copy of a *Burning Bright* script on the dresser. That reminded me of the two scripts I'd swiped from Hall's place which had so mysteriously disappeared from my car. And then I felt guilty for having taken them in the first place, and guilty for losing them, and guilty for hopping into the sack with a young actress who was probably just living out some bizarre teenage fantasy about sleeping with Sandy Salt. Or was there something more to it? Why the hell *had* she come to see me? Why *would* she so readily play park-the-pink-Pontiac with a clapped-out old geezer like me? What the hell was going on with *The Devil on Sunday,* anyway?

By the time Lissa bounced back into the room balancing a bottle of Coke, a big glass of apple juice, and a super-sized Mr. Goodbar, my mood of rapturous satiation was as gone as my woody.

See? The brain's a bastard.

"Gaawwd," Lissa said, hopping onto the bed, "I *really* shouldn't do this." She was unwrapping the chocolate bar. She looked more excited than when she had been unwrapping me. Shut up, brain!

"Why are you doing this?" I asked.

"Huh?"

"Don't get me wrong here. I thank you from the tips of my toes to the split ends of my thinning hair. With an extra dollop of gratitude from the underutilized naughty bits in the middle. But you know, it's not often that the likes of you takes an interest in the likes of me."

"Come *ooonnnnn.* You have your own show. Don't tell me they don't throw it at you."

"Oh, they throw it. But some things you don't want to catch."

"You caught me pretty well. Quick hands."

Lissa ran her tongue back and forth across the Mr. Goodbar, and I couldn't help but note that her nipples had gotten hard again. It was a little distracting.

"How'd you know to come here? Where I live?"

"I have my sources," she said with a devilish smile.

"Did Kevin Ryan Paul send you?"

That didn't come out right. I knew it right away. It's what I wanted to know, but not the way I should have asked it. Lissa froze, a smear of chocolate like a shit-stain down her chin. The humor fled her eyes. She got up, one foot on the floor, the other knee still on the bed.

"What do you mean by that?"

"I just meant did Paul give you my address."

"That's not what you meant at all. What do you think I am?"

"I . . . I'm not . . . I don't know. I don't know you."

"What the fuck do you mean you don't know me? You just had your dick in my mouth. What don't you know? You think I'm some kind of whore?"

"No, of course not. That's not what I'm saying."

"No? You think I came here to fuck you for Kevin Ryan Paul? You think I whore for him? Who do you think *you* are? What kind of balls you got thinking that?"

"No, Lissa . . ."

"I can't believe this. I came over here because I want to meet you. I always been sort of sweet on you and think maybe we can get along. I blow you, I fuck you, and you think what? I'm Kevin Ryan Paul's whore now?"

"That's not it at all." Actually . . .

"So what is it?"

"It's"—it was driving me crazy—"Lissa, you've got a big glob of chocolate on your chin."

"And you got pussy on your breath. So fucking what?"

"Lissa." I reached out for her hand, but she pulled it away. I touched my fingertips to her knee, still on the bed. "It's not you, it's me. I'm . . . I'm going through a tough time. A friend of mine just died and it's messed up my head a little. I'm just . . . I guess I'm just feeling old, you know? Like what would a gorgeous young woman like you want with a decrepit old thing like me."

"Your friend died?" she asked, softening.

"He wasn't that much older than me. It sets you to thinking, you know? And stuff like what happened here tonight, between us, that doesn't happen to me too often anymore. It threw me a little."

"Yeah?" She sat back down on the bed.

"Yeah. I just . . . I'm doubting myself a little and it came out like I was doubting you. I didn't mean anything by it. I'm sorry."

"Who was your friend?"

"He was a writer. Hall Emerson was his name." Lissa looked away. "You ever hear of him?"

"No," she said. But she didn't meet my eye.

"Kevin knew him, too. He never mentioned the name?"

"I don't think so."

I didn't believe her. Lissa Torres had a face and body to become a tower sniper for, but I tried watching *Lupé Garou* once, and the girl can't act for spit.

"Anyway," I said. "I wasn't saying anything bad about you. Just me."

"Okay."

"Are you all right?"

"I'm okay," she said, and smiled. "I'll drown my sorrows in chocolate."

Lissa snuggled up against me and devoured every bit of the big Mr. Goodbar, chasing it with loud slurps of Coke. I prayed she wasn't a purger. I put my arm around her and gave her a squeeze.

But still I wondered how she knew where I lived.

Lissa vanished in the night like a dream. I didn't hear her get up and go. She left her panties behind, and I suspect it was deliberate. I felt like a perv, but I gave the crotch a sniff. More clearly intentional, she also left the wrapper from the Mr. Goodbar on the inside of which she wrote "You're not old to me." I started to crumple it up, stopped, and smoothed it out. I stuck it in my night table drawer.

God, men are sad.

Once I was up and about, I called Detective Khan. Wouldn't you know the son-of-a-bitch has voice mail. Soon we won't need people at all. As it happens, he called me back before I could work up any kind of decent lather about the subject.

"How'd you get on at Emerson's place?" the cop asked me.

I tried to play it cool. "Why? What do you mean?"

"Find anything of interest?"

I took a deep breath. "Not really, no. I'd never been to Hall's place before. I found it revealing about his character."

"That bedroom's something else, ain't it?"

"I think if Hall could have compartmentalized his life as neatly as he did his living space, he might still be alive."

"Maybe. But it's one thing to put your books in order, a whole other to do it with your life."

"I know. Made me sad, though."

"Suicides *are* sad, Marty. Because of all the unanswered questions they leave behind. And when you try to answer them, well, usually it just makes you sadder."

"You may be right. But the thing is, I still have some questions."

"Oh?"

"And I was thinking that you might be able to do something to help me answer them."

There was a pause, then: "Depends what they are."

"I want to know about Connie Clare's murder."

Along silence ensued. "Why?" is what finally came back.

"I'm not sure. I feel like there's some big missing piece to Hall's life story—something that had to lead him to do what he did. You're still sure about the suicide, right?"

"For all intents and purposes, the case is closed."

"But that doesn't mean the questions are answered."

"I don't see what Connie Clare's murder is going to tell you."

"I don't either. Nothing, probably. But is it possible to find out?"

Khan exhaled a little tune while he considered it. "It's almost fifty years ago. I don't know if we keep records that long."

"Could you find out?"

"I don't know if I want to, if it's something that you should be looking at."

I sighed. "I sort of didn't want to tell you this, but maybe it'll help to convince you. I got . . . threatened I guess you'd call it. Last night."

"What? By who?"

"One of Hall's buddies. I think he's one of those unsavory types you mentioned to me from Hall's past. You remember the guy who howled at the funeral?"

"Big beard, big belly. What happened?"

"Nothing much. He and a couple other biker types stopped by to suggest that it might be nice if I didn't ask too many questions about Hall's life." I thought it best not to mention my broken glass door.

"I don't follow you here. What exactly have you been doing? You just went to Emerson's place, right?"

"Ahhh, I also went to see Melly Dougherty."

"For Christ's sake! Why? What do you think you're doing?"

"I just wondered about some stuff. Dougherty's the only one I could think of who could tell me."

"Marty. You are not a police officer. You are not even a private investigator. You are an actor. And you have no business going around making inquiries into a death."

"It's not illegal to ask a person questions."

"It is if you're interfering with a police investigation."

"You just told me the case was closed."

I could sense Khan fuming on the other end.

"I'm not trying to make trouble for you, Detective. I just . . . want some answers."

"Why?"

"Why?"

"Yes, why. You told me that you and Hall weren't that close, more acquaintances than friends. From what you say you didn't take that great an interest in him when he was alive. So what's changed now that he's dead?"

I thought about the question before I replied. I'd been thinking about that myself for a couple of days, and while I wasn't entirely sure of my motivation, I had come to a partial conclusion.

"You know what Hollywood is, Detective?"

"I've got a few choice words."

"It's a victim machine. They call it the dream factory, but that's always been a lie. The Business sucks in innocents from all around the country, all across the globe, and chews 'em up and spits 'em back out as victims. Oh, there are a chosen few who make it out the other side okay, but even they've got their scars if you know where to look. I'll show you the molar marks on my butt, if you don't believe me."

"I believe you. I just don't follow."

"Hall Emerson was a victim supreme. He was born into The Business and into victimhood. His mother went to the top of the victim list when he was just a baby. The machine gnawed on him for fifty years, and in the end it swallowed him up. I was a victim, too. But I got lucky. I got chewed up and spat out quick."

"And you've come back for more."

"I was blind before; now I can see. I got lucky, Detective, in a way that Hall never did. Because Hall never escaped. At least, until he escaped the hardest way of all. I could have been Hall. Hell, who's to say I won't be yet? There but for the grace of God and Rupert Murdoch. If there's any difference."

Another long silence from the cop's end of the line ensued. Then: "I think you're taking this way too personal."

"How are you supposed take a suicide?"

"You don't. You shake your head, shed a tear if you must, and then you let it go."

"I can't seem to do that. I admit that me and Hall weren't close, but I still feel a kinship I can't explain. Maybe it's stupid or irrational, but it's there."

"The past is a funny place to visit. The maps are always wrong, the beds are lumpy, and the food sucks."

"That's why I'm asking you for directions."

"I don't like the trouble you might be getting yourself into."

"I'll be a good boy, Detective. At least, I'll try. Will you find out about Connie Clare?"

"I don't know. Are you going to keep your nose clean?"

"Call me Mr. Hanky."

He called me another name entirely. But he agreed to think about it.

I called Kendall next. Even on a Saturday morning she was in the office. I told her about the *Burning Bright* meeting, but she already knew the details. I didn't fill her in on my other activities—and certainly not my evening with Lissa Torres. Kendall would most definitely not approve. Hell, I wasn't sure *I* approved. And I didn't want her to think I was acting based on what had gone on in my bed.

"I want you to call Kevin Ryan Paul and express my interest in *The Devil on Sunday*."

"What? I thought you were off the idea completely."

"I might not have a job now."

"I'll find you something else, Marty. Don't take this for the money if you don't like the part or the property. Or Kevin Ryan Paul."

"I'm not. In fact, I don't want you to agree to anything right now. Just make sure he knows that I'm interested. String him along a little if you can."

"We have to be careful here, Marty. You don't have to sign a contract to be committed, you know. There are legal precedents . . ."

"Just trust me here, Kendall. You do trust me, don't you?"

Good thing I didn't hold my breath, because I'm still waiting for her answer and blue is *not* my color.

Nine

I knew that my explanation to Carl Khan as to why I wanted to know more about Connie Clare's murder might not be satisfying to him. I don't know what I expected to find out, what *could* be found out so many years after the fact. But the truth of the matter was that the more I learned about Hall Emerson, the more I felt an affinity with him. And the more I wanted to know what might have driven him to do what he did. I knew as well as anyone the trauma of a life dominated by The Business. I live well enough at the moment, God knows, but the truth of the matter is that if I had a chance to do it all over again—to choose a path outside of the industry—I would do so in an *Entertainment Tonight* minute. Show business is a perverse world, and a difficult one not to be perverted by. Some manage it, of course, but most fall prey to the sickness endemic to it to greater or lesser degrees. You almost can't help it. In other walks of life the deadly sins are what you strive to avoid being seduced by. But in Hollywood, they constitute the minimum requirements for the big roller-coaster ride. It should be sign-posted, like the amusement park that it is: You must be greedier or more envious than *this* to get on board.

I think Hollywood is most difficult for those who are born into it, as Hall was. There are obvious advantages to being to the manor born—the movies are a tough nut to crack if you don't already have one foot, two hands, and a sturdy shoulder in the door—but at the same time you're laden down with the burden of other people's often busted dreams. I know firsthand how hard it is to turn civilian when you've been brought up in The Business. If anyone had ever had good cause to avoid the family business, surely it was Hall. His mother had been murdered as a young actress; his dad, though nominally successful, was at least something of a fraud. Hall himself had knocked around for thirty years and managed no better than a pile of overdue bills and a narrow bed in a rented shack in the shadows of a better part of town. But still he had that drawer marked "In Development," so he clearly hadn't given up. Hope springs eternal and all that jazz. Or at least it did until he walked into the garage, cranked the engine, and breathed carbon monoxide until he died. What was he thinking as he sat in the car and the air grew thin and his vision dulled? Was he so wrecked he didn't know what he was doing? Or did he sit there and play back the direct-to-video of his life and suck those fumes all the harder?

I'd never know, of course. But I realize that is the particularly cruel brand of pain suicides leave behind. I've never lost anyone very close to me by their own hand, though I know enough people who have, and I've seen them torture themselves asking over and over again: what if, could I, should I, why didn't I . . .

I won't pretend that Hall meant enough to me to suffer that kind of torment, but at the same time, I knew I was the last person to see him, to talk to him before he took his life. You can't be in that position and *not* feel some guilt, wonder if there was something you said or didn't say, whether you were too sympathetic or not sympathetic enough.

Could I, should I, why didn't I?

What if?

I've learned—the very hard way—that there is more to life and living than the messy meat and water shells we walk around in. Despite some of the things I've seen and done in my life, I'm not a religious person, but I am respectful of the greater mysteries. I didn't think Hall was looking over my shoulder or that his soul was dragging around chains of torment or anything like that, but I couldn't help but feel that maybe he'd rest easier if some of those questions got answered. And even if he didn't, I knew I would.

The envelope that Harry Blanc had given to me sat where I'd left it, atop of a pile of junk mail on my hall table. I opened it up and took out the black-and-white studio glossy of Connie Clare. It was a posey shot even by the artificial standards of publicity stills, with Clare looking distinctly uncomfortable despite her mile-wide smile. The photo was dated April 1, 1949, about a year before her murder. Hall would have been just a year old. Connie Clare didn't look much like a young mom. Indeed, knowing The Business as I do, I suspect she would have done everything she could to ensure that no one knew she had a kid. Motherhood is hardly the right image for a sexy young starlet-to-be. Was she a good mother? Did she love her baby? Or as in the case of so many actors and actresses that I've known, did The Business come first?

More questions, but ones which I believed might still be possible to answer. I went and found some of the materials I'd copied at the UCLA library, including the picture, from 1947, of an even younger Connie Clare in the company of one, very dapper MacArthur Stans.

I knew exactly where to begin.

Well, sort of.

I wanted to talk to Mac Stans, but I didn't have a clue where he lived. Detective Khan must have known, but I didn't think it would be a good idea to call and ask. I was already counting the number of steaks it would cost me if he agreed to help with the police records on the Connie Clare murder. I wonder if it's cheaper to buy entrecôte by the dozen?

One especially delightful perk of celebrity is to have minions at your beck and call. Actually, I don't have minions of my own, but I'm entitled to full access to the studio's minions, and their minions are legion. You just need to have their cell phone numbers. Fortunately, I had the number for the minion assigned to *Burning Bright,* a nice enough kid named Hap who prided himself on knowing every trivial fact about any movie or TV show you might mention. I think he fancied himself a Tarantino in the making, but I didn't see big things in his future. Then again, I'd never have made Elliot as a two-million-dollar man, so who can say? As hath become sacred writ in Hollywood: Nobody knows anything.

Whether or not Hap ever ends up directing Pam Grier, he's good at what he does now, because in less than thirty minutes he called me back with the address and telephone number of Mac Stans. A glance at the Thomas Guide indicated that Stans lived in Laguna Beach, a lovely seaside burg, indeed, but a little bit far to drive on the off-chance I would catch him in. I hated to give Stans the chance to blow me off, but the only thing to do was to call and ask if he'd see me.

"Hell*ooo,*" a voice purred.

The image of that red-haired Venus floated to the top of my mind on a mother-of-pearl half shell.

"Ohhh, hi," I said. I forgot to say something more.

"Yes?" the voice asked.

A thousand ships were launched.

"I"—what the hell was I calling about again?—"yeah, I'd like to speak with MacArthur Stans, please."

"Who is calling, please?"

"My name is Marty Burns. Mr. Stans doesn't know me, but we have . . . had a mutual friend, I believe. Hall Emerson."

Silence on the other end. No! Come back, please . . .

"Hello?"

"Yes?" she said.

"Is Mr. Stans in?"

"Mr. Stans is unable to come to the phone at the present moment."

"I would really like to speak with him. About Hall Emerson."

"I see."

"Do you think that would be possible? I'd like to talk with Mr. Stans in person."

"Just one moment, please."

Before I could say anything else, hold music played down the line. Swing isn't my thing, but I think it was Glenn Miller. I don't know anyone who has hold music on their home phone. I decided I didn't like it.

"Mr. Burns? Are you the same Mr. Burns who appears on television?"

"That's me."

"And your association with Mr. Emerson was professional?"

"Actually, no. It was personal. Hall was a friend."

"Just a minute."

Back to swing time. I can't believe this stuff has actually come back. Though I always did love the look of stocking seams and garter belts. Oh, and . . .

"Mr. Burns?"

"Still here."

"When would be convenient for you to see Mr. Stans? Could you come to the house?"

"Absolutely. I can do it any time that works for him. This afternoon if that's not too soon."

"Should we say three-ish?"

"That would be perfect."

"Do you know the way?"

Ever-faithful a companion as the Thomas Guide may be, I don't know Laguna at all. And those canyon roads can be very difficult to find. I wrote down the directions.

"We'll look forward to seeing you at three," she said.

"Delighted," I said.

And with that voice turning the dirty windmills of my mind, I was.

The drive down took longer than I expected. The South Bay beach communities are lovely, but getting to and from them is an ever-loving bitch. There's always a tailback where the 5 and 405 freeways meet up, just north of the exit for Laguna Beach, and on a sunny Saturday afternoon it was more no-way than freeway. I then missed the turnoff which the Voice told me to be careful not to miss and I ended up having to drive into Laguna Beach proper. It's a pretty seaside town, but suffers from too many tourists and even more "U-turn Prohibited" signs. By the time I got turned around and back to where I needed to be, heading back up into the brown hills above Laguna, it was already three-thirty. I got lost again and ultimately had to ask someone where to find Brilliant Drive, only to be told I was already on it. At least I located Stans's private road on my own, found that the iron gates at the entrance had been left open for me. Someone—the Voice?—had even tied a bright red balloon to the mailbox to indicate, or so I assumed, that this was, indeed, the place.

The road up to the house was canted at one of those impossible seeming grades that I find terrifying to ascend. My usually well-behaved Lexus growled as I cautiously drove up—the road was single lane, hugging the hill on the right, with a sheer drop on the driver's side that would dent more than your insurance premium if you let the wheel slip. Not that there was much chance of it escaping my white knuckle grip. As I came up over a final, particularly steep rise, Mac Stans's house came into view: an immaculate concrete and glass vision in white that shimmered like a desert mirage in the SoCal sun.

The house wasn't huge by overblown Hollywood standards, but it was plenty big. God knows how they got the construction materials up that road to the top of the hill; maybe they dropped it all in by helicopter. The approach widened out into a huge drive in front of the house. There was enough parking to accommodate a modest theme park, though the only car out front was a gleaming red 4×4 with the vanity plate HONEY D. I parked beside it, but walked to the edge of the paved area when I got out rather than toward the house. I had to take in the view from Olympus which was, it probably goes without saying, breathtaking. A handful of other houses, all big but of notably varying design, dotted the hilltops, but none was higher in elevation than Stans's place. Laguna Harbor glistened golden below and the endless blue of the ocean beyond seemed like nothing so much as the roiling grounds of Stans Manor. A stiff sea breeze buffeted me, tousling my hair and making me squint, but I felt like I wanted to stand there forever and just watch. Suddenly, my treasured beach house in Hermosa seemed small and pathetic, and I realized that I had ascended not merely up into the hills of Laguna, but into the rarefied atmosphere of the monstrously wealthy. MacArthur Stans might look like an old man with a hole in the side of his face, but in this supposedly classless society of ours, he was in an entirely different league from me. I might be famous and comfortable, but this sonu-vabitch was *rich*. Spectacular and pleasing as the view was unto itself, I was grateful, too, to be reminded of that fact before I went in to talk to him.

Of course, the redhead was reminder enough when she opened the door wearing nothing but a warm smile and a bathing suit which, neatly folded, could have been packed inside a Silly Putty egg with room to spare for nose plugs. I suppose it was a bikini, but frankly I don't think the atom bomb blast that inspired the name could have seared my eyes any more fiercely. As I took in the sight of her—she had a copy of the *Wall Street Journal* tucked under her arm and wore little granny reading glasses that made her look even sexier—I some-how managed not to blubber "hummina-hummina-hummina." I think.

"Mr. Burns?" she said, and held out her hand. "I'm Honey."

You make up the punchline.

"Call me Marty."

"Won't you please come in. You're a bit late."

"I'm sorry about that. I got a little lost. I often do."

"No matter. But Mac's having a rest at the moment."

"Is he okay?"

"He's fine. He just needs to recharge in the afternoon. He asked me to set up the video for you until he comes down. Would you come with me?"

Video? What the hell was this? "Thanks," I said.

Honey turned and led the way. My sexist, piggy eyes tracked down her silky, tanned spine to the ample perfection of her rear. "Thank you *very* much."

She shot me a glance over her shoulder. It wasn't coy or warm or playful. I got the message.

As she led me down the hall, I stole looks through open doorways where I could and saw that, except for a notable preponderance of very large mirrors everywhere, the house had that stripped down, ultra-white, minimalist design that says, "no one makes ka-ka here," and judging from the pages of the Sunday magazines (which is as far as my knowledge of design goes), has been trendy for far too long. Even the mirrors all had simple, stainless steel frames. I don't know how people can live in such Spartan surroundings. It's neat and precise, sure, but whose life is so neat and precise? No one I know. Maybe that's the whole point: However messed up your life and your head and your relationships might be, at least your house is in order. But me? I like my stuff sprawled around me. I'm not arguing for roaches in the deep pile, but I think *some* disorder is the sign of a life lived right. And if you have the moolah for a spread like this—on top of a mountain with a view of the sea—surely you don't need to consign yourself to some Beverly Hills trendoid's idea of how to live.

But hell, maybe the old boy really liked it. Or the redhead. I imagine you'd put up with a lot to please a woman like her. Or was she just another bit of furniture? I had sort of assumed so coming in, but that one over-the-shoulder look had me thinking twice.

Honey led me into a small den with a large wall-mounted video screen, a white leather sofa that looked as if it had never been sat upon, and a curvy glass coffee table with nothing on it. She bade me sit down, then went back out. A few seconds later, the screen flicked on, went to static then black as a tape got going. When the program proper came on, I saw it was not of broadcast standard. The camera wobbled a bit, and zoomed in and out before settling on a medium wide shot of a banquet dais. The sound was grubby. An emcee who I didn't recognize stood up at the podium and began reading from some cue cards. It seemed I was about to be graced with the rare opportunity to watch the thrills and chills of the 1983 Writers' Guild of America Lifetime Achievement Award Dinner. No prize for guessing who the guest of honor was.

Honey came back into the den. "Would you like something to drink?" she asked.

"Oh, *I* think so," I said, eying the screen. "Beer if you've got it."

"Certainly." She offered me a mildly sympathetic smile. "Mac thought you'd enjoy watching this."

"Of course," I said. What could be more fun than a tape of a twenty-year-old awards banquet with garbled sound?

"Be right back."

In fact, it was a good fifteen minutes before she returned with a large bottle of Budweiser. The Budweiser was the *real* stuff, Budwar from the Czech brewery, not the domestic slop sold by frogs and lizards. She put the bottle and a glass down on the coffee table and headed back out.

"Aren't you going to keep me company?" I asked.

"I've seen it before," she said. And disappeared.

The tape was interminable. Lots of old codgers, and a couple of young ones, heaping praise on the genius and courage of Mac Stans. A few of them told funny stories, but the punchlines were mostly inside jokes that I didn't get. Or were only amusing when Ronald Reagan was president. Wasn't that a time? After thirty minutes, my beer had been drained, the label read, reread, and neatly peeled off the bottle, and I began to scan every corner of the room for some measure of diversion. Nothing. After another fifteen minutes of banquet—with no sign of the ancient evening approaching its end—I heard voices from out in the hall. Shortly thereafter Honey reappeared.

"Mac's up and about. He's waiting out by the pool."

"Great!" I said, jumping up fast enough to pool blood in my ankles.

"Of course, if you'd like to watch the end of the tape . . ."

"No, no," I all but shouted. "I'm looking forward to seeing the great man in person."

It was very fast, but Honey definitely gave me a little wink. Good God, this woman was walking Viagra.

The pool was modest as these things go, no more than a quarter Olympic size. As we strolled around the concrete path, I could feel the thrum of the filters beneath my feet. A wrought-iron picnic table was set off in the grass to one side, sheltered from the sun by an enormous canvas canopy. At the far end of the pool were two chaise longues and a wicker chair which must have been purchased at the Sidney Greenstreet estate sale. One chaise longue was draped with an extra-large beach towel imprinted with the image of a smiling dolphin.

Mac Stans, in his white suit and Panama hat, straddled the other. He was leaning back in the chair, but his feet—clad in white canvas shoes; we called them "skips" when I was a kid, and woe betide the poor bastard whose mom made him wear them to gym class—were planted on the ground on either side. It took him a little while, but he managed to stand up as we approached him. His gold jewelry rattled almost as much his bones, though he looked haler than he had that day at the cemetery.

"Mr. Marty Burns," Honey said, gesturing elegantly at me with a manicured finger. "MacArthur Stans."

"How do you do, sir," Stans said, holding out his hand. I took it, but it had hardly any weight. He barely gripped my fingers as we shook. I don't know how he lifted it at all with the fat gold ring he wore.

"It's Marty, please. And it's an honor to meet you, Mr. Stans."

"Pah. Everyone calls me Mac. Though not many people call me at all, these days." He laughed uproariously and indicated that I should sit in the wicker chair. I forced a polite chuckle.

"It's still good of you to see me, Mac. I'm sure you've got better things to do with your time."

"You see how I spend my days, Marty. I lie out here in the sun, read the trades, and survey my . . . domain." He made an extravagant gesture with his hand that vaguely took in the sumptuous surroundings, but more particularly suggested he was referring to Honey.

"Nice work if you can get it," I said, managing not to ogle the redhead.

"It didn't come easy."

"I know it never does, believe me."

"How'd you like the tape?"

"Huh? Oh, very interesting. Quite an honor to be accorded."

"Yes."

We stared at each other, each seemingly waiting for the other to say something more. Honey, bless her, saved the day.

"Drinks?"

"I never say no. But Honey can vouch for that." The old man gave me a truly nasty wink. "Gin and tonic?"

"I'll have another beer if I might."

"I think we can oblige," Honey said. She slunk off toward the house, the little motor in that fabulous rear of hers humming like a rotary engine. It was no fun tearing my eyes away, but I watched Stans watching her. He practically drooled.

"Is that a sight, my friend?" he said. "One to rival my ocean view?"

"She's a very beautiful woman."

"That she is. Smart as a cat-o'-nine-tails, too."

"I believe you."

"Sucks cock like it's going out of style."

Honey disappeared into the house and Stans looked up at me. He flicked his tongue out past a vile grin. The concave side of his face collapsed beneath the ugly leer, but I was more put off by the comment than his appearance. What kind of thing was that to say to a stranger? How was I meant to respond?

"I see," I said.

"Think an old man can't get it up?" he asked.

"I . . . don't have any idea." In fact, I'd bet Honey could raise the *Titanic* surer than Jim Cameron, but looking at the old man, the mere thought made me queasy.

"I can still put it to her, don't you worry." Phew, now I wouldn't lose any sleep tonight. "She could be big."

"Pardon?"

"Honey. With what she's got? Those tits, that ass, her . . ." He pursed his lips, stuck his tongue out, then made a sucking noise like Anthony Hopkins as Hannibal Lecter; for a moment I thought I might toss my cookies into his pristine pool. ". . . star quality. Says she's not interested, though."

Honey emerged from the house, carrying a silver tray with a shaker full of gin and tonic, two highball glasses, and another large bottle of Budweiser along with an honest-to-God toby jug.

"Thank you, darling," Stans said, all sweetness and light. "You're too good to me."

Honey smiled at him. She handed Stans his drink first, then carefully poured my beer into the stein. The thing was ugly as sin and awkward to drink from, but the beer still tasted nice. Honey poured herself a drink, but just set it aside and lay back on the other chaise longue, closing her eyes.

"I collect them."

"What's that?" I asked. How many Honeys could one old pervert own?

"Beer steins." He reached over and tapped the nose of my toby jug. "I own over five hundred of them. Seventy-five tobies alone. If not for some damn dentist in Santa Monica, it would be the biggest collection in the state. Been chasing after them for years and years. Got a special room upstairs."

Why? I wondered. "How interesting," I said.

"The one you've got there's only a minor item. Worth . . . fifteen hundred, tops."

"Fifteen hundred dollars?" I tightened my grip on the stein.

"Only paid seven for it. Insure it for twenty-five, though. Just in case. The market is volatile."

"Who'd have guessed?" I said, very carefully putting the stein down on top of a copy of *Variety*. The metal table wobbled slightly and I emitted a little gasp. Stans seemed not to notice, but Honey, peering through a half-open eye, coughed to cover a laugh.

"You're in TV," Stans said.

"Well, I'm *on* it. *In* it makes me think of quicksand."

"Never did TV myself. Don't watch much, either. Except *60 Minutes,* of course. Still a vast wasteland?"

Actually, one of the bios I'd read mentioned that Stans had written several scripts for *Philco Television Playhouse* through a front during his blacklist period. It seemed uncouth to remind him of it now.

"I've never shared that view," I said. "Though my show's on Fox, so maybe I can't see the desert for the mountains of sand. I don't like to poop where I eat, pardon my French, in any case."

"How's the money?"

"Beg pardon?"

"The money. The big green was in the pictures in days gone by. Now I hear TV money's better than it used to be." He tapped the copy of *Variety*. "If you can believe what you read."

"I've got no complaints," I said. "Hell, a bum like me, I'm stealing my paycheck."

"Had an idea for a show. War story. Could be big, like that Spielberg thing. Sans the schmaltz."

"I'm sure there'd be great interest in anything with Mac Stans's name attached. Do you still write much?"

"Old writers never die," he said. He flicked a glance at Honey, then winked at me. "We just put fresh lead in our pencils."

Stans laughed uproariously again. I smiled along, noting that Honey didn't find it necessary to humor him. Indeed, my initial feeling was that the great Mac Stans was a revolting old bastard.

"Speaking of writers," I said, "I came up here because I wanted to talk to you about Hall Emerson."

All trace of humor fled Stans's face. He sucked in his remaining cheek, and through the taut, thin skin I could see the shape of the skull that, before too much longer, would be all that was left.

"A damn shame. A goddamn shame."

"You were at the funeral. You and . . . Honey are hard to miss."

"Had to go pay my respects. I don't get out much these days, it's tough for me with my circulation and the angina. But I felt an obligation."

"Did you know Hall well?"

"Old friend of the family. Knew him since he was knee-high to Hedda Hopper."

"Had you been in touch with him recently?"

"No, not for many years. We had a bit of a to-do."

"What about?"

"That's none of your business. With all due respect."

"Fair enough. But you don't know what Hall was working on just before he died?"

"Should I?"

"A question isn't really an answer."

"Isn't it?"

I got the feeling that Stans was enjoying the game of Ping-Pong, though I don't know what the pleasure was. Maybe he just didn't have many people to talk to.

"You know that there's a remake of *The Devil on Sunday* in the works," I said.

"As you can see, I still read the trades."

"Hall was working on the script for it."

"Is that so?"

"You don't find that . . . interesting?"

"Is there some reason why I should?" Stans smiled wide enough to show me all his false teeth. They needed a Polydent bath.

"You're still pretty slick for a guy who doesn't get out much, Mac."

"Just because I don't get out, don't mean I ain't been around the block a few times. Got more than a few miles on these veiny old gams."

Okay, to hell with subtlety. "Hall told me something interesting about *The Devil on Sunday*. The original, I mean. You are familiar with the picture. And don't ask me if you should be."

Stans looked very serious now. "I know it."

"Is that all?" I glanced at Honey, who was sitting up, eyes wide open. I turned back to Stans and raised an eyebrow.

"Say what you have to say," he told me.

"You wrote *The Devil on Sunday,* didn't you?"

Mac Stans turned to his Honey, but her gaze was locked on me. He scratched at the bristly skin stretched across the hollow cavern of his cheek and fiddled with the big ring on the little finger of his right hand.

"Hall told you that," he said.

"Yes, he did. He said that you wrote it during the blacklist and that Frank Emerson was your beard or your front or whatever you call it."

"You were a good friend of Hall's."

"Not really. We used to play cards."

Stans looked genuinely puzzled now. For the first time since we met, he seemed less than confident.

"Had he lost a bet to you? Owed you a lot of money?"

I shook my head.

"Fucked your wife?"

"I'm not married. And Hall usually walked away from the card games flush, while I'm a break-even poker player on a good day. And for what it's worth, I don't think Hall was a wife-fucking kind of man."

"Everyone is if the woman's right. Why in heaven's name would he tell you such a thing about me?"

"It's true, isn't it?"

"Will you answer my question first?"

I thought about cracking wise, decided it was not the play. "I think

Hall decided that I was a kindred spirit. I didn't appreciate it at the time, but he might have been right. He asked me to help him find out some stuff about the original picture and about his mother. Though he already knew you had written it and his father hadn't."

Stans let out a long breath and leaned back in his chair. He looked to Honey again for support, but if he found some I couldn't see where. The pair had an interesting relationship.

"*The Devil on Sunday?*" I prompted.

"I did write it."

I waited for more. It didn't come.

"And you knew that Hall knew?"

Stans nodded. "He found out when his father passed. Frank and me agreed to keep it our little secret, but I gather that Frank left some papers when he died and Hall read them all. There was something in there about *Devil* and Frank's role in it. I'd known Hall since he was a baby. Knew Frank *and* Connie Clare. Hall was upset when he found out the truth. I don't know why, it was so long ago, but he felt his dad had betrayed him somehow by not telling him, not coming clean."

"Hall had an overdeveloped sense of honor."

"I don't know about that. He came up to me all hot-headed and outraged, like I'd committed some personal offense on him. He demanded to know why the truth about *The Devil on Sunday* had never come out."

"And why didn't it? Why hasn't it?"

"I'll tell you precisely what I told him: None of your goddamn business. It was a thing between Frank Emerson and myself, and as far as I'm concerned it remains so. A man who understands honor, who appreciates and cares about such things, wouldn't ask me to betray the sanctity of that agreement. But Hall didn't much like that."

"Is that the to-do you mentioned before?"

Stans nodded.

"And this was how long ago?"

"After Frank Emerson's liver cancer. Twelve, fifteen years? I don't remember anymore."

"And you never spoke with Hall after that?"

"Wouldn't say that exactly. You know how small this town is." If you're in The Business, though you might be having the conversation in Pinprick, Idaho, *this town* can only mean one place. "We bumped into each other over the years. We never had much conversation, and the subject never came up again. Though I felt it was always there between us."

"Yet Hall honored your confidence."

"How do you mean?"

"You're telling me that he's known . . . knew for a dozen or more years that you were the real author of *The Devil on Sunday* and he never told anyone. Until he told me. And clearly his state of mind those last few days wasn't all it should have been. I found some books about you that aren't that old, and there's no mention at all of *The Devil on Sunday,* so the secret's still safe. If Hall had been really pissed off, if he hadn't honored your . . . pact, or whatever it was, he could have told. Given your name and the fuss about the blacklist and all, there would have been interest. Maybe even some money in the story, and Hall always needed money. But he didn't tell."

"A chip off the old block, I suppose."

"Frank Emerson? Or Connie Clare?"

That drew a very sharp look indeed. "What's that supposed to mean?"

"Nothing at all. But Hall's mother was one of the things I wanted to ask you about."

"So you mentioned. I don't know what there is to say."

"What was she like? You must have known her pretty well."

"What makes you think that?" Stans demanded.

"I found an old newspaper picture of you and her from 1947. A film premiere or something. So you must have known her for several years before the murder. And certainly when she was married to Frank Emerson, cast in the movie you'd written."

"Why do you want to know all this? What kind of actor are you, anyway?"

"You obviously haven't seen my show: I'm a lousy actor. But a curious one. And it looks like I'm going to be in the remake of *The Devil on Sunday.*"

Stans's eyes went wide. He sat back in his chair, looking lost for a moment, then he turned to Honey. She'd been following the conversation very carefully, but offered Stans only a shrug of her lovely, bare shoulders.

"Kevin gave *you* a part?"

Say what? I thought, but played it cool. "I shouldn't say anything, because the contract isn't inked, but it's certainly looking like a done deal."

"So this is, what? Research you're doing? Are you one of those Strassberg types?"

The only method *I'm* concerned with is how best to get beer nuts out of the jar. But Stans looked confused—suddenly seemed a very old man, indeed—so I went with it.

"I like to know all I can about these things. That's why I went to see the original *Devil on Sunday*. Between that and Hall, I got interested in Connie Clare. I play opposite the girl who has the Clare role in the remake. So I've been wondering about the original performances, the production."

Stans shook his head as if he couldn't quite follow the conversation.

"I thought you came because you were a friend of Hall's," Honey said. She didn't look a bit confused.

"I did," I said. "I've been upset since his death and have been hoping to find some better clue as to why he killed himself. No one seems to have a decent answer. In the course of asking around about Hall, Mac's name came up. Hall wanted to know more about his mom and that made me curious. The truth is I couldn't think of anyone else who might have known her. Of course, there's *also* the new picture. So I figured why not kill two birds with one stone. So to speak. Come straight to the horse's mouth."

They both nodded. There's no act of selfishness, venality, or greed that cannot be readily understood by anyone in The Business as a necessary condition of getting a movie made.

"Connie Clare was a nice girl, a *beautiful* girl," Stans said. He was staring over my shoulder—over the *ocean's* shoulder—somewhere into memory. "George Gaines introduced me to her."

"Gaines was the producer."

"George G. Gaines. What a piece of work. I did three pictures with that bastard, and he still shafted me when the red shit hit the fan. He was after Connie himself, but she wouldn't touch him. He only fixed me up with her because he was convinced she was a dyke. That was George Gaines's idea of funny."

"Sounds like a charmer."

"When you lift up a rock and the bugs come scurrying out, you think they're running from the light. No, they're just afraid it's George Gaines might have picked the rock up."

"Yet you worked with him over and over."

"That's The Business."

"He must have known that you were the real writer of *The Devil on Sunday*."

"Of course. How could the producer not know? But Gaines also knew he was getting a Mac Stans script for a fraction of what it should have cost him. And Frank Emerson took half of that for fronting."

"Nice racket."

"What do you think the blacklist was? You think it was anything but a racket? When a Mac Stans or Dalton Trumbo script got stuck in front of a studio boss's nose with Joe Blow's name on the title sheet, you think Warner or Cohn didn't know who typed those words? They were buying in at ten cents on the dollar so what did they care? Do you think McCarthy and Nixon and Thomas and all those politicians weren't in it for the skim? Darling, only lunatics act without an eye on the big score. These guys were nasty, yes, and a few were stupid, but you better believe that none of them were crazy."

"I never thought of it in those terms."

"You should never have to live through such a time."

"I've always wondered what I'd do in your circumstances. If I'd have been brave enough to act as you did and tell them to go stuff themselves."

Stans looked me square in the eye now. "You wouldn't believe the things you can do. If you have to."

The conversation had drifted rather far from Connie Clare. I wanted to steer it back.

"Were you able to stay close to the shoot on *The Devil on Sunday*?"

"Huh? No, not really. Gaines knew I wrote it, and surely the studio, but I'd just been in jail. I couldn't go near the lot."

"So you don't know much about the production."

"What's to know? It was a low budget shoot. Twenty-one days in the can."

"It's what went into the can that I'm interested in. Do you remember seeing the picture when it was released?"

"I saw it, sure."

"Do you know anything about any missing footage or extra scenes that have been cut or lost in the years since?"

Stans' gaze drifted back to the sea. The sun was getting low in the sky, adding that much more value to the view. "Hall again," he said.

"Sorry?"

"Hall wanted to know this, didn't he? This is what it's all about."

"Yes, he did want to know. He was looking for some footage of his mother. He was sure there was another scene with Connie Clare."

"He was haunted, that boy."

"Not too hard to understand, is it? Pretty rough way to start your life with your mom dead in the street. And to finish it."

"I wrote a scene Frank didn't like. It was with Clare and John Dall. A sex scene—hot for the time, but today, well, it could be on *Sesame Street*. Frank thought it was too much and he took it out before he passed the script to Gaines. I once gave Hall a copy of my original script"—a little ball of ice dropped down into my gut—"and he thought they shot it. He was desperate for any coverage of his mother. I can't blame him. But the scene never made it into the shooting script. He was chasing a phantom."

"And Connie Clare's . . ."

"Mac," Honey said, reaching over and taking the old man's hand. "You're looking tired. I think maybe it's time for you to rest."

"Hah?" Stans said. He studied his . . . girlfriend? Life partner? Master? Pet? I don't know. Something passed between them. "Yes. Honey knows best."

"Yesss," she purred, "you know Honey knows best."

"Can I give you some advice, Marty?"

"Please."

"Don't get old. But if you do . . ." Stans reached over and gave Honey's muscular thigh a squeeze. I'm probably just an ageist, but the sight of his withered old claw on her tawny, young skin gave me the creeps. "Make sure you've got one of these."

He winked at me, and Honey helped him into the house.

"You can show yourself out, Mr. Burns?" she asked over her shoulder.

I usually do.

Ten

We hadn't organized a poker game for Saturday night—I don't think anyone was quite up for it yet—so no-date Burns spent a quiet evening with a pizza (extra cheese), the Dodgers (no starting pitching), and his pal Henry Weinhart (convenient six-pack). A pleasant time was had by all. Except the Dodgers, who got shut out. The Mets sure looked happy though.

I fell asleep on the couch, as I often do, and woke up to the harsh light of a sunny sabbath and a ringing in my ears. I always feel extra-dopey when I sleep on the couch—maybe because it usually follows evenings with that convenient Mr. Weinhart—so it took me a moment or two to realize that the ringing in my ears was, in fact, the doorbell.

"Just a minute," I yelled. I scooped my watch off the coffee table and saw that it was quarter to ten. I don't expect visitors at the best of times, and Sunday morning definitely does not meet that qualification. My first thought was Gabbo and his buddies, but they didn't seem like doorbell ringers. Then it occurred to me that perhaps Lissa was back. I hadn't changed the linens after Friday night because I liked looking at the stains we'd left on the sheets. I'm a pig, I know. I was suddenly aware of my morning breath, mussed hair, and two-day stubble. Also I had to pee.

The doorbell rang again.

"All right," I called.

I smoothed my hair back with my hands and wiped the gunge out of my eyes. A chewed wad of Wrigley's Spearmint gum sat where I'd spat it out a day or two before in its wrapper on the edge of the coffee table. I pulled it out and popped it into my mouth, thinking it might do something for my breath. It was none too easy to chew, though, and rather lacking in spearminty freshness. I returned it to its resting place.

Another ring.

"Fuck me," I muttered and answered the door. I suppose I was hoping that it *would* be Lissa.

Kevin Ryan Paul awaited me. I peered around the edges of the door, but the rest of his stock company weren't in evidence.

"Hey, Marty," Paul said. He was wearing wraparound shades and some bizarre ur-disco white jumpsuit thing that hurt my still-sensitive eyes.

"Where's the rest of the Sunshine Band?" I asked.

"Just me. I brought cappuccino and croissants." He dangled a couple of brown paper bags in front of me and smiled broadly.

"Almond?"

"Two plain, two almond, two chocolate. And a bear claw, just in case of emergency."

"You may definitely come in," I said.

I led Paul into my living room. It was an awful mess, but he offered the obligatory, "Nice place."

"Usually," I told him. "But I host cock fights on Saturday night and the cleaning girl doesn't come until Tuesday."

"Usually have to go to West Hollywood for cock fights," he said. I raised an eyebrow and he smiled. "I'm kidding, of course."

"Good one. Listen, I got to hang Wally real bad."

"A man's got to do what a man's got to do."

"Make yourself at home. Smoke 'em if you got 'em."

I padded my way to the can, wondering what in the world Kevin Ryan Paul was doing sitting in my living room with a portable dessert cart on an early Sunday morning. I took a long and satisfying whiz, washed my face, combed my hair, and brushed the taste of nighttime and old chewing gum out of my teeth. I thought about putting on fresh clothes, but decided Kevin Ryan Paul was someone who didn't merit a change of underwear.

The coffee table had been cleared and the croissants neatly arranged on a plate when I returned to the living room. Paul handed me a cappuccino.

"Thanks. Where'd you find the clean plate?"

"I washed a dirty one. Hope you don't mind."

"Spoil yourself." I took a big sip of the frothy joe. I prefer plain coffee, but didn't wish to seem ungracious. "Well, this is an unexpected surprise."

"If you expected it, it wouldn't be a surprise would it?"

"This is true." I grabbed an almond croissant and took a bite. A blizzard of powdered sugar fell on my lap. Just as well I hadn't changed. Good pastry, though.

"I know it's presumptuous of me to just drop in like this . . ."

"Mm," I said, nodding. *Damn* good pastry.

"But I only did it because I know we have this connection thing happening between us."

The almonds turned bitter in my mouth. Is it arsenic that's supposed to have that taste or cyanide?

"There's *some*thing going on," I said.

"Huh? Huh?"

"Maybe I'll try the bear claw," I said. Paul handed me the plate.

"Marty . . ."

"Where did you get that suit?" I really had to ask, lest I wander into the shop by mistake.

"Huh? Oh, is this the haps or what? A designer named Ozzie makes them for me. He's new and he's a genius. Gamma turned me on to the guy."

"I should have guessed. Do all his friends just have the one name?"

"Don't you be dissin' the Ozmeister. He's very exclusive, but mark my words: In six months time everyone'll be wearing these."

"So is white the new black?"

"Hmmm? No. No! But I'll let you in on a little secret. Sun-dried linen is the new rock and roll."

I studied Paul hard; searching, *praying* for some indication that he was joking or having me on. If so, Paul was more stone-faced than Buster Keaton. I swore for the millionth time this year that yes, I really, really, *must* leave Los Angeles in search of signs of intelligent life.

The temptation to ask about sun-dried linen was considerable, but all I said was: "I'll make a note."

"Marty. I've come here this morning because I have to talk to you about Mac Stans."

Ding-ding-ding-ding! The daily double. That's what happens when you select "nasty old codgers" for a thousand. My, oh, my, but word travels fast on this coast. Stans must have called Paul as soon as I left. It's a wonder the producer waited until morning to come see me.

"Mac Stans?"

Paul dropped his chin and peered up at me through his eyebrows. I half-expected him to grate his fingers at me and go "tsk-tsk." He did give a slight head shake of chastisement.

"Yeah, I saw Mac Stans yesterday," I said.

"I know that. May I ask you why?"

"If you know I saw him, you probably know why already."

"If I knew why would I be asking you?"

"If I wanted you to know, wouldn't I have told you?"

Paul crossed his arms and shook his head more forcibly. "Marty, Marty, Marty. I think we've got too good a thing going on to play silly games. Don't you?"

"I treasure what we have."

"I know you do. And you know *I* do. That's why I'm here. Talking to you hombre-to-hombre. No one else to listen, no one to get in the way. Just you and me. *Communicating.*"

"We cannot *not* communicate," I said. I once read it in a fortune cookie I got at a dim summery in Chinatown. My lucky lottery numbers were printed on the back.

"That's a beautiful thought, man."

"Thank you."

"No, thank *you*." For a terrifying second I thought Paul was going to lean in and give me a hug. Mercifully he reached for his coffee instead. "Mac Stans," he whispered.

"How well do you know him?" I asked.

"He's co-producer of *The Devil on Sunday*."

"What?" I think I yelled.

"Don't tell me you don't know that."

"How in the world would I know that? You never mentioned it. You've never mentioned Stans's name to me. For Christ's sake, I'm still waiting to see a complete script."

"Details. I must have mentioned it."

"I think I would remember that, Kevin."

"I guess with this amazing connection we've got, I just assumed you knew. My mistake, Marty."

"Stans didn't mention it, either," I said.

"He can be a little forgetful."

"Oh? He seemed pretty sharp to me."

"He goes in and out, has good days and bad. He suffers from that old timer's thing. Which is why I'm so concerned that you're bothering him. He's very sensitive and easily disturbed."

"I just went to ask him some questions."

"About?"

I considered my answer. "Connie Clare," I said.

"What?" Paul looked puzzled. "Why?"

"Just curiosity. I like to research my roles very carefully." What the hell, it worked with Stans.

"I'm not sure I follow you."

"I got curious about the picture, you know? I rented the original to check it out. I was fascinated by Connie Clare, got to wondering what she was like and how her murder might have affected Hall. I've been thinking about Hall a lot since the suicide. Brooding a little, I guess. And I got to wondering why Stans was at the funeral. Then I found out that Stans knew Hall since he was a little kid. He knew Connie Clare, too, of course. So I went to ask him about her, see what he remembered."

"What did he tell you?"

"Nothing much," I said, straight faced. "He just told me some old stories. Made me watch a videotape of some award he once won."

"Been there, done that, snorted the coke to stay awake," Paul said.

"I tried not to spend the whole visit staring at Honey's tits."

"Been there, too," Paul said, with a smile that made me feel cheap.

I wondered exactly how much Paul did know about Stans. It had stunned me when the old man casually mentioned Paul's name to me during our talk. I let it pass because I didn't want him to know that *I* didn't know he was connected to Paul.

"How does Stans come to be involved with *our* picture?" I asked. I said a mental mea culpa for the use of the possessive.

"Just Hollywood luck. He owns half the rights to the original property."

That made sense if you knew that Stans was the real author of *The Devil on Sunday*. *Did* Paul know?

"*Half* the rights?"

"Mm. He and Uncle George owned the rights between them."

"I don't understand," I told him. "How did Stans come to own any of the rights to your uncle's picture?"

"They worked together on a bunch of projects. Uncle George surrendered some rights in lieu of payment when he came up short on a budget. Stans kept hold of them all these years. Wily old man."

"And so now you have to be in bed with him."

"Whoa! I don't mind a little reach-around now and again, but it's not like I'm gonna let him slip me the wet, wrinkly one. Of course, if he'd agree to a little three-way action with that pussy machine of his, well, I wouldn't say no to that. Hey, don't tell Sade I said that."

"You know you can trust me, Kev."

"I do. I know that. And that's why I have to ask you not to bother Stans again. He's a funny old man and we don't want to spook him. This project is happening my friend, with a capital *h*. We have to be sure not to upset the applecart. We can't risk any bad publicity right now. Huh? Huh?"

"They say there is no such thing as bad publicity."

"*They* don't always know their ass from a . . . jar of *honey*. But *we*—you and me, baby, that spells *us*—are not *them*." Paul gave me a big wink. "So you keep clear of Mac Stans, right?"

"Hey," I said, pointing at Paul with one finger, myself with another, "you and me. We happen."

"Beautiful."

Paul smiled and put on his shades. He held out his hand and we shook. I followed him to the door. As he was about to go out, I said: "Hey, Kev."

"Mar?"

"Did you see that piece about Hall Emerson in the *Reporter* the other day?"

"Ahhh, don't think so."

"It had a bunch of quotes from you about the picture. It was sort of nasty about Hall, though. Is that the kind of bad publicity you're worried about?"

Paul took hold of my shoulder, slid his shades up over his forehead. I hate when people do that.

"They misquoted me," he said, lying to my face. "The bastards took it all out of context. That's why you've got to be careful with the press. Don't make waves when Charlie don't surf."

"I'll try to remember that," I said.

Paul winked at me and patted my arm. He slid his shades back down with a practiced flick of his neck, and in a white-suited jump, he was gone.

Talk about your out of context.

Carl Khan rang me on Sunday night.

"You ever get any time off, Detective?" I asked.

"Like rust, justice never sleeps. Though it does nap. And it stops for doughnuts, of course."

"Maybe it just needs someone to tuck it in."

"Or put it out of its fucking misery."

"Oh, dear. You sound like you've had a bad day."

"Despite what some people think, Celebrity Affairs is no bowl of Cherry Garcia. I spent the whole day riding shotgun on a shoot for a music video."

"This is my tax dollars at work?"

"It was a rap video. KKK Snuff-E Smith."

"I'm unfamiliar with that particular gentleman's sound. But then I'm told by those who know that my finger lies not on the throbbing pulse of popular culture."

"Good for you. Apparently Snuff, as he likes to be called, is feuding with some other noise merchant whose name also defies the laws of the King's English. Death threats were issued. Fortunately—though not to my ears—no shots were fired."

"A job well done, Detective."

"Maybe. But I suspect parents across the country would curse my name if they knew I was responsible for preventing the guy who makes that awful noise from taking a whack. Shit, after eight hours of that racket I considered doing him myself."

"A lawman's lot is a lonely one," I said.

"Where's that line from?"

"The pilot episode of *Burning Bright*. Surely you've committed it to memory?"

Khan cleared his throat. "I was actually calling about your request yesterday. About the Connie Clare murder."

"Yes! What did you find out?"

"I'm still not sure I like you asking about this stuff, but I did put a request in for the file. It doesn't exist."

"Rats," I muttered.

"They really don't keep much beyond twenty-five years. Some old stuff is preserved for historical reasons, and really high profile cases often survive because no one can bear to toss the files, but everything else gets scrapped."

"A murdered film star isn't high profile?"

"Christ, Marty, she was less famous than you are when she got punched out. I doubt the investigation was all that big. Probably made some good tabloid headlines at the time, but who's even heard of her today? And let's face it, it's going on fifty years now."

"It's a bummer though. The newspaper stories I looked up didn't offer any real details about the murder."

"Well, there you go—that sort of proves my point. Though if it was a rape or sexual assault, they would have played that down back then. The scandal sheets are probably a better bet for info than the straight press."

"I hadn't thought of that. I appreciate you looking into this, Detective."

"Just how much do you appreciate it?"

Uh-oh, I smelled steak.

"What do you mean?"

"I made a couple phone calls, asked around a little. Doing that voodoo that Celebrity Affairs does *so* well."

"And?"

"The detective who worked the Clare case is still alive."

"You're kidding."

"No, his name is Bill Caldwell. He must be in his eighties, but I spoke with him and he sounded pretty compos mentis. At least, he remembers the case. He lives with his daughter in Alhambra."

"Louis, this could be the start of a beautiful friendship."

"I don't know abut that," Khan said, "but you've managed to pique my curiosity with this stuff. I don't have time to get into it myself—or the justification—but I'd sort of like to know what the old cop has to say about things. You interested?"

"Very much so." I flashed on the scripts I'd swiped from Hall's place that had then been stolen from my car and felt a heavy pang of guilt.

"He said he'd be willing to talk to you. Just remember that he's an old guy, and from what I can gather, he was a pretty good cop."

"Don't worry, old people love me," I said. Then I sighed. "They're our best demographic."

I spoke with Caldwell's daughter, whose name was Loretta Young ("Not the actress," she chuckled), on Monday morning and she said that her father would be happy to see me after his afternoon nap. She sounded pretty excited to be talking to me, which always makes me nervous, because I invariably prove to be disappointing in the flesh. They lived in a big, Spanish-style house on one of those absurdly wide boulevards halfway between Alhambra and South Pasadena. The street was lined with the tall, thin palms that look as crazy as giraffes and make you wonder just how and why evolution works. It was a balmy seventy degrees when I left my house in Hermosa, but naturally by the time I got off the freeway at South Pasadena, the car's A/C was cranking away. I like the San Gabriel Valley—it's pretty and feels cozy and homey in a way that the rest of LA doesn't—but I could never live there for the heat and smog.

Caldwell's daughter, Loretta, was in her mid-fifties and greeted me at the door with The Look. Most Angelinos try to be cool about celebrities, but you can't be on TV or in the movies without learning to spot The Look of the terminally star-struck. It's often followed by a curious bouncing motion on the balls of the feet, and most disturbingly in extreme cases, by a dog-whistle squeal emanating, one hopes, from the mouth. Loretta hopped a bit and tended toward the giggly, but fortunately didn't summon the hounds. She pumped my hand hard enough to draw water from a well, but seemed like a nice enough suburban lady.

Bill Caldwell sat in a wheelchair out in the back garden. Despite the warm weather, he wore a stripey red track suit with the jacket zipped up to the neck, and a blanket folded over his lap. His hands were gnarled with arthritis and his face drooped with Bell's Palsy. He had a full head of thick silver hair, though, and sharp eyes. He was gazing thoughtfully up at a pair of hummingbirds zooming in and out of the trees at the back of the yard. The house was a shotgun shack stacked up against Mac Stans's world-beater of a hilltop spread, but didn't seem a half-bad place to play out the remainder of your days. Loretta opened up a folding chair for me and offered drinks.

The old man wanted mineral water, so I said that was fine with me, too.

"It's very nice to meet you, sir," I said. "Detective Khan told me you're a hell of an officer."

Caldwell took a good study of me. His droopy lip trembled slightly, as did his hands, but there was nothing soft about the way he sized me up. "You want to know about Connie Clare," he said. So much for small talk.

"Yes. I'd like to know about her murder."

"Why?"

"I knew her son. He killed himself last week."

"And?"

"And . . . I don't know. I've been trying to make sense of what happened. He—her son—asked me to try and find something about his mother for him, but he died before I could do it. I suppose I'm just following through on what I started."

"What were you looking for?"

Old as he was, Caldwell struck me as a guy not to lie to. I imagined he'd spent a lifetime around liars and could sift bullshit easier than flour.

"A piece of film. Clare's son, Hall Emerson his name was . . ."

"I know his name."

"Right, sorry. Hall thought that there was some missing film footage of his mother that hadn't been seen in years. Leftover shots from an old movie. He thought I could use my connections to help him find it. Unfortunately I couldn't. Or what he wanted doesn't exist anymore."

The Devil on Sunday."

"That's right. Hall believed that there was a missing scene with his mother. He said he wanted to see it because it was all he had of her. Of course, Hall was in pretty bad shape toward the end. The truth is that I suppose I feel a little bit guilty about what happened."

"Are you?"

"Huh? Am I what?"

"Guilty."

He said the word like he was passing judgment at the gates of heaven.

"I don't know. I don't *think* so. Or I don't know what of. But what started as a little favor for a friend is turning into a long and very complicated story, and I'm afraid I'm losing the plot. I thought you might be able to fill in some blanks for me."

"You're an actor."

"That's what I claim on my tax return, along with sixteen imaginary dependents. Critics have been known to disagree, however. Fortunately, I haven't heard from the IRS."

"I gave up on TV." Another rating point down the drain. "This isn't some stunt? Some studio hype you're up to?"

"No. I can promise you that. The network and I aren't all that close."

Caldwell stared back up into his trees. The hummingbirds were gone. Some of the focus fell out of his eyes and I thought he might have drifted off. I glanced back at the house for his daughter, then he spoke.

"I remember the little boy."

"Hall?"

"He was a whiner, one of those brats who never shuts up, never stops complaining. Always after attention. He made terrible noises when he didn't get it. Inherited his mother's looks, though."

"What was she like?" I asked. Foolishly.

"Never met her alive. I only knew the body, fair piece of flesh though it was. 'Course it didn't look too good by the time I saw it."

Caldwell's daughter brought out a tray with a big bottle of Perrier and two glasses with ice and lemon. And a bowl of blue tortilla chips with some salsa from Trader Joe's. I thanked her and she giggled some more.

"Loretta watches your show," Caldwell said when she'd walked away.

"Thank God someone does."

"She's not too particular."

"Beggars can't be choosers," I sighed.

"Didn't mean anything by that," Caldwell said. "But you should meet my son-in-law."

"Does he watch, too?"

"Couldn't say. Likely not, though. Watches a lot of the soccer on satellite. I can't stand it myself. Up and down, up and down. Nobody ever scores. Don't mind pool, though. But not that nine-ball crap."

"I'm a dyed in the wool baseball man."

"Dodgers?"

"Sadly, yes."

"Would you believe I can still remember when they moved out here? I walked a beat near Chavez Ravine before there was a ballpark."

"I was born up in the valley, but I'm afraid my cognizance of Dodgers' history starts with Sandy Koufax."

Caldwell nodded. Then he asked: "What do you know about Connie Clare?"

"Not too much. She had a few bit parts in the late forties, early fifties. *The Devil on Sunday* was supposed to be a big thing for her, but she was killed during the shoot and they had to work around that. I've gone back and looked at the newspapers of the day, but there's not that much about the murder. I know she was raped and strangled and that her body was found in South Central. And that the killer was never caught."

"Never arrested, anyway."

"What do mean by that? You know who did it?"

The old cop took a deep breath, let it out with a low moan that sent his lip to greater quivering. "Not such that I could prove it. Or so they'd let me."

"Which 'they' are we talking about here?"

"They come and they go. Just follow the money, you want to know who they are. Same as it ever was. Hell, son, you work for them. You must know that."

"I suppose I don't like to think about things that way."

"No one does. That's the magic trick keeps the lady in the air."

"So who killed Connie Clare?" I asked.

"I don't have proof positive, you understand," Caldwell began. "For one thing, Connie Clare got around some. She was no stranger to the casting couch. Or anything else that was horizontal and padded. I don't even know if the padding mattered. She was generous with her favors, as we used to say."

"She slept around."

"If it got hard, she humped it. Sometimes even if it didn't."

I shrugged. "Sounds like an ambitious young actress to me. I've known a few."

"True enough. But when you've got a dead body, you look for connections. You start with whoever's closest to the victim. Clare was in the middle of a film shoot, surrounded by men: some handsome, some influential. Not many are both. It didn't take long to find a baker's dozen . . . ah . . . *close* enough to her that you couldn't slip a piece of paper between them without it getting wet. The director, the editor, the cameraman. Christ, the truck drivers."

"The writer, of course," I said, thinking of Frank Emerson.

Caldwell made a cacking noise in this throat. "Of course, most of the men she . . . knew were easy enough to clear, but two could never account for themselves to my satisfaction."

"Who were they?"

Caldwell shook his head. "One of them's still alive, so far as I know. I won't say the name. The other's dead and I only curse the fact that I wasn't there to see him put into the ground, maybe do a little dance after. Fellow named George Gaines."

"Uncle George," I said.

"Excuse me?"

"Nothing, sorry. You think Gaines killed her?"

"Heard of him, have you?"

"Only bad things."

"Not surprised. Like I say, I had another suspect I couldn't strictly clear, but in my gut I knew that Gaines strangled her. It's always gnawed at me that I couldn't nail him for it."

"Why would Gaines have killed her?"

"He was a vicious fellow. He beat up women for kicks, usually paying for it. Buy anything in Hollywood, you probably know. Found one street girl he busted her jaw. Another had . . . well, damage to her gentle bits. And Gaines tried to strangle both, but didn't go all the way. Gaines had a more serious thing for Clare, though. And she went for it, up to a point."

"How so?"

"Well, she was sleeping with him. That was established. She liked it rough, too, according to some of her other partners. I think she and Gaines stoked each other up and it got out of hand. I can't say for sure that the murder was premeditated, but talking to people I came to believe that Gaines had been working his way up to a killing and that Clare just fit the bill."

"But he needed her for the picture. It would be crazy to kill one of your actors in the middle of a production."

"Film got shot, didn't it? She wasn't that big a part of things."

"I don't buy it."

"I'm not selling," Caldwell said, a little bit angry.

"I know, I'm sorry."

"There were other things, too. Gaines had a rep for jealousy. He insisted that Clare stop . . . sharing her favors, but she wasn't a one-man gal. He went nuts when he found out she was still putting it around. Also, he had another gal—a black woman—had a place he paid for two blocks from where Clare's body got dumped. The black gal disappeared right after the murder. Spent a long time looking for her, but bodies are easy to lose. We got us a big ocean conveniently located by the beach here."

"He didn't lose Clare's body," I challenged.

"No. He wanted that to be found. I think that was part of the thrill for him. Not to mention that buzz it gave the picture."

"No publicity is bad publicity."

"You're in the business. You ought to know."

I refilled our glasses and noshed on some chips and dip. Caldwell was starting to look tired, but there was more I wanted to ask him.

"So if you had all this, why didn't you charge Gaines for the murder? You didn't, did you?"

Caldwell laughed. A tendril of spittle spilled out of the palsied side of his mouth.

"Charged. I was lucky to ask him three questions. Gaines had protection."

"Protection? From who?"

"You've got to remember the times, son. People were seeing Reds coming out of every sock drawer. You were on one side of the fence or the other. If you were on the right side, you could do no wrong. If you were on the wrong side, well, you know what happened."

"I don't follow you. What's that have to do with Gaines?"

"Oh, don't you know that Gaines was big in the anti-Red movement? He was buddied-up from here to Washington, District of Columbia. George Gaines was Ronald Reagan's producer, you know. He was in with all that so-called patriotic crowd. That's how Gaines moved out of the low rent end of town. He rode the scare right up to respectability."

"But surely murder, even if it wasn't premeditated . . ."

"You believe those types cared about a dead little starlet who liked it rough and put it around? That they wouldn't protect one of their own first? No, that's not the way things worked. I'm retired twenty-two years but I don't believe it's different today. Some things don't ever change."

The hummingbirds came back and we sat and watched them for a while. I once read that a hummingbird flaps its wings over a thousand times a minute. I always wonder who could be bothered to count.

"You, ummm, made a funny noise before when I mentioned Connie Clare's husband."

"Who?" Caldwell asked.

"Frank Emerson. The writer. You sort of coughed. Or were you just clearing your throat?"

"The faggot?"

"What?"

"Sorry, that's not a nice word these days, is it? I try not to act my age all the time, but I can't quite bring myself to talk about *gay*. Jeanette MacDonald, she was gay. I don't think sodomists are so damn gay."

"Wait a minute: you're telling me that Frank Emerson was . . . a homosexual?"

"Bent as a rusty nail in a fun house mirror."

"No, you must be mistaken. He was married to Connie Clare."

"And?"

"He was Hall's father!"

"Busted clock's right twice a day. I suppose it's possible he's the sire. Not likely, though." Caldwell leaned forward and lowered his voice to a whisper. "If Frank Emerson ever saw the inside of a pussy, he must have taken a can opener to a cat."

I shook my head; I didn't know what to make of this information. Caldwell's memory seemed solid, but how could this be true? Surely, Hall would have known. He hadn't mentioned, even hinted, at anything like it.

Caldwell's daughter came back out and told him that dinner was just about ready. She invited me to join them—pepper steak—but I politely declined.

"Can I ask you one more thing?" I said, after she'd gone again.

Caldwell nodded.

"Your other suspect in the Clare murder—the one you think is still alive—was it MacArthur Stans?"

One eyebrow, on the non-palsied side of Caldwell's face, rose a quarter of an inch when I said Stans's name. "How do you come to ask me that?" he said.

I shook my head. "Was it?"

"Yes," he said.

"Why did you suspect him? Because he was a Red?"

"Stans was no Red."

"Okay, but he wouldn't rat his commie buddies out, would he? That must have made him look suspicious."

"Never could figure that. Him putting on the high hat and all. Didn't seem in character to me."

"What? How so?"

"He didn't strike me as a principled kind of feller. Something . . . unctuous about his nature, I thought. Even for show people, no offense. 'Course he went and made himself a hero, so-called, so what's my opinion worth?"

"Quite a lot, I should think."

Caldwell looked me over again, as if for the first time, then turned back to look for his hummingbirds. After a little while he said: "You know, I just might have to watch your damn show after all."

Eleven

I took a chance and stopped by Jon Conlon's place on my way back from Alhambra. I felt a little bad about ringing the bell unannounced given the recent string of drop-ins at my place, but I wanted to ask Conlon a question. Fortunately, the lights were on and Conlon's partner, Susan, opened the door. She looked surprised, but not unhappy, to see me.

"Jon's just on the phone," she said, leading the way to the living room. "Come and sit down."

Sure enough Conlon was pacing back and forth between the living room and the kitchen, a cordless plastered to his ear. He nodded at me, then shook his head and rolled his eyes as he pointed at the receiver.

"No . . . no . . . no . . . impossible! Listen to me: he's a fucking barbarian, right? So how would he know how to decipher ancient runes? . . . No, he's not an *educated* barbarian. What the hell does that mean, he has a degree from UCLA? . . . No he does *not*! . . . Because that's the archmage's role. If the archmage doesn't free the silver goddess then there's no point in having him in the episode at all . . . So why don't you tell me at the start that you want to save the money? I know he's an asshole. I . . . Listen, I got company just arrived, so put it in an E-mail. Yeah, okay."

Conlon flipped off the phone, then threw it hard at the couch.

"Remind me again why I went into this business," he said.

I counted off on three fingers. "The money's great. The work isn't really that hard. No one will hire you to do a real job."

"Oh, yeah. Still, I wonder sometimes."

"Art not keeping you sane?"

"Did you know that I won an O'Henry Prize for short fiction when I was just twenty-one years old? I was named by Philip Roth as one of the ten brightest prospects on the literary scene in an article for the *New York Review of Books*. Granted, that was in 1985."

"So what are you saying? You could have been a contender?"

"Instead of a bum which is what I am," Conlon recited. "Christ, Marty, I spend my days writing for babes in breastplates."

"So did Richard Wagner."

"Great. I'll probably end up as Pat Buchanan's speechwriter."

"Have I come at a bad moment, Jon?"

"Hah? Nah, I'm just whining. I'm thinking about giving up my amateur standing."

"I'm no scout, but I think you've got a shot at the big time."

"Thank you, thank you very much. So, can I offer you something in a beer?"

"Normally I wouldn't impose, but I hate to break some little bottle's heart."

Conlon fetched a couple of Asahis from the fridge.

"No beer stein?" I asked when he handed me the bottle.

"Huh?"

"Nothing. Just that I've been keeping some peculiar company lately."

"Elliot?"

"Much worse. Let's see"—I started counting fingers again—"Kevin Ryan Paul, Lissa Torres, Mac Stans . . ."

"Whoa! You met MacArthur Stans?"

"You're not interested in hearing about Lissa Torres?"

"Not unless . . ." Conlon glanced over his shoulder to make sure Susan was out of earshot. "Not unless you fucked her stupid."

"That's the only way I know how to do it, my friend."

"You dog. Or are you shitting me?"

"I don't shit; at worst, I excrete daintily. And being a gentleman, naturally I don't wish to get into the sweaty details, but Ms. Torres and I spent a lovely weekend together one recent evening."

"Man, if I wasn't so significantly othered, I could go for a piece like Lissa Torres. I love that furry cleavage."

"You are aware it's just a CGI shot."

"Awww, don't ruin it for me. You know, I pitched an episode of *Lupé Garou* a few months back."

"Any luck?"

"The climax was going to be a cat fight—she-wolf fight, I suppose you'd say—in a strip joint. The producers accused me of being too brainy for their audience."

"They must know about that O'Henry Prize."

"I *broke* the telephone I threw after that call. Missed the couch and took out a glass coffee table. I'm still nervous about walking barefoot in here. So tell me about Mac Stans. Did you see his babe, too?"

"Her name is Honey," I said.

"Bull. Shit."

"Nope. I was down at Stans's hideaway in Laguna. Amazing place. Honey was in attendance, of course, and wearing a bathing suit that would have made Angelyne blush."

"I think I have to sit down."

"You are sitting."

"Not all of me. What were you doing there? What's Stans like?"

"He's a funny old guy, but not in the George Burns sense. He's so full of himself you wonder how he eats."

"I'm wondering what he eats. Or should I say who?"

"You're a degenerate, Jon. But then that's why we love you."

"Ignore me," Susan said from behind us. "Just passing through." She went into the kitchen, emerged with a bottle of Evian and a package of Chips Ahoy. "You may now carry on discussing cunnilingus," she said and went into the bedroom.

"She deserves better than you," I told him.

"Don't say it too loud," Conlon whispered.

"I already know," Susan called from the bedroom.

Conlon shrugged. Then said: "Honey."

"Stans says they enjoy a healthy sex life."

"He *told* you that?"

"In rather less delicate terms than I just used."

"That's kind of disgusting."

"You should have been there."

"What were *you* doing there?"

I puffed my cheeks, expelled a long breath. "I'm still chasing around after Hall."

"What? What in the world for? What's to chase?"

"I don't know," I said, and laughed.

Jon squinted at me and shook his head. "What are you doing, Marty?"

"Did you know that Kevin Ryan Paul's uncle may have killed Hall's mother?"

Conlon closed his eyes, then shook his head like a dog. "You want to run that by me again?"

"George Gaines, the producer of the original *Devil on Sunday,* was Kevin Ryan Paul's uncle. An old cop just told me that he always suspected Gaines of the murder of Connie Clare. You know that Clare was Hall's mother."

"Holy cow! So why wasn't he arrested for it?"

"The detective claims that Gaines was protected by the industry powers-that-be at the time. Clare was killed in 1950 and Gaines was a big wheel in the anticommunist movement and so it was covered up. Also the cops had another suspect and couldn't actually prove which of them had done it."

"So this cop isn't really sure about any of this."

"He's an old guy now, but I think he is pretty sure. Don't you want to know who his other suspect was?"

"Ummm, Ralph Meeker."

"Not a bad guess, but no kewpie doll for you. Mac Stans."

Conlon's jaw literally dropped. "No. Way."

"The cop didn't say the name, but he didn't contradict me when I suggested it to him."

"That's what you went to see Stans about? To ask him if he killed Connie Clare?"

"No, no. I did go to talk to him about her and about Hall, but I had no idea that he could have been involved in Clare's murder at that point. See, I just spoke to the cop this afternoon. Actually, there's no reason to think Stans was involved. This cop is about ninety-nine percent sure it was Gaines. But I have to say, having met the legend—and I include within his own mind there—I came away less than dazzled. That doesn't make him a killer, God knows, but I do think he's kind of a creep. Who can say what he was like when he was younger?"

"Goddamn, you've been a busy boy. You trying to write a script or something? That what all this is about?"

"No, nothing like that. Writing is for chumps, no offense. The closest I ever got to an O'Henry is the candy bar."

"Goldenberg's Peanut Chews are my preferred poison."

"Really?"

"I scarf 'em by the dozen. So how the hell did you come across all this?"

"Mostly by accident. I've been feeling bothered by Hall's suicide, you know? I find something out only to have it raise six more questions. I just wanted to know why he did it. There's a bunch of stuff that didn't make sense."

"And does it now?"

"Not really. It just gets murkier and messier. This old cop I talked to, he said he thought that part of the reason Gaines killed Connie Clare was for the publicity. For the picture I mean. *The Devil on Sunday.*"

"That seems like a stretch."

"Maybe. But it got me thinking: Like uncle, like nephew?"

"What? Kevin Ryan Paul killed Hall and made it look like suicide for the PR? It didn't work, if he did."

"You haven't met Paul, right?"

"Not to know him."

"He's an idiot. A Hollywood idiot—you know, he might be worth a hundred mil and wear thousand-dollar jumpsuits, but you wouldn't trust him to tie your shoelaces without knotting it up."

"Jumpsuits?" Conlon asked.

"It's a long story, never mind. I'm just saying he's the kind of guy who could mess up gravity. Maybe he just misplayed the PR angle with Hall. He did manage to get a piece in the *Reporter* out of it. Maybe he expected more buzz."

"You're leaping across some awful big canyons here, Mr. Knievel. Do you have any proof to link Paul to Hall's death?"

"You know that Hall wrote a draft of the remake script for *Devil on Sunday?*"

"Yeah."

"Well, Paul denies it. Says Hall was hired for a polish which he never delivered. But I've seen Hall's full script."

"Interesting."

"Paul and Hall had some nastier run-ins, too. Paul swore out a police complaint against Hall a little while ago."

"That I didn't know."

"Paul said he only hired Hall because his uncle always felt guilty about what happened to Connie Clare. Not that Paul suggested that Gaines killed Clare, mind you. He said he figured he owed Hall something because of Clare's death during the original shoot, so he gave him a chance with the remake. *And* the PR might play, of course."

"Of course. You gone to the cops with this?"

"Not exactly. Officially, they've closed the case on Hall."

"I don't mean to offend, Marty, but do you think you know better than them?"

"I used to be a detective, you know."

"Hey, I used to be a rising star in the literary firmament."

We stared at each other for a little while.

"You think I'm nuts," I said.

"I wouldn't say that. But maybe you've been spending a little too much time in the land of network detective drama."

"Fox network," I reminded him.

"Exactly my point."

"You're probably right," I said. "But that doesn't take the tiny niggle out of the back of my skull."

"That's why the good Lord created beer. And harder stuff if the niggle won't drown like a newborn kitten."

"Been there, done that, taken the cure. It's not a satisfactory solution anymore."

"So what then?"

"You remember that fat biker bastard who howled at Hall's funeral?"

"Oh, yeah."

"Hall ever mention him to you? He calls himself Gabbo."

"How do you know that?"

"Turns out he's a fan. Hall ever mention him to you?"

Conlon started to nod. "Yeah. I didn't know that was him, but I do recall Hall talking about a Gabbo. They used to raise some hell together."

"Do you have *any* idea where Hall knew him from? Where I might be able to find him?"

"None whatsoever. Can't exactly look in the phone book under 'G' can you?"

"Actually, I tried. There are over fifty Gabors in LA—there's either a wave of Hungarian immigration or those sisters bred like jackrabbits—but no Gabbos."

"Hall's ex might know."

In fact, I was sure she did. I realized it had to be Melly Dougherty who sicced Gabbo and his buddies onto me in the first place. She must have told them about my visit to her. I didn't want to explain all that to Conlon, though. "Anyone else?" I asked.

Conlon held up a finger. "Got me an idea."

Conlon grabbed the phone off the couch and walked out of the room. I heard him shuffling through some drawers, then the one-sided half of a telephone conversation. He came back in with a piece of note paper.

"Don Grady. He says he once went to a biker bar in Long Beach with Hall. The kind of place he thought he'd never get out of alive. They met Gabbo there."

"Great," I said.

"Maybe. Don said this was about three years ago. He doesn't know if the place is still there, much less if they'll know Gabbo. It's slim."

"It's a start," I said. I studied the address.

"He also said that, absent Hall, he wouldn't walk into the joint without a SWAT team for backup."

"Yeah," I said, "but Don doesn't possess that old Marty Burns charm."

Conlon looked worried.

"Two SWAT teams," he said.

I stopped at home to change: a pair of old jeans and a work shirt; nondescript cowboy boots and a battered leather bomber jacket. Not exactly biker chic, but the least inappropriate outfit I could find for where I was headed. I figured that just about anything else I owned was likely to net me a cue stick across the back of the head before I could get three steps inside the door. Even so, I double-checked that my health insurance card was in my wallet because it was more than passing likely I'd end up in a hospital before the night was through.

I hate Long Beach. The best thing you can say about the place is: "Nope, never been there." It's an ugly, squalid, dirty, gang-infested, crime-ridden, white-black-and-Latino trash, trafficky wart on the pockmarked face of the Southland. It used to have the Spruce Goose, but that's gone. It still has the Queen Mary, but who cares?

There isn't even a decent beach there.

It's not *just* that Long Beach is butt ugly and ungodly dangerous. One of the worst things that ever happened to me, happened in Long Beach.

I got the shit beat out of me by a kangaroo.

Manny Stiles was behind it, of course. In the dying days of *Salt & Pepper,* Manny's publicity gimmicks got more and more extreme. There was a big outdoor festival along the harbor front and as part of a charity event (though I believe the "charity" proved to be the Manny Stiles Retirement Fund), I was coerced into participating in a celebrity boxing match with Skippy the Bush Kangaroo. Skippy starred in a syndicated series from Australia that was being launched in America that summer, so it was a double PR stunt. It wasn't meant to be a *real* boxing match. I was instructed in how to dance around the ring with the animal, and poke it lightly in the shoulder a few times. Skippy, I was assured, would merely hop up and down a little, wave to the crowd and pull some confetti out of its pouch. I still remember the kangaroo's trainer—an old rummy who looked like he'd taken one too many return hits to the noggin from his boomerang—telling me there was nothing to worry about. ("Kid," he said, "this 'roo's doped up better than Judy Garland.")

Once inside the makeshift ring I followed the script. It went well and was kind of fun for a while. Skippy hopped on command, and I jabbed him a few times without reply. Kind of cute, actually. But then I got cocky. I fancied myself Muhammad Ali and started winding up, bolo-punch style, on the poor animal. I didn't really mean to do it, but I caught Skippy a pretty solid blow to the snout. I've always thought that if it had *just* been that, the kangaroo might have shook it off. But for some reason, Skippy was having trouble with the pouch confetti—was it allergic?—and started getting frustrated. When I caught the kangaroo on the nose, the bouncing suddenly stopped. Skippy went all quiet and looked me square in the eye. Then the creature rocked back on its tail, raised its feet, and kicked me halfway to San Pedro.

I can still remember the astonishing feeling of flight. And the searing pain from my cracked ribs.

As if that wasn't enough, the maddened kangaroo leapt out of the ring after me, braying like a wounded donkey. It landed right on top of me and started to pummel my body with its feet. The trainer tried to pull it off, but Skippy lashed him with his tail. Just when I was sure that the crazed syndie star was going to mash my face, the trainer's assistant nailed it with a trank dart. I don't know what kind of Jones the animal had, but I swear it went down with a big smile on its puss. It was only later that I learned that this wasn't even the *real* Skippy, who never left Australia. Apparently they used dozens of kangaroos for publicity. Hell, who beside their mothers can tell one of the miserable things from another?

So that's another reason to dislike Long Beach.

The bar that Don Grady had visited with Hall was on Seventeenth Street, toward the Carson end of things. Believe it or not, that's the even *less* handsome side of town. I wasn't fool enough to drive my Lexus down, but was none too thrilled to leave even my beat up old Subaru on those streets. This was one of those rare occasions when I wished I did have a cell phone, with 911 programmed into the speed dial. Also lacking a stun gun or a can of pepper spray, that old Burns's charm was suddenly feeling like a thin shield.

Still, in for a penny . . .

The bar—at least *a* bar—called Haw-Haw's stood where Grady said it should. In front there was a row of thirty or more gleaming bikes, mostly Harley's, in a perfect line down the length of the street. No one stood guard. But then, even in LA, you might not find anyone stupid enough to mess with them. The requisite headbanger music spilled out of the open front door, along with the smell of reefer and stale beer. The other businesses on the street were dark, even the three tattoo parlors. If you were seriously in need of permanent scarring at this hour, Haw-Haw's was obviously the place to go.

With a deep breath, a shake of my head, and a quick prayer to the administrators of Blue Cross, I walked inside.

My hope, I suppose fantasy might be a better word for it, was that I'd walk in and find Gabbo propping up the bar. Naturally, he was nowhere to be seen. I tried to take in the place without looking too much like a narc, studying faces for Gabbo's buddies. The trouble was everyone in the joint looked and dressed almost exactly the same. I always thought bikers fancied themselves rebels and nonconformists; this crowd, with their leathers, long hair, and tattoos, were as uniform in appearance and demeanor as a roomful of high school cheerleaders. Though not as perky. I walked slowly toward the bar, drawing a look or two, but none especially menacing. The crack of cue balls could be heard over the "music"—though it didn't meet my definition of the form, I'll be generous—but mercifully the thud of cue stick against skull wasn't as imminent as I'd feared.

I ordered a bourbon and a Bud from the bartender, which seemed about right. No one bothered me at the bar; no jostling or hassling or making fun of my manifestly declasse ensemble. The bartender was polite each time he refilled my drinks, even saying "thank you" as he made change. The noise level inside was gratingly high, and there was the odd bit of raucous behavior from time to time, but the general mood of the place was clearly live-and-let-live-and-have-a-swell-time.

After a couple of hours of losing brain cells to the juke box fury, not to mention the bourbon, and with no sign of my quarry, but a seemingly decent rapport happening with the bartender, I casually mentioned Gabbo's name.

I swear the "o" of Gabbo had barely passed my tongue when the barstool was kicked out from under me, and a very big and angry looking man in a leather vest had me pinned to the floor with his smelly boot on my throat.

"Who the fuck are you?" he growled. He pressed down on my windpipe such that I couldn't have answered if I wanted to.

A couple of other bruisers, big as Samoans, had materialized, forming a leather screen between me and the rest of Haw-Haw's. I glanced up toward the bartender, but couldn't see past the thick leg that held me down. The pressure on my throat eased up a notch.

"I'm trying to find Gabbo," I croaked.

Wrong answer.

"That's not what I asked you, cocksucker." The big man took his foot away, but he moved fast. Before I could even raise my head, he had dropped down to straddle me, pinning my shoulders to the floor with his knees. He had a knife in his hand, a wild look in his eyes, and—I very much suspected—a Judas Priest song in his heart. He pressed the tip of the blade against the corner of my eye. All I could see was sharp pain and a lifetime of books on tape. Possibly a *short* lifetime.

He began to press the knife. "Now, motherfucker . . ."

"I'm a friend of Huck's," I shouted. I don't know how I thought of it. The brain can be a smart cookie, God bless it.

"Huck?" the big man asked. He backed off with the knife.

"Yes. I was a friend. That's why I need to find Gabbo." The big man looked unsure. "He *knows* me," I added. I didn't mention that he knew me only to *threaten* me. One misstep at a time.

"Canny," the man said. I thought he was complimenting my perspicacity, but it must have been one of the Big-as-a-Samoans's names. The BaaS reached down and grabbed me by the collar.

"Take him in back," the lesser big man said.

The BaaS helped me along past the end of the bar and through a door marked "Privates." I don't know if it was a misspelling, a joke, or an indication of what they kept inside. The BaaS threw me onto a wooden chair, wagged a finger at me, bared his teeth, and walked back out. He locked the door behind him.

"Huh-boy," I said, and checked for damage. Amazingly, I hadn't wet myself. How could Fox even *consider* cancelling my show?

There wasn't a lot in the room with me. A stack of metal beer kegs; some busted-up furniture; a dozen cases of "Mary's Vodka" (was I ever glad I hadn't ordered a screwdriver); a half-naked woman . . .

Rewind.

Lying atop a pool table that had been stripped of its baize was a woman who had largely been stripped of her clothes. She wore only a leather halter top and a gold ankle bracelet. Rainbow snake tattoos coiled up both her legs. The woman was very still, either passed out or dead. I wasn't sure I really wanted to know which, but I got up and walked toward her. As I approached, I could see the rise and fall of her chest. I could also see that the snakes on her legs went all the way up, their forked tongues hissing at her shaved pussy. Just above her cunt was another tattoo: like a traffic sign, but with an arrow pointing to the crack between her thighs.

"Abandon hope all ye who enter here" the gothic lettering read.

Just then, with me studying her crotch, her eyes opened. She let out a little gasp, then licked her lips and dragged herself to a semi-sitting position. The pool table rocked on its unsteady legs. "Twenty bucks," she said.

"Huh?" I replied.

"To fuck. Twenty bucks. Ten for a blow job. Five for hand."

"What do I get for two-fifty?"

"A kick up the ass."

I read the sign on her abdomen again. Who, I wondered, in this great, wide, oh-so-weird world of ours—even in Long Beach, home of pissed-off kangaroos—would be so unwise as not to heed the words emblazoned there?

"No, thanks," I said and smiled.

"Okay," she shrugged.

And lay down and went back to sleep.

I scurried back to my chair.

Snake Lady snored. Loudly. I considered waking her, but decided better the devil you know. I tugged at the door a couple of times, but it was solid. Even if I could open it, there was no chance of sneaking out through the bar. There were no windows and only a tiny ventilation grate in the ceiling. There was nothing much to do, either. I found a copy of *Beaver Express* (usually, I prefer to take the local) tucked under a beer keg, but the pages were stuck together, which was something I would have rather not learned. I cracked open a bottle of Mary's, but this Madonna was no virgin. I don't care for straight vodka anyway.

I'd been sitting there, shaking my head at myself for over an hour when the door opened and Gabbo came strolling in. Pud, the bruiser with the bum rotator cuff, was with him. The extra-large gentlemen who'd escorted me into the back room were not in evidence.

"Sitcom Boy," Gabbo said. I'd stood up when the door opened, and Gabbo shoved me back down in the chair. He pulled up a chair of his own and dropped himself onto it with a little grunt. The chair complained rather more loudly. Pud went around to stand behind me. "You mentioned my name. Looking for a new face?"

"Actually, I've come with the estimates."

Gabbo shook his head.

"For the sliding door. I got three because I don't want you to think I'm trying to pull a fast one. One estimate's a little bit high, but I think it's worth paying for quality work, don't you? After all, your home is your most valuable asset."

Gabbo cocked his head to one side in a birdlike way and squinted at me. He looked up at Pud, then back at me. Then he broke out laughing.

"Okay, Sitcom Boy, so you really are a funny fellah. And you got chutzpah. You saved yourself a beating. For now. So why you looking for me?"

"I want some information about Hall. Huck."

Gabbo narrowed his eyes some more, but didn't speak.

"I'm trying to figure some things out," I continued.

"What kind of things?"

"I'm trying to make sense of Hall's life. And death."

"And what would that be to you?"

"I was his friend," I shrugged.

"Bullshit."

"What?"

"Huck never so much as mentioned your name."

"We only got to know each other some right before he died. I . . ."

"Pud," Gabbo said. He suddenly seemed to notice the girl asleep on the pool table. He pointed at her. "Get that out of here."

Pud went over and kicked the pool table. The girl didn't budge, so he poked her in the side. She raised her head, opened her eyes and yawned.

"Egg it," Pud told her.

The girl got up, moving slowly. She threw her tattooed legs over the side of the table, then went down on her back again.

"Pud!" Gabbo ordered.

The big man grabbed the girl's hair and yanked her off the table. Her legs went out from under her, but Pud held her aloft by the hair. "Oh, oh, oh," she moaned, as Pud dragged her to the door and threw her out, still naked from the halter top down. I heard laughter and applause through the briefly open door; saw the girl do a little curtsy and then scamper off before Pud slammed the door shut again.

"Charming," I said.

"Skank city," Gabbo complained. "You didn't let her blow you, did you? You can't imagine where that mouth has been."

"I thought about it, but she couldn't make change for a quarter."

Pud laughed uproariously. Gabbo studied me a little harder.

"I don't often say this," Gabbo told me, "but I honest to God don't know what to make of you."

"I'm a tortilla wrapped in an enchilada."

"You are one of the strangest damn fellas I ever met. And I know a few."

"Stranger than Hall?"

"*Why* are you asking about Huck?" Gabbo asked, with what I took to be sincere puzzlement.

We started a staring contest, but Gabbo was the Mark McGwire of the blank look. I turned away. "You think I'm some kind of threat?" I asked.

"Wasn't sure at first. I couldn't figure out what you were after."

"And now?"

"Only threat you pose is to cultural standards."

"Hey!"

"I looked at your program. You ain't no Jim Rockford, Sitcom Boy."

"Who is?" I muttered.

Gabbo shrugged.

"I'm just trying to figure some stuff out," I confessed. "I . . . you're right: Hall wasn't my best friend. He was barely my friend at all. But he asked me to do something for him, to find something important to him, and then he died before I could do it. I think I was maybe the last person he ever talked to on this earth and knowing that, and knowing what he did—likely did—I feel like I'm still carrying some obligation to him."

"What do you mean *likely* did?"

"I'm not entirely sure that Hall killed himself."

"Fuck," Pud said.

Gabbo silenced him with a look. "Why do you say that?" he asked me.

"I can't give you anything solid. Hell, I barely have a liquid. And I'm going through a lot of gas."

"I already told you you're a funny guy. You can stop now."

"Sorry. The thing is, Hall just didn't seem like the kind of guy to kill himself, you know? Everybody I talk to says the same thing about him. All his friends have trouble with the idea, 'cause it doesn't seem to fit with his personality, his way of thinking and doing."

"That it?"

"No. He was involved in a bit of a mess. He got hung out to dry by a producer on a movie deal. I think Hall's death came at a very convenient time for this producer. In more ways than one."

"Kevin Ryan Paul."

"Yeah, that's him. He was dicking Hall around. Did Hall tell you about this?"

Gabbo ignored my question. "Paul say anything to you about Huck?"

"No, not really. But it turns out Paul has a funny connection to Hall's past. It's an awfully long story."

"You got no place to go. Not so as to *walk* to, least."

So I told him. About the favor that Hall had asked of me. All about George Gaines and Connie Clare and Mac Stans. I told him the things that Hall had told me about *The Devil on Sunday,* holding back only the details of the deal between his father and Mac Stans. But I told Gabbo about Bill Caldwell's theory as to who killed Connie Clare, and about Kevin Ryan Paul and Mac Stans and the high profile of the new version of *The Devil on Sunday.* I told him until there was nothing left to say.

Gabbo took it all in without saying a word. When I was done he got up and walked over to the wall. He leaned forward, closed his eyes, and rested his head against the filthy bricks. Then he started banging his forehead against them. Harder and harder. I saw a trail of blood crawl down the side of his face, but still he went on banging, like some crazed Hasidic Jew at the Wailing Wall.

All at once he stopped.

"Tidgy Pud," he said, and flicked his head toward the door. A drop of blood flew off, adding another bodily fluid to the pages of *Beaver Express.* The big man slipped out into the bar, and Gabbo fell back into the chair across from me.

"Oh, Huck," he moaned.

I always have tissues in my back pocket—allergies, don't you know—so I pulled one out and offered it to Gabbo. He looked at me like I was nuts, and I thought he thought I was offering it him to blow his nose. Like he was crying or something. I pointed at the cut on his forehead. He took the tissue and dabbed at the blood.

"Something I said?" I asked.

Gabbo shook his head, almost laughed. "You been working this ain't you?"

"Yeah. I mean, what the hell, there's nothing good on TV."

"Hall never did so much as mention your name to me."

"I'm not surprised."

"Maybe he should have. Seems to me you're maybe a good friend to have."

"I've been told I have an overly developed sense of responsibility."

"Not many do. Not many left who care about such things."

"I don't know if there ever were," I said.

"Maybe. Let me ask you something: Is this the reason you went to see Mel? To find out about this stuff?"

"Mel?" Then the penny dropped. "Melly Dougherty. Yes. I thought maybe she could fill in some of the blank spots in Hall's life for me. She wasn't too helpful, though."

"She's cautious. Rightly so."

"She just made me more curious. I've been feeling like I still owe Hall something, though I can't say why. Call it . . . I don't know, a *death* debt. Or just that overly developed sense of responsibility. Whatever, I spoke to all the friends of his that I know, but they're all Hollywood people, industry friends and acquaintances. I wanted to talk to someone who maybe knew about the rest of his life."

"So you come looking for me."

"Dougherty told you about my seeing her, didn't she? That's why you busted up my door."

"Yeah. I'll get it fixed, too."

"That doesn't matter."

"It's my *responsibility*."

"Whatever."

"I'm Hollywood people," Gabbo said.

"Sorry?"

"Where you think I know Huck from?"

"I don't . . . Oh, God," I wheezed, "don't tell me you have a screenplay."

Gabbo laughed at that. "Not anymore. I have had a few produced, though. Directed some myself."

I shook my head in utter bewilderment. Gabbo held out his hand to shake. As I took it, still puzzled, he said, "Danny's my real name. Daniel. Daniel Gabowitz."

"Oh. My. God."

"Yeah," he said.

"The Final Flicker."

Gabbo took a small bow.

If LA were any smaller a town, you'd be able to stuff the whole damn thing—Hollywood sign and all—inside the belly-button of an angel dancing on the head of a pin. And still have room for fluff.

"I almost worked for you," I said. I took a slug out of one of the bottles of beer that Gabbo had Tidgy Pud bring in for us.

"Yeah?"

"I remember when *The Final Flicker* was *the* hot property. After you hit it with *Wild Star* and before you started shooting, of course. My agent was desperate to get me the part of Kid Cinema."

"Please, it hurts in my belly just to hear you speak the names," Gabbo said.

"But you refused to work with any professional actors—really, I would have fit the bill. No sets, no props, all location shoots. No script, as I recall. Amazing that you got a studio to stump up for the thing."

"Viva la revolution. Them were the days."

"I was always able to take a certain comfort from knowing that nothing I ever did got reviews as bad as *The Final Flicker*. And I worked with Forrest Tucker on three different shows."

"My artistic career wasn't in vain then."

My mouth opened. I was just about to ask Gabbo what had happened. What had gone wrong? How did he get from the Hollywood Hills to the back room in Haw-Haw's?

I caught myself.

Because it's the question they used to ask *me* all the time. The lawyers and claims adjustors and bail bondsmen whose nickel and dime scutwork I took on in order to eat and maintain a roof over my head. The scumbags who loved it because they had a fallen star in their grasp, a *former* celebrity at their beck and call, and who never quite managed to suppress the superior smiles as they asked: How did you end up here? What's it like to have climbed the mountain and seen the promised land, only to come down in Barstow?

What went wrong?

"So how'd you meet Hall?" I asked.

Gabbo narrowed his eyes at me again, studied me long and hard. He'd been waiting for the scumbag's question, expecting me to ask it. I could see it on his face. He was looking at my mouth and I just knew he was watching for the slightest tremor of a superior smile in formation. I know, too, that he didn't find it.

He nodded, and something elemental passed between us. Gabbo wasn't some biker thug threatening to rearrange my features in a seedy bar. I wasn't a star, reascendant, lording my good fortune over him.

We both relaxed.

"Aw, me and Huck both moved in the same wild man circles. We shared a vision of what living the good life ought to be. And we did it."

"You had a certain reputation for chemical adventuring as I recall." Gabbo nodded. "You?"

"I went for the booze. I don't know if I was too stupid for drugs or they were too stupid for me."

"Smart boy. Me, I can't remember anything that happened between 1971 and 1976."

"At least you came around for the bicentennial."

"*November* 'seventy-six."

"Oh. Well. It wasn't that great. Lots of tall ships and such. Nice fireworks."

"Huck and me fancied ourselves the Lewis and Clark of the pharmaceutical wilderness. We had a manifest destiny to conquer it all. It's what led me into my current line of work."

"Can I ask you something? Why Huck? What's the name mean?"

Gabbo snorted a laugh. "Hall was Huck and I was Tom. Finn and Sawyer, right? Mel dubbed us. Got to be a joke between us ever since."

"I don't see it myself."

"Had to be there, maybe. I had a clean-cut look about me at the time. For the money-men, don't you know."

"And Hall?"

"Hall. Huck was a man on the run. I think that's why Mel gave him the name."

"What was he running from?" I asked.

"What do you got? Huck was never happy. We both of us had our periods of success in town—the money, the drugs, the poontang—but I don't believe Huck ever really enjoyed it. I don't think he ever got past being born."

"That's a hell of a thing to say about a man."

"I know, and it hurts me to say it. When I tell you Huck was my brother I mean it. I got no blood kin to speak of, though knowing the story of Huck's life maybe that ain't such a bad thing."

"You mean his mother's murder."

"Sure. Hall felt tortured by that all his life. He was always looking for a woman to replace her, but there's a fool's quest pure and simple. Mel tried to play the role, but it's what drove 'em apart in the end. You can play mother or you can play whore, but you can't play both.

Even a diehard movie maverick like me knows that much about narrative motivation."

"Do you know if Hall ever tried to find out about Connie Clare's murder?"

"I know he looked into it some. Fact that he had you searching for that damn film shows it never really left his mind in all the years. I don't know if he ever spoke to your cop friend. Probably not. If he'd known what the cop suspected he would have killed George Gaines cold, instead of just talking about it. He couldn't stand the bastard."

"Hall wanted to kill Gaines?"

"Used to go on about it all the time. I am going back some now. Gaines took his deep-six holiday a lot of years ago, but Huck didn't do him. Heart attack, if I remember right. Though Huck said he didn't believe the bastard had a heart or if he did, why it wouldn't have attacked him years before."

"Do you know why Hall hated Gaines so much?"

Gabbo shifted in his chair. "Huck blamed Gaines for his mom's death, though not the way you mean it. I think Huck knew that Gaines had a thing with Connie Clare. He knew his mom was kind of a slut, but it was easier to blame Gaines for her ways than his mom. It'd always been assumed that's what got her killed after all—sleeping around till she got tangled up with some crazy man. Though, Huck also talked about how Gaines fucked his father over."

"In what way?"

"Standard industry practice. Gaines was a producer, Frank was a writer. Ain't no business like show business after all. Big fish eat little fish, ad infinitum."

"Did Hall talk a lot about his father?"

"They didn't get along too good. Huck hardly ever saw the old man. I think he resented Frank for allowing his mother to slut off and die. Stupid, sure, but there's shit you just never get over, never forgive. I knew Frank, always thought he wasn't a half-bad guy. Troubled, but well-meaning. Or is that a horrible thing to say?"

"You just described ninety-five percent of the American public."

"No I didn't. Most people aren't well-meaning at all. Just like to believe they are."

"The cop I talked to, Caldwell—he told me that Frank Emerson was gay."

Gabbo didn't look surprised. He nodded. "Frank wasn't the most manly man in the world. I guessed he swung both ways at least, not that it was any of my business. Though as far as I know he spent most of his time alone. Never heard mention of a partner of either persuasion."

"Did Hall know?"

"Hell, yeah. It's another thing he resented Frank for. Huck figured Frank being a little light in the loafers was what sent his mother looking for the apple in the baby's fist someplace else."

"Did Hall ever talk about the possibility that Frank Emerson wasn't his father?"

"Not in so many words. Not even to me."

"But you think he suspected."

Gabbo nodded. "You'd have to think it, wouldn't you? Let's face it: Connie Clare was a sperm bank in ankle-strap wedgies."

"Criminy, there's an image," I said.

"I once asked Huck if he thought maybe George Gaines was his dad."

"What did he say?"

Gabbo leaned forward, pulling the hair away from above his right ear. An ancient, but deep scar ran two inches up the side of his head.

"That's an answer," I said.

"We was pretty far gone on mescaline at the time. Even so, I didn't ask him twice. My head's only so thick."

I stood up and paced around the little room. I found the spot where Gabbo had been banging his head into the wall. I stared at the bloodstain.

"I'm going to tell you something I haven't mentioned to anyone else, not even the cops. You busted up my place, virtually held me hostage here tonight, and I assume you're a drug dealer and a reprobate of no small proportion. But in a weird way, I feel like I can trust you."

I turned around to look at Gabbo. He offered no reaction.

"It's something Hall told me right before he died. He said he'd never told anyone about it, and asked me to keep it in confidence. But I think it may be important. Hall told me that Frank Emerson did not write *The Devil on Sunday*. He was a front for MacArthur Stans."

Gabbo blinked once, then looked away.

"Did you know that?" I asked.

"No," Gabbo said, very softly.

"Hall never told you?"

Gabbo shook his head. He looked hurt.

"What do you make of it?"

Gabbo didn't say anything.

"Did Hall ever talk about Mac Stans?"

"He had some business with him, I know that."

"What kind of business?"

"I don't know. Huck went a little funny when the subject came up."

Gabbo stood up, raised a finger to indicate for me to wait, and walked back out to the bar. I spotted a cue ball on the floor, and kicked it back across the room, under the pool table. Gabbo came back in carrying a Jiffy Bag. He tossed it onto the table in front of me.

"Yours," he said.

I opened it up. Inside were the copies of the two *Devil on Sunday* scripts that I had pilfered from Hall's library, and which had, in turn, been so expertly stolen from my car.

"*You* took these?" I said.

"My boys."

"You were following me."

Gabbo nodded. "Picked you up after Mel called about your visit. I was worried your interest in Huck might have something to do with our, ah, chemical business. That's why we braced you at your place, too."

"Shit. Why'd you take these?"

" 'Cause you took them from Huck's place. Wanted 'em back. When I saw what it was, I couldn't figure why you lifted them. But it's 'cause of Stans, ain't it?"

"And Paul. I've been trying to figure out who's zooming who in this mess. Or is it whom? I can't tell the liars without a scorecard. Hollywood, don't you know. I wanted to compare the scripts to see if it might grant a little insight."

"You take 'em," Gabbo said. "You're doing all right. Maybe you should keep on at it, see what else turns up."

"Damn, that practically makes you a client. Just like old times. Of course, there's no money in it. Hell, it's *exactly* like old times."

"I'll pay you," Gabbo said.

"No! I don't need or want your money. I just want to know what's going on. What's *been* going on."

"You need any help, you let me know. I got some unusual connections around town." Gabbo scrawled a phone number on the back of the Jiffy Bag.

"No E-mail address?" I asked.

Naturally, he scribbled that down below it. "But someone *always* answers that phone," he said.

Something occurred to me: "How'd you break into my car so neatly? The alarm was still on when I got back to it."

"Slice of Entemann's. About as tough as getting into Lissa Torres." I think I might have blushed. Gabbo offered me a wry smile. "I hear she gives great head, but her pussy's loose enough to stash a pair of bowling balls."

"I couldn't possibly comment. You're not going to keep on tailing me, are you?"

"No reason for it. Just keep in touch."

I nodded and picked up the scripts, but wasn't quite ready to go.

"You ever think of getting back into The Business? Out of the one you're in now?"

"Never. It would be too big a step *backward* in personal integrity."

I snorted my understanding. I locked eyes with Gabbo and asked the question that I'd been wanting to ask, needing to know his answer to before I could leave.

"Do you think that Hall . . . Huck killed himself?"

Gabbo didn't blink—it wasn't in his character—but I do believe it was something other than early morning dew I saw in his eyes.

"Yes," he whispered. "Yes, I do."

We shook hands. In the bar the Snake Lady was on top of another pool table, though this one was covered with red felt. I suspect she welcomed the padding because she was busy indeed, earning her keep twenty bucks at a time.

The very, very hard way.

Twelve

The next morning I tried to call Mac Stans first thing. I wanted to try to pry more out of him about George Gaines and the murder of Connie Clare, maybe even confront him with some of the things the old detective had told me. I wasn't sure what good it would do, or that Stans wouldn't just laugh in my face, but I continued to feel a nagging sense of incompleteness about everything I'd been looking into. And the stirrings of the kind of festering, unearned moral outrage that has gotten me into serious trouble in the past.

The phone rang and rang, but no one picked up, not Stans, not Honey, not even an answering machine. I thought about getting into the car and driving down to Laguna again, but it was an awfully long way to go on the off-chance that Stans *might* be at home. Better to call again later and cordially try to arrange a face-to-face so I could look the dirty old bastard in the eye.

The copies of the two *Devil on Sunday* scripts sat on the kitchen table where I'd tossed them upon getting home. I hadn't had the energy to look at them when I'd got in, and though I ran my hand over the leather binding of the old Mac Stans version, I found I still didn't have the stomach to sit down and read through them. I don't know why I was avoiding the task, but the scripts felt as welcome as incomplete tax returns on April fourteenth. I knew I had to be in the right frame of mind to face up to tackling them, and I was too antsy for it this morning. In any case, I'd been struck by inspiration earlier, while sitting on the crapper—I've been told that my bathroom benefits from excellent feng shui, by the way. I've also been told the correct way to pronounce feng shui; so I've got all that going for me—and wanted to follow through on the porcelain epiphany. I spent ten minutes scampering around for my address book, and then dialed Olivia Sullivan's number. I asked her if she wanted to get together for lunch and she happily accepted. I arranged to meet her at a little patisserie in Santa Monica with an ocean view and a decent cup of coffee.

Olivia is eighty years old (at least, that's what she admits to), but doesn't look a day over seventy-nine. The great thing about her is that you can say stuff like that to her face and get a laugh and a playful punch in the arm. Though it might leave a bruise afterward. Olivia has been in The Business for over sixty of her eighty-whatever years, almost all of them as an extra. By her own count she's appeared in a couple of hundred movies and more than twice as many television shows. We met under slightly (actually *extremely*) peculiar circumstances when she was cast in a bit part as a bag lady on an episode of *Burning Bright.* Improbably, we got to be friends. I insisted that she be written in as a semiregular on the show, and she became Hermione, my wizened, all-knowing contact-on-the-streets. She was still a bag lady and meant to be English (for reasons known only to the story editors), but Olivia does such a bad English accent that they had to drop that bit. The "Hermione" stuck, though. It may not be the best part in the world—though it could be the most-clichéd—but by her own admission, it's the solidest, best-paid work Olivia's had since Roosevelt was president. And I'm told that Olivia's become something of a gay icon, though these are things I don't understand. I still don't get what they saw in Bette Midler. Olivia herself has told me that there are several dozen Web sites about her. When I asked her how many are devoted to me, she changed the subject. This is yet another reason why I dislike computers.

In her largely invisible, extra's way Olivia has worked with or around just about every big and small name in Hollywood since the coming of sound. She danced for Busby Berkeley, swam with Esther Williams, skated with Sonja Henie, cowered from Vincent Price, and took a custard pie in the face from Sammy Petrillo. She saw James Dean do naughty things with Sal Mineo near Griffith Observatory, and John Ford bawl like a baby at a screening of *The Yearling* at Grumman's Chinese. In a drunken moment, Olivia even claimed to know the truth about Garbo, but she passed out before I could get the scoop. Sober, she denies any such knowledge. Though she will tell you an upsetting story about Montgomery Clift's penis if you know which brand of Belgian chocolate she loves.

They say that life imitates art, so if Hermione can point the way for Marty Burns (PI) to reach the end of every episode, who better than old Olivia to help Marty Burns (DNR) to wind my way through the dark fens of Hollywood history?

"You think *Burning Bright* is art?" Olivia asked me when I explained this rationale to her.

I blushed slightly and poked at my croque monsieur, which only a patisserie in Santa Monica could get away with calling a ham and cheese sandwich. I think they charge an extra buck for the French.

"Art is in the eye of the beholder," I said.

"*Who* told you they think *Burning Bright* is art?"

"It's just an expression, Olivia. Forget it."

"Don't get me wrong, Marty, you know I love you dearly and I'm very grateful to be a part of the show, and I'm as concerned as anyone about whether the network picks us up. But art? Paul Cezanne is art. Pablo Picasso is art. Even that strange British man who puts dead cows in glass cases might be art. But *Burning Bright* is . . ."

"More coffee?" a passing waiter asked.

I had to refrain from standing up and kissing him on the lips. "George Gaines," I reminded her when the waiter had gone and before she could pick up her train of thought and set it back on its nasty rails. "Did you know him?"

Olivia leaned back and rubbed the palm of her hand in a circle over her cheek. "Unfortunately," she said, and looked the other way.

"Why unfortunately? What can you tell me about him?"

"George Gaines, everybody loses."

"Sorry?"

"That's what they used to say about him. Bad things always seemed to happen on a George Gaines set, but Gaines himself merrily rolled along from movie to movie. George Gaines, everybody loses. It was always said with a laugh, but there was nothing funny about that man. George Gaines was a rancid little monster, and the only thing that surprised me when he died was that it wasn't a homicide. Disappointed me, too."

"Can you be more specific? How was he a monster?"

"Well, he was a producer of course . . ."

"And the sky is blue."

"Yes. But Gaines was especially unpleasant. Mean, I'd say."

"Hollywood mean?"

"Yes, of course. He was always trying to stiff the extras. And how much money did that ever save? But Gaines wasn't just mean on the set, he was *life* mean."

"I'm not sure I follow you here."

"Movies are a funny business. And yes, I know: The sky is *very* blue. But it's funny because the make believe quality extends past the act of moviemaking. Everyone plays a part when they get on the set. Not just the actors, but everyone from the director to the fat grip with the hairy ass crack. There's just something about it: *show business,* you know?"

"I suppose."

"It's even worse in the theater, though I've only spent a handful of days there relatively speaking. All that lovey-dove phoney baloney. Feh! But when you're working on a movie or a TV show, you're so busy creating a new little world that even when the lights are off and there's no film rolling, it's hard to ever shake your part. Some of it sticks to you when you leave the set—that's why show people have such a hard time dealing with civilian life. But if you don't remember that you *have* to turn it off, slip back into the real world when you walk through your front door and open your mail, well that's when you get into real trouble. The *big* stars suffer the worst from it, but they're mostly rich enough to get away with it. They can buy extensions of fantasy in the real world. After all, that's the big payoff of fame, isn't it? The rest of us just have to cope."

"And George Gaines?"

"Gaines didn't understand that there were two worlds. Because he was lord high muckety-muck on the set and around the lot, he believed the same had to be true off as well."

"Sounds like the usual tinseltown power tripping to me."

"Maybe it does. But I've worked for lots of producers and directors who were mean as snakes while film rolled and the meter was running, but reverted to human form when the lights went off. George Gaines, though: He'd bark orders at you walking down the street as if every step you took was still costing him money, and he had the right to tell you where to put your feet. There was something missing in the man. A sense of . . . I don't know: empathy. Simple humanity and decency. Maybe he spent too many years spinning fantasies and it took over his life. But I think there was something worse in him. Something dark and evil."

"So let me get this straight, Olivia: You didn't care for George Gaines."

I said it with a wry smile, intending a little levity because Olivia had gotten herself so worked up. A mood-breaker.

Olivia crossed her arms, clutched her elbows. Her face puckered up like she'd just been force-fed a bowl of lemons. She suddenly looked rather more than eighty years old.

"George Gaines tried to rape me," Olivia said.

Smilin' Marty Burns. Now you know why the sobriquet never took.

"Flbbbpth," I think I said. Or maybe it was "Qllrrmm." I know it was all consonants. If Vanna White had been there buck naked with fifty large tucked between her silky thighs, I still couldn't have bought a vowel.

"Nineteen forty-six," Olivia said. She stared into her Caesar salad, poking at the dry chicken bits and soggy croutons as if raking through the mists of time. I wanted to tell her to stop, but I still couldn't do a vowel movement.

"*Kiss the Night* was the movie. Richard Conte and Robert Ryan. No speaking part, of course, but great exposure. A nice little picture, too. Very moody. There was a long scene in a downtown diner. I was the extra in the booth behind the leads. The scene ended with some gunplay and there was a complicated tracking shot. The director couldn't get it right and Gaines was going crazy. Three days I got out of it. Good for me, huh?

"On the last day Gaines insisted they lose the fancy shot. He got into a big fight with the director, fired him in front of everybody. Humiliated him, naturally. They had to close down for the day, which made Gaines really crazy. I was happy because I thought I might get another couple of days work out of it. They'd have to reshoot the scene, after all. I deliberately hung around; a little face time, you know, maybe get called back, but the set emptied fast. The others knew. I was back in wardrobe when Gaines stormed in. I wasn't half-dressed or anything. I wasn't playing any games with him, flirting or anything. It was never my style, not in all those years. It was just . . . face time."

"I believe you," I whispered.

"Gaines saw me and stopped. His hair was all on end. He had curly hair anyway, but it was standing out as if he'd been pulling it. Literally pulling at his hair. Like Larry Fine in the Three Stooges. I worked with them, you know. That Shemp was a dog, though I would have married Larry if he'd asked. Anyway, Gaines didn't look soft or harmless like Larry. Not harmless at all. I saw that right away.

"He looked at me and he only said one word: 'Extra,' he said. I nodded and he nodded back. Then he walked over and slapped me so hard across the face that I fell over into a rack of clothes."

"Jesus."

"Before I even realized what happened, he was on me. He ripped my skirt off and got on top of me. He . . . he started to . . . he was a . . . backdoor man, if you know what I mean."

"Yes."

"I felt the tip of his . . . against my . . ."

"Olivia," I said.

"He didn't get to do it, though. He didn't get it inside me. You know why?"

I shook my head.

"Someone came in. The first AD. A little fellow, had one leg shorter than the other. I can still remember the funny way he walked, can you imagine? The little thud-thunka sound his shoes made. He came in and saw and he said that the head of studio was on the phone. The little man saw me lying there in a tangle of clothes, crying and screaming, with George Gaines climbing on my back, his little thing poking out of his pants. Gaines got up, tucked himself away, and walked out the door, just like that. That little AD just stood there and looked at me. I had to cover my . . . down belows with a fedora I found on the floor. Only then did he go after his master. Thud-thunka. Thud-thunka."

"I'm sorry, Olivia. I'm so sorry. If I had known . . ."

"How could you know?" she asked. And managed a wry smile of her own. She pushed away the remnants of her salad. "How could anyone know?"

I felt awful for having made her dredge up the awful memory of George Gaines. She must have seen it, because she reached across the table and took my hand.

"It's all right, Marty. It was a very long time ago, and it taught me a valuable life lesson. I learned only I could look after me. No one else would. But you know what?"

I shook my head.

"To this day, I don't know which of the two of them was the worst: Gaines because he tried to rape me, or the little man with the funny walk for the way he looked at me after. And even after all these years I don't know what lesson to take from that."

"Hollywood sucks?" I suggested.

"Maybe," Olivia said. She found a morsel of chicken and popped it in her mouth. "Still, it's the only one we've got."

Something Olivia said clicked with me, but not until after I'd left her nursing a fifth cup of coffee at the patisserie. It was her remark about bad things happening on the sets of George Gaines's pictures. I assumed she was thinking of the Connie Clare murder, but when I mentioned Clare to Olivia, she shook her head and said she couldn't even put a face to the name and was certain she'd never met her. She knew who Mac Stans was, of course, but then who didn't? I thought it interesting that unlike most, Olivia wasn't bowled over by Stans. I told her about the less-than-sensational impression he'd made on me and she nodded agreement.

"I never knew him, of course," she said. "I hardly moved in the same circles he did. I was Pluto to his Mercury at best."

"Huh?"

"You know, like closest to the heat of the sun?"

I shrugged.

"The planets, Marty. You are familiar with the solar system?"

"Oh, right. Of course."

"I sometimes forget that you were taught by studio tutors."

"I wish *I* could. But then, at least I learned how to deal three-card monte at an early age. The teacher told me it was a far more reliable skill than anything taught at the Actor's Studio."

"Too true," Olivia said.

"So what was it you didn't like about Stans?" I asked.

"It's not that I didn't like him; as I say, I didn't know him. But I knew girls who knew him. And they didn't say such nice things about him."

After dredging up the memory of her encounter with George Gaines, I was afraid to delve further. Olivia seemed to sense it and patted my hand.

"It's okay, Marty. There's no personal trauma involved. I just remember stories about Stans being . . . self-absorbed. He liked mirrors. He liked to watch himself in the act, if you know what I mean. Or so I was told."

"Harmless, if tacky."

"Mmmm. He liked to humiliate women, too. Make them . . . do things."

"Things?"

"Use your imagination."

The strain must have shown on my face, because Olivia rolled her eyes and let out a sigh.

"He liked to pee on them," she whispered. "And stuff."

I didn't pursue the "and stuff." But I got the idea. And frankly it only confirmed the icky impression I got of Stans from our meeting. The great man didn't just have feet of clay, he was pretty damn loamy from the neck on down. No wonder he and George Gaines got along so well. I thought that the old detective, Caldwell, may just have known what he was talking about when he had the two of them down as his prime suspects in the Connie Clare murder.

I wanted to find out more about George Gaines's various productions. I thought about stopping off at the Santa Monica library, then had a better idea. I hopped onto the freeway and scooted across town, back to Hollywood. It would be proper and fitting to be able to say that all roads lead to Hollywood in LA, but that would be only a metaphorical truth. In fact, Hollywood's a pain in the ass to get to from the west side, which is where most of your upscale white population lives. What with the usual bottleneck around La Cienega and some street repairs where I made the ill-advised decision to cut north on Highland, it took me near an hour before pulling up to Blanc's Noir. Dame Fate was smiling on me, though, because I nabbed a parking spot right out front with time on the meter and everything. Only thirty minutes, but if worse came to worst, it would prove a convenient excuse to get out of the store.

Harry Blanc was sitting on his stool by the register surrounded, if possible, by even larger stacks of files and envelopes than last time. An old guy in a loud Hawaiian shirt and too-long/too-short shorts (they were long enough to look silly, but short enough that you had to see his veiny legs) leaned on the counter and watched Harry sort through a pile of lobby cards. He looked like a regular, but the kind who doesn't spend any money. Harry's face lit up when he saw me and he came running out, arms spread wide, booming, "Marty! Marty Burns!"

I was afraid he was going to hug me, but he merely shook my hand with vigor. The old guy scowled a bit. I got the feeling my appearance ruined his day.

"Hi, Harry. How's business?"

"I'm still buying lottery tickets."

"Beats show biz."

"You're a card, Marty, you know that? Say, I'd like you to meet someone." He steered me over to the old guy, who was looking less happy by the second. "Marty Burns, this is Dicky Dolan."

"A pleasure," I said, and shook the old man's already shaky hand.

"D'ya do," Dolan said.

"You know who Dicky is?" Harry asked.

Oh, Christ, I thought, *why didn't I just go to the library?*

"I'm afraid I don't."

"Dicky?"

"Aw, don't bother the man, Harry. Nobody cares."

I studied the old bird, but he didn't look at all familiar. He had a surprisingly sweet, high-pitched voice, though.

"You ever see *To Have and Have Not?*" Harry asked.

"Yeah, sure," I said. " 'You know how to whistle, don't you, Steve? You just put your lips together and *blow.*' "

"Right! Well, you remember the scene where Lauren Bacall sings in the hotel bar with Hoagy Carmichael?"

"Eh, more or less."

"Dicky did the vocals."

I glanced at the old guy again. He briefly caught my eye then looked down. His face showed the oddest admixture of embarrassment and pride I'd ever seen. What a claim to fame!

"Wait a minute," I said. "I thought that was Andy Williams."

"He recorded it, too," Dolan said, "but they didn't use his track. Always claimed it was Bacall's real voice afterward. It was me, though."

"Wow," I said. I had no idea whether to believe him or not. It was, admittedly, a bizarre claim to make if it wasn't true, but then I remembered I was on Hollywood Boulevard and nothing is too odd for the locale.

"Is that something?" Harry asked.

"That is something."

Harry nodded, still smiling. I shook my head in feigned wonderment. The old guy just studied the dirty floor.

"Can I maybe have a brief word with you, Harry?" I asked, to move things along.

"Sure, sure. Delighted."

Dolan took the hint and got up. "I'll see you tomorrow, Harry."

"Righty sure, Double D." Harry said.

"Nice to meet you," I called. The old guy gave me a little half-wave as he limped out. He started softly singing "These Foolish Things" as he went and I swear it sounded like angel-song. I knew, too, that the tune would swirl around my head for days to come. Could be worse.

"What's up, Marty?"

"I'm looking for some information about George G. Gaines."

"Still chasing after *The Devil*? You find that missing scene?"

"No, I don't think it exists. But I've expanded the hunt a little. I'm curious about other of Gaines's movies. Someone told me he had a reputation for bad luck on the sets of his movies. Bad things happening."

"Yeah, Gaines got known as a trouble magnet. The Clare death was probably the most notorious, but there were mishaps on a few of Gaines's pictures."

"Mishaps?"

"As I recall, couple of stunt men died in a plane wreck on a war picture he made. Let's see, *Thirty Minutes over Broadway,* I think it was. Then there was the fire on the set of *Summertime Sizzlers.* Took out a whole section of the old Republic lot. Don't even know if you can find a copy of the picture these days. I seem to remember there being one or two other things, but it's gone off the top of my head."

A too-familiar, queasy sensation did the cha-cha through my gut. Little bells started to ring in the back of my head.

"Could you find out more for me?" I asked. "I mean, I'd pay you, of course."

"What is it you want to know exactly?"

"Whatever you can find out. Any George Gaines movie that ran into some unusual problem. Especially if he got any publicity out of it. Get me whatever you can on the movies and people involved. Press books, photos, any newspaper or scandal sheet coverage if you've got it. Can you do that?"

"Yeah, sure."

I was worried he would ask what I wanted it for, but it occurred to me that running this shop and hanging out with the likes of Dicky Dolan, Harry Blanc wasn't the kind of guy who would find any request too unusual.

"How soon can you put it together?"

"End of the day? Maybe tomorrow morning."

"That's perfect. Can you send it all over to me?"

"That's what you want. Write down your address, I'll messenger it over."

I started to write down my home address and then thought better of it. I didn't think it was such a good idea to let the likes of Harry Blanc know where I lived. I could just imagine Harry and Dicky turning up one evening for pinochle. I put down Kendall's office details and asked him to send the items there.

"Might cost a bit," Harry warned me. "Gaines pictures aren't that collectable, but some of this stuff is still rare."

"Can you keep it all under a thousand?"

"Oh, yeah," he said. And the look in his eyes told me that my credit card was likely to get debited precisely $999.99. Screw it.

"And if you could maybe write down any other stories you might remember about Gaines or his movies that come to mind, that would be a help, too. Rumors, legends, gossip, whatever."

"No extra charge."

Uh-huh, I thought. "Thanks, Harry," I said.

As I got back in the car, a brand new bullet train of thought speeding through the mountain passes in my head, I nonetheless found myself humming "These Foolish Things."

Or maybe not so foolish, after all.

I tried again to call Mac Stans when I got home and got a busy signal. I dialed it an hour and a beer later, but it just rang this time. I still wanted to confront him again, though I decided it could maybe wait a couple of days until I got the information I was hoping to find from Harry Blanc. Kendall called me to say that Kevin Ryan Paul was very antsy to have me sign the contracts for *Devil on Sunday*. I told her to keep the stall on and also to expect a delivery from Blanc's Noir.

"What did you buy from Harry Blanc?"

"You *know* Harry?" I asked.

"I know everybody, Marty, that's my job. And Harry Blanc is a real gonif."

"Gonif? This is an official warning, Kendall: Your certified shiksa status is now in serious danger of being revoked."

"When in Hollywood . . ." was all she said, and hung up.

I goofed around the house for a while, pretending to tidy, turning the TV on and off, sorted through the mail. All the little things you do when there are big things that you don't want to do. Trouble is, every time I looked up it seemed like I was in eyeshot of the two movie scripts that Gabbo had returned to me. I don't know why I was afraid of them—I'd taken them, after all, because I *wanted* to read them—but I had a feeling of foreboding about picking them up. It wasn't so much the old Mac Stans script as Hall's rewrite. I was curious as hell about it, yes, but also fearful. Of what, I couldn't clearly say. Perhaps, simply, that it wouldn't be any good; that Kevin Ryan Paul was exactly right and that a drunken old writer had merely pissed a few bitter words out on the page to make a quick buck. I didn't want the script to be worthless. I didn't want Hall's last effort to be crap, to be hackwork. To disappoint. I had no good reason to feel as I did. As everyone kept reminding me, Hall was never that much of a friend. But bizarrely, I felt closer to him now than ever I did when he was alive. If on the night of that last poker game someone told me that Hall had hacked out a crappy screenplay, I'd have shrugged my shoulders and said: "Really? Did the sun rise in the east this morning?" But if I discovered now that his work was garbage I knew I would feel deeply depressed. Let down. Hurt, even.

I know, I know, as Kendall might say: I'm meshuga.

I needn't have worried.

I read the Stans's script first, and like the film it was a competent piece of noir. The shooting script had clearly followed Stans's version very closely, as there were only a few scenes where I remembered the actors speaking slightly different lines. There was, indeed, the sex scene Stans told me about which was not in the filmed version, but as the old man explained, it couldn't be what Hall was looking for. It wasn't a bad read, as scripts go, but like the picture itself there was little to mark it out as anything more than engaging.

Hall's script was fucking brilliant.

Staying true to the basic story, and without adding any characters and only a few settings, Hall had turned musty old *The Devil on Sunday* into a modern morality play full of sharp edges and dangerous curves. Hall had Tarantinoed up the structure some—events didn't unfold in a strictly linear fashion—but the little tale of a dangerous drifter caught up in all that double-and-then-some-cross in a tiny town was transformed by Hall into a complex exploration of the meaning of masculinity, friendship, and faith in a world without honor. I couldn't figure out how he did it, but he'd found some internal philosopher's stone which enabled him to turn genre dross into gold. Even some of the dialogue was word for word out of the original, though typically put in the mouth of a different character than originally spoke it. It felt like Hall's whole life, everything he thought, believed in, held true, and mourned for losing, had been distilled down into this one, potent piece of work.

How could Hall have been anything other than a bitter bastard when he could write like this, yet had to pay his bills off Elliot's lousy poker play?

The first time I read through it, I got caught up in the rhythm and flow and enjoyed the script for the sheer pleasure of the storytelling. But the second time through—and I paused in between readings only to take a whiz and pop open a beer—I recognized aspects of Hall talking through the mouths of his characters. I found the pain and the heartache and the disappointments of a man whose life was lived too long under a black cloud. And in the final, acrid twist of the shock ending I felt a genuine sense of the bottomless chasm of despair that must have driven him to his death.

I put away the beer—in my stomach, strictly for reasons of public safety—and started on a big, beautiful bottle of Jack Daniels.

I don't remember going out to the beach. I don't remember it at all. But there was sand all around me and a whispering ocean in front of me, so I must have wandered out at some point.

I had no idea what time it was, but it had to be very late because the sky was black, without even a sliver of moon to light the way. I couldn't see anyone else around. Not the drug dealers who ply their trade on the south coast beaches at night, nor the cops who pretend to hunt them down between coffee breaks. There were no bums scouring the sand for butts and half-sandwiches and dropped coins. Not even a flickering campfire marking the flocks of teens who come at night to buy the drugs and evade the cops and beat up the bums and get high, and do the things that give southern California the reputation that it has. When I turned around, I couldn't even pick out my house. Everything, everywhere was dark. There was nothing, no one.

Nada.

And then Connie Clare said to me: "You're not from around here, are you?"

"Hah?"

She was standing between me and the ocean, which I could only hear and not see at all. I don't know how I was able to see *her,* because it was still dark as pitch, but there she was, plain as day. She was dressed in the outfit she wore in *The Devil on Sunday*: a white waitress skirt showing just too much leg to be safe and a matching top, two buttons undone on the blouse with a push-up bra taking care of the rest. She didn't have an order pad, but she stood with her elbow tucked in at her waist, her hand held palm up as if waiting to inscribe my order in her flesh.

"You're not from around here, are you?" she said again.

Her first line from *The Devil on Sunday.*

"Connie?" I said.

"Stranger than what?" she said, and raised the corner of her full lips.

I'd blown my line. I was supposed to have said: "I reckon you could say I'm a stranger." It was in both scripts. And the film. But then, I was feeling a mite confused.

"Connie," I said again. I tried to get up, but couldn't move out of the sand which was damp all around me. I felt pins and needles everywhere, as if my whole body had gone to sleep.

"A preacher! Guess I'd best watch my sinful ways. And my sweet little mouth."

I looked up and down the beach again, but there was nothing to see. No sound other than the words Connie Clare spoke in character. The little breaths she issued between lines.

"What are you doing here?" I asked. "What do you want?"

"Little towns are full of nasty, little men," Connie recited. I had no idea what my line should have been. "I got no use for little men and their little . . . ways. I think big. I *like* big. Are you . . . *big*?"

"Are you here because of Hall?" I asked. "Do you know about Hall?"

"I seen some things, and you will too, you stick around. It's that kind of a place, don't you know. You gonna stick around, stranger?"

"Connie, please. Did Hall kill himself? Can you tell me anything?"

She looked over her shoulder in the direction of the ocean. I couldn't hear it at all now. Light caressed the curve of her neck, though there was no source of light to be found. She turned back to me and there was fire in her eyes.

"I want a man who can stay the course. It's all I ever asked for. A man who'll go the limit for me." I realized the line was from another scene. A line Connie Clare never spoke in *The Devil on Sunday* because she was killed before she could shoot the scene. I'd read it in the script, though.

"Did George Gaines kill you?" I asked.

"I'm going now, but I'll be with you always. You got me inside you now and I ain't letting go, no sir. You have to wait for me to come back, stranger. In the flesh."

"Connie . . ." I pleaded.

She looked past me and her eyes went wide. Without thinking, I turned around to follow her gaze. When I looked back she was gone.

I was the kind of kid who always fell for the finger in the chest routine, too.

"Hey, buddy."

I turned back around even as I noticed I could hear the sea. The sky had lightened some and a flashlight beam shone on my face. I raised an arm against the glare and realized I could move again.

"Wha-?"

"What are you doing here?"

Two cops on beach patrol were getting out of their vehicle. They approached me slowly.

"Where did she go?" I asked. "Did you see her?"

"See who? Who are you? Let's see some ID."

I looked all around, but there was only the beach. I could see my house across the sand, lights on upstairs and down.

"I live there," I said, pointing.

"Uh-huh," the first cop said. "ID."

"Hey," his partner said, still picking me out with his flashlight beam. "I know him from TV. You're that infomercial guy, right? The car wax that won't burn up to a thousand degrees? That stuff really work or what?"

I felt slightly less disoriented, but very, very drunk. It must have shown.

"I live there," was all I could say. I managed to get to my feet on only my second attempt. Fortunately, my wallet was in my pocket and I fumbled it out. The cop checked the address on my driver's license and nodded.

"Had a snoutfull, friend?"

"Yeah. Maybe I did. You didn't see anyone else with me? A woman?"

"Lost your girl? Not surprised smelling like you do. Maybe you head back to your house, you'll find her there. Maybe you should get inside before something bad happens."

I stole another look around. No one else about.

"Too late," I said.

Thirteen

I woke up on the couch. Well, almost. One leg was on the couch, the rest of me was on the floor next to the couch. I hadn't even managed to pull any cushions down with me. This is precisely why I ignored the carpet salesman's entreaties at the time and went for the deepest pile shag they had in the store.

My head felt like it had hosted the Nuremberg Rally, with Burning Man held on a second stage. The pitter-patter of tiny jackboots continued to goose-step about my frontal lobes as consciousness mercilessly returned. My leg had gone to sleep as well and plopped stiffly to the floor as I swiveled my hips and tried to negotiate a sitting position. Morning light—nasty, evil, treacherous morning light—streamed through the windows. Why, oh why, does glass have to be so clear, anyway?

At least I didn't have any carpet burn. The shag may look like it came off the set of *Superfly* and be a bitch to vacuum, but it more than redeems itself on those mornings-after you've elected Jack Daniels führer-for-the-night.

Christ, but this was an excellent reminder of why I shouldn't drink hard liquor.

And then I remembered Connie Clare.

"Oy-oy-oy-oy-oy," I whimpered. I probably spend too much time talking to Kendall.

Another man, a more sensible man, perhaps, would have merely dismissed the events of the previous night as the bourbon-ignited flight of fantasy it almost certainly was. That sensible fellow would have thought about it and realized that the vision of the dead actress— Hall's long-ago murdered mother—was surely a consequence of too much stress, too much worry, and too much time spent chasing after feral geese in the name of I-don't-even-know-what. That Florsheims-on-the-ground chap would know that the dead don't come back from wherever it is they've gone to deliver Chinese Whisper telegrams to the living, especially when the living—and can you really call this living?—have been fool enough to polish off the best part of a quart of Kentucky sippin' sauce. People see things when they're drunk. Hell, I knew an actress who claimed to have once seen a studio exec walk past an orphan without laughing. Then I found out she'd downed a bottle of mescal at the time. And the worm.

The story of my life, of course, is that I've never been a sensible man. And the older I get and the more I see, the more I've learned— the hard way, trust me—that we do not live in a sensible world. There's nothing simple or straightforward about the way life works and having seen and done things that many a pragmatic man would dismiss as madness, I don't shake anything off casually. I saw Connie Clare on Hermosa Beach last night. She may have been a figment of my bourbon-addled head, or she may have been something more than that. I don't care to say for sure, because I don't rightly know. But either way—unconscious mind sending missives to my (semi-) conscious self, or Oogy-Boogy made manifest—the message wasn't one I was prepared to ignore.

Or the image of her something I was likely to forget.

Whether the experience was simple or complex, inebriant or epiphany, the message I took from it was straightforward: I was meant to keep on keeping after Hall. Connie said she wanted a man who'd go the limit for her. Maybe that's what Hall had been trying to do, in his way. I think maybe his script—that beautiful rewrite of *The Devil on Sunday*—was part of the effort. I felt determined to carry on with things, because I guessed that few had ever done so for Clare in her too-short life.

I was determined, when it comes right down to it, to be . . . *big*.

The phone rang and I let the machine handle it. It was Kendall, but she hung up before I managed to get to my feet. She wanted me to call her when I woke up. She made it sound pretty serious and I feared that a reckoning over *Burning Bright* must have come. I could definitely wait to hear about that.

I shambled into the bathroom and did the things a man has to do. This morning that mostly involved scarfing down a handful of Tylenol. I ran a shower but it hurt my head too much to do more than dance in and out. I thought about shaving, decided that if this was the day they were canceling my show, I could live with stubble. I studied myself in the mirror, didn't like what I saw and picked up the razor after all.

The fridge needed to be stocked with real food, but there's always a bottle of apple juice somewhere in the house so I poured myself a big glass and chugged it down. I considered what my stomach could cope with and settled on that safe, old settler: Cap'n Crunch. It's a funny thing, but I always feel funny buying Cap'n Crunch in the store. I keep reading about how you can do food shopping on the Internet these days, and it's the one thing that would tempt me to become computer literate, just to avoid the look the cashiers give me as they scan the big cereal box past the laser thingee. I don't know why it embarrasses me so—I have no problem going into the video store and renting porn, so my shame threshold isn't *that* low—but buying Cap'n Crunch turns me Crunchberry red. I don't really know about these things, but I think maybe this is what is called the post-modern condition.

Having fortified myself with the three most important food groups—juice, milk, Crunch—and with the pounding in my head reduced from orchestral timpani to be-bop brushes, I picked up the phone.

And I dialed Mac Stans's number.

"Hello," a Honey-drenched voice purred.

"Honey, how are you? This is Marty Burns."

Dead silence. I felt like I was back in high school.

"I was wondering if I might be able to have a word with Mac."

More silence, then. "That's not possible right now."

"Okay, the thing is I'd really like to see him again. It's very important. When might be a good time to . . ."

"He can't see anyone now. No one at all."

"I . . ."

Click. Brrr.

"I wondered if you might, you know, like to go out to a movie or something. With me. Sometime. With me." I like to play these scenarios out to the bitter end. "Bitch," I said, and hung up.

I was just about to call Kendall when a loud thud hit the front door. Then twice more. Like a good detective, I went to investigate.

Gabbo's pal with the bum rotator cuff stood on my front step.

"Tidgy Pud," I said, recalling his name.

"I prefer just Pud."

"Who wouldn't?"

"Gabbo sent me over with something for you."

For half a second I expected him to pull out a gun. Instead he handed me an envelope.

"Gabbo says he forgot to return it to you at the bar the other night. He says he's real sorry."

"He's a gentleman and a scholar," I said.

"You think so?"

I cleared my throat and opened the envelope. It contained the file labelled *Better Red Than Dead* that I had lifted from Hall's place along with the *Devil* scripts. I'd completely forgotten about it.

"You waiting for a tip or something?" I asked Pud.

"I wouldn't mind using your head."

I did mind some, but felt obliged to let the man pee. I waited for him by the open front door.

"You got any message for Gabbo?" he asked. "You want me to mention that gentleman and scholar thing?"

"Ah, no. Just tell him I said thank you."

"Okay."

"How's the shoulder?"

Tidgy Pud's expression suddenly went all soft and his eyes widened. I wondered if anyone had ever asked after his own welfare before.

"I got to have"—his features betrayed a hint of strain—"arthroscopic surgery."

"Tough break."

"I hate doctors."

"Me, too."

"And I got no health insurance."

"Doesn't Gabbo provide benefits?"

"Oh, yeah," Pud said. "But health insurance ain't one of 'em."

I didn't ask. Off he went, rubbing his shoulder.

I started to glance at the file when I remembered I was about to call Kendall. I picked up the phone.

"Marty! You're up early."

I glanced at the clock: 10:37. I've got to do something about my reputation.

"A condemned man doesn't want to while away his final hours asleep. Dead man sleeping is even worse than dead man walking."

"What are you talking about?"

"Isn't this the *Burning Bright* call? You heard from the network, right?"

"No, Marty, though I hope to by the end of the week. What made you think that?"

"Nothing. I'm feeling generally hinky. Reading entrails before the guts have been spilled."

"Well, take off your haruspex and put on your reading glasses."

"What? Harry who?"

"*Haruspex.* It was . . . never mind. Have you seen the trades yet?"

"You know I don't get the trades, Kendall, they depress me. I only like the comics and the Jumble anyway and you don't get that in *Variety.* Oh yeah, and the box scores."

"The *LA Times.* You still get that, don't you?"

"Most days. I don't have it delivered anymore, though. I felt it was too much of a commitment, made me feel tied down. I don't know if you know this about me, but fundamentally, I'm a rambling man."

"Marty . . ."

"Just tell me what happened, Kendall."

"Gamma. He's been shot."

"Where?"

"In West Hollywood."

"Actually, I meant where on his person. Though that's interesting, too."

"He was shot in the head, walking down the street yesterday afternoon. They're calling it a drive-by. Marty, you still there?"

"I'm here, Kendall. I'm just thinking."

"Kevin Ryan Paul called me this morning. He wanted to assure me that the picture was still a go."

"Was he frantic?"

"No, he was amazingly calm."

"Maybe not so amazing. What did he say?"

"Only that he wanted to assure all participants that the production was going to happen regardless. He said he'd direct if need be, but that film will roll. The show must go on and all that."

"I've never really known why. I mean, I like Ethel Merman as much as the next guy, but so it's *not* on with the show. Who'd give a gaffer's ass?"

"You're not a trouper, are you Marty?"

"Never claimed to be, no. What's the word on Gamma?"

"The papers only report his condition as serious, but my morning scuttlebutt says that he may be a vegetable."

"May you grow like an onion with your head in the ground."

"What?"

"It's an old Yiddish curse, Kendall. I thought sure you'd know it."

"You don't sound too shocked by any of this."

"No, I don't, do I? Call it the postmodern condition."

"Marty, you been reading the *LA Weekly*?"

"Perish the thought, Kendall. Did Paul say anything else?"

"He nudged me about the contracts again, but under the circumstances he didn't make a fuss when I hemmed and hawed. I imagine this Gamma shooting will buy us a few more days, but we have to wee-wee or get off the pot pretty soon."

Wee-wee! God, I love Kendall.

"Just don't agree to anything until I've told you to."

"Of course not."

"And Kendall: Don't go spending your commission off *The Devil on Sunday* just yet, okay?"

"I don't even use my credit cards, Marty. That's the way I am."

"Good girl. Hey, did you get that package for me?"

"I don't know, let me check." She put me on hold. Bless her, Kendall's hold music consists of themes from old TV shows. I got "The Ballad of Gilligan's Island." "Yes, Marty, there's a big box here from Blanc's Noir. I told you . . ."

"I know, I know: Never pay retail. Can you send it right over to me?"

"Sure. Is everything okay, Marty? You sound funny this morning."

"It's just the hour, Kendall. I'm right as rain."

"It never rains in Southern California."

"But like Morton's salt, how it does pour," I said. And hung up.

I dashed outside to the newspaper vending machine on the corner. The nice thing about living in a monopoly town is that you never have to go far to find a copy; the bad thing is that it's the *Times*. I dropped my quarters in and took a paper, then yanked out another to prop the door open with. Others could then make the moral decision about whether or not to pay for their copies. This is as close to anarchy as a a man with a half-million dollar beach house is likely to get.

The Gamma shooting didn't make the front page, but a blurb for it did. When I turned to the inside, I nearly passed right over the story because of the accompanying picture of a grubby looking little man with a scar on one cheek and a ring in his nose, wearing one of those woolly, Mike Nesmith ski caps pulled low over his ears. I reckoned it must be about gangbangers, but sure enough, this was Gamma. He looked like a thug. Even Gabbo might be taken aback by his appearance, and I felt sure the Directors Guild would deny all knowledge of Gamma's existence.

The story didn't offer much beyond what Kendall had already told me. Gamma was shot while walking alone down a residential West Hollywood street. No witnesses had come forth, but an unnamed police source speculated that the shooting might be linked to a music video Gamma had directed for an also-shot-in-the-head rapper. Gamma's various media credits were noted, including his anticipated participation in *The Devil on Sunday*. In fact, there was a long quote from Kevin Ryan Paul about the "tragedy." (Their words, not mine. A dead child is a tragedy. A flood in Bangladesh is a tragedy. A movie director with a bullet in his head is at worst unfortunate, at best worthy of a round for the house.) I noted, with some interest, that Paul managed to get the picture's name in twice in the space of a single paragraph. The story concluded by noting that Gamma was widely regarded as "the face of the new Hollywood."

I took another look at that photograph. It might as well have been an e-fit or a mug shot. Certainly worthy of hanging in any post office.

Call me a grumpy fart, but the *old* Hollywood never seemed quite so appealing.

A second bowl of Cap'n Crunch later, I dialed Mac Stans's number again, just for the hell of it. No answer. Then I called Carl Khan, but he wasn't there, either, so I left a message. By the time I skimmed the rest of the paper and straightened up the living room, the messenger with my box of stuff from Harry Blanc had arrived.

It was quite a big box. Harry was obviously determined to give me quantity if not quality. He had the good grace to put the invoice on top, and I saw that he'd hit me up for nine hundred bucks out of the thousand limit. A little steep, in that I didn't actually want most of what he sent me, but I suppose he could have gone for the last C-note, too. The invoice included a detailed list of the items enclosed and though I wasn't fully conversant with the complete George Gaines's filmography, I suspected that Harry sent me at least one item from every single film. Mostly, he sent lobby cards and one-sheets and I put them aside. Maybe there'd be something worth framing and hanging up out of it all, but that would be a bonus. I only told Harry to send them to make the effort worth his while. I went more carefully through the press books, though these, too, were largely uninteresting, written as they were in pure PR-ese. Few consisted of anything more than plot summaries, star bios, cast lists, and absurd claims as to the shimmering wonderfulness of the movie at hand.

One padded envelope inside the box offered me my money's worth, however. There wasn't a lot inside, but it was exactly what I'd been hoping, even expecting, to find. There was also a note from Harry:

Dear Marty,

I've sent along a nice taste of goodies from George Gaines's pictures. I've limited the package to items held in stock. "You never draw a blank from Harry" is my motto. (Ha, ha, ha.) I can get you more if you want, but it will take a few days. Please let me know.

The items in the envelope are the only newspaper cuttings I could find quickly. Really, they're mostly from magazines and scandal sheets. Those were very big at the time as you probably know and they can be very collectable. I've taken the liberty of xeroxing a few things to keep the price of the package down. The truth is, if you want a real search of the newspapers and magazines, it will take time and cost more money. I can do it, of course, but we would have to discuss it in greater detail. I am, naturally, at your disposal. Good service at a fair price is my other motto.

Taking another look at the invoice, I was tempted to ha-ha myself, but it wasn't funny.

You also asked if I knew any stories about Gaines. I made a few phone calls to my "contacts" and dug the dirt. We all agreed that Mr. George Gaines was not a nice man. The thing they always said about him was "George Gaines, you lose."

Almost exactly what Olivia said.

I don't like to tell tales or speak ill of the dead because they're too much a part of my living. But one story an old union hand told me may sum things up for you. He worked on a George Gaines horror movie called Curse of Darkness *(one-sheet is enclosed). The fellow who played the vampire villain was hit by a car in the middle of production and was killed. As you know, this is usually the worst catastrophe that can happen to a producer. On the day of the accident. Gaines gathered the cast and crew to break the bad news. He was very sorrowful as he did so, and told them that shooting was finished for the day and the set would be closed as a mark of respect. My friend was stuck up on a catwalk at the time in an awkward position. By the time he got himself disentangled, everyone but Gaines had left the set. When the last person walked off and he thought he was all alone, Gaines let out with a roar of laughter. The union guy had started to come down, but froze where he was when he saw the producer. (Everyone on set lived in fear of Gaines, he told me.) Gaines laughed so hard he fell down on the ground. The set was made up like a graveyard and when Gaines finally managed to stand up, he walked over to the grave that was supposed to mark the final resting place of the character played by the dead actor. And he did a dance on the fake grave, laughing while he jitterbugged. My friend said he never saw anything like it in his life. The film shut down and got paid off by the insurer and though he had opportunities, my friend swore he'd never work for Gaines again.*

I don't know if this is of any use to you. As I say, if I can be of any additional assistance, please do not hesitate to call or to call in. And any stories you might care to tell me will always be happily listened to. Fill in the Blanc, as I like to say.

Warm Regards,
Harry Blanc

Criminy.

I went through the clippings that Harry sent me and they served to confirm what was now a very solid suspicion. It was no coincidence that everyone lost as George gained. No coincidence at all.

It was time to talk to someone about it.

Many species are creatures of habit. There are birds which migrate thousands of miles, yet land on the same patch of ground every year along the way. Salmon notoriously swim upstream against the forces of nature and incredible odds just to spawn where they were born. I once saw a documentary on the Discovery Channel about a kind of twenty-four-hour dung beetle which virtually tore itself to pieces in its frenzy to return to a particular hunk of shit when it was time to die. You'd think it would have better things to do with its day.

I found Kevin Ryan Paul propping up the bar at Blönde.

Kant and Sade were with him. Kant was shoving into his mouth what looked to me like pigs-in-blankets, but which no doubt went by a fancier Blönde name (and price), and had a big glass of some crème-de-menthe-type whore's drink in front of him. What the hell was this guy's story? Sade and Paul shared a bottle of white wine that floated in a translucent ice bucket on the bar between them. Paul was talking to her—or at her—but Sade was preoccupied with watching Kant eat, an expression of abject horror on her skeletal visage. I reckon the big plate of cocktail weenies was enough to feed an entire African village for a week. Or Sade for a year. Kant saw her watching him and wickedly dangled a frank, its nitrate-red glans poking obscenely from the filo pastry foreskin, in front of her. I thought she might purge on the spot. Chivalry demanded an intervention.

"How's it dangling, Kev?" I said, scarfing up the offered snack.

Kant harrumphed as Sade squealed with delight. I kept my eye on Paul, though. His face morphed from surprise through annoyance to patently manufactured bonhomie in less time than it takes to swallow a minidog. I could practically see the little crane straining to hoist the false producer-smile as he put out his hand.

"Marty, my man of men. The I-Ching said something good was going to happen to me today and you. Are. It."

"Kev, you are a beacon of light in a land of darkness." I turned to Sade. "And you, my darling, are a golden rainbow."

Another squeal. How could a rainbow, starring the colorful Mr. Roy G. Biv, possibly be golden, you ask? You'll obviously never be a starlet, is my reply.

I ignored Kant entirely. The feeling was mutual.

"You don't normally hang out in these parts, my friend. To what do we owe this orgasmic pleasure?"

"They say blöndes have more fun," I said, and waved at the surrounding. "Just trying it on for size."

"Well, grab yourself a chair and join the party. The drinks are on M-E."

I pulled over a stool and sat down, ordered a large Seven-Up. I thought about a beer, but with Jack Daniels's footprints not yet faded from the inside of my head, I played it safe. The large Seven-Up turned out to be a marginally oversize shot glass. I *hate* restaurant bars.

"Have yourself a real drink," Paul urged, raising his wine glass.

"I'm all right. But you're awfully chipper for a producer who just lost his director. What are you going to do without Gamma?"

"I'll tell you the truth, Marty. Gamma's a genius. Huh? Huh? And it's a hell of a thing that happened to him. A damned disgrace. The streets haven't been safe since they loosed the Juice, if you ask Mama Paul's little angel. But, and this is just entre nous mon etoile, maybe it's for the best."

"Getting shot in the head walking down the street is for the best? What might the worst be?"

"It's a tough break for the G-man, that's for sure. A genuine personal disaster, no argument. Hard to get happy when someone leaves a lead suppository in your nut."

"I'll say," I said.

"But I saw creative differences, like storm clouds, on the horizon. Gamma's a pistol, pardon the expression, but he's got no safety. Maybe what happened is an omen."

"I hear from my agent that you're thinking of directing the picture yourself."

"They're big shoes to fit, but I've got big feet." He glanced at Sade. "And you know what they say about a man with big feet."

"The trouble with big feet is you got to be damn careful what you step in."

"I don't think I follow your simile, Marty."

"Your uncle George might know."

That furrowed his brow. "Uncle George?"

"Seems like maybe you're walking a little bit close in his footsteps, don't you think, Bigfoot?"

Paul put his glass down and scratched at the little furrow above the middle of his lip and under his nose. I've always meant to look up what that bit of us all is called.

"Why don't you take Sade shopping," Paul instructed Kant. "I'll see you both later at la casa."

Kant was on his feet in a flash. Sade looked disappointed, but a stern glance from Paul sent her on her way. She stopped to air-kiss me on both cheeks, and was gone in a puff of bulimia.

"Something I said?" I asked Paul, when they'd gone.

"Let's sit over there," he said, pointing to a corner table. It was conspicuously isolated from prying ears.

"I'm sensing a certain equivocation on your part, Marty. Huh? Huh? Is there some problem I should know about?"

"I don't know what you mean."

"Please. My friend. Do not insult. I wasn't born yesterday and I didn't just come across the border under a load of watermelons. You have commitment issues."

"Meaning?"

"I don't have your name on the dotted line. That funny little agent of yours has been dancing me up and down the Hollywood freeway for a week now."

"In high school, Kendall was voted most likely to boogy-oogy-oogy till she just couldn't boogy no more."

"Marty. I thought we'd agreed that we were past the game-playing."

"I like to think that's true, too, Kev."

"Beautiful, baby. So talk to your Uncle Kevin. What's the problem?"

"Like I say, it's not so much Uncle Kevin as Uncle George that has me worried."

"You mystify me, Marty."

"I don't mean to, Kev. You know how they always say that history repeats itself?"

"That's a Kevin Williamson line if I'm not mistaken. From *I Know What You Did Last Summer*?"

"Something like that. See, I'm a little worried we're moving straight into a rerun here with *The Devil on Sunday*."

"I remain mystified."

"Your Uncle George wasn't a lucky guy, was he? Or rather, he wasn't good luck for the people around him."

"You're still thinking about Connie Clare," he said, shaking his head. "Why?"

"Did you know that George Gaines was the prime suspect in the Clare murder?"

"What?"

"The other suspect was Mac Stans."

"You're having fun with me now. Am I on *Candid Camera*? I thought Alan Funt kicked it?"

"This all news to you, Kev?"

"Where did you get this stuff? Marty, if you have a substance abuse problem please tell me now. We can get you help. I care."

"Lots of bad things happened to people on George Gaines's shoots. Car accidents, plane crashes, fires. Rapes."

Paul started shaking his head. "You know how people live in this town. *Lived.* It's an edgy place. Isn't that why we're here, the kick that we do it for? Uncle George . . . he liked to push the envelope, no doubt about it. And he liked to work with people who did the same. So occasionally some of them pushed things too far. Was that his fault? Shit happens isn't just a bumper sticker, you know."

"Maybe. But it's not one of the three laws of thermodynamics, either."

Paul shrugged. "What does any of this have to do with the price of hookers in Chinatown?"

"Your uncle knew about PR, didn't he? Knew how to play the press?"

"He was a producer for thirty years."

"And he didn't hesitate to capitalize on all the . . . shit that happened around him."

"What are you, a virgin? You do whatever you can to talk up a picture, to make it happen, give it a buzz. That's not just the golden rule, it *is* a law of movie thermodynamics. You think they'd still be cranking out that *Crow* shit, have a syndicated series out of it, if Brandon Lee hadn't caught a bullet? If you have to sell your mother to the Arabs to push a picture, it's Osama bin Laden mama. If you don't know that . . ."

"Is there anything *you* wouldn't do to sell your movie? To give it buzz?"

"What are you saying here, Marty? What are you accusing me of?"

"Connie Clare was found dead in the street halfway through the shoot of *The Devil on Sunday*. Gamma never even saw film roll."

Paul stared at me for a moment, then broke out into hysterical laughter. He doubled over, grabbing onto my bicep to stop from falling out of his chair.

"Oh, Marty," he said, wiping the corner of his eye with a cocktail napkin. "You are too, too much. I love you, kid."

"I say something funny?"

Paul stifled a further guffaw. "You think *I* shot Gamma? Huh? Huh?"

"I didn't say that. I'm just remarking on some curious coincidences I find troubling."

"Gamma hung with gangbangers. He did it for street cred and because he's very fond of certain illicit substances. Some breakdancing motherfucker busted a cap on him."

"Mmmm. They talk like that, don't they. Do they even *do* break-dancing any more?"

"He thinks I shot Gamma," Paul said, addressing some imaginary audience.

"First Hall, then Gamma. Can't help but think that *The Devil on Sunday* is developing quite a nasty little . . . buzz."

The levity drained from Paul's face. "That's what this is about, isn't it? Hall fucking Emerson. That dead bastard just won't leave me alone."

"The dead can be funny that way."

"He badgered Stans about Connie Clare, too. He was drunk, but . . ."

"What? When did Hall see Stans?"

"We took a meeting. The three of us. I told you Stans was on as a producer. He suggested bringing Emerson on. You already know this, Marty."

I most certainly did not. Stans told me he hadn't seen Hall in years; that they'd long since been estranged. "Of course," I said. "I forgot."

"Emerson couldn't let go of the Clare thing. And he's still got his hooks into you, too. She was his mother; okay, I can appreciate that. But what is your trip?"

We staged a brief stare-down, but I'm no good at those things. I could see Paul try to suppress a smile when I looked away. It pissed me off.

"I've read the script," I said.

"What? Of course you have. I sent it to your agent weeks ago."

"You haven't actually. Not all of it. But I mean Hall's script. I read that. The one that you told me he never delivered."

Paul's smile was a distant memory. "Now, listen to me, Marty . . ."

"Something stinks here and it's not just the terrapin soup. The saying—and trust me, it's not from Kevin Williamson—is that history repeats itself, first as tragedy, then as farce. Well, I don't want to be a part of either."

"You want to be careful here, amigo. You may not have signed the papers, but you've made a verbal commitment to the picture. Don't think you can just walk away from that. And don't think you can spread this shit about me and the picture around town. I'll sue your ass for that, too. You are in this, my friend. Remember what happened to Kim Basinger."

"I hadn't thought of that," I said, and Paul nodded knowingly. "God, what could be worse than marrying a Baldwin?"

Before Paul could say any more, I got up and headed for the door. Paul mewled something at my back, but I ignored it.

I don't care what Elliot says: You can't top going out on a Baldwin brothers line.

"Hi, Lissa?"

"This is Lissa."

"It's Marty Burns."

A brief pause on the line then: "Oooh. Hi, Marty."

"I've been thinking about you."

"Dirty, filthy thoughts?"

"Among others. I was wondering if I could maybe see you."

"Ummm, we're shooting tonight on location. It's a full moon, you know."

That threw me. Then I recalled that *Lupè Garou* was a werewolf series.

"I really just want to have a chat. It's kind of important."

"*Just* a chat?" she cooed, and mudslide of dirty, filthy thoughts tumbled down the crumbling palisade of my frontal lobe.

"Well, I *can* rub my tummy and pat my head at the same time, so I probably can talk and . . . do other things."

"With your mouth?"

"Huh boy."

"Why don't you come by now? The studio limo doesn't pick me up until five."

Limo? I have to drive myself to the set. *And* I have a crummy parking spot. Of course, *Lupè Garou* is on a real network.

"I'm coming," I promised.

"Only if I come first."

Hummina-hummina.

I had to be careful what I said, but I felt obligated to try and warn Lissa about Kevin Ryan Paul. Despite his laughing denial of any involvement in the Gamma shooting—and, indeed, despite my having no evidence whatsoever to implicate him beyond suspicions about his uncle—I was worried that another "accident" might befall those involved with *The Devil on Sunday.* And given what had happened to Connie Clare, Lissa Torres seemed a good bet for the firing line.

It took a while to get down to conversation. Lissa greeted me in crotchless panties and a smile. I've never been big on the whole novelty lingerie thing, which always strikes me as trying a little too hard—and can you still legitimately call them panties once they've been de-crotched? I mean, can you have footless socks?—but Lissa Torres could sell fur G-strings to the Eskimos. And when you come right down to it (and we certainly did), like most men I'm a slut at heart. Would I be in show biz if I wasn't?

In the postcoital glow, which admittedly came largely from me, I mentioned Gamma to Lissa.

"I'm *very* disappointed," she said. "We were supposed to get pierced."

"Huh?"

"Pierced, you know. I was going to do my labia and he was going to have one of those blocky things put through the head of his cock."

"Ai-ai-ai."

"No, it's supposed to be incredible. My girlfriend had it done and she says she just comes all the time. Once while she was eating soup!"

"Condensed?"

"What?"

"The soup."

"She didn't say. Wow, you think it makes a difference?"

"I don't really know about these things."

"Anyway, I'm too chicken to go do it on my own. Unless . . ."

"No, no, no, no. The only thing that pierces Mrs. Burns's little boy is Martin Lawrence's rapier wit. And I promised my moyel I'd never let any other man touch my willy."

"Oh. I suppose if you *promised* . . ."

"Gamma," I tried again. "What do you think about what happened to him?"

"I wasn't tight with him, but we, you know, *partied* a little. He hung with some bad boys."

I didn't like the way she said "partied," but people who live in crotchless panties shouldn't throw stones. Or something like that.

"Does Kevin Ryan Paul count as one of them?"

"Kevin? Don't be silly. Kevin's a puddy-tat."

"You sure?"

"Kevin's a big old teddy bear. Well . . ."—she lowered her voice, though there was no one else to hear—"not *that* big." And she giggled.

Explains a lot, I thought. Not that I shop in the big man's section at Codpieces 'R Us. Though I did start to wonder if there was anyone Lissa *hadn't* slept with. And knowing that I'd screwed the same woman as Kevin Ryan Paul made me feel a little queasy.

"It's just that stuff seems to happen around Kevin. Bad stuff I mean."

"I don't think so."

"Hall Emerson died, and now Gamma's in the hospital."

"So?"

"You know that Kevin's uncle was a producer? George Gaines?"

"I don't know. He might have mentioned it."

"He was. And lots of bad things happened on his sets. Things which he then used to help publicize his pictures. I can't help but wonder if Kevin hasn't taken a page out of his uncle's script."

"This is a joke, right?"

"Maybe. But maybe not. Uncle George had a thing about pretty actresses. He liked to see nasty things happen to them. I'm just . . . I guess I want to let you know about my concerns. I don't want to see anything bad happen to you."

Lissa threw her arms around me and gave me a sloppy, little girl kiss. "You're so sweet, Marty."

"I come in a diet version, too."

"But Marty?"

"What?"

"You're loco. Kevin could never do anything bad like you're saying. I know he didn't shoot Gamma because I was with him at the time."

"That's convenient."

"What do you mean by that?"

"Nothing. It's a joke. But I wasn't suggesting that Kevin himself went out with a gun. Doesn't mean he didn't make it happen."

"I can't believe you're saying this."

"I don't say it lightly. And I admit I don't have any hard evidence. I'm just saying I'm worried."

"How you going to work for Kevin, you think like this? How you going to be in the picture?"

"Maybe I am, maybe I'm not. Nothing's been signed yet."

"I thought you wanted to work with *me*? I thought that meant something to you."

"It would be a delight to work with you, Lissa. I'm just saying I don't know about Kevin. And telling you . . . asking you to be on your guard."

"I think you should go now."

"Lissa . . ."

"Just go."

I made for the door, but Lissa called my name.

"You don't *really* think Martin Lawrence is funny, do you?" she asked.

The answer, as any sane person would acknowledge, is a no as big as the great outdoors, but I just shrugged. Ever the tortilla.

Out I went.

I felt bad because obviously Lissa had taken personally what had nothing in particular to do with her. But I was also worried that she would ignore my warning. She'd looked angry. I hoped she wasn't mad enough to do something stupid.

I sat in my car across the street from Lissa's place, mulling it all over. I hadn't planned to sit there for as long as I did, I just felt unsure of what to do next. Which is by way of saying that tailing Lissa Torres *wasn't* a part of my plans. It just happened.

I was surprised to see her come out of her house and get into her car at four-thirty. She'd said the limo was due to pick her up at five. Was she popping out for milk? Cigarettes? An iron-on crotch patch for those panties?

I decided I wanted to know.

It had been a while since I'd done any mobile surveillance. It's not hard exactly, but it can be tricky. You have to be ballsy but not obvious, and willing to risk the inevitable tickets which will come for blowing through stop signs and red lights in order not to lose your subject. I used to do it all the time when I made my living investigating worker's comp claims, but I drove the Subaru then, and felt a little more protective of my Lexus now. And true to type, Lissa drove like a maniac. I've yet to meet an actress who didn't. She wasn't one to take yellow lights seriously, even when they were half a block away. If not for the fact that there was only one logical route into town from her part of the Hills, she'd have lost me for sure. As it was, I had two old Hasidim to thank for getting into a fender-bender at the corner of Fairfax and Melrose and backing up traffic, or I'd never have caught up with her. She absolutely floored it when she got onto the westbound Santa Monica Freeway, but her red Beamer had too low a series number to worry me on acceleration. I tailed her off onto Bundy and straight up into Brentwood from there.

Brentwood gives me the creeps. It's too posy and too sick-making quaint. And it's silly, but to me Brentwood is still tainted by OJ. I always expect to see Nicole's ghost wandering the streets, wailing her fury. Or Ron Goldman labored down by that fatal set of sunglasses, like the chains on Jacob Marley.

Also the traffic in Brentwood really sucks and you have to know your way around, which I don't.

Lissa tore around the expensive residential streets as if she was still on the freeway. I had a hard time keeping up, and then almost rear-ended her (and, no, it wouldn't have been the first time; happy?) when she jerked to a stop in front of a large, gated property. I drove past and pulled over half a block on. In the rearview I watched her hop out of the car and buzz the intercom at the entrance. A moment later she disappeared inside the gate.

I hung a huey, and pulled over next to her parked car. It wasn't possible to see the house behind the gate or any of the property through it. I thought about waiting there for a while, but what was the point? I wrote down the street address on an El Pollo Loco bag I found on the floor in back, and drove off regretting, for once, that I don't keep a cell phone on me. You don't find payphones on Brentwood corners and I had to drive all the way up to Sunset before I spied one. I called Kendall.

"Hey, Marty," she chirped. She always chirps. "No news yet on the show."

"That's okay, I'm calling about something else. Would you know where Kevin Ryan Paul lives?"

"No idea. If I had to guess, I'd say he rents a big house he can't afford in Bel-Air."

"Or Brentwood?"

"That'd be second best, but would fit. Why?"

"Can you find out where he lives?"

"I suppose so. What . . ."

"Can you do it *now*?"

"*Right* now?"

"Yeah."

"Marty . . ."

"Please, Kendall? I don't make a lot of stupid, spoiled actor requests."

"What about that Thai beer?"

"*Other* than that."

"Okay, hold on a minute."

In fact, it took her three minutes. Which is still pretty good.

"Is that what you wanted?" she asked after giving me the address.

"That's perfect. Thank you, Kendall."

I don't know if it *was* perfect, but the address she reported matched what I'd written on my greasy chicken sack.

To quote Mel Allen: How 'bout that?

• • •

I stopped at Johnny's in Culver City on my way home and treated myself to a pastrami sandwich and fries. And a Coke and a thick shake. I suspect that much food would have killed Sade outright, but I briefly considered ordering a second shake. I decided to go healthy and just took a refill on the Coke.

The answering machine blinked at me when I got home. A message from Kendall wanting to know if everything was all right—I knew she'd be freaked by that call from the pay phone. And a terse message from Detective Khan returning my earlier call. While I was standing by the phone, I dialed Mac Stans again. It was practically becoming a habit.

No answer.

I turned on the TV to occupy my attention for a while. I was tired of thinking about this whole mess I'd gratuitously immersed myself in, and tired period. An old *Rockford Files* episode briefly diverted me—now *that* was a show; I really do want to be Jim Garner when I grow up—but when even Stuart Margolin and Joe Santos can't hold your attention, you know you've got troubles. I found myself wandering over to the table where I'd piled the materials that Harry Blanc had sent me. Idly, I leafed through a batch of stills I'd put aside before, mostly studio glossies with a few oddities mixed-in.

Including a photocopy from an old scandal rag called *Picture Privies*. I'm sure Harry sent it because of the article—a puff piece about an alleged affair between George Gaines and Judy Holiday—but it was the photograph accompanying the article that caught my eye like a *Texas Chainsaw* meat hook: George Gaines and Mac Stans with their arms draped around Unknown Hollywood Starlet #23,261—her smile as fake as the Mona Lisa with a Walkman—standing between them. The magazine dated from 1948, before Stans had fallen beneath the wheels of the Red Scare, so there was nothing unusual about he and Gaines being seen together. And I already knew that they'd worked on several projects before *The Devil on Sunday*.

But something about the picture bothered me. It drove me crazy as I studied it, poking at my brain like some cartoon demon with a pitchfork. I stared at Gaines's face, then at Stans's. I took an extra long look at the starlet's bubbies. They were nice. And they were neatly framed by the two "gentlemen's" dangling hands.

And that's when it struck me.

I tore through the chaos of my living room looking for the folder containing the pages I'd photocopied at the UCLA library. I couldn't find them anywhere, then remembered I'd been looking at them before going to sleep one night. Sure enough, the manila file was on the floor atop yet another unread issue of *Entertainment Weekly*. I sorted through the pages and found the sheet with the picture of baby Hall Emerson held in some big man's hand.

A hand with a gold pinky ring.

The same pinky ring that adorned Mac Stans's finger, pressed ever-so-lightly, but-oh-so-pointedly against the curvaceous swell of the breast of UHS #23,261.

The ring which I now remembered him nervously playing with when we spoke at his poolside in Laguna.

The thunderbolt knocked me out of my figurative chair. In the more literal world, I got up and made a phone call.

"Bill Caldwell," the old cop answered.

"Detective, this is Marty Burns. We spoke a little while back about the Connie Clare case."

"I remember."

"I have another question to ask you, if you don't mind."

"Go ahead."

"Your two suspects were George Gaines and Mac Stans. You knew they were friends, right?"

"I knew they worked together, sure. I don't about friends, though."

"Did you know that Mac Stans was the actual screenwriter of *The Devil on Sunday*?"

There was an intake of breath, then a lengthy pause. "No, I didn't know that. Is it true?"

"Without a doubt. Does that information make any difference to you?"

"Hard to say. Gaines still stands out as the perp. I suppose that he and Stans could have done it together, but I never had any reason to think that before. There'd be no way to even start to look into it now."

"No, I realize that. But don't you think there's something odd about Gaines and Stans being friends? After all, you told me Gaines was in with the anticommie crowd. How would it have looked if it was known he was buddies with a leading red?"

There was another pause while the old cop considered the question.

"Son," he said, "I worked homicide for twenty-odd years. Was a cop in this town ten years beyond that. And you know what I mostly learned?"

"What is that?"

"When it comes to Hollywood, ain't nothing too odd to believe."

I got myself a frosty cold one, sat down, and had a good think. I thought I had almost everything worked out in my mind about Hall Emerson and Mac Stans, and what went on between them, but something continued to jar. Then I remembered the file that Tidgy Pud had dropped off in the morning, the TV treatment titled *Better Red Than Dead*. I retrieved it and started reading through it.

And the last piece of the puzzle fell into place.

I made another call.

"Carl Khan," the detective answered.

"It's Marty Burns."

"Hi-ho, Silver! How's the Lone Ranger?"

"Does that make you my faithful Indian companion?"

"Native American."

"Sorry?"

"These days I'd have to be your faithful Native American companion. And you can forget that Jay Silverheels pidgin English crap. Lawsuit city or what?"

"Whatever you say, Kemo Sabe. I want to ask you something. A couple of things."

"Fire them silver bullets."

"What can you tell me about the Gamma shooting?"

Khan cleared his throat. "You ask some funny questions, boy."

"I'm not looking for a scoop, just something more than is in the paper."

"Why?"

"Would you believe it has to do with Hall Emerson?"

"Not really, but you'll tell me over entrecôte."

"Deal," I sighed.

"Or lobster. There's a new seafood place in the Marina I've been hearing about. Trés expensive."

"It's your call, boss. Gamma?"

"Cut and dried. Some rapping mofo that Gamma dissed meant to throw a scare into your boy. Rapmaster Dickhead's aim was either better or worse than he thought."

That threw me. "You sure about this?"

"Yup. You disappointed?"

"Sort of. It's . . . not what I expected. There's no doubt? No chance that someone put the shooter up to it?"

"Like who?"

"I'm . . . just asking."

"No, it's just a stupid hip-hop thing. Pardon the redundancy. Hey, you know what Gamma's real name is? Norman. Norman Spolansky. Is that great or what?"

"Is . . . Norman going to make it?"

"Looks that way. The world remains safe for pretentious commercials. Close one, huh?"

There was silence while I mulled things over.

"Was there something else, Marty?"

"Yeah. Did you ever interview Mac Stans after I told you about his relationship with Hall?"

"No. Should I have?"

"I think so."

"Well, it's too late now."

"Huh? What do you mean?"

"Stans had a stroke the other day."

"What?"

"Yeah, very serious. That scraping sound you hear is the obit writers sharpening their pencils."

"Shit," I said.

"Sorry, Marty, was I breaking bad news to you?"

"How do you know this?" I asked, ignoring Khan's question.

"I've told you before. I'm CAD, and we know everything." He laughed.

"Maybe not everything," I told him. "In fact, maybe nothing at all."

I paused to enjoy the abrupt termination of the detective's chuckling before I hung up the phone.

Fourteen

It took a little doing, but I tracked down Mac Stans. Never underestimate the currency of star power, even if that star is fading into the darkness of a probably-going-to-be-cancelled series. I was later told how a few cans got rattled obtaining the information, but Stans was recuperating from his stroke in a private hospital in Palos Verdes. Three times I got lost trying to find the place—Palos Verdes is a rich man's community designed to confuse and discourage those who don't already know where they are going—but the "hospital" proved to be a converted mansion high atop a hill in Palos Verdes Estates with a stunning view of Lunada Bay and the ever restless ocean beyond.

Not a bad place to check out if you've got to go. Certainly beats the hell out of taking the gas pipe in the back of an LTD.

They didn't want to let me up the drive at first, but a little sweet talk from "Sugar Lips" Burns and the gates buzzed open. Basically, I lied like hell. The property was expansive enough that the gas gauge visibly twitched toward "E" just driving up to the main building. On grounds like this even my Lexus felt like a battered old Gremlin; nothing less than a Rolls or Bentley would have felt right. The visitor parking was some distance from the house and I walked up a winding path through immaculately landscaped gardens to get to the entrance. For all the splendor around me, there wasn't another soul to be seen.

I had to buzz again at the front door—just who did they tend to in this joint?—but got admitted without any problem. The inside was done up in the style I like to think of as *Beverly Hillbillies* baroque, including a grand, circular staircase that might have led straight to heaven. A chesty blonde in nurse's whites sat behind a big mahogany desk at the bottom of the stairs and smiled at me. I sidled on up and gave her that patented, Marty Burns wink.

"I'm here to see Mac Stans."

"You're his son, you said."

"That's right."

"Our records indicate that Mr. Stans doesn't have any children."

I heard a footfall behind me, glanced over my shoulder at a burly security guard who now stood between me and the front door.

"Afternoon," I offered.

He fingered the stun gun on his belt. He had that over-buffed, steroid induced, Village People look common to his line of work, right down to the how-does-he-trim-it-so-neat mustache. He didn't look up for a chorus of "YMCA," though. Maintaining my most pleasant smile, I turned back to the receptionist.

"Your records must be mistaken," I said.

"No, we're very careful about these things. But I think the police will be interested in your story."

She nodded at the guard who moved fast and grabbed me around the neck from behind. I did what I'd always understood you're supposed to do in such a situation and went limp even as I carefully aimed a sharp heel blow at the guard's instep.

It's probably a good response in many such situations, but it presumes that you are not wearing four hundred dollar, "guaranteed softest leather in the world" Bruno Magli shoes. And that your assailant is not shod in toughest-leather-in-the-world jackboots.

Village Person had his stun gun in hand before I could squeal "ouch."

"It's all right," a new voice called out. The stun gun was crackling like power lines on a rainy night. I swear he singed an ear hair. "Let him go."

The guard did as he was told. Honey, dressed in skintight black leather that no Avenger—new or old—would have dared to wear, posed on the sixth step of the staircase.

"Mr. Burns," she said.

"Hi, Honey, I'm at the home," I offered.

"So I see."

"I'm sorry Miss Duel, I didn't realize you know this gentleman," the receptionist said. "He was telling fanciful tales."

"That seems to be his business," Honey said. "Would you like to come upstairs, Mr. Burns?"

"Definitely."

I flashed a smug look at the receptionist, who rolled her eyes. The guard had already disappeared to wherever they stashed the Indian chief guy and the construction worker. Honey came down the remaining stairs and offered me her hand as I approached, and very delicately we shook. Her skin was softer than my shoes, but it wasn't my feet I would have chosen to wear her on. She gestured for me to head upstairs, paused to whisper something in the receptionist's ear, then joined me.

"Your last name is Duel?" I asked.

"Yes."

"Honey Duel?"

"That's right."

"Any relation to Pete?"

"Who?"

"Never mind. Junior high must have been hell."

"Not at all. I was an early developer."

"Yowza," I muttered. I couldn't help but sneak a glance her way as we went. I had no idea how she was able to climb stairs in pants that tight, but God love her for making the effort. She caught me looking.

"Of course, one need not *be* in junior high to endure the puerile sensibility."

"Right. Sorry."

"It's nothing at all," she said.

We turned right at the top of the stairs. Two more burlesque queens-cum-angels of mercy idled at a nurses' station. If they ever green-light *Baywatch Nurses,* this is the place to cast.

"Quite a joint," I said as we went on down the hall.

"Don't be fooled, Mr. Burns, this is the finest private clinic in Southern California. I wouldn't allow Mac to be cared for anyplace else."

"So how is he?"

"Not very well. He suffered a stroke, a series of them actually, two nights ago. He's lost feeling on his right side and is largely immobile. Much of his vascular system is near collapse. The doctors are not hopeful. Nice of you to ask, though."

"I see."

She pushed open a door near the end of the hall which I expected to reveal Mac Stans's sick room. It was, in fact, nothing but a small sitting room. Honey gestured me into a chair and sat down across from me on a grotesque, green divan.

"You're quite tenacious, Mr. Burns, but what is it that you want here? Why are you lying about your relationship to Mac?"

"I need to talk to him. Obviously."

"Need?"

I thought about it for a moment. "Yes, need is the right word. It's definitely long past want. Yeah, I don't really *want* to be here. Most of the time I don't even want to be me. But like the singer says, I *gotta* be me. And I *need* to talk to your . . ." It struck me that I didn't have a clue what Honey and Mac were to each other, though my suspicions must have shown on my face.

"Sugar daddy?"

"Whatever. It's your choice, ninety-nine cents."

"Mac and I regard ourselves as partners, Mr. Burns."

"Partners, huh? Like Lerner and Loewe. Or is that Leopold and Loeb? I was never big on musicals."

"You're not a nice man, are you."

"Hey, I'm not criticizing, Honey. I like things to be spelled out neatly, too. I've even got it in my contract they have to put a jar of M&M's in my dressing room every damn morning. Plain, not peanut. Though I'm not picky about the colors. I mean, they all taste the same anyway."

"Why should I let you see Mac? You're going to upset him, aren't you?"

"Oh, I think so, yes."

"Is that all you have to say about it?"

"I don't know that the rest is anything he'd want you to hear. I have no idea what's in *your* contract."

"You don't know a single thing about me."

"That's true. I shouldn't make assumptions. It's bad detective work."

"But you're an actor, not a detective."

"We're all of us detectives in one way or another, *Honey.* Don't you know that's the deep dark secret of the genre's success? Though not necessarily among eighteen to thirty-fours."

"I have no idea what that means. But I can tell you that there is nothing about Mac that I don't already know."

"That may be. But it doesn't mean you—or *he*—want everyone else in the world to know, too. And know it they will if I don't get to see him today. Now."

"You're here about Hall," she said, the life drained from her voice. "Again."

I nodded.

She looked around the small room. If it was for help or guidance, I don't know where she expected to find it. The Hockney swimming pool print on the wall was pretty, but didn't offer a lot of answers. At least, none that I could see. Then I realized it was an original and not a print. In the end, Honey simply stood up, her leather creaking lasciviously (oh yes, it *can* do that), and gestured for me to follow.

"Isn't that outfit kind of uncomfortable?" I had to ask, as we walked back up the hall. She stopped in front of a big oak door and gently brushed her knuckles against it. She opened the door without waiting for any response from within.

"Extremely. But as you say, you have *no* idea what's in *my* contract," she said. And ushered me inside.

Stans didn't look good, no doubt about it. If he'd looked like walking death at Hall's funeral, he was crawling death today. And it was crawling pretty damn fast. Stans's tan had gone to seed, leaving nothing but the bony old man underneath. The side of his face that wasn't sunken before had collapsed as well, emphasising the sharp edges of bone beneath the withered skin. The lip and eye on his left side drooped, too; from the stroke, I assumed. Stans was awake and propped up in his sumptuous bed, but there was major cyborg action going on, what with hoses running into his nose and both arms, all attached to jazzy machines that beeped and blipped ominously. I noted with interest that the ten pounds of gold jewelry he usually wore was all gone. Except for the pinky ring.

He didn't smile when he saw me. Thank God.

"Hi-de-ho there, Mac. How's it hanging? Getting much?"

Stans narrowed his eyes at me as best he could. In fact, the left eye appeared to be completely dead, and the half-squint left him looking like a central casting Igor from some low budget *Frankenstein*. Recognition was not imminent. Honey helped out.

"You remember Mr. Burns, Mac? He paid us a visit at the house."

Nothing.

"He watched your award tape. And you spoke with him out by the pool about Hall."

At mention of Emerson's name a little light came on behind the fuzzy eyes.

"Hall," he sputtered. "Ah do emeber."

"What'd he say?" I asked.

"He said he does remember," Honey translated. Then to the old man: "Mr. Burns was very insistent about seeing you today."

"Don' feel vel," Stans said.

"I know," Honey said. "He says he doesn't feel very well. But I think you'd best listen to what Mr. Burns has to say."

"Don' feel vel."

"He said . . ."

"Got it. I'm a quick study in dialects. Feeling a little punk today, huh, Mac?"

He nodded.

"Yeah. Well, that's probably for the best. You look like canned shit and it'd be a shame to look like that and feel *good*."

Stans shook his head as best he could manage.

"Is this really necessary, Mr. Burns?" Honey asked. I ignored her.

"Reminds me of an old joke. You know it? Dim fellah named Jackson is going around town and everywhere he goes people tell him that he's looking real bad, but the thing of it is that Jackson's feeling real good. So he goes to visit a friend of his named Bones. First thing Bones says to him is: 'Jackson, my man, you are looking *real* bad.' Jackson just about shits a brick. 'Goddamn,' he says. 'Everybody keeps telling me that, but I'm feeling really, really good. What the hell is going on?' Bones he says, 'Know what? I got one of those medical encyclopedias. Let's see if we can't look up your condition.'

"So Bones he finds the book on his shelf and gets it down. He starts whipping through the pages, zip-zip-zip. He says, 'Let's see here: looks real good, feels real good.' He looks at Jackson. 'Nope. That's not it.' Zip-zip-zip. 'Ahhh, looks real good, feels real bad. Nope, that's wrong.' Zip-zip. 'Looks real bad, feels real bad. We're getting warmer.' One last zip and: 'Looks real *bad*, feels real *good*. That's the ticket! Let's see what it says here. Hmmm. Hmmmm. Hmmmmmmmmmm!'

" 'What is it?' Jackson asks.

" 'My goodness, me,' Bones says.

" 'What?' Jackson pleads.

" 'Who'd of thunk it?'

" 'Tell me, Bones,' Jackson screams.

" 'Jackson,' Bones says, 'You're a vagina!' "

Honey made an unhappy noise behind me. Stans continued to look blank for a moment, then the working side of his mouth turned up ever so slightly in a smile. With the other half drooping, the effect left him looking like a cross between the Joker and Two-Face from *Batman*. He actually laughed out loud.

"Don't know that one, huh? I thought you'd like it. If only because you're such a fucking cunt yourself."

"Mnphscorgin," Stans spat. Even Honey couldn't translate. I shot her a glance, not sure how she'd take it, half-expecting her to run screaming for the security guard. But she only watched and let me go on.

"Or do you think that's unfair of me?" I asked.

Stans took three deep breaths and concentrated his energies.

"How dare you," he said. I was getting better at understanding his stroked-out garble.

"Who dares wins, baby."

"Honey," he called.

"Hear him out, Mac. You have no choice now."

"She's a cold one, isn't she, Mac? Not surprising, though. I reckon she knows how you talk about her to strangers. And, of course, it's always hard to get good help." I didn't hazard a look at Honey, but she didn't make any sound or move. "Then again, you're something of an ice man yourself, I'd say. Not even all these years in the California sun has raised your temperature above freezing. Reptiles are like that, though. Sunning on rocks doesn't make them warm-blooded, either."

"You bastard."

"Not me, boss. I know who my mother and father are. I confess, there were years when they didn't admit to having a son—*Bazooka Beach Massacre,* what could I have been thinking?—but then that's something you'd know a lot about. Seeing as how you're Hall's dad and all."

If there'd been any color in the old man's face it would have drained out the catheter along with his pale piss. He slipped down the bed a ways.

"Not having a heart attack or anything are you?" I glanced at the bank of monitors. They whizzed and whirred just as before. "No such luck."

"Hall," the old man muttered.

"It took me a while to put things together, but here's the way I got it scoped. Ready? You were banging Connie Clare like the proverbial screen door. Nothing unusual there, 'cause everything I hear says she put out like an asbestos blanket on a kitchen fire. But you and she went back a ways, didn't you? A few years before Hall was born at least. I found a picture of the two of you in a paper from the mid-forties. You must have slipped up or ridden bareback on the wrong day, though, 'cause you knocked her up. So Connie Clare is pregnant with your kid, but uh-oh! She's a wannabe starlet on the make and can't have it known she's an unwed mother. She sure can't marry you because you're already married at the time, aren't you? So she—or the studio—rigs up a marriage with Frank Emerson, who is as gay as an April day in Paris. Perfect cover. I couldn't figure what was in it for Frank, but son of a gun, along comes HUAC and the Red Scare. Suddenly, D-list Frank Emerson is getting some A- and B-list jobs. Of course, he's not actually writing the pictures, he's just fronting for the poor blacklisted bastards whose lives are being destroyed. So maybe it's not the cleanest paycheck he's ever earned, but money is green wherever it comes from. That's the first rule of Hollywood. How am I doing so far?"

He shook his head, but I swear Mac Stans was shriveling in front of my eyes like The Incredible Shrinking Man. Lucky for him a spider didn't come along and attack just then.

"So let's see now: Connie Clare has your baby, but everyone thinks it's Frank Emerson's. Since Frank is already bearding for you as a father, who better to play the front when *your* name goes on the blacklist. Of course, that's a con, too, but we'll come back to that.

"Frank Emerson's safely in the bag because he's a queer and going public would be the end of him. Your old pal George Gaines knows all about it—you told me yourself that he introduced you to Clare—but George is an interesting guy in his own right. He was a sociopath, wasn't he? And not just in the usual producer way. He liked to hurt women. I know that for a fact because he casually tried to rape a friend of mine. But you had some peculiar predilections, too, didn't you? Water sports, is what I hear. Is that right, Honey? Or do prostate problems take the fun out of that?"

No reply. Stans got some color back in his cheeks now. One of the monitors was starting to beep a little faster, too.

"Now, Gaines, he didn't just like doing bad things to women—he liked doing bad things period. He learned early on, maybe by accident at first, I don't know, that there really is no such thing as bad publicity. There is *only* publicity. So if no one had the good grace to crash a car or fall off a cliff or OD on a Gaines set, he arranged for it to go down. And then he cashed in on the press coverage he made certain would happen. George Gaines, everybody loses."

"Mr. Burns . . ."

"I'm still not done, Honey, so shut the fuck up. I'm *sure* that this isn't covered in your contract."

"I'm going to get the guard now."

"Mmmm, you might want to ask Mac about that first. What do you say, Mac? Should I tell all this to the cops? 'Cause there's an old detective in Alhambra who still thinks you might have had something to do with Connie Clare's murder. He's convinced that George Gaines did. And I think he's right. Do you know there's no statute of limitations on murder in California?"

"Sit down, Honey," Stans said.

She did as she was told.

"The thing I couldn't figure about any of this was your relationship with Gaines. Okay, so you whored around together in the forties, indulged your nasty habits. No big thing, it's a zany old town and there's nothing new under the sun. And you made some bucks off each other in the movies, you writing and Gaines producing. But Gaines was a walking heap of manure with no regard for anyone or thing other than his own pleasure and enrichment. So why did he stick with you after you got hit with the blacklist? I can guess why he liked Clare; she had the looks and she liked to play rough herself. And it figures that Gaines would get extra jollies from screwing her knowing that she was your punching board. But why continue to work with you on *Devil*? It just didn't make any sense. Especially since Gaines himself was so deep into the anti-Red movement. Why in the world would he risk shooting a script he knew was written by MacArthur Stans—*the* man of liberal conscience—at the height of anticommie fervor? *The Devil on Sunday* wasn't even a big budget shoot, so money doesn't explain it."

I waited for an answer from the old man. A nod, a wink, an acknowledgement of any kind.

"Shall *I* tell *you*?"

Bleep-bleep-blip went the machines.

"It was all a lie, wasn't it? A massive con. You and Gaines were in it together all along. You were no hero, no man of conscience. You weren't just a writer, you were an actor. And man alive did you ever play the part."

Stans held his head in his palsied hand now. His whole body was shaking.

"Hall knew. I don't know how he found out, but he did. The big hero of the blacklist—his real dad, for Christ's sake—was a fraud and a traitor to everything he supposedly believed. You were a plant. You played the man of conscience, even did a little jail time, to get inside the old Hollywood left, the better to rat them out secretly later. The great man of honor was a man to whom honor meant nothing at all. But you know that it meant *everything* to Hall. Irony or what? And being a good and true son of Hollywood, you know what Hall did when he found out?"

I pulled the pages of the treatment—*Better Red Than Dead*—out of my pocket and tossed them on the bed at Stans's feet.

"He wrote a goddamn movie about it."

Stans reached down for the pages, read the title, then pushed them aside.

"It's a classic Hollywood story. Venality, lust, greed . . . all the usual suspects. It's set during the time of the blacklist—go figure!—and tells of a man who plays a hero, but who's really a rat. Like *On the Waterfront* in reverse. I wonder who it could be based on?"

Stans stared vacantly at the clean white sheet which covered him. I imagined how it would look when they pulled it over his head.

"Hall knew you were his father, didn't he?"

That sheet sure was interesting.

"*Didn't* he?"

Stans nodded. "He came to see me a few weeks ago. I don't know how long he suspected, when he figured it out. I tried to deny it, of course, but he knew the truth. I couldn't dissuade him."

"And that's why you and Kevin Ryan Paul killed him."

"Wha-?" the old man gasped.

"You *idiot*," Honey said to me.

"Well, you did, didn't you?"

Stans let out a moan that came from someplace very deep inside. I think maybe he'd been saving it up for many years.

"Hall killed himself," Stans said.

"Bullshit."

"It's the truth."

"Why did he do it?"

"Didn't you just tell me?"

"*You* tell me, you miserable old fuck!"

Stans shook his head and stared some more at his sheet. I turned to Honey for help, but she just sat in the corner of the room, watching the old man with a look that would rust stainless steel.

"I've got a friend," I said. "His name is Doug Hughes and he writes the 'Gone Fishing' gossip column for *Variety*. If you don't give me the straight story here and now I'm going to tell him everything I know about this. I have a feeling you don't want to check out remembered as the man who made Elia Kazan look like Princess Di."

Stans snorted. "And if I do tell you?"

"I'll think about that. The truth is I don't give a shit about you or your reputation, or Honey or George Gaines or Kevin Ryan Paul or any of it. I just want to know what happened to Hall." I reached over and raised up Stans's chin to make sure that he was looking at me. "And Connie Clare. I *want* to know."

Stans weakly pushed my hand away. I was happy to remove it because his skin felt like soggy sandpaper. I sat back and waited for him to speak. It was a long wait and he very nearly ran out of time.

"I am . . . was Hall's father, you're right about that. How did you find out?"

"It's all out there to be found. I don't think anyone ever cared enough to look, other than Hall. If you must know it was the ring that clued me in." I pointed at the gold ring which looked loose on the old man's shriveled pinky. He raised his shaky hand up to look at it, then gave it a little kiss.

"You're kidding me, right?" I said.

"Connie Clare gave me this ring." Another little head shake, possibly for effect. Possibly not. "Connie and I had a long running affair. Gaines introduced us and was furious when we hit it off. Connie was . . . a lot of woman, the love of my life. The best woman I ever knew."

Stans glanced at Honey, but she'd turned to stone.

"What really happened to her?" I asked.

"I was married at the time, you're right, and Connie got pregnant. I wanted her to lose the baby, but she wouldn't do it. She might take on a bar full of sailors for kicks, but she wouldn't have an abortion. Catholics," he said, and rolled his eyes.

"Frank Emerson came into it like you said. Gaines fixed it all up, threatened to expose Frank as a homo if he didn't marry Connie, promised him big things if he did. Frank wasn't a bad fellow, but he wasn't up to Hollywood. Not big enough. He should have quit town. Gone back to where he came from and taken a job with some little newspaper or taught college. He took the deal, instead."

"Why'd Clare go for it?"

"What could she do? She was ambitious, she was pregnant. She wanted to be a star. Gaines offered her a way to get what she wanted. She didn't even have to screw Emerson, not that that would have been any obstacle. It was a business arrangement, pure and simple, and it was common as muck at the time."

"So what went wrong?"

"Connie overplayed her hand. She found out about . . . my arrangement with Gaines."

"You mean she knew you were a fraud and threatened to expose you."

"Yes. She went to Gaines with it, told him she'd bring us both down if he didn't make her career. So Gaines killed her."

"Just like that."

"George was a sick man. He was involved with many awful things. Killing Connie meant nothing to him."

"Or to you."

"No. It was terribly difficult for me. I loved her very much."

"Is that a violin I hear playing? It sounds like a very small one."

"You don't understand. You've never lived through a time like that. It's a thin line separating hero and villain. It all seems so easy looking back, making judgments from the comfort of the here and now."

246

"So murdering the mother of your child was okay back then, is that what you're telling me?"

"I didn't kill her."

"But you knew about it."

"I suspected, yes. I never asked George flat out."

"But did he ever tell you?"

Stans's tired eye filled with hate. "You are a bastard," he said.

"I'm not a nice man, either. Or so I'm told. But coming from the likes of you I'll take it as a compliment."

"Gaines would have destroyed me, too. Me, Emerson . . . Hall."

"So you did this all for Hall, is that your story?"

"Connie's death was a warning. To Frank and to me. George would have killed the boy. Or worse. He had friends in Mexico."

"Where life is cheap? Okay, we'll add 'ignorant racist' to your list of hobbies in the Who's Who of Twentieth Century Shits."

"You would have done the same if you'd been there. There was no other choice."

"Let's say that's true. I'll give you that twisted, anorexic benefit of the doubt for the moment. So why, with Gaines gone these many years, did you not come clean, set the record straight? With Hall, at least? You obviously kept track of him over the years. You must have known how tortured he was. If you and Kevin Ryan Paul really didn't make it happen, how could you allow him . . . allow what happened to Hall to happen?"

"None of us could ever tell the truth. While Gaines was alive, the risk was too great. I had a reputation and a career. Frank was stuck in his closet. He raised the boy and did a fine job of it. How could we tell Hall growing up all that had occurred? What would it have done to the boy?"

"What did it do to the man?"

Stans had no answer to that.

"What did you think when . . . if Hall really killed himself? How did that make you feel?"

"I felt regret, of course. *Feel* regret. But Hall made his own decisions through the years. Most of them bad."

"And this was just another bad decision? You must have known you were driving him to it. Working with Paul, helping to screw him over."

"*The Devil on Sunday* is a very important project. It's going to be big."

"Oh, well that's all right then. A big opening weekend is worth driving your son to suicide for. What jury would convict you?"

"I had no idea that would be the consequence. I thought I was giving Hall an opportunity. Kevin Ryan Paul is headed for the heights. If I learned nothing else, I learned you have to hitch your wagon to the right star. I'm executive producer of *The Devil on Sunday*. When I get out of here and get my strength back my name is going to mean something again, something more than ancient history. *The Devil on Sunday* is the start for me. A *new* start. I've been waiting for it for a *long* time."

"Kevin Ryan Paul is a loser. He's a jackass. You sold out your only flesh and blood for a ticket on a fairground kiddy ride."

"I don't think a TV actor is anyone to talk. If I'd listened to the likes of you over the years, I wouldn't be where I am today."

"And what a place this is. You're a hideous coward, Mac. You're every bit the monster that George Gaines was. Maybe worse: Gaines never disguised the fact that he was walking pond scum. But you've been posing behind a facade of heroism for forty years. Everything about you stinks of lies."

"I'm a man of my time."

"So was Vlad the Impaler."

"That's unfair."

If I'd a had a bit more straw with my lunch, I might have shat a brick.

"You"—I felt myself sputtering like Jack Benny's Maxwell. A wave of fury rode through me—*"producer."*

"Are you going to tell your friend at *Variety*?" he asked. "It would jeopardize everything I've worked for. I'll never get back in if you tell it now. Paul will ditch me."

Only then did it truly strike me that I was trying to argue conscience with a man whose dictionary had no entry for "shame," and which naturally fell open to the definition of hubris. MacArthur Stans was little more than the shell of a human being. Something small and ugly quivered inside.

"You'll be the last to know," I said.

I looked over at Honey, but she refused to meet my gaze. How much of all of this, I wondered, did she know about? Did any of it matter to her? Or was she only obliged to attend to strictly contractual matters?

I realized I didn't care. I got up to go.

"Mac," I called.

He didn't respond, so I yelled his name again. He looked up at me, his eyelids now heavy with exhaustion.

"I want to know one more thing. If you tell me honestly, maybe I won't spill any of this."

His eyes opened a little wider.

"The missing footage that Hall was looking for, *The Devil on Sunday* scene with Connie Clare. Do you know what he was after? Does it exist?"

The old man looked as glazed as a Christmas ham now. I wasn't sure if he heard, or understood, the question.

"Mac? Was the scene ever shot? Do you know what Hall wanted?"

"Yes," he muttered. I didn't know which question he was answering. But he was out of it, and Honey stood up and made clear that she wouldn't let me ask any more.

I left them there, deserving each other.

And ran into Kevin Ryan Paul locking his SUV in the parking lot. No coterie, today. Though Paul was wearing another one of those ridiculous jumpsuits. Fire engine red this time.

"Marty Burns! Still on the case, I see."

"Like Shakespeare said to Nathan Hale, I always get my man."

"Huh?"

"Nah, I didn't figure you for a Marx Brothers fan. Tell me something, Kev: Do you even *like* movies?"

"Since when has that ever mattered?"

"Maybe never. But it sure seems like it should."

"You telling me you're a slave to the art of the one-hour detective drama? I have seen your show, you know."

"I like to think I do the best I can."

"That's not the same thing, is it? Remind me how much they pay you every week?"

"Far too much. And nowhere near enough."

"Congratulations, Marty. You just encapsulated the philosophy of the business in ten words or less. Your career hasn't been in vain."

"That means a lot coming from you."

Paul kacked up a patently false laugh. Then: "I thought I told you not to bother Mac Stans anymore."

"Told? What are you, my mother?"

"*Asked.* Is that better?"

"Well, like God, sometimes my answer is 'no.' "

"God, huh?"

"I feel you're never too old for role models. Mine used to be Paul Winchell. Then I found out that Jerry Mahoney was just a dummy."

"You are a piece of work, I'll admit that. I think I didn't give you enough credit."

"It's okay, I gave you far too much."

"Still trying to prove I killed your buddy Emerson?"

"You did, didn't you?"

"Marty."

"Okay, so you didn't conk him on the head or drop a roofie in his hootch and stick the gas pipe down his throat, but you might as well have. You set the poor bastard up for the fall. You and big daddy in there."

"What did Stans tell you?" he asked, looking a little more concerned.

"Not much. He's just a sick old man. But he has big dreams. Apparently you're his ticket back onto the Hollywood A-list. Think they'll reserve an iron lung for him at Blönde?"

"Nothing he says means a thing."

"I don't know, I think there might be some interest in it. Hey, Miramax loves developing projects from true stories, maybe I should pitch it at them? I've even got a treatment, thanks to Hall. Now who could we get to play you? Too bad J. T. Walsh is dead. Maybe Dan Hedaya."

"You know, you never signed that contract for *The Devil on Sunday.*"

"Well, duh."

"I think maybe we're gonna recast. You don't have the equipment for the part."

"Do you think there are any circumstances under which I would *take* the part? After what you've done?"

"What, exactly, have I done, anyway? You keep dancing around it, because you've got a big hole where your third act should be. You've got nothing, Marty."

"God, how I hate three-act structure. You think Irving Thalberg worried about crap like that? And what I've got is you and Stans doing every little thing you could to drive Hall to his death. You fucked him over on the script, but that wasn't enough, was it? I couldn't figure why, after so many years, Hall got the bee in his bonnet about Connie Clare. She was his mother, sure, but he'd had a lifetime to come to terms with what happened to her. And it couldn't have just been *The Devil on Sunday* getting remade. How is it, when hardly anyone even remembers the film and no one has ever heard of any missing scenes, that Hall suddenly got obsessed about the idea that one with Connie Clare existed?"

"Maybe a little bird told him," Paul said. He smiled so ugly I had to stop myself from knocking his teeth in.

"A little shitbird, I'd say."

"We'll never know, will we?"

"You had to get it from Stans. There is no one else. You pried the whole awful story out of the old monster, didn't you? And you used it to bait Hall. That was the real price of Stans's executive producer credit."

"Actually, it's only *co*-exec."

"So you're a chiseling bastard, too. I could have guessed. You must have figured you'd get something out of Hall. If not a good script on the cheap, then maybe some publicity."

"I already told you that much. Hall being Connie Clare's son had to be good for something."

"You're a liar. You knew Hall, worked with him before. You must have known he was desperate and unstable. So maybe a little push here, a shove on the right psychological button there, and he'd go over the edge. And man did he dance for you. That poor, sad son of a bitch. You played Hall like Miles Davis on the trumpet, didn't you? And you got your stories in the papers out of it. And Gamma to boot! You learned very well at your uncle's feet."

"You're in fantasy land now, Marty. This is all pure speculation."

"La-la land, yes; there's no escaping the gaze of the Hollywood sign. But it's no fantasy. If Hall hadn't obliged so faithfully in the back of his car, what would you have done? Did you have some other button to push on him, or were you going to sacrifice the old man? Spill his story for the coverage?"

"Can you imagine the PR that'll get? Mac Stans, the great liberal hero, is a ratfink. A double agent for the dark forces of the McCarthy right. What attention might a story like that get for a picture if it came out, say, the week before *The Devil on Sunday* opens on three thousand screens?"

I felt my mouth drop open. I hadn't thought it possible, but I'd underestimated Paul's loathsomeness. The lizard meter didn't go high enough to register his like.

"You know," Paul said, "it's a shame that you didn't sign the contract for *The Devil on Sunday*. Not that you were ever going to play the part. I was looking forward to firing you on the first day of shooting, though."

I could only shake my head in confusion.

"You don't think that I like *Burning Bright,* do you? That you *impressed* me in it? Though Sade, the silly bitch, really does watch the show. It doesn't make her come, though. Only George Clooney can do that for her."

"So what . . ."

"I had to know what you knew. Lissa did Emerson—she'll pretty much shove any dick-shaped object into one hole or the other—and he mentioned your name and how you were helping him with *Devil.* I had to know what he told you. That's why Lissa banged you, too. Sorry to break it you, kid."

"I take back what I said: I think Uncle George might even have learned a thing or two from you."

"You've got to move with the times, *Mar* old pal. I know Uncle George would have. And speaking of moving, I got to see the old buzzard before he goes ripe on me. So if you'll excuse me . . ."

"What makes you think I won't spill all this? Tell it to the trades or the *Times*? Fuck with your scenario?"

"Two reasons. First of all, you're screwed on your commitment to *Devil.* This conversation never happened, so as far as I know, you've agreed to take the part. Make trouble and I get the lawyers out. Maybe you'd win in court, but I don't think you want to try. Or pay the bills. Ask your agent what it would cost. By the way, I would dearly love to come in her mouth. Ask her for me will you?"

"What's the second reason?"

"It's even better. I don't give a shit. I want to control the timing, sure, but if you tell now, it's just that much more publicity. The money's set, the picture's happening. You go and spill your guts now, well, that's just two blasts of PR the picture gets. Marty, it's a win-win situation."

Paul winked at me and stared up the path toward the hospital.

"Do you feel anything, Kevin?" I called out after him. "About Hall or Stans or Connie Clare?"

The producer stopped in his tracks and mimed deep thought. Then his eyes went wide and he raised up a finger as if to say: eureka!

"I feel good, ba-da, ba-da, ba-da, bop," he sang, and did a little spin step. It was a more than passable James Brown. Of course, the jumpsuit helped.

I watched him disappear into the garden. I didn't feel good at all. In fact, I felt pretty damn black.

And not the least bit proud.

Fifteen

H oly Moly!" Jon Conlon said.

We sat in his living room, where it had taken three-quarters of two six-packs for me to tell him the whole story. I had to talk to someone about it, and while I considered confiding in Kendall, I decided Jon was more likely to understand. Also, Kendall would insist I do the *right* thing, whatever that might be. And I wasn't sure I wanted to do that.

I waited for Jon to expand on his exclamation. He didn't.

"Is that it?" I asked. "Is that all you have to say? 'Cause pithy as it is, I might as well talk to Elliot if that's the best you can muster."

Jon shook his head. He looked shell-shocked. I couldn't blame him.

"It's, uh, a lot to take in. Maybe I shouldn't have had that last beer," he said. And then he opened two more.

"Thanks." We ritualistically clinked bottles. "But what do I do?"

He was still shaking his head. "I don't know, Marty. What do you *want* to do? Shit! I've been waiting years for a chance to use that line and I blew the reading. May Paddy Chayefsky forgive me."

Conlon chuckled, but I wasn't in a laughing mood. I'd been moping around the house all week, waiting for a revelation to knock on my door. The only thing that arrived was a telegram from the production company officially informing me that Fox were pulling the plug on *Burning Bright*. And wasn't that just the wind beneath my wings. Kendall called, too, to confirm it and commiserate. And Carl Khan. He wanted to know when he was going to get his lobster dinner. I told him that with the show eighty-sixed I was leaning towards filet o' fish and did he want fries with that? He wasn't amused. Naturally, I didn't tell him what I'd learned about Hall. Which made me feel guilty.

"Do you like movies?" I asked Jon.

"Huh? Sure, of course. Ahhh, what do you mean?"

"I mean, do you *like* movies. And TV. The stuff you write. Do you do it because you like it, or because you do it and it pays well?"

"Oh. In other words, am I a little Kevin Ryan Paul? I don't know, are you?"

"I don't know." When Paul asked me that question, whether I was devoted to *Burning Bright*—while there still was a *Burning Bright*—it threw me. I was getting all high and mighty on him, and suddenly discovered maybe it was *me* who was standing in a ditch. "I know it's not the greatest show in the world. The stories are hackneyed, the jokes are obvious, the endings are always telegraphed, and the characters are just that little bit too thin. But you know, I really *do* do my best, however pathetic that may be. And I wouldn't do it if I didn't think that there was something there. Something, I don't know . . . *worthwhile*."

"It's not just losing the paycheck that makes you feel bad then."

"Hell no."

"I feel the same way, mostly. But it's hard not to get jaded and cynical doing this stuff. I sometimes think back to when I was in high school and college, when I really got into movies, the *idea* of movies. My folks lived in New York and when I went home for summers and breaks and stuff, I used to go into the city every day and see as many movies as I could. I'd catch all the first run stuff, old movies at rep houses, the Museum of Modern Art, wherever. This was before VCRs, of course. Some days I'd literally race from theater to theater to see everything possible. There were good student discounts back then, so it wasn't even that expensive. It just felt so"—Conlon offered me a wry smiled—"*worthwhile*. Important, even. It was such a thrill."

"And now?"

"Now I'm in the business and—it's a business, isn't it? I know what it takes to get those words and images on the screen and, yeah, I admit it: It doesn't feel so thrilling anymore. But I'm not eighteen years old and I've seen and been a lot of places, and I don't thrill so easy. That's just life, isn't it?"

"I *am* big," I drawled, "it's the *pictures* that have gotten small."

"Maybe yes, maybe no. This business is run for kids. Too much of it is run *by* kids. But maybe that's all right. That's who it's all meant for."

"You haven't answered the question: Am I a little Kevin Ryan Paul?"

Jon laughed. "To be honest, I think the fact that you ask the question is a damned good sign. It's when you stop asking, you better start to worry."

We drank our beers in silence for a while. Both of us, perhaps, considering the trails that led us to where we are today.

"What do you think I should do?" I finally asked. "Do I tell the tale?"

Conlon put his beer down and ran his fingers through his thick, dirty-blond hair. He thought long and hard, staring at me the whole time. Neither of us blinked.

"I understand why you want to," he said. "I think I'd want to, too. It feels like the only way to get some justice for Hall."

"I don't think it's justice."

"Retribution?"

"No. Well, a little."

"Equanimity?"

"That's it. God, Jon, you oughta be a writer."

"But the equanimity is for you, isn't it? Not for Hall at all."

"I suppose. Your answer is no, then?"

"Didn't say that. I said I understand why you'd want to tell. And maybe it's the right thing to do. But maybe not."

"Say more."

"I don't know if Paul's right; if telling the story would just earn more PR for the movie. I think he was bluffing you a little, that it might not work to his benefit like he says. I'm sorry, but there *is* such a thing as bad publicity. Just ask Pee Wee Herman. It's a tough call, though. It'd be awful if you went through the heartache of all this only to boost *Devil's* opening by ten mil."

"Yeah."

"I also agree that Mac Stans deserves whatever he gets. He is a monster, you're a hundred percent right. It makes me sick to my stomach to think that I regarded the guy as a hero for so long."

"Take a number, boss."

"But much as I hate to say this—and it really makes me feel that my youth is forever gone—maybe Mac Stans needs to still be a hero. Maybe the model that he serves as, the virtuous and noble man that people think him to be, is more important than the truth. Who's a hero these days? Movie stars? I don't think so. Politicians? Pthheww. Athletes? Soldiers? No, there's no one. I'm sorry, but Tiger Woods taking a hundred mil to plaster Nike swooshes on his ass does not fit my definition of hero. But Mac Stans, not the real one, I grant you, but the Mac Stans of the public mind, the popular imagination— well, *that's* a fucking hero, buddy. Almost as good as in the movies even."

"You think anyone under the age of forty even knows who Mac Stans is?" I asked.

"You think if you tell them the truth, that anyone ever will?" Conlon said.

"You're no help."

"I'm sorry, Marty. I'm just a humble script doctor. You want better you got to pay bigger money. It's the best I have to offer."

"I know. I appreciate the input."

Jon went to fetch more beers. He brought snacks back with him from the kitchen, but I had no appetite.

"Do you understand why they did it?" I asked.

"The usual, I should think: power, lust, *greed*."

"Paul, okay. He's a mid-level producer hot to make it to the front ranks. He has no conscience, no morals, understands no limits. And he's from bad blood. *Hollywood* blood. I think, maybe, he's something like his uncle: a sociopath."

"I'm not sure a clinical psychologist would second that opinion."

"Maybe not. But what about Stans? He's an old man, obviously in poor health even before the stroke. He's a universal hero. He's got that fabulous house in Laguna, millions in the bank, a priceless stein collection"—I slapped my palm to my forehead; Conlon laughed— "and *Honey*, of course."

"Of course."

"What the fuck does he want back in the business for at his age? How could it possibly be worth all that it cost him?"

"Ohhh, Marty. You're scaring me, now."

"What? Why?"

"I'm starting to think that you don't understand greed."

"No. No, it's funny. I never really have."

"That's because you've been poor. You've gotten by without much, you know you could do it again if you had to. Only the rich really understand greed, work at perfecting it."

"But that doesn't make any sense."

"Oh, yes it does. The richer you are, the more you think you deserve what you have, that you're entitled to it. And the more terrified you become that you'll lose it or have it taken away. Greed has to come naturally, like blond hair, or it's just not the same. To reach the pinnacles of greed you have to be born with it. Like Down's Syndrome or muscular dystrophy. It's something to behold in its pure form. And it's a medusa; once gazed upon, you're stoned forever. You'll never reach the top in this business if you don't understand that."

"Probably explains a lot."

"Hell, yeah. I've always thought they should tear down the Hollywood sign and refurbish Mt. Lee. Five big little letters: 'G-R-E-E-D'."

I smiled. "And then they could rename the merchandising operations. Instead of Warner and Disney boutiques, they could merge them into one overpriced outfit. Call it *Greed & Stuff.*"

"Now, you're cooking with gas. Somebody make this man a studio exec."

"I haven't got the suits for it."

Another clink of bottles.

"So what *are* you going to do?"

I blew out a big breath. "I still don't know."

"Glad to have been such a big help."

"You have helped, Jon. Thank you."

"So you wouldn't be all upset if I turned on the TV for a minute? Just to catch the scoreboard?"

"No! Go ahead. Maybe a Dodger victory will provide the sign I need."

Conlon zapped his big TV on and punched up Headline News. He was just early for sports, but right on time for the Hollywood Hickey or whatever the hell they call their sixty seconds of entertainment news.

"Legendary screenwriter and hero of the McCarthy era, MacArthur Stans died this evening at the age of eighty-nine of complications following a stroke," the announcer read.

Conlon and I looked at each other.

"Holy Moly," we both said.

．．．

Those old Quinn Martin shows, like *The FBI* and *Streets of San Francisco,* always concluded with an epilogue, clearly labeled: "Epilogue." I always liked that.

So here's mine.

Four months after that night at Conlon's, I was back at work on *Burning Bright.* Fox gave it the kibosh, yes indeed, but all you have to do in this town is click your ruby heels three times—and agree to cut your budget by thirty percent—and TNT will pick you up for sure. I confess that after all that soul-searching at Jon's, I wasn't sure that I wanted to do another season of the series, but Kendall talked me into it, using her keenly honed talents of persuasion.

"What could it hurt?" she said.

The only downside was that it cost me the deal with Schmears 'R U.S. Turns out they had agreed a big campaign with the network: Fox 'N Lox. It simply wouldn't fly with TNT. I tried to get Kendall to convince them that a new tie-in could work, too: "Shmears is Dyn-O-Mite" was my suggestion for the campaign. They didn't buy it. I reckon it's because there was no apostrophe in there. "Dyn-'O-Mite," perhaps? I should have thought of it sooner.

The Devil on Sunday went into production within days of my encounter with Kevin Ryan Paul. Paul, as promised, took on the direction himself, trumpeted by full-page ads in the trades. The shoot ran into some trouble, though. On day one of filming, an attorney from the Writers' Guild served court papers on Kevin Ryan Paul on behalf of the Hall Emerson estate. It seems the Guild came into possession of Hall's script of *The Devil on Sunday* and felt that Kevin Ryan Paul's shooting script—of which they also had a copy—just might represent a breach of copyright. I can't imagine how the Guild ever came to know about Hall's script. Or rather, I couldn't imagine if I hadn't been the one to send it to them.

The lawsuit didn't shut the picture down, though; the fire did that. Though I didn't start it.

Myself.

Exactly.

I debated very strongly whether or not I wanted to tell Gabbo everything I'd learned. I felt that he deserved to know—he was undoubtedly Hall's truest friend—but I feared that he might rush out and kill Paul, and much as I detest the producer, I didn't want anything like that on my conscience. Still, I felt Gabbo should know. So I arranged to see him and before telling him the story, made him swear—on a copy of *Huckleberry Finn*—that he wouldn't kill Kevin Ryan Paul or arrange to have him killed. Gabbo almost didn't go for it, but curiosity got the better of him. So I told it all.

The fire struck the set four weeks into the shoot. As an old movie man himself, Gabbo knew what to do to maximize the loss. The fire happened late at night, but I knew about it before it made the next day's news. A thud woke me up at five in the morning. I couldn't figure out what it was at first, then saw the package—the enormous package—balanced against the rail of my sundeck. I knew what it was as soon as I rapped a knuckle against the wrapping paper. I tore it off and admired my lovely new sliding glass door. I admired, even more, the photographs taped to the glass: lovely action shots of *The Devil on Sunday* set going up in flames. It wasn't signed exactly, but a Post-it note was also attached:

"He ain't dead. Yet. (PS: It's double glazed)."

That "yet" scared me, but I think it was just Gabbo playing gruff. He also plays mean: incendiary materials linked to the fire were later discovered in Kevin Ryan Paul's garage. The cops haven't charged Paul yet, but the insurance company is refusing to pay off. The producer may get off in the end, but his movie's as dead as a good writer.

Lissa Torres came out of it okay, though. Until those tits start to sag, she always will. She's signed up to do a feature version of her TV show: *Lupé Garou: Deep Fur*. Gamma, I read, made a full and somewhat miraculous recovery, having had a kind of religious experience in the hospital. Apparently, he's renounced Hollywood and taken refuge in a Buddhist temple near Encino where's he learning to become a Zen master. Good luck to him. Sade is doing well, too, as hostess of a new game show on ABC. She's even put on a few pounds.

I don't know what happened to Kant. I don't care.

In the end, I decided not to break the true story of Mac Stans. I had (lobster) dinner with Carl Khan—would you believe the bastard ordered a caviar appetizer, too?—but only told him that, like the reporter in *Citizen Kane*, I never really found the key to Hall's life.

Or death. Khan smiled at me knowingly, said he understood, and ordered another cognac. He's a decent cop, but he's still LAPD. He already knows more than is good for him.

My decision to keep the true version of events secret ultimately had less to do with Conlon's speech about the need for heroes than with the question he posed to me about who I'd be telling the story for. I don't hold much stock in heroes myself; don't know that it's such a bad thing for people to be the heroes of their *own* stories and not look to anyone else to be the good guy. But the question of Hall—still; maybe forever—vexed me.

Much as I might like the truth about Hall to be known, I'm not sure it's what he would have liked. To tell the story, to have the unpleasant details come out and be pored and pawed over in this awful little town of ours, would not do Hall any credit. He would look like a sap and a loser and a pathetic sad sack who's entire life was a series of pratfalls and misfortune leading to one, giant banana peel exit. It wouldn't go a jot toward letting people know what Hall Emerson was: a mighty hellraiser, a pretty good writer, a decent friend to those who still believe in honor.

And a man who deserved better than what he got.

So I kept my trap shut. Kevin Ryan Paul hasn't spilled the story, either. But given his troubles, I don't think his word means much any more.

I thought it was all behind me, though sometimes late at night I'd find myself still haunted—figuratively speaking—by that vision of Connie Clare, until one Saturday afternoon, in the depths of SoCal winter (sixty-six degrees in the shade), there came a rap-rap-rapping at my chamber door.

I paused the PlayStation and went to answer it.

Honey stood on my doorstep.

She looked like an additional million dollars. I don't know how many million that makes—all of Mac Stans's I suppose. She wasn't wearing a microbathing-suit, or skintight leather; just a sycophantically flattering—and dead conservative—more-than-a-grape-picker-earns-in-a-year pants suit. She could be any lady-of-a-certain-standing, out for a day at the club or a shop on Rodeo Drive.

Okay, not any lady. Grace Kelly, maybe.

"Honey," I said, genuinely startled.

"Mr. Burns," she said and nodded.

"Ah, would you like to come in?"

"Under no circumstances. I've only come to give you something."

"What caliber?"

"*Trés amusant.* It's in the car and it's heavy. Could you come and take it?"

"I suppose."

I followed her to the car—a spanking new Jag—and she opened the trunk. A bulky film canister rested inside.

"What is it?" I asked.

"I'm sure I don't care. It represents . . . the fulfillment of a contract," she said. And very nearly smiled. She closed the trunk when I removed the canister, then got into the car and drove off without another word. Her vanity plate, I observed, read:

PDNFULL

"Call you sometime?" I said to the wind.

I schlepped the case inside and opened it up. Sure enough a single reel rested within. Thirty-five millimeter film, and no more than a few minutes worth, I estimated. Suddenly, I got all excited. I thought I knew what it was. I unrolled a length and held it up to the light. Academy leader. I unspooled just enough more to see the footage proper was in black-and-white. I was tempted to roll it all out, but restrained myself and carefully spooled the film back onto the reel. A quick search for my car keys and I was on my way to Burbank, where TNT rents space to shoot *Burning Bright.* They wanted to move the show to Vancouver, but I put my foot down. If David Duchovny won't live there, why should I?

It was tough finding anyone around on Saturday, but after threatening a snit fit, they set me up in a small, executive screening room. The projectionist looked as if I'd woken him from a twenty-year sleep, but then they always do. He took the reel from me and threaded it up.

As I sat there, in the dark and the cold, waiting for that magic light to come flickering on, I thought about Hall. I glanced over and imagined him sitting next to me.

Someone had stuck a plug of gum on the seat of the adjoining chair. Suits!

The scene only lasted six minutes. But that's plenty of time for a star to be born. And that's exactly what Connie Clare would have been. Tom Neal brought down the tone, no denying, but she had such presence, such authority, that even Neal's decidedly B-talents couldn't wreck the work. Clare was sultry and sexy, strong yet vulnerable, wicked, wild . . . wonderful. The camera loved her. It does that for some people: falls in love. You can't fake it, you can't make it, and you can't buy it. You either have it or you don't.

Connie Clare had it.

As I watched that brilliant scene—it couldn't have made it into the picture because of a technical fault—I saw, or imagined I did, Hall's face in his mother's. I also saw the tragedy of his life reflected in hers. I saw all the possibilities for both of them, the things that could have been and should have been, but which didn't happen because of the greedy, awful men who always have and always will run Hollywood.

"That's a funny clip," the projectionist said over the speaker. "I like the girl, though. Want me to run it again?"

I did. I did want to see it again. Again and again and again.

And I would tell him so.

As soon as I stopped crying.

About the Author

JAY RUSSELL was born in New York City in 1961. After graduating from college, he moved to Southern California, where he received a PhD from USC. Some of the many jobs he's held include editor, video slave, and researcher for a private investigators' agency. He reviews for *Tangled Web UK* and his short fiction has appeared in various anthologies and collections, including *Dark Terrors, Dark Detectives, White of the Moon,* and *The Year's Best Fantasy and Horror.* He lives in London with his wife and daughter and avidly follows the fate of the New York Mets from overseas.